all this TIME

ANNABELLE McCORMACK

To my sister, Christi.
No, this isn't about me. Yes, I promise. But maybe skip the
steamy scenes because that's just awkward.

all
this
TIME

CHAPTER ONE

SEVEN MONTHS. That's how long Sam Redding had been promising her sister that she would be at the hospital for the birth of her newest niece. Trust a freaking snowstorm in November to get in the way. *I hope Laura's in a forgiving mood.*

The heels of Sam's boots clopped against the tile, a mix of shuffles and loud *thunks* as she attempted to fling off the snow clinging to them. Sam stopped and glanced back at the trail of dirt and slush she'd streaked from the hospital lobby to the front desk to the elevators. She grimaced, then glanced around.

If the lady at the desk had noticed the mess, she didn't appear to be concerned. The security guard by the door, on the other hand, watched her warily.

The elevator chimed and Sam jumped in, away from his scrutiny. She didn't need one more person irritated with her. She wanted to be excited about meeting her niece, but all she felt was the nauseating burn of apprehension in her stomach. Laura had been annoyed when Sam had missed Bella and Carson's births. *"You're my only sister, Sam. You couldn't have tried to be there?"*

With the door closing, Sam rolled her shoulders. The soft mechanical whir lulled her, despite the odd scent combo that could best be described as locker room sweat, green pepper and onion pizza, and heady men's cologne. The smell only made her feel worse.

Would Laura be mad? Her texts had been terse. She had to know Sam couldn't have done anything to control the weather. Sam had wanted to be here the last two times. But work had interfered and she hadn't been experienced enough to know how to stand up to her boss for well-earned leave. This time, Sam had been more prepared.

She made her way down the hallway and found the room number, then took a moment to gather herself.

The door squeaked as Sam opened it a fraction. She tucked a loose strand of dark hair behind her ear. "Hey. You awake?"

"Sam? Come on in." Laura's voice was quiet but enthusiastic.

That sounds promising. Relief flooded her. When her relationship with Laura was peaceful, their bond was unshakeable. Sam was desperate for that camaraderie. She missed her big sister's friendship when they argued.

Sam pushed open the door, then slid aside the curtain giving privacy to the room. Laura lay on the bed in the center with a plastic bassinet beside her. Laura grinned, her face wan. "Finally here to meet your newest niece?"

Sam edged closer to the bassinet and placed a hand over her heart. "Oh my goodness, she's absolutely beautiful." She peeked at the soft dark hair sticking out from under the newborn cap. The baby had a heart-shaped face, a bit like her sister's, the only thing visible from the tight swaddle. "I'm sorry I couldn't be here sooner. I left New York as soon as Mom called me. The train stopped somewhere in New Jersey, and we stayed on the track for three hours without a single update."

"It's fine, Sam. It's my third baby. I figured I wouldn't be in labor long this time anyway." Laura pushed a button on her hospital bed to sit upright and winced. "Of course, I never expected an emergency C-section, but here we are." She smiled lovingly at the baby. "I named her Charlotte."

"After Mom? Wow, she must be thrilled." Sam glanced at the sparse furniture for any hints of her mother's presence. "She's not here?" She removed her coat and backpack, setting them on the window ledge in the room.

"She's watching Bella and Carson. Mark just left to take over so she can come in and meet the baby." The corners of Laura's mouth turned downward. "Though I'm a little worried about how this C-section is going to affect things for Mom. I won't be able to help her for a while, and Mark only gets a week of paternity leave."

Sam focused her attention on the baby. Laura wasn't asking, but she knew what the expectation would be. Not that they didn't need or deserve Sam's help. But her family still wanted her to make Brandywood her home again. They'd probably always want that. *But I don't live here anymore.* "Let me see what I can do. I don't know if I can help for more than a week because I have a social media shoot for *This Charmed Life* in a few weeks. I have to style, shoot, and edit everything, and—"

Laura held out a hand. "Don't worry. I know you're busy. We all know you're busy. And I'm sure any help you can give will be perfect, thank you."

Sam relaxed and sat on the bed beside Laura. "I'll do as much as I can."

Laura's dark eyes were unreadable. "I know you will. You always do."

If it had been anyone else, the barb in the comment wouldn't have been obvious. But it was Laura. Ninety-five percent of the arguments they'd had in the past few years were about the same topic. Maybe eventually Laura would understand that Sam really was doing all she could. She was just a visitor to her hometown now, one whose trips here required vacation time.

Now wasn't the time to argue. Or to take the bait. Sam brushed the baby's soft cheek with the knuckle of her forefinger. "Can I hold her?"

"Of course." Laura's entire demeanor shifted as she turned her attention back to her daughter. "I'm so excited to snuggle her. I know Carson is only two, but the newborn phase is my favorite."

Sam lifted the sleeping baby from the bassinet. Her heart squeezed as she gazed at her new niece. *She's perfect.* The first time she held Bella, she hadn't felt like she was missing out by not living here. With each subsequent child, that seemed to shift. "You and Mark make the cutest babies."

"I know." The smile on Laura's face came from a depth Sam was certain she couldn't tap. "You and Eli could make babies almost as cute if you two would get married. I've never seen two people drag their feet more. Are you guys even together right now?"

Not this. As though it were that simple. Sam shrugged. Sam had shared with Laura her dreams of having children someday —that wasn't the problem. Unfortunately, Laura assumed Sam had found the right guy and just hadn't gotten around to it. "Not really. He was in LA working as a showrunner for some new project a few weeks ago, but he's back in New York now. We had lunch recently."

"Ah." Laura's eyes brightened knowingly. "Lunch? Sounds like a date."

"Nope. Just lunch. The timing is never right, you know?" Sam shrugged, pressing the infant closer. She'd better change the subject before she got the comment about not getting any younger. In New York, no one blinked an eye at her being twenty-seven without babies, but here in Brandywood, that practically made her an old maid. "Mmm . . . I love that newborn smell."

"Or it means you have a fear of commitment." Laura tugged off the striped pink-and-blue newborn cap, revealing a shock of dark hair resembling both Redding sisters. "Look, she's got Mark's crazy widow's peak." She pulled the cap back on. "You can't let Mom's experience continue to screw you up for all relationships. Everyone knows you and Eli are the endgame. You always have been."

"Maybe. Either way, I'm not in a rush. And neither is Eli." *There's an understatement.* Sam sighed, rocking the infant in her arms. "I'm happy with my life the way it is. New York City is great. Brandywood folks may not believe it, but city life is fun. I haven't cooked in about six years. Everything I could want to eat is minutes away and better than I could ever make it."

"Yeah? I guess dining options trump having family nearby —and getting to know your nieces and nephew." Laura arched a brow. "Or being there for your mother. Mom's been slowing down lately."

Her new niece let out a mewling wail, and Laura extended her arms for her daughter.

Sam's arms tightened reflexively around Charlotte, not ready to let go of the source of calm. *Will we ever get to a point where Laura doesn't guilt-trip me within minutes of seeing me?*

Sam carefully placed the baby in Laura's outstretched hands. "Mom slowing down just means she's finally moving at normal human speed." Sam leaned over and kissed the top of the baby's head. "And you know I love your kids. I have a lot on my plate right now."

Laura grunted and shifted to a more upright position. She winced again. "This incision is going to be a pain. Hand me that pillow on the rocking chair, will you?"

Sam fetched the pillow and averted her gaze as Laura nursed. No matter how many times her sister reassured her it was fine to watch, it was hard for Sam to understand how motherhood meant being so comfortable baring one's boobs. "I promise I'll try to help. I'll give Rachel a call and see if she can box up all the styling elements I'll need so all I have to do is slide in with my props and camera gear at the last minute."

"Thanks." A few beats passed and Laura added, "You know I give you a hard time because I miss you, right? We're all very proud of you."

These softer moments did the trick of making Sam feel those twinges of guilt and doubt. The fast pace of her life made it easy to drown out what she missed from Brandywood. She cleared her throat. "I miss you too."

Laura chuckled. "I'm hormonal, so if I cry, don't pay any attention." She sniffled and stretched out her hand toward the tray by her bedside. "Can you push that closer to me? I need some water."

Sam adjusted the rolling tray, and Laura ripped the lid off the Styrofoam cup with one hand. She guzzled the water and flashed a smile. "I'm so thirsty when I'm nursing." Checking the clock on the wall, Laura frowned. "I wonder where Mom is. Mark left here an hour ago. She should have been here by now."

"You want me to call her?" Sam pulled her phone from her purse. *Crap.* Eight missed calls from Mark.

Sam's stomach dropped. Was something wrong?

Fighting a flash of panic, Sam gave Laura a tight-lipped smile. "I'm going out in the hall to give you some privacy while I call."

She slipped out before Laura could protest. What if one of Laura's kids was hurt?

The door clicked shut behind her as she punched in Mark's number. He picked up on the first ring. "Oh, thank God, Sam. You with Laura?"

"I'm at the hospital, but I stepped out of the room when I saw you'd been trying to reach me. Everything okay?"

"I'm fine. In the car with Bella and Carson. Listen, don't say anything to Laura yet, but your mom—uh—I don't know what to say exactly, but she's on her way to the hospital. In an ambulance. I think she might have had a heart attack."

Mom was in an ambulance? Sam covered her mouth, gasping. She glanced over her shoulder at the closed door to Laura's room. Tears pricked her eyes. *Not Mom.*

"What happened?" Sam's voice felt tight. Had the ambulance arrived at the hospital yet?

"I don't know. I got here to watch the kids and found her facedown in the living room. Bella was crying in the playpen, and Carson was stuck in his high chair. He was asleep, so I don't know how long they were there alone. I don't want to say anything to Laura yet because she'll freak out."

Mark breathed out as though he needed to vent. "I swear to God, finding Carson in that high chair was worse than finding your mom. I saw your mom first, then Carson. Sam, I thought someone must have broken in and shot them both."

Sam squeezed her eyes shut, trying not to imagine the scene Mark had so vividly described. It was too horrible for words. "I won't say anything." *But Laura's going to be upset if I don't.*

"I'm dropping the kids off with the babysitter, and then I'll be there and tell her." Mark blared the horn, then swore under his breath. "Your mom might already be in the ER if you want to check on her."

Sam started walking. She had to find out where Mom was.

Oh, God. What if she died? "I'm on my way to the ER now. I'll call you when I have an update."

She hung up and found the nurses' station, where they gave her directions. Rushing toward the elevators, Sam tried to stay calm, but she failed badly. *Not Mom. Please don't let her die.*

She pressed the call button for the elevator a few times, her hand unsteady. How could Mom have had a heart attack? She was too young, wasn't she? Only fifty-four. She went to the gym every day.

The elevator bell dinged too slowly, and she pushed into the crowded car. *Stay calm.* As the elevator stopped at other floors, irrational resentment curled in her chest at those alighting and getting on. Why couldn't it be empty like it had been last time? *Stay calm.* Others probably had their own catastrophes too.

When she arrived on the ground floor, she peeled out into the hallway. She rushed to the ER front desk. "Hi, my mother, Charlotte Redding—they brought her here. A few minutes ago, I'm not sure. In an ambulance."

The woman behind the desk stared at her computer screen. "Can I get your photo ID?"

Sam reached for her wallet, then paused. She'd given it to the woman when she'd checked in to visit Laura. *Of course.* Frustration bubbled, and she rubbed her eyes. "I don't have it."

"Sam." A deep and familiar male voice came from behind her as someone tapped her shoulder.

She turned, startled. *Garrett?* What was Garrett Doyle doing there? She hadn't seen him for five years. He seemed taller, broader. His dark-brown hair was longer, but he'd just graduated from Army Ranger School the last time she'd seen him.

The memory curled out of a place where she'd buried it deeply. Standing there on the porch of The Dutchman, the restaurant where Katie and Garrett had planned their rehearsal dinner. The fallout of that conversation had haunted her for years.

She shook her head, the ugly memory clearing.

His eyes were the same. Light brown, flecked with amber. They'd always held a mixture of humor and sarcasm when she'd looked at them most of her life. But not now. There was concern. Even sadness.

"Garrett, what are you doing here?" The sight of someone so familiar undid her composure. Tears slipped from her eyes, and she dashed them away. "My mom . . ."

Garrett stepped forward as though his impulse was to hug her. He stopped and stuffed his hands awkwardly into his pockets. "I know. I came over with her in the ambulance."

What? Why would Garrett have come in with Mom? Sam stepped back, trying to hide her shock. She wiped her eyes again. "Laura's upstairs, as she just had a baby, and I gave my ID to the desk staff there and . . ."

Garrett tugged at her visitor pass hanging from the bottom of her sweater. "I think you're covered." He flashed it at the woman behind the desk and tilted his head. "Come on. I'll take you back."

Of all the people she *didn't* want to share this moment with, Garrett ranked near the top of her list. But this wasn't the time. Her curiosity burned at his presence. "So you rode in the ambulance? How did that happen?"

"Yeah." Garrett checked over his shoulder. "Your mom hired me to do some work on a few cabins. I saw the ambulance pull up. Mark couldn't ride with her, so I volunteered."

Why would Mom hire Garrett? *Katie would be so hurt if she knew.*

"Have they said what happened to my mom?" A few nurses ran past her.

"Not sure yet. But she's stable now." Garrett slowed and put a hand out to stop her.

Sam followed his gaze. Several nurses rushed toward a room, one of them hastily pulling the curtain closed. She gripped his forearm. "Is that my mom's room?"

The muscles in Garrett's forearm tightened, and he nodded slowly.

The space in the hallway seemed to narrow as alarms beeped wildly amid running footsteps and voices shouting out orders. Orders that had something to do with Mom.

The area around Sam seemed to spin as nausea rose in her throat.

More nurses ran toward the room. *Mom!* Her silent scream resounded in her brain like a thunderclap.

Garrett's eyes widened. "Sam. You okay?"

Sam dug her fingers into his arm. Then she threw up.

CHAPTER TWO

THE DOOR SQUEAKED OPEN, and Sam looked up from the couch in the living room. Eli stepped inside the house and shook the snow from his dark peacoat. She sat up straight, her eyes half open. "Eli—" *How did he find out?*

"Garrett called me. I hopped on the first flight I could get out of JFK." Eli hung his coat on the hanger by the door and started forward. He stopped mid-step and kicked off his loafers. "I forgot how much your mom hates shoes in the house." After crossing the room in his socks, he sank onto the couch beside her.

Garrett and Eli still stayed in touch. They'd been best friends since grade school, but she hadn't expected Garrett to make that call. She was too relieved to see Eli to care about whether Garrett should have done it.

Sam wiped her eyes and let Eli pull her into a tight embrace. *This. This is what I've needed. Thank you, Eli.* "I'm so glad you're here."

Eli didn't let go, his hand stroking her back. "How is she? Was it a heart attack?"

"She's out of surgery. They said it went well. The doctor said the blood was causing too much pressure on her brain from when she'd hit her head falling, but they're still not sure why she fell in the first place. They didn't think it was a heart attack, though. Garrett brought me home at four in the morning so I could get a few hours of sleep." Not that she'd slept well, despite her exhaustion.

Every time she closed her eyes, she relived the scene of her mom crashing in ER, the scramble to get her to surgery, the long, quiet wait, and then how still Mom had been post-surgery. *When will I find out more?*

"It was a relief to know Garrett was there. A surprise, but still a relief. Especially since Laura and Mark couldn't be there with you." Eli kissed her temple, the scruff of his trim sandy-blond beard scratching her.

Sam chewed on her lower lip. Seeing Garrett had been strange. Especially because she hadn't seen or talked to him since he'd walked out on Katie so many years before. Sam had been on the receiving end of many years' worth of Katie's rants about "the asshole." Katie had spent a long time trying to get over Garrett. And even though the passing years had led to distance in Sam and Katie's friendship, Sam still felt loyal to her childhood best friend.

But it had been a relief to have someone she'd known forever with her in such a terrifying moment. Someone who'd been present at almost every single significant event in her life. Garrett may have been the boy she'd spent a lifetime bickering with, but there had been none of that last night. Just calm. Kindness.

She shook her head, pushing the thought away. "He was the last person I expected to see in the hospital, to be honest. But he was helpful. Didn't even yell at me when I threw up on his shoes."

Eli chuckled and put his arm around her shoulder, drawing her to rest against him as he leaned against the couch. "You never did well around hospitals. I'm surprised you didn't pass out like that time I talked you into giving blood with me."

"Well, I hadn't eaten." She yawned. Despite all the difficulties of their romantic relationship, it was so easy to fall into a familiar rhythm with Eli. She knew him better than anyone—and vice versa. She combed her fingers through the tangles in her hair, then pulled the elastic out from her ponytail and hastily redid the messy bun.

She yawned. "Follow me to the kitchen. I'm going to need an entire pot of coffee to get through the day."

They made their way into the familiar kitchen. Sam paused at the counter, running her hands over the smooth butcher block. For all those times she'd advocated to upgrade to granite or quartz, she was glad Mom hadn't listened. She had so many memories of standing at these counters, clumsily helping her mom chop vegetables. Making projects for school. Watching Mom work out numbers for the cabins on that old dinosaur of a calculator she still used.

Sam had even shared her first kiss with Eli in this kitchen.

She dug the canister of coffee beans out of the freezer. Eli came up beside her and took the container from her. "Sit. I'll make the coffee. You look exhausted."

She gave him a grateful smile and shuffled toward the kitchen table. "I meant to ask you—how's the new show going?" The old chair creaked under her weight, sounding as though it'd seen better days. Had Eli come from work? He wore a button-down shirt, collar open, untucked over his jeans.

"Great." Eli fished around in the cabinet under the range until he found the coffee grinder. "We'll be getting ready to shoot the pilot right after Christmas." The grinder's loud whir cut him off. "I have a good feeling about this one."

Her gaze settled out the window, unable to process Eli's words. From here, she could see the sign for the cabins and the main entrance. Her eyes were bleary. "Sounds great." She'd been four when they'd first hung that sign. The joy on Mom's face was something she'd never forget. A short-lived joy that had disappeared a few months later when the world came crashing down around them.

"Eli. What am I going to do?" She barely heard her own question.

Eli was beside her in seconds. He pulled out a chair and sat, taking her hands. "It's gonna be okay. We'll figure it out."

Tears threatened her. "But what if she dies? I don't even know what's wrong with her." For the many years she'd been gone from home, she'd always assumed Mom would be there waiting when she came to visit. Now, everything felt far less certain. She wasn't ready for any of it. Guilt hung over her head.

"She won't die, Sam. It'll be all right."

He meant the words as a comfort, but it was a phrase so trite that she tossed him a glare. "You don't know that. No one knows that."

He ducked his chin, chastened, and shifted hair from his eyes. He could use a haircut. "You're right. I can't tell you if she's going to live or die. But it *will* be all right. No matter what happens. Because if there's one person I know can get through anything, it's you."

"But what about the cabins? There's no way she can manage everything by herself when she leaves the hospital—not with Laura recovering from a C-section. Mom barely makes enough to scrape by. And her employees are depending on her." The coffee maker hummed as the pot filled with the steaming brew, and a deep and robust scent floated toward her.

"I know what you're asking. And I think you already know the answer." Eli smiled tightly. "But if you don't want to leave your life in New York City behind to help around here, I don't think it's unreasonable. You have a job. I'm not sure you won't catch hell for it from your family, though."

He was right. This wasn't the type of thing she could say she was too busy for. If she didn't come home to help now—then when? She'd claimed the flexibility of her new job gave her the chance to go back home when needed. And she was *needed* right now. "I know."

Eli winked. "You ready to become Brandywood's most reluctant resident again?"

Anger flared at his attempt at humor. "There's nothing funny about this."

He sobered. "Sorry." He kissed the back of her hand. "You're a good person, Sam. The best I've ever known. I know Laura gives you hell about why you left, but deep down I think she wishes she could have escaped too. You shouldn't feel guilty about the choices you've made. You've always been here when it matters."

She wished she could agree. But his words didn't make her feel better. "Unless, of course, my mom dies. In which case, I'm that daughter who avoided home for years."

The coffee machine hissed to a stop and Eli headed toward it. He poured her a cup, then set it in front of her. "Your family also doesn't understand the life you live in the city. You don't get to your level without working your ass off. Leaving the city at the busiest time of year isn't exactly easy."

The acrid sweetness of hot coffee greeted her as she sipped it. "You're not kidding." She groaned thinking of how little she'd brought with her for this trip. Hopefully, her assistant would help. Thank God she'd given Rachel keys to her apartment. "I have to call Rachel and see if she'll send me some things. And"—she grimaced—"I should call Maren. Maren is going to kill me when I tell her I won't be back until the Christmas cookie shoots." Her editor wasn't known for her empathy.

"Christmas cookie?" Eli raised his brows. "Something you want to tell me?"

Sam cringed. *Dammit.* She must be more tired than she thought. This wasn't the way she had wanted to tell him. "Yeah, so I asked for an assignment with the food photography team. I wanted to try something different. The magazine is doing a 'Twelve Days of Christmas Cookies' social media campaign I'm supposed to shoot starting December seventh." Only a couple of weeks away. Her editor would definitely kill her. Maren had done her a favor by putting her in for the job ahead of the contracted food photographers.

Eli took a measured look at her, his eyes unreadable. "And that's what you want? To shoot food?"

She wrapped her hands around the mug, delighting in its warmth. Glancing at her bare feet, she frowned. Mom always kept the thermostat low in winter to save money. She'd need to go through her old room and dig around for some warm wool socks. "I-I thought it would be fun. A break from all the normal pics. The magazine is doing this thing where they're baking the cookies live on social media, and I'm taking pictures of the baking process and final product."

Eli rolled his eyes. His tolerance of what he called the *"schmaltzy side of Christmas"* seemed to grow thinner by the year. "I'm sure they can find another food photographer, even last minute."

It was probably true but not something Sam liked to think about. She didn't want to be replaceable. Especially not when she'd worked so hard to get the job as the lead staff photographer for *This Charmed Life*. But she wasn't ready to tell Eli she didn't want this to be a one-time thing. "And if Maren decides she likes the new photographer's style more? Or the campaign does amazingly, and they give that photographer more assignments? I'm out of a job." *Or they won't give me any more food shoots.*

The corners of Eli's mouth tipped in a smile. "Would it be the worst thing? I have a friend with a great in at *Lands and Oceans*. That could be the next big step for you in landscape photography."

Sam held Eli's light-blue gaze. Not so long ago, the news that *Lands and Oceans*—or any major wildlife magazine— wanted to work with her would have been enough to float her spirits to the moon. But she didn't want that anymore. "I like what I'm doing now."

Before Eli could answer, the doorbell rang. "I'll get it." Eli left her, disappearing through the doorway.

Moments later, Katie rushed into the kitchen. "Oh, honey —" Katie stretched out her arms. "I'm so sorry." Katie bent and hugged Sam tightly.

How had Katie heard? Sam hadn't even thought to text her yet. Garrett couldn't have been the one to spread the news. If Garrett was back in Katie's life, Sam would have heard. "Who told—"

"It's all over town. The babysitter Mark left the kids with? Her mom is good friends with my mom." Katie straightened and pushed back a strand of ashy-red hair from her cheek.

All over town. She should check in with Laura. People would be reaching out to Laura and Mark right now. *She must be overwhelmed.*

"I didn't want to barge in, but I didn't know Eli would get all the way here from LA first, and I didn't want you to be alone." Katie blew a kiss toward Eli. "You're amazing for coming out here so fast."

Eli smiled and kissed Katie on the cheek. "It's good to see you. But I came out from New York, actually. I've been there the last couple of months working on a new show."

Katie nodded distractedly and sat in the chair Eli had vacated. She peeled off her coat, directing her full attention to Sam. "Is your mom okay? What happened? Can I visit her?"

If it had been anyone else, the peppering of questions would have felt annoying. But Katie's eager, pretty face wore concern. "She's alive. I think she's stable for now. I haven't heard from Mark. And I don't know about visits." Sam swallowed another gulp of coffee. "I figured I'd take a nap and shower, then head back to the hospital."

"Okay. I'll go with you." The determination on Katie's face indicated she would argue the point. "I can drive you both. Knowing you two out-of-towners, you don't have cars here."

Sam smiled, looking from Eli to Katie. How the years could pass and the same two people could be by her side in the same kitchen . . . she was lucky. As her emotions bubbled and twisted her gut, she managed, "You two really are the best of friends."

Katie's green eyes teared. "Why don't you go upstairs and grab that shower and nap? Eli and I will monitor your phone for updates."

Give Eli my phone? Sam hesitated.

Eli rolled his eyes. "Don't worry, I don't even know what your passcode is anymore."

That was true. He could only answer incoming calls. She nodded and slid her phone toward Katie. She stood.

Katie palmed it and laughed. "Good God. This thing is huge. It makes my phone look like a tiny baby phone." As she examined it, Sam's phone rang.

Sam furrowed her brow as they both looked to see who was calling.

Katie stiffened and Sam's stomach sank.

Even though Sam had kept the generic label of "asshole," Katie knew exactly who that referred to. She'd been the one to change the contact's name on Sam's phone.

Garrett.

CHAPTER THREE

DAMN WOMAN.

Garrett stared at the flashing number on his phone. Sam had ignored his call. Of course. Even though her lack of derision in the hospital had given him a moment of hope, he'd known better than to get too optimistic. She'd been upset, and he was the closest thing she'd had to a friend.

His boots hit the snow-covered gravel parking lot beside the Redding Cabins guest service house, and he slammed the door to his pickup. He followed the sidewalk to the one-room brick building and opened the door. The whole parking area and sidewalk needed shoveling—something he wouldn't have time for. The bell on the knob jangled.

"Oh, thank God you're back. How is Mrs. Redding?" Jen popped up from behind the front desk, her bleached-blond hair sticking up in odd directions from her messy bun. She threw her diaper bag strap over her shoulder, then grabbed Colby from his playpen. The toddler grinned, a pack of fruit snacks in his hands.

"Alive. Barely." Garrett slipped his fingertips into the back pockets of his jeans. "Out of surgery."

"I was so scared for her." Worry lined Jen's face. She swung Colby onto her hip. "I'm so sorry I can't stay longer. A guest came in from cabin twelve and asked about getting the water turned on for the hose outside. Took his bike through some serious mud and wants to rinse it off."

Garrett nodded. "You have another job to get to." He ruffled Colby's hair, and Jen walked past him. He motioned toward the snow. "You need a ride back to town?"

"Nah, my dad insisted I bring his truck last night. I'm good. But if you're around later, stop by Bunny's. I'll make up a big old cup of hot chocolate, and we can hang out."

He hesitated. The last time her brother Dan had seen them hanging out at Bunny's Café, he'd pulled Garrett over for a traffic violation—to tell Garrett to stay away. Since then, Garrett preferred to keep their hangouts to moments like this, when they were both working at the cabins. "I don't think I can today. I have to be on the job site."

"Okay, well, I'll see you around. Oh! I brought you chocolate peppermint truffles from Bunny's. They're behind the desk." Jen winked before she walked out, the bells on the door bouncing noisily.

"You're a saint." He spied the truffles on the counter, and his stomach growled. He hadn't eaten dinner. Or breakfast.

"I don't know about that." Jen's clear laugh was silenced as the door shut.

Garrett watched her svelte figure through the glass door as she navigated toward her car, taking big steps over the snow. He should have offered to help her to her car. Colby's legs dangled from her hip. The kid still had pj's on. She caught Garrett watching, then smirked.

Since he'd moved back to town a few months ago, he'd struck up an unexpected friendship with Jen while working at Redding Cabins. Unexpected, because she was several years younger—and a Klein. Growing up with Dan Klein was reason enough to avoid her. And given she'd had a kid with some deadbeat two years ago, her brothers threw murderous looks at anyone who approached her. Everyone still thought of Jen as Dan's baby sister. A twenty-two-year-old woman should be able to make her own decisions.

He found the bag of truffles she'd left and untied the ribbon. The plastic crinkled in his hands. Popping a truffle in his mouth, Garrett closed his eyes. Chocolate and peppermint. Best damn combination on the planet.

Garrett rubbed the back of his neck and glanced at his phone again. Running guest services for the cabins hadn't been on his agenda for the day. He had a job he was supposed to be managing in town. The homeowners had been adamant he supervise everything, no matter how many promises Garrett made about Luis being trustworthy. They were the type of homeowners that detonated red flags, and he'd wanted to say no to the job, But things had been slow lately, and his crew was desperate for extra work before Christmas.

His eyes burned with exhaustion. Maybe Sam was sleeping and hadn't declined the call. She had to be as tired as he was.

He wished he could leave. This wasn't his problem; it was hers. He didn't know squat about running the cabins.

But he wasn't about to do that to Mrs. Redding.

Walking over to the small coffee bar opposite the main desk, he pulled a pod out of its space on the rack and popped it into the coffee maker.

The machine gurgled as his phone rang. He dug it from the pocket of his jeans—it didn't surprise him to see the caller.

"Hey, man, what's up?" he answered.

Eli cleared his throat before speaking. "You have no idea."

His voice sobered. "Katie was here when you called Sam. If your ears have been ringing—that's why."

Aw, shit. Garrett cringed. He should have known Katie would be the first person to flock to Sam's side. "Chernobyl?"

"Pretty much." Eli chuckled. "I have to give it to you. The way Katie talks about you, you'd think you'd dumped her yesterday."

He hadn't just dumped her, though. He'd walked out from their rehearsal dinner and driven four states away. *Which is why everyone took her side.* Not that he hadn't deserved the heat he'd gotten for it. But Garrett had never won awards for his intellect and getting engaged to Katie had by far been the dumbest thing he'd done.

"I need to talk to Sam. I'm supposed to be at work this morning." Garrett wiggled his Styrofoam cup out from under the coffee maker and ripped open eight packs of sugar. Not enough for his taste but it was a start. Cradling the phone, he searched the office fridge for creamer.

"And where are you instead?"

"At the front desk cabin. Jen Klein worked the night shift, but I took over for her because she has to be at her other job at eight. Someone's gotta be here for checkout this morning at least. Laura normally does it."

"All right, let me talk to Sam. Can you hold down the fort for another half hour?"

Garrett groaned inwardly. He didn't want to seem like a jerk, even to Eli. Then again, Eli wasn't writing the reviews for his business. "Yeah, I'm not going anywhere until someone comes and takes over. But if it's too much longer than that, I'll have to put a sign on the door with an emergency number."

"Sit tight. Katie or I will probably come to take over for you. Hopefully, Katie will know how to run things. Sam needs her rest."

As Eli hung up, Garrett found the creamer in the back of the mini-fridge and stood. French vanilla. At least it was flavored.

He stirred it in, not wanting to think of facing Katie. They'd done a decent job of avoiding each other since he'd moved back to town.

Growing up as the only daughter of one of the most influential politicians in town, everyone had handled Katie with silk gloves her whole life. You didn't look at Katie the wrong way. And you *really* didn't dump her the night before her wedding.

That was what it had been, after all. Her wedding. Not theirs. She'd planned the damn thing while he was at Ranger School, from the location to the purple vest he was supposed to wear. Garrett wasn't sure what she had been madder at—being dumped or losing all those pictures she planned to put on her social feeds.

He sat at the chair behind the front desk and flipped on the TV. The morning news shows were on, which was good since he needed the distraction.

Seeing Samantha Redding again had jolted him.

How did she keep growing more beautiful?

He sipped the coffee and made a face. Still a little under-sweetened and bitter for him. Better than nothing though.

When he'd moved back to Brandywood, he'd known it was a matter of time until Sam and he would run into each other. Truthfully, the encounter had taken longer than he'd expected. She rarely seemed to come home.

And the circumstances of their meeting were much, much worse.

The last words Sam had spoken to him years ago resurfaced as though someone had recorded them and hit Replay in his brain.

They'd been standing on the porch of The Dutchman.

"Love makes nice women like your mom and my mom marry morons like your dad and my dad. You may have forgotten what it was like growing up as the kids of the town drunk and the town criminal, but I haven't. The only thing that was good about your dad was that he made people gossip about mine marginally less. Oh, and that because of him, you ended up looking out for me."

Sam hadn't minced words, and he'd left her standing there on that porch in the cold air by herself.

But throughout the rest of the rehearsal dinner, those words had rung through his head. He'd kept telling himself marrying Katie when they were both so young was okay because they loved each other. But it wasn't what Sam had said that was the problem. It was the memories that had surfaced.

He hadn't forgotten what each of their fathers had put them through as kids. The first fistfight he ever got into was over what a second-grader said about Sam's dad. He'd been in first grade. In middle school he'd been suspended while defending Sam again when another kid told her everything her family owned had been paid for in blood money. As though Mrs. Redding hadn't been scrimping to survive the horrible financial position her husband had left her in.

Sam didn't get book fair money and wore hand-me-downs from the thrift shop—just like him. They'd been the only two kids who didn't go on the annual eighth-grade ski trip. Neither of their families could afford it.

He'd always had her back. He'd always wanted her friendship because his dad had been as loathed as hers.

But Eli had been the one Sam saw as something more than a friend. Hell, Samantha Redding had never even seen him as a friend—only Eli's annoying friend. And, later, as Katie's annoying boyfriend. Garrett leaned back in his seat and gulped another burning swallow of coffee.

When he went back into that rehearsal dinner, he'd known he couldn't marry Katie. He'd understood a deeper part of him had never let his feelings for Sam go. Because he was still very much in love with her.

He glanced at his watch and stood. Not that any of it made a difference now. It hadn't made a difference back then. Sam and Eli were too close, and he could have never betrayed his best friend by making a play for his girl. And that wasn't even factoring Katie into everything.

The pathway to Sam had always involved a drop off a cliff. He'd put those feelings of youthful infatuation to rest a long time ago.

Sudden movement outside the front door caught his attention, and his stomach lurched. Katie exited her silver Jeep Cherokee. She strode toward the door, her red hair seeming to streak behind her like a fireball.

Dammit, Eli.

Katie yanked open the door, the bell clanging harshly. She threw him a disdainful look. "You can get out now. I'll take over."

Garrett gave her his best, most charming smile. "Good morning to you too, beautiful."

She cut her eyes at him. "Oh, shut up."

Garrett gathered his coffee and the truffles Jen had left him. "I know I'm not who you want to see. But we can all get along, can't we? For the Reddings?"

"What the hell are you doing here?" Katie crossed her arms. "Why, of all the idiot contractors in this town, are you the one here?"

"Ran into Mrs. Redding at the grocery store. She mentioned she needed some help repairing a few cabins. I offered my services." Garrett scooted past her, and the tension between them seemed to amplify at their proximity.

Katie stalked away from him toward the desk. "I'm sure Sam or Laura will be in touch if you're still needed. Which you probably aren't."

"Okay." Garrett winked and pointed toward his truck. "I'm gonna stop by cabin twelve and put the outside water on for the guest there. But make sure someone turns it off. You know, it being winter and all."

"Like I said"—Katie tossed her thick hair over her shoulder—"I think we got it. Bye."

The door shut behind him as he stepped back out into the cold air. Truthfully, it had been frostier in that room with Katie.

She might never stop hating him. He shook his head and headed toward his truck. It made him sad she hadn't moved on, if he was honest. Yes, he'd done her wrong, but wasn't she glad they hadn't made a bigger mistake? *Because how can you say you love someone one minute and tell them what an unlovable asshole they are the next?*

"Even your dad knew what a worthless piece of crap you are, Garrett." Katie's voice rang through his head.

He checked his rearview mirror as he put the truck in Reverse. Katie was no longer visible. Thank God he'd dodged that bullet.

CHAPTER FOUR

SOFT FOOTSTEPS STIRRED Sam from a deep sleep. She bolted upright, barely glancing at Eli approaching before she checked her watch. A sinking feeling fell through her, and she leaped out of bed. "Oh crap, my online meeting with Maren was three hours ago."

Eli held out her phone. "Laura called." His face hinted of worry.

Sam searched under the old wooden footboard for the socks she'd found earlier. "What did Laura want?"

"She's upset about your mom. Wants you to come back to the hospital." Eli squatted beside her. "Direct quote—'I can't believe Sam left the hospital.'"

Stopping her futile search, Sam gaped. "She realizes I was up for twenty-four hours straight, right?"

"Yeah, but she's just had a baby, so you won't win in the great One-Up Battle." Eli grimaced. "What're you looking for?"

"My socks." Sam curled her toes against the smooth wooden floorboards. The One-Up Battle was the joking term Eli had given to the way Sam, Laura, and their mom responded to all things. The sisters had probably unconsciously learned it from their mom, and now Sam's therapist was working on helping her unlearn it.

"Listen to what others have to say," Sylvia had said. "Don't make a comparison to something you've experienced."

Flattening her feet to the cold floor, Sam palmed the phone and scrolled through her missed calls and messages. Nothing from Maren.

Which meant she was probably upset.

Maren rarely sent a reminder for meetings. She didn't believe it was her responsibility to remind the people working for her what they should have scheduled. She certainly wouldn't have gone hunting for Sam.

Sam went over to the window and pulled back the curtains. The clear sky and last traces of brightly colored fall leaves against the snow didn't match the dimness of her spirit.

"Found them." Eli stood behind her, socks in hand. "What else can I do? I feel useless. Katie took over manning the guest lodge, and I shoveled the walks and parking spaces."

Sam pulled the socks on and smiled gratefully. "You being here is a big deal. I know you can't stay, but it means the world to me."

Eli approached and hugged her. "You'd be here for me if the roles were reversed. Why don't you come on downstairs? We can eat a late brunch, and then I'll ride with you to the hospital."

She wrapped her arms around his neck and let him hold her. Maren and Laura both needed tending to, but Sylvia's voice, with its deep, smoky tone, continued running through her head. *Don't always rush to put other people's needs above your own emotional ones.*

Pulling back, she stood on her tiptoes and pressed a gentle

kiss to Eli's lips. Surprise registered on his face but he returned the kiss, his arm tightening around her waist.

Maybe this was the time to lean on Eli. When he'd suggested they give it another go in the summer, she hadn't been ready. But here he was, like always. *Yet, he's never indicated he wants forever with me. We always let each other go.*

She wasn't even sure she could change her mind to let him back in. The last time, her heart had been left so bruised she'd sworn she couldn't put herself through another round with him. The pain of it outweighed the pleasure.

They broke apart, and Sam slipped her fingers into his as they left her room. For most of high school, this had been their haven. Where they'd watch movies and dream of him being a famous director and she, the award-winning cinematographer, at his side.

"Do you think things would have been different if I'd gone to Hollywood with you instead of going to New York?" Sam dropped his hand, and he followed her down the stairs.

Eli sighed. "You mean, would we be making blockbusters by now? Probably not. I think we were both a little naïve about how easy it would be."

In the kitchen, Sam pulled eggs and milk from the fridge. Eli slid a bowl across the counter toward her. She cracked eggs, falling into the familiar routine of making breakfast with him. Familiar felt good right now. She didn't want to think about her mom. About change.

She took a fork from the drawer and handed it to Eli. He always did all the cooking when they spent extended time together. Not that she didn't enjoy cooking. Rachel had suggested she take a few cooking classes if she wanted to go into food photography.

As though she had the time.

She fished a pan out from under the oven and lit the burner. "How long are you planning on staying in town?"

"Probably only a couple of days." Eli finished mixing the eggs and then brought them over. His brow furrowed as he poured them into the pan. "So . . . uh . . . you missed a few calls from a credit card company while you were asleep."

Crap. Stiffening, she focused on mixing the eggs in the pan with the spatula. She should have remembered before giving Eli her phone. "Oh, yeah?"

Eli leaned against the oven door. "I picked up. Because the number kept ringing. I wasn't sure who it was."

Except that the name of the credit card company shows up when the call comes through. "So you thought it would be better to do some snooping?" She raised a brow. She shouldn't let it bother her this much. This wasn't like last time. The heat from the burner rose against her wrist.

But he also knew better than to invade her privacy. *Or he should.*

Eli's expression softened. "Hey now. Listen, I know the past few years haven't been the easiest, and the rent is expensive in New York. If you need help, I just want to let you know I'm here."

So she was behind on her credit card payment this month? What business was it of his? She was great at paying her bills ninety-five percent of the time. "I don't need help." She handed him the spatula and stomped toward the toaster.

"There's no need to get defensive about this—"

"Who says I'm being defensive?" She untwisted the tie on the bag around the loaf of sandwich bread. It didn't give, and she gritted her teeth. She twisted the other direction. *Damn twist ties.*

Eli watched her with a guarded expression. "I'm just saying I'm here."

"Yeah, now you are," she muttered, ripping the plastic below the twist tie. "But who knows what your plans for tonight are?"

He flipped the burner off and scraped the eggs onto a plate. Turning his back to the oven, his arms flexed as he crossed them. "Seriously? You want to do this right now? We weren't even talking about that—"

Humiliation crept up her throat and into her cheeks. "Me giving you my phone doesn't mean you can snoop. Not to mention, I don't need or want your financial help. Yes, I was late paying a bill. But that's partially why I asked Maren for this extra job doing the cookie shoot. Most of the food photographers are contractors, and they get paid for one shoot five times the amount I get in three months. I'm fine."

"Somehow you turned me into a bad guy for trying to care about you." Eli's eyes narrowed.

"I don't know, Eli, it's awfully hard to get over the last time you snooped through my phone, misinterpreted what you saw there, and then blew us up." She went over to the sink and started washing the pan and spatula.

His jaw clenched, Adam's apple bobbing as he swallowed. After all the years he'd known her, he shouldn't have misinterpreted a friendly message. *And he shouldn't have gone to someone else.*

"Stop already. I don't want another four months of you not talking to me."

"Well, if you don't walk out of here and jump into bed with another woman within six hours, I think we're good." She clenched the spatula in her fist, feeling every anger management technique Sylvia had taught her careening toward a precipice. "Unless you think you're incapable."

"You're blowing things completely out of proportion. And stop holding on to that spatula like a baseball bat. Settle down.

Your mom probably won't enjoy having to replace a window or television."

Sam's jaw dropped, her fury now molten hot, and she slammed the faucet off. "How dare you bring that up to humiliate me?" If she didn't get away from him, though, she might prove him right. Before Eli could answer, she stalked away into the hall. "God, and you think I'm guilty of pulling things off the shelf? But, no, you bring up what happened in February again. That was your fault and you know it."

He followed her, as she'd known he would do.

"*I* didn't bring it up. And I won't keep apologizing for that. We weren't dating. And we're not dating now. You made it clear you don't want to be together this summer."

How on earth could he act like it was all her fault they weren't together? Sure, he might have come heart in hand this summer, but he'd broken her heart on Valentine's Day, of all days. She'd gone to him, hoping, for once and for all, to figure things out. She glared over her shoulder as she hurried toward the front door. "And I'm not trying to get together now, either. In case you misinterpreted what was going on here this morning. You should have known better than to snoop. And have the common sense not to bring it up if it was as accidental as you pretend."

"Wait. Stop." Eli caught up with her as she grabbed her boots. He took her by the elbow. "Please, come on. Wait up."

She whirled around to face him but didn't make eye contact. "You know, I appreciate you being here. I really do. But I can handle this. And, to be honest, it's probably better if you go back to New York. I don't need to deal with 'us' in the middle of figuring out what the heck is going on with my mom and what I'm going to do about work."

Pain etched Eli's wide blue eyes, his expression tired. "You know I love you. I don't want to hurt you. Not anymore. I can't do that to you anymore."

She dashed away tears. "I need to talk to Maren and get back to the hospital. Need me to call you an Uber?"

"Don't do this. I cleared my schedule for a couple of days. Let me stay and help you." Eli put a hand on her shoulder. "You don't have to do this alone."

Sylvia be damned. The ugly anger spread through her and she was too tired, too frustrated, and too embarrassed to push it back. She grabbed Eli's coat from the coatrack. Fisting the thick fabric, she shoved it against his chest. "Thanks, but you've done enough."

"Sam . . ."

She let the coat fall to his feet and moved away without looking back. "You know where the door is." She didn't stop until she'd reached the kitchen and had nowhere else to go but out the side door.

Cold air smacked her, prickling at the wet trails of tears on her cheeks. She wiped them away with her palm, and her shoulders heaved. Realizing she was still holding the damned spatula, she threw it. It sank into the snow next to the side door.

So much for breakfast. She might have ruined everything with Eli for good this time. He'd said he wouldn't put up with her temper.

How could he have brought up her throwing things?

Like you brought up his cheating?

A part of her wanted to turn around and bolt back into that house. Chase him down and apologize. But her feet stayed glued to the shoveled steps.

Shivering, she started down the stairs. The front guest lodge was a quick walk. She could sit and vent to Katie until Eli left. Call Laura from there and plan to go back to the hospital and find someone to cover the guest service desk.

She pulled her phone out and called Maren.

Maren answered on the second ring. "I don't appreciate you leaving me sitting in front of a computer for the twenty minutes I graciously afforded you before giving up."

"I'm so sorry. I—" Sam paused, scrambling to think. She should have done that before calling. Too late now. "My sister had an emergency C-section, so I came down to Maryland to see her. While I was here, we found my mother unresponsive and unconscious in her house. I spent the night in the hospital."

"Are you in the hospital now?" There was a note of curiosity in Maren's voice.

Sam's breath frosted in front of her. The snow crunched under her boots, but the day was otherwise gorgeous. Snowy days at home like this had always been her favorite. "Not right this second. I came home to rest and find someone to cover for my mom's business. I'm heading back to the hospital shortly."

"So you were sleeping during our meeting," Maren said. Sam pictured her sitting at her desk, tapping perfectly manicured fingertips against the desktop. "Not that I'm not saying I don't understand. Sounds like you had a terrible night."

"It won't ever happen again." She hadn't expected any sympathy from Maren—the woman seemed as allergic to that attribute as she was to excuses. Her display of some level of understanding made Sam feel strangely guiltier for missing their meeting.

"Of course it won't. You know better than to think I'll tolerate it. But, given your difficult circumstances, I'll let it slide today. I am sorry to hear about your mother. When do you come back to the city? We can talk over lunch."

Sam smiled. For the inexperienced person, lunch with Maren would appear to be an honor. But Sam knew better. She invited people out to lunch when she wanted to see them squirm. Online meetings were for those in her favor.

Time to be brave. "I'm going to stay through Thanksgiving, actually."

A long pause followed.

"Maren?" Sam asked after about ten seconds.

"I'm still here."

"Ah, I didn't hear anything."

"I was trying to process what you said." Maren cleared her throat. "Are you not planning to do the Christmas cookie campaign?"

"Yes, of course—"

"I'm about to nix you from the whole thing. As it is, the test kitchen and the camera crew are pushing back about having to do it live. They want an additional fifteen grand to convert an area to an appropriate *live* space—whatever the hell that means —and now you're basically unavailable. I don't want the whole thing blowing up in my face."

"I fully intend to be there after Thanksgiving. I had put in for vacation because I knew my sister would be having her baby. All my assignments are in, and the only thing I'm working on is editing a few images for February's blog." Sam curled and uncurled her fingers, her skin aching from the cold.

An approaching car caught her attention as it crept up the driveway. The car Eli had called. She pointed it toward the main house and kept going. *Go after him, Sam. Don't be an idiot.*

Maren was silent for another beat, then sighed. "I'll have to keep you updated. What's going on with your mother?"

"They haven't told me yet. She was in surgery last night, but everything was so rushed, I didn't completely understand it. Something about fluid in her abdomen and pressure on her lungs caused her oxygen levels to drop. She hit her head, which caused a brain injury. But they said they needed to test the fluid from her abdomen. I have no idea."

"Oh, that doesn't sound good, honey." Something in Maren's tone hinted at genuine concern. "That happened to my sister. She was gone six months later. Cancer."

Sam stopped in her tracks, a hollow ache in her chest. *Cancer?*

Mark's description of how he had found Mom haunted her. *No. It couldn't be cancer. A heart attack or stroke, sure. But not cancer.*

"I'm so sorry for your loss, Maren. I— I doubt it's cancer with Mom. She's super healthy, so I'm hoping she'll be up on her feet soon." *I'm hoping she'll be alive and well.* Sam hated the not knowing.

"Of course, it could be something entirely different." Maren's tone had shifted. "But you take time if you need it. Get her to write things down. Like recipes. That's what I wish more than anything I'd done with Iris. She made the world's best challah, and I swear I miss it more and more every year."

Sam couldn't imagine Maren baking anything. She did brag about making fantastic Matzo ball soup, though. "You must miss her so much. My mom is pretty good at handing recipes down. She hosts a big Christmas cookie exchange every year and invites all her friends to bring their favorite recipe cards—I have some killer cookie recipes from it."

"That's such a marvelous idea."

Sam chuckled. "It's not an uncommon Christmas tradition." She stopped by the guest lodge, stomping her feet to stay warm.

"Yeah well, you know . . . Jewish. I didn't grow up with those things." Maren cleared her throat. "Okay, let's chat again in a couple of days when I have all this figured out with the test kitchen. I'll send you a link to the meeting. But, don't forget, these Christmas campaigns are some of our most important ones. I didn't give you a shot for a contract job to have you blow it. We'll need you back here immediately after Thanksgiving."

I have no idea if that will be possible. "Thanks for your understanding, Maren. And sorry about missing our earlier meeting." Maren didn't respond, which was nothing unusual.

As Sam hung up, she looked back toward the main house. The hired car was making its way back up the driveway.

"You know I love you. I don't want to hurt you. Not anymore. I can't do that to you anymore . . . you don't have to do this alone."

Sam swallowed back tears, her brain feeling dull. "That's where you're wrong, Eli. You've always made me feel like I was doing this alone."

CHAPTER FIVE

GARRETT STOMPED the snow from his boots as he held the door to Bunny's Café for an exiting customer. After a long day working in a cold attic, he wanted a giant bowl of cream of crab soup to help him thaw out. And no one did cream of crab better than Bunny.

Fall leaves decorated the glass display shelf with decadent cakes and pies displayed for the upcoming holiday. He made his way toward the register and stopped. Eli sat at a table in the back corner, staring into his laptop, headphones on.

What is he doing here?

He detoured from the line and headed toward Eli, who noticed him when he was a few feet away. Eli stood with a smile.

"Didn't think I'd get to see you this go-round," Garrett said as the two men greeted each other. "Getting some work done at Bunny's? I figured you'd be with the Reddings at the hospital."

Eli shook his head and sat once more, extending a hand to the empty chair. "Sam got a little mad and sent me packing. I couldn't get another flight out until tomorrow morning, and my parents have their house tented for termites and are in a hotel, so I came here to get some work done."

Garrett hesitated at the empty chair. After the long day and even longer previous night, the only thing he wanted was to go home to his bed. But Eli was his oldest and closest friend, and who knew when he'd see him again? His aching legs hating every motion, Garrett sat. "What happened?"

Eli stowed his laptop and headphones in a leather backpack. "Women." He rolled his eyes. "It's always something with Sam. I don't know. We got together too young, probably. And both of us were too independent and ambitious for country life." Eli scrunched his nose. "Not that I'm putting it down."

Garrett slumped back in his chair. "I'm not offended. I've seen enough of the world to know Brandywood is too small for people who have big dreams." He frowned. "But—and I'm probably the last person to give advice about women—don't you think Sam needs you right now? Let her cool off a bit. She's got a lot going on with Laura and her mom."

Eli shook his head. "Nah. She made it clear she wanted me gone." He sipped from his coffee mug. "I probably need something stronger than this."

Garrett knew the routine well enough. He was the only one Eli usually went to when he needed to vent about Sam. He grinned half-heartedly. "We can go over to Yardley's. Get a beer."

Eli nodded and finished packing his bag. "Let's do it."

Gesturing toward the wall behind Eli, Garrett chuckled. "It's too intimidating sitting here with you anyway. I swear half that wall is about you."

Eli rubbed the back of his neck, turning toward the wall of framed newspaper clippings and magazine articles. Bunny proudly displayed the townsfolk's accomplishments. Most articles were from the *Brandywood Register*, the local newspaper, but there were some big-city ones too. Lots of articles were about Eli. Almost the same amount was about Sam. "It's embarrassing. More people need to spread their wings from Brandywood."

Garrett's lips curled. Bunny had even snagged a picture when he'd graduated from Ranger School. Probably from his mother. Thankfully, you could barely see him.

The two men stood. Eli fished a couple of bills from his wallet and left them on the table. On the way out, Bunny caught sight of Garrett. "You leaving with nothing?"

"I'll be back for the cream of crab later. Don't close without me." He winked at the silver-haired plump woman.

"Yeah, we'll see. When Tweedledee and Tweedledumb go on the prowl, fat chance they're coming back." Bunny laughed. "Good to see you back here as a team."

Eli and Garrett exited into the frosty night air. Garrett shook his head. Their teen years were far behind them, but in the eyes of those who had known them as children not much seemed to have changed. They weren't the troublemakers in school. More like the goofballs who occasionally pulled over-the-top pranks.

They fell into step together down the slick sidewalk of old-town Brandywood. Eli squinted at a book club meeting inside Wordsworth's Bookstore. "Nothing ever changes here, does it?"

Garrett shoved his hands in the pockets of his jeans, wishing he'd brought his gloves from his truck. "I don't know. We've both changed, haven't we?"

Eli smirked. "Have we, though? You're still charming your way through life. I'm still dating the same woman from high school. Sort of, anyway."

Garrett lifted his brows. "You're dating again? I thought you were taking a break."

"I don't know what the hell she wants." Eli's gaze fell to his feet as he avoided a patch of ice on the sidewalk. He nodded toward Yardley's Pub, still a block away. "Christmas lights already? Thanksgiving isn't until next week."

Garrett shrugged. The magical line people drew about Christmas decorations forbidden until after Thanksgiving was mystifying. As though the rest of the world paid attention to Thanksgiving.

Even more confusing? Eli and Sam. They'd *somehow worked* according to Eli, yet, mostly, they didn't. *And Eli always blamed Sam.* "But she sent you packing so . . . another fight?"

"It's been the same fight for most of the last year." Eli stopped and tugged on the strap of his backpack in a self-conscious way Garrett recognized from high school. Didn't matter how fancy the backpack got. Eli didn't resume walking again. Maybe because he didn't want to have this conversation so openly.

Garrett crossed his arms and waited until a woman walking a dog passed them on the sidewalk. Main Street in Brandywood wasn't terribly busy at this hour. With the snow, there wasn't much street parking, and mounds of snow filled every three spots. "Sounds like you're both holding on to whatever is making you mad."

Eli's expression was rueful. "It's complex. We'd broken up for a few months, and then, last Valentine's Day, she showed up. So we hung out, but then I had a date with the woman I'd been talking to casually."

For a reason he didn't fully understand, Garrett's pulse increased. He stared at the passing cars. With the nighttime temps dropping, ice formed everywhere, and the cars moved slower. "I'm no genius with women, but what the hell were you thinking?"

Eli cringed. "I was in LA, and Sam was in New York. We hadn't been together for months. I was talking to someone else and didn't want to leave the woman hanging."

"So you chose to go on a date with a woman other than your long-term girlfriend on Valentine's Day?" He restrained his surprise that Eli hadn't told him about that. But he'd been in the Army still, finishing his last deployment. There hadn't been time to talk to Eli.

"Yeah, and uh . . . not just a date." Regret filled Eli's face.

Despite his attempts at listening to Eli with a sympathetic ear, Garrett couldn't help feeling like punching his longtime best friend. No wonder Eli had described their relationship as "rocky" the last year. Garrett leaned back against the stone façade of a historic shop along the main. "You slept with the other woman?"

Eli's shoulders hunched as he leaned back beside him, and the two men faced the street, not looking at each other. "Yeah, when Sam found out, she was furious." Eli broke off a small icicle from a window frame. "I've never seen her that mad."

He wasn't used to thinking of Eli as an asshole, but Garrett couldn't help himself. He watched Eli break the icicle into pieces and toss them on the sidewalk, waiting for a response. Garrett measured his words carefully. Hopefully, Eli had already beaten himself up for the mistake. "I have to admit, I can understand her anger." They started forward again.

"It didn't help that I had gone through her phone earlier that day. Seen her texting a guy friend from work, and I jumped to the conclusion they were sleeping together—" Eli loosened his scarf.

Garrett grimaced. Eli had always been jealous of other guys talking to Sam.

"I know. I'm an idiot. But that's why I'm trying to not be an idiot right now." He turned to face Garrett. "I'm not what she needs during this situation. Maybe not even at all. I want her to be happy. She needs someone who doesn't come with all the emotional baggage that I do. Much as it's killing me not to be there for her now, she was right to ask me to leave today. Things are too complicated for us. I messed things up with her in February, and I don't think she's ever going to forgive me for it."

Even from several feet away, Yardley's radiated with warmth. The owner, Peter, had installed a couple of outdoor propane heaters near the exit to accommodate smokers and people who didn't want to wait for a table inside the always-crowded waiting area. They slipped into the restaurant, heading for the long bar.

Garrett stared at the back of Eli's head as he followed him. The nagging feeling of anger toward his friend bothered him. "I'm not going to lie, Eli. That was a dick move. But you know that, and maybe you're right. If you wanted that freedom to date another woman even when your longtime girlfriend was in town, maybe that's your brain telling you your time is done."

"Yeah, I think you're right. I don't want to hurt her anymore, and that's all I seem to do."

As Garrett pulled out a stool and sat, he asked Eli, "Where's Sam now? In the hospital? Have you heard anything about her mom or a diagnosis?"

"Radio silence all day." Eli lifted his chin. "Do you think . . . ?" He hesitated. "Would you be willing to help her? Be there for her a bit? I know you said Mrs. Redding has you working on the cabins. It might be a good excuse to check in on Sam over the next week."

"You really think she needs the sarcastic asshole who left her best friend at the altar around?" Garrett squinted. "She'll probably tell me to go to hell."

Peter Yardley approached them from behind the bar, two coasters in hand. He slid them in front of them. "The usual, Doyle?" By the look of him, outsiders wouldn't guess Peter was beloved in town. He appeared to be a gruff, lumbering old man who would yell at kids for walking on his lawn. The reality couldn't be more different.

"Nah, I'll take whatever seasonal you have on draft."

"The usual?" Eli quirked a brow, then ordered the same thing.

As Peter walked away, Garrett shrugged. "I live in town."

Eli chuckled. "I guess that's true." He sighed. "Anyway, Sam might not see it, but I know you're a good guy. And I need your help, if you're willing. You've known her forever, and that's the sort of person she needs. Someone steady—with roots."

At least twenty things were wrong with this plan, foremost being the elephant in the room. "And Katie? Why not ask her?"

"Katie will be around. But Sam'll probably ask her not to tell me anything. And I want to"—Eli's face looked pained—"*have* to know she's okay. I'm not proud of the things I've done to hurt Sam. I hate that I can't be there for her."

Garrett squinted into the headlights of a passing car. When he'd left Katie years ago, Eli had practically been the only person who had stuck by him. Even some of his siblings had taken Katie's side. Until he'd moved back, Garrett felt like a *persona non grata* in Brandywood. Katie had made sure of that. And she had the influence to alienate him. Her father was the mayor now, and Katie knew how to use that to her advantage.

About a year after the breakup, Garrett's father had sobered up, and Garrett had said to hell with Katie's attempts to keep Garrett from town. His family had needed him. Ironically, whatever hesitations folks in town had about Garrett seemed to vanish the more he showed up for his family.

He sighed. "All right. I'll try to do what I can. But I can't guarantee Sam won't slam the door in my face."

Eli's relief was palpable. "Thank you, man. It means the world."

Peter reappeared with two foaming beers. "These two are on the house. Good to see you kids back here together." He set his hands on the bar and leaned forward. "What can I get you to eat? Got some good happy hour specials. Shrimp and wings over at the buffet are free for another thirty minutes, but we also have some new appetizers on the menu."

He pushed a happy hour menu toward them before moving on down the bar.

Eli sipped his beer with a shake of his head. "I didn't appreciate the man's genius enough when I was younger, but no wonder this place is packed every night."

That's for sure. "My buddy Luis works as a bartender here once a week. Says Yardley encourages them to comp a lot of drinks. They aren't hurting for happy customers."

"These prices—totally different from twelve-dollar beer night in the city. Almost makes me want to move back."

"Somehow, I doubt that." The pint glasses Yardley served were so cold that Garrett shuddered. He'd forgotten how much he'd been longing for that cup of cream of crab from Bunny's. It would have to wait. Garrett checked his watch and saw it was just before six. If he cut things short here, he might still catch Sam at the hospital. "Should I try the hospital and see how things are after this?" He could make it a quick visit. It might tire him out less than staying out at the bar with Eli for too long. A few beers would have him snoring by ten o'clock.

"Sure." Eli scanned the menu. "You want to split a crab dip?"

Garrett nodded, then dug into his pocket. "Hey, since your parents are in a hotel, why don't you go crash at my place when you leave here? Take the key to my house. I can let myself in the back and drive you to the airport in the morning."

Eli took the house key and tucked it away in his wallet. "Thanks, man. And thanks for your help with Sam. I just want her to be happy." He frowned. "Even if that means she's not with me."

CHAPTER SIX

SAM REACHED over the hospital bed for her mom's limp hand. In the busy ICU, the bed felt exposed. The privacy curtain did little to help and fluttered each time a nurse walked by.

Mom stirred and blinked, turning an unfocused gaze on Sam. A plastic tube was inserted in her nostrils, delivering her oxygen, and her head was wrapped with gauze. She looked frail and thinner than Sam remembered. *And I feel both powerless and terrified.*

"Did you get some sleep?" Sam squeezed her hand gently. She was thankful for the opportunity to talk to her mom. When she'd first come to the hospital earlier in the afternoon, Mom had been surrounded by medical personnel. Then Mark had come by for a quick visit, and the nurse had given her mother pain medication that had caused drowsiness. But now they were finally alone.

She nodded. "Some." She closed her eyes and wiped a tear from her cheek. "I don't understand how this happened." The familiar lilt of her voice comforted Sam. Other people said her mother had a Spanish accent—she'd come to the States as a young adult from Venezuela—but Sam couldn't hear the accent.

Sam searched the room for tissues. Finding a tiny box on the bedside tray, she yanked out a thin, stiff tissue and pressed it into Mom's hand. "The doctor said you had fluid in your abdomen, and it caused you to have trouble breathing. But he's sent out a sample to the lab, and they'll know what caused the problem."

Mom dabbed her eyes. "I already talked to him earlier today. They don't need to. I know what's causing the problem." She drew a long, unsteady breath. Meeting Sam's eyes, she said, "I have ovarian cancer. I found out about it three weeks ago."

Sam's jaw dropped open. Cancer? Maren's words returned hauntingly. "But . . . " She struggled with what to say. Three weeks? Why hadn't she said anything? She searched Mom's watery dark gaze. "Does Laura know?"

Mom shook her head. "No, that's why I was waiting to tell you. I didn't want to put stress on Laura while she was pregnant, and I figured I would see you soon anyway with the baby coming." Mom swallowed, her fingers shaking as she wiped back tears. "And I wanted to tell you in person."

As self-sacrificing as her mother's reasons had been, Sam felt frustration curling within her. "Mom, I can't believe you didn't tell me. We need to get you to an oncologist and started on treatment as soon as possible."

Mom crumpled the tissue in her hands. Her voice was almost inaudible. "Who do you think gave me the diagnosis?"

The noise of the ICU grew quiet as Sam leaned closer. She could barely wrap her head around what Mom was saying. "Okay, and what did the oncologist say? What's the treatment?"

Mom's chest rose and fell with shallow breaths. "There

isn't any." She turned her palm up, reaching for Sam's hand. "I have stage four ovarian cancer, *mi amor*. It's metastasized to my lungs. They can do chemo to extend my time a little, but there's no cure. They said at this point the chemo is a palliative treatment."

Sam's heart thumped painfully. "Palliative? What ..." Her mouth felt dry, and she swallowed. "What does that mean?"

"It's to manage my pain levels. Make my last days more comfortable."

Sam pulled her hand back, stunned. The sweater she wore felt thick and hot. "So you're not going to do anything?" she choked out. "Just . . . die?"

"Honey, please don't feel so betrayed. If I had a good shot at getting better, I would be the first in line for treatment. But I don't. There's nothing they can do."

"You can get a second opinion. Or we can find trials. Experimental treatments." *Something!* Sam raked her fingers through her long hair and stood. She turned, unable to face her mother. How could this be possible? Mom was so healthy. So vivacious. How could she be dying? Tears stung her eyes.

"Honey, I've talked to some of the top doctors in the state." Mom's dark eyes were wide and somber, tearful. "Do you think I would give up without a fight?"

"But you are giving up. And three weeks, Mom? *Three weeks?*" Even if Mom hadn't wanted to tell Laura, she could have told her.

Before Mom could answer, the privacy curtain slid back. Both Redding women looked up. Garrett stood there, holding a flower arrangement in one hand. "Is this a bad time?"

Sam's gaze traveled from the flowers to Garrett's work boots. His presence didn't seem as surprising as it had the day before, but why was he here? She couldn't decide if his timing was a welcome interruption or an intrusion, but she nodded stiffly. "Um . . . come in."

He addressed her mom. "How are you feeling?" His gaze dropped to the tissues in her hand and her red eyes. His stance shifted. He clearly realized he'd come at a bad time.

"I'm all right." Mom attempted a halfhearted smile. "Mark told me what you did for him. Thank you, Garrett. I'm so grateful. I couldn't have asked for a better person to accompany me to the hospital during an emergency."

Sam crossed her arms. She didn't want Garrett, of all people, here, but his presence had helped break the desperation of the previous moment. As Garrett moved closer to the foot of her mother's bed, chatting familiarly, Sam dropped back. She splayed her fingers over her heart and tried to take a deep breath.

Mom is dying of cancer.

Her brain refused to assimilate the information. Wouldn't Sam have known? It had to be a misdiagnosis.

Her gaze shifted to Garrett. Then again, she hadn't known something as basic as Mom hiring Garrett. She combed her memory, trying to recall if her mother had complained about her health. She hadn't said anything, had she?

How many times had she ignored Mom's phone calls? Slid the call button to silent because she was too busy?

A deep knot twisted in Sam's gut.

She had so many questions. How much time did Mom have left? What could they do in the meantime to ease her symptoms? Were there any treatment options that she would consider?

There's so much I want to talk about with her.

Giving Garrett a hard look, Sam rejoined the space she'd unoccupied. "Sorry, Garrett, it really isn't a good time. I need to talk to my mom."

"*No seas así*," Mom whispered. *Don't be like that.*

Something odd passed over Garrett's face, and he held out the flowers. "No problem. I wanted to stop by. I can go. It's been a long day."

The privacy curtain drew back, and a nurse appeared. She introduced herself, as shift change had just happened. Then she looked at Sam and Garrett. "I'm sorry to tell you all this, but visiting hours are ending. You can come back tomorrow from eight to noon in the morning or four to eight in the evening."

"Thanks, they gave us the schedule this morning." Sam's voice was less than thankful.

Mom's look was sharp. "Garrett, would you do me a favor and take Sam home? It would put me at ease to know she'll get there safely instead of using those rideshare apps."

"I'd be happy to." Garrett smiled politely in her direction.

Sam gritted her teeth and gathered her things. "Thanks." She didn't want to leave yet. And going back with Garrett was the last thing she wanted. But Mom looked exhausted, her face wan.

She was injured, of course, but dying—no. She couldn't be.

"I'll be back at eight." Sam leaned over the bed and pressed a kiss to her mom's cheek.

"Come in the afternoon," Mom said. "Mark wanted to come in the morning, and I'm hoping to have time to talk to Laura. They said they might wheel her over from the maternity ward."

Sam nodded and wiped the mist from her eyes. Laura had as much right to know about Mom's diagnosis. And the ICU only allowed two visitors at a time. She kissed her mom again and left with Garrett.

Garrett fell into step beside her, but she couldn't look at him. She rubbed her eyes, not wanting to cry in front of him.

They got into the elevator wordlessly. Somehow, the walk to Garrett's truck at dawn hadn't seemed so tense.

"Sorry I didn't call you back this morning," Sam finally said as the elevator doors opened on the ground floor. "Eli said he took care of what you needed."

Garrett put his hands in the pockets of his coat. "Were you and Laura able to find people to cover at the cabins? I know Jen Klein will help where she can."

"Jen Klein. There's a name I haven't heard for a while. Mom and Laura never told me she was working at the cabins." She'd left Katie to handle finding coverage for the night shift for today. Sam fidgeted with the strap of her purse. The "never told me's" were piling up.

"Yeah, she does about half the night shifts. I think it's convenient for her because your mom lets her use the back room to keep a playpen for her son to sleep in. She doesn't have to find a babysitter and still can earn an income."

Sam's eyes drifted over the cars in the parking garage. It didn't seem that long ago she'd worked the night shifts during high school. Garrett was right—it was a simple job. It mostly meant manning the phone and getting up if someone had arranged a late check-in or had an emergency. "I don't know why my mom bothers to keep the position. Cell phones make it unnecessary. It's not like Mom lives on the other side of town. Her house is right there."

Garrett cleared his throat. "Uh—yeah, I think she does it for Jen's sake."

Sam stopped mid-step and gaped at Garrett. Then, what he'd said before clicked. *Jen has a kid?* She had to still be in college, didn't she? "How old is Jen's kid?"

"Two. Colby." Garrett turned back and frowned. "And, no, the dad's not involved."

No wonder. Jen was a perfect charity case for her mother.

She didn't comment on it, though. Garrett seemed to be unusually close to Jen. "You two dating or something?"

Garrett raised a brow. "Nope."

"Do you want to be dating?"

He chuckled. "Have a sudden interest in my love life, Redding?"

"Nope." *You're being a brat, Sam.* More gently, she added, "Just curious. Anyway, I think Katie volunteered to take a few shifts this week when she doesn't have clients scheduled. But it's a tough week for her. Apparently, everyone wants a hair appointment before Thanksgiving. I'm going to stay for the week and take the other shifts."

Garrett didn't respond. His truck beeped as they approached, and the locks opened with a click. He didn't hold the door for Sam and slid into the driver's seat. As Sam climbed into the passenger seat, he wrestled a mess of papers and tools into the backseat.

"Sorry it's such a mess." He lifted a few empty cans of energy drinks and tossed them into a plastic bag from a convenience store.

She had a dim memory from a long time ago of climbing into her dad's work truck as a little girl. The scent of grease and pine tree air fresheners and who knew what? Her fingers curled into fists. She didn't want to think about that bastard right now.

Buckling herself in, she leaned back and closed her eyes as Garrett maneuvered his way out of the parking garage.

Sam turned and peeked into the backseat. Tools and building materials took up all the space. "So when did you take up construction work?"

Garrett turned the wheel around a sharp curve and stopped at the parking attendant's booth. "Home improvement, not construction." He waved a salute-like good-bye to the parking attendant and pulled off. "I did it as a hobby. Then this summer, I got out of the Army and my dad's business was floundering, so I bought him out."

"Weren't you like a pilot or something?"

"Warrant officer. Helicopters." He quirked a brow. "I'm surprised you knew that."

Did he think Katie had been keeping her up to speed? She rubbed her hands together to keep them warm. "Eli told me." The fractals of ice on the windshield threw patterns into the truck's cabin as they passed a streetlight. *Perfect for macro shots.* "So, what? Did you not want to fly helicopters anymore?"

Garrett glanced at her. Then he said noncommittally, "Something like that."

"Do you still have your pilot's license?"

"Yup."

Garrett had never been a scintillating conversationalist, but he wasn't giving her much to work with. Then again, she'd been rude to him in the hospital. She lowered her hands to her lap and rubbed her thighs. "I-I'm sorry. I wasn't trying to be a jerk back there. You arrived at a bad time."

"I figured." Garrett adjusted the heat on the dash. Thankfully, as he hadn't been in the hospital long, the engine hadn't had too much time to cool, and the air was warm. "You can shift that vent toward you a bit." He pointed toward it.

She lifted her hand to turn the vent, and his fingers collided with hers. The slightest of brushes, but the hair on her forearm seemed to stand, her skin tingling.

Sam pulled her hand back and stared at her hands. "You seem pretty friendly with my mom."

"Your mom is a great lady. She needs the help."

Sam's head snapped up, and she gave him a hard stare. Mom hadn't told her or Laura about her diagnosis, but had she told other people? Her friends?

"Do you know?" She squinted, trying to make out his features more clearly.

Garrett's brows lifted. "Know?"

"That my mom has terminal cancer." The words spat from her mouth, flat.

No sooner had she said it than she realized from the shock on his face that, no, Garrett hadn't known, and she'd ensured the second person to find out about this was him. "God, no, Sam, I'm so sorry."

He turned the wheel to round a curve when the tailgate fishtailed, taking a hard slide to the right and straight toward a speed limit sign.

Sam stared out the windshield with shock, unable to bring the scream in her throat to life.

Garrett let out a string of expletives, and his right hand shot out across the center console to hold Sam back as they mowed down the sign. A snowbank stopped the truck, but it leaned at an angle with the right side higher than the left.

"Son of a bitch," Garrett breathed, shoulders heaving. He glanced back at Sam, his hand still across her. He lowered his hand slowly. "You all right?"

She nodded numbly. "What the hell was that?" She blinked rapidly, unable to process what had happened.

"Black ice. I couldn't see it. I'm so sorry. Are you okay?" Garrett stared at her with concern.

The slick, nearly invisible ice was everywhere on a night like this. Being in Garrett's truck had likely helped keep them from flipping.

The sudden rush of adrenaline had tempered her urge to cry, but it was now replaced with anger. "No." Her fists clenched. "I'm not okay. My mom told me she's dying of cancer, and she's not going to do a thing about it to get treatment. And my boss is mad at me, Eli's a jerk, and I'm back here in fucking Brandywood. I don't think I'm going to be able to leave soon, and I'll probably lose my job." She yanked the scarf from her neck, overcome by the feeling of suffocation, then peeled off her coat.

But it wasn't enough. Desperate and feeling as though she teetered on an emotional precipice, she pushed open the passenger side door, finding resistance against the snowbank. She climbed out, and immediately her boots sank into the snow until she was engulfed up to her thigh.

The snow soaked through the fabric of her jeans, and she yelped. She tried to lift her legs, but the snow was too deep. She was stuck.

A bubble of laughter erupted from the cabin, and she turned back to see Garrett, still in the driver's seat with a grin across his face. "Asshole." She narrowed her eyes.

"I'm sorry," he managed through a chuckle. "Do you want some help?"

"No, I'd like to stay here all night." Of all the people, why did Garrett keep having to be the person around in these situations? She shook with cold and crossed her arms. "And nothing about this is funny."

"Says you." Garrett moved to the passenger seat and swung his feet onto the sideboard. He leaned out and slid his arms around Sam's waist. "Now, face me and put your hands on my shoulders."

She did as he instructed, and he lifted her, pulling her back into the cab with him. She rested against him, half-frozen and simmering with fury and sadness. As though he felt the emotions seeping through her skin, Garrett tightened his arms. A sob broke from her chest, and tears filled her eyes. After a moment, she took a grief-filled breath.

"My mom's dying," she said as though speaking the words

again would help her believe the unbelievable. Her breath was a shattered, shallow attempt at air.

"I'm so sorry." He stroked her back, letting her cry into his shirt. With the truck bell dinging repeatedly to tell them a door was open, the cabin filling with the blast of cold air from outside, the comfort he offered was unexpected.

It occurred to her that Garrett had never hugged her before. Not once. Yet she'd always known him. Somehow, the realization made her feel as though this should be more awkward than it was. A flash of red and blue lights caught their attention, and they raised their heads as a police officer exited his car and approached them.

Sam disentangled herself from him and wiped her eyes.

The officer reached the driver's door, and Garrett scooted back into his seat. He unrolled the window, and the officer lifted a flashlight to peer into the cab, shining it directly into their eyes.

"Everyone okay?"

She recognized the officer after a moment—Dan Klein. He'd been in their class in grade school. The idea of him coming to their aid was ludicrous. He'd been the biggest bully in school. "We're fine." Garrett's voice didn't hold a shred of friendliness. "Hit some black ice."

"Good, then you don't need my help. You know you can't park here, Doyle." Dan smirked.

Garrett chuckled humorlessly. "Good one, Klein."

Dan leaned farther into the window, clapping his hand against the window frame. "And is that Sam Redding I see? I thought you were too good for this town."

"Good to see you too, Dan." Despite her best efforts, Sam's teeth chattered. She leaned halfway out of the truck and pulled the passenger door shut with some difficulty.

Garrett noticed her shivers and turned the knob to blast the heat. But with her jeans soaked, she doubted she'd warm up until she got home and took a hot shower.

Dan straightened and shone the flashlight down the truck's length. "You been drinking at all tonight, Doyle?"

"Nope." Garrett's jaw set. Garrett and Dan had never liked each other—and that was putting it mildly. They had always seemed to share lunch detention together most days, though. Usually for fighting each other.

"Well, how about you step on out and prove it?"

Garrett glared at Dan. "Probable cause?"

Dan returned a steely look. "You're a Doyle, aren't you? I'd say that's cause enough."

Sam rolled her eyes. "He wasn't drinking, Dan. He came from the hospital with me."

"Then a little test won't hurt." Dan clapped the window frame twice. "Come on out."

Sam sank into her seat as Garrett swore under his breath and opened the driver's side door. Wiping her sniffly nose with the back of her hand, she searched the cabin for a tissue. She settled for a fast-food napkin tucked into the passenger side door and watched the lights from the police car glint off the snow.

When Dan had finished humiliating Garrett, he left, and Garrett climbed back into the truck. "God, I hate that guy." He scrubbed his eyes with his fingertips and put the shifter in Reverse. "Worthless use of air. You'd think he could have at least asked if we needed help getting out of this ditch."

"This is all my fault." She shivered again.

Garrett didn't respond to her claim. "I don't think they'll fit, but I have a pair of sweatpants in the backseat you can borrow. Seeing as you won't be home for another half hour."

"If they fit, I'm never eating again." Sam chuckled unexpectedly at the ludicrous thought. Garrett was at least a foot taller than her and had a masculine build. But he was right—the trip home would be miserable in these pants. "All right."

He fished them from the backseat with one hand, then continued pulling out of the snow. Sam unlaced her boots, clumps of snow falling onto the seat. She brushed them onto the floor mat. "I'm sorry about Dan again." She wiggled out of her jeans, conscious she was going to be half-naked in front of Garrett. *As if he would even notice or care, Sam.* She didn't, especially if it meant she wouldn't be so cold. "It's a good thing you hadn't been drinking anything tonight. I'd hate to see what he would do if you had a beer or two before coming to the hospital."

"Actually, I grabbed a beer earlier, but it was only one. And if it had been more, I would have refused the breathalyzer and told him you'd drive me home. He would have had to order me to submit a test." Garrett shrugged, almost as though that exact scenario had happened before.

She shook her head and smiled. "Well, you would have been stuck there. I still don't know how to drive."

"Really?" Garrett ducked his chin. "You never got your license?"

"Nope." She shrugged. Distant memories of Katie talking about driving lessons with her dad resurfaced. "It never seemed important in high school, and we didn't have enough money for me to have a car anyway. And then I went to New York for college and stayed there. No one I know who lives in the city has a car."

"How are you planning on getting around in Brandywood?"

"Rideshare." She waved her cell phone. "Turns out I don't really need to know how to drive most places."

Garrett looked skeptical. "You want me to teach you?"

Trust a man to want to solve a problem. She furrowed her brow. "Didn't I just tell you I don't need to know how?"

"Didn't you just tell me you don't know how long you're going to be in Brandywood? Rideshare will get expensive, especially back and forth to the hospital. Plus . . . " Garrett hesitated and then said in a gentler voice, "With your mom as sick as she is, she may need you to drive her around. You'll probably be able to use her car. It could be important."

Oh. Despite her snap judgment, his logic wasn't as terrible as she'd initially assumed. "Um . . . you think so?"

Garrett nodded, his large, dark eyes serious. "I think so." At her silence, he added, "I can come over on Saturday morning. Around ten? I have a job I'm managing, but I don't need to be there all day tomorrow, only for a few hours in the morning to get my guys started."

Sam ran her fingertips along the soft fabric of the sweatpants. Would Katie be angry if she found out? Accepting the favor Garrett was offering would be relatively easy otherwise. Would Katie think Sam was being disloyal?

Garrett's point about her learning to drive was valid. It would also probably help Mark and Laura if she could drive. If she didn't take Garrett's offer, she'd have to enroll in a driver's ed class, and God knows when one would start. Garrett might get her on the road sooner rather than later.

She bit her lip. "Okay, thanks." She would have to deal with Katie later.

CHAPTER SEVEN

"YOU KNOW, your guys tracked a gigantic mess from the front door to the tented space in the master bedroom yesterday." Trisha Sanders's silky voice seemed to materialize from nowhere.

Garrett lifted his head abruptly, searching the space for her. His gaze narrowed. She was in a satin pearlized light-blue nightgown—a revealing one. She wore a robe, but it was open in the front and untied. He looked away from the voluptuous breasts below her crossed arms, his fingers tightening around the tape measure in his hands.

What in God's name is she doing up here dressed like that? It's freezing.

He smiled tightly. "Sorry about that, Mrs. Sanders. I'll tell them to do a better job cleaning up today."

She approached, then stopped a few feet from him, tilting her heart-shaped chin. She was an attractive woman, about fifteen years older than him, but she took great care of her appearance. "Let's not let it happen again. And please, call me Trisha."

Oh, fuck. She was clearly not wearing a bra. Garrett attempted to keep his eyes level with her light-green eyes. He'd known there were red flags—but he had not expected this. "I'll make sure of it."

"Good." A little smile hinted at her lips while her eyes were flirtatious. She wore bright-red lipstick. For the briefest flash, she bit her lower lip, her top teeth tugging gently back with a knowing look.

Yeah, he was definitely not mistaken about her intentions. He glanced uneasily behind him. Where the hell was Luis when he needed him? Then he remembered he'd sent him to the hardware store. And Kevin was running late this morning.

"I'd better get back to work." His smile was polite. *No way in hell, lady.* The last thing he needed was a rumor started that he got mixed up with a married woman.

Trisha rubbed her arms and tossed her highlighted, light-brown hair over her shoulder. "It's freezing up here. You must be so cold. Do you want a cup of coffee or something?"

If she wasn't up here in a barely-there nightgown, she wouldn't be so cold. The thought drew his gaze, momentarily, to her hardened nipples showing through the fabric. He blinked away as an unwanted wave of lust passed through him. Not that he found her unattractive. She was clearly beautiful. And how long had it been since he'd had sex? Had to have been at least a year.

The hesitation was all she needed. She stepped closer to him. "Why don't you come down for a bit while your guys are out at the store?" She set a hand on his forearm. "The kids are at school, and my husband is at work. It's always nice to have company during the day."

Except Trisha didn't want company.

Think clearly, you moron, Garrett scolded himself. If he

made mention of her attire, it would invite more conversation. He needed to shut this down right now.

To his relief, footsteps sounded on the attic steps. Trisha sprang back and tied her robe shut as Kevin appeared. "Let me know if I can get either of you a cup of coffee." Trisha smiled again, without flirtation this time, then hurried past Kevin down the stairs.

Garrett's face flushed. He turned back toward the area he'd been measuring when Trisha had interrupted. Flustered, the tape measure fell on the plywood boards they'd set up to walk around on in the attic.

"Everything okay?" Kevin set his tool belt on the floor.

"Yup." Garrett snatched his tape measure from the floor. As much as he trusted Kevin, it wouldn't do to give him any reason for an awkward exchange around Trisha. And what would he say anyway? That she'd come onto him? She'd touched his forearm, not flashed him. If he talked about the nightgown, it would only make it appear he'd been looking.

Kevin popped open a can of energy drink. "Drywall? If you want to get the mud up on Monday, we should get all the sheets and tape up by the end of today. Luis says Gus plans on mudding next week."

"Sounds good." Garrett tried to focus. He removed his work gloves and rubbed his hands together. This was the last thing his business needed, so he'd have to do his best not to be left alone with Trisha Sanders again.

His cell phone rang and he pulled it out of his pocket. Speaking of wrong women. "What's up?"

Sam's voice came through the line in a panic. "There's a disaster in a cabin, and I'm not sure what to do about it. It's like the pipes froze or something. Water is everywhere, and I've got some furious guests on my hands. Any chance you can come?"

Katie. She must not have told Sam about the water being on

—or turned it off. Garrett winced. "Was this cabin twelve, by any chance?"

"How did you know?"

"Long story." Garrett pulled his knit hat from his head. "Dammit. Call a plumber. Actually, scratch that. I'll call the guy I work with and have him meet me at the cabins. Are you going to be there?"

"Yeah, I'm at the guest lodge."

Garrett hung up and turned toward Kevin. "I have an emergency I need to head out to. You think you and Luis can handle things here?"

"Yeah, but where is Luis?"

"He's—" Garrett swore to himself again. He didn't want to leave any of his guys around Trisha. Not that she would hit on them. But he did not want to risk putting them in that position. He'd have to tell Luis about what had happened and make it clear they needed to work at least in pairs on this job. Much as he hated to do it to her, Sam would have to wait.

Luis returned a half hour later, and Garrett took him to the side. "Listen, the lady of the house." Garrett zipped up his coat. "She hit on me. If either you or Kevin needs to go to the store or anywhere, go together. I can't afford that sort of liability. And let's see if Dean can work on this job with us. I think it'll be useful to have another set of hands. Get this done as quickly as possible."

Luis grinned. "I told you, man. You're cougar bait." He shook his head with a laugh. "Every damn time. I wish I could be so lucky."

"Until you end up doing twenty 'fixes' on this job because she wants us to keep coming back." Garrett rolled his eyes.

"Good point." Luis sobered. "I'll keep an eye out. Don't worry."

Garrett didn't answer as he headed down from the attic and to his truck.

The drive to the Reddings' house returned his thoughts to Trisha. From the outside, the Sanders looked like a perfect family. Joe Sanders was a successful real-estate agent—had sold Garrett his house. He shouldn't have avoided addressing the flirtation. He should have shot her down. He blamed the lack of sleep in the past forty-eight hours. Not to mention, he'd faced major ghosts from his past over the past couple of days.

He pulled into the Reddings' driveway twenty minutes later, rock blaring from his windows. Music always helped drown out his thoughts. When he'd been flying helicopters, it had been his constant soundtrack. *God, I miss being in the air.*

Sam was waiting by the steps of the guest lodge. Garrett killed the engine and climbed down from the truck, the door slamming behind him. "Sorry it took so long." He closed the space between them quickly. "Water shut off yet?"

Sam's look was blank. "I-I'm still waiting for the plumber to arrive."

"Oh . . . dammit." In his rush to get here, he'd completely forgotten to call John. He didn't want to seem like a total screwup, though. "Let's see what I can do before John gets here." He'd shoot him a text on the way over. Tell him he'd pay double if he got out here in the next twenty minutes.

"Should we take a UTV?" Sam was already uncovering one in the parking lot. She shook the snow from the canvas covering, then unzipped the side.

"Sure." Garrett grabbed some tools from his truck and tossed them in the back of the UTV. "Been a while since I rode in one of those things."

Sam handed him a helmet, holding another one in her hand. "You'll have to drive. Mom says you need a license for one now. Which is ironic, considering I was driving these things when I was fourteen."

"Yet another reason for you to get your driver's license." Garrett fastened the helmet and climbed into the driver's side. "But you were never planning on returning to Brandywood long term, were you?" With her dark hair in a long ponytail, jeans, and a plaid shirt, she looked like she'd never left.

"Nope." Sam smiled tightly and jumped in beside him. "I had all I want of small-town life as a kid. Movies make it look so charming. They don't show you what it's like when you're the topic of all the gossip. When everyone knows your last name because your dad got thirty years in prison for dealing."

She was right. People in town had gossiped about his family too. *"Poor Rebecca Doyle. Seven kids and a deadbeat drunk for a husband."* Garrett started the engine of the UTV. Things had gotten substantially better for his family when his father had sobered up a few years ago. Most of his siblings even attended family functions enthusiastically now. Being in the Army for nine years had made it hard to attend.

But being back home now, his family expected him to be there.

Sadly, Garrett found everything a little less easy to forgive.

The wind rushed against the UTV's camo-colored frame as it bounced through the snow toward the cabins. When they'd been kids, Eli and Garrett had always loved it when Mrs. Redding hired them to work around the cabins and let them drive the UTVs. The wintry day made it more nostalgic now, though. The air stung his eyes, drawing tears, and he glanced over at Sam to see her dark hair whipping across her red cheeks.

Despite the odd circumstances, he couldn't help but think how pretty she looked. The drive through the snow was refreshing. The icy air made his lungs ache, but the outdoors and the sun had a magical look, especially with everything blanketed with snow and sparkling ice.

They arrived at cabin twelve, and Garrett parked the UTV. "Is the guest still there?" He removed the helmet and grabbed his tools.

"No, I moved him and his family to another cabin and gave them a refund on one night." Sam combed through the tangles in her windblown hair with her fingers. "So how did you know it was this one? You said long story?"

One I'm ready to be done with. Katie's continued war felt juvenile. Katie and Sam's friendship had never really made sense to Garrett, as they'd always seemed to be complete opposites. But he still had to be careful with what he said to Sam. She might be more like Katie than he realized.

Garrett threw a sardonic grin as he walked toward the cabin. "Because it started five years ago when Katie and I broke up. The guest at this cabin came by yesterday and asked for the exterior water to be put on so he could wash the mud from his bike. I turned it on but told Katie to tell you it had to be shut off. She was in a hurry to get rid of me, and my guess is she didn't even listen to what I said. The pipes must have frozen overnight and burst."

Sam stopped in her tracks. "Oh." Her dark eyes narrowed with a flash of irritation. "So Katie ignored you?"

Garrett tried to gauge her response. Was she mad at Katie . . . or him? Or did she not like the implication it was Katie's fault? *Which it is.* "I'm not trying to blame her. I probably should have reminded you last night about it, but I was so tired I forgot. Not to mention, that whole denting my front bumper in a snowbank thing."

She brushed past him to the cabin. Opening the door, they found the cabin with several inches of water on the floor. Water had seeped through the back wall. This would require total cleanup.

"Be right back." Garrett left Sam standing at the doorway to the cabin and went to the back. Finding the external water valve, he shut it off. Like it or not, he was partially to blame for this. He'd turned the water on. He should have made sure it was off. Insurance would cover this, but he doubted Mrs. Redding needed the expense of her deductible on top of everything else she had going on right now.

He found Sam inside the cabin. "Water stopped." She turned to face him. "So I guess that's good."

Garrett nodded. "I shut it off." His boots sloshed as he came closer to her. Unfortunately, the brunt of the damage was on a drywalled area of the cabin. He stood next to her, inspecting the damage. "John can fix the pipe, but you'll need a water remediation company to come out here and clean this all up. Insurance will cover it. But I'll pay the deductible."

Sam gaped at him. "I can't let you do that."

"I'm partially to blame." He took out a pocketknife and cut away some of the soaked drywall, peering behind it. He remembered the look Sam had given him when he'd mentioned Katie a few minutes earlier. "Or fully. Who knows? Either way, I'm not letting your mom pay anything for this. And I'll do the repair work for free. We'll have this cabin up and running in four weeks."

Sam set her hands on her hips. "This isn't your fault at all. I'm sorry if I gave you the impression I thought that." She stepped closer to him. "Garrett, I know I haven't been the nicest to you in the past, but this is on Katie. She shouldn't let her anger at you impede telling me something important." A distant look clouded her eyes. "And to be honest, it seems like it's about time she let things go."

Her lips twisted. "I hope to God none of us are the same

people we were in high school. If I could tell Katie she needs to let it go, I would, but you know how she is. She'd think I wasn't being supportive."

Garrett smiled ruefully. Was Sam hinting she'd forgiven him? If so, it was more than he'd expected from her. "Twenty years won't make a difference. The last thing I wanted was to hurt her. I never should have let things get as far as I did. Asking her to marry me was dumb and impulsive. You were right."

Her eyes faltered, and she stepped back. She swallowed, hard and visibly, and turned away. "You know Katie read me the letter you wrote to her when you left that night. You used almost the exact words I said to you on the porch of *The Dutchman*."

Garrett flipped the blade back into his pocketknife and clipped it into a belt loop of his jeans. "That's because I couldn't get your words out of my head all night."

Sam shifted, her shoulders drooping.

The sound of dripping water continued, seeping from the over-saturated drywall.

Drip.

Drip.

Almost as though it had synced to his breath as he waited for her to say something.

She swallowed again. "Katie." She moistened her lips, and her words came in a rush. "I never told Katie I talked to you that night. She would have blamed me. And I've felt my share of responsibility for what happened. I shouldn't have said those things to you. I was in a bad mood and frustrated with you, but it wasn't true. You loved each other. I mean . . . look at the most significant relationship of my life. Ten years and we still can't make it work. I'm probably the least expert in love ever."

Ripples formed in the water as Garrett turned to face her.

"You have nothing to blame yourself for. You did Katie a favor. Marrying would have been a mistake for both of us. Things would have eventually fallen apart. She would have been more hurt in the long run, especially if we'd had kids."

She nodded. "Maybe so. But somehow, it feels less like a favor when I know Katie would hate me for it." She turned to go back outside, then her foot slipped on the wet tile near the fireplace. A yelp left her as she tumbled toward the floor. Garrett reached out to catch her, but she slammed against him. The toe of his boot slid forward on the tile, then his leg shot out from under him.

They both landed on the floor with a small splash, and a ripping sound followed. The wind was knocked out of him. Garrett let out a grunt as icy water seeped through his clothes. "Ahhh!" He grimaced, his body stiffening, the water feeling like pinpricks against his skin.

"Holy crap, what the heck?" Sam hovered inches above his face, draped half on him, half in the water. She shifted her legs onto his. "Oh my God, this is cold." She shivered, her eyes scanning his with alarm.

Despite the circumstances, he could hardly help the snicker bursting from his mouth. "I feel the need to insert some cheesy movie line like—'we have to stop meeting like this' or 'if you wanted me on my back, you could'a just asked.'"

She gave a short bark of laughter, then shook her head. "I. Am. Freezing." She peeled herself off him. "*Asshole*. But thanks for catching me."

Something about the way she swore at him sounded affectionate. The corners of his mouth tipped in a smile.

The loss of her proximity only meant the removal of the only warm thing near him. And he hadn't minded her touch. "Anytime, Redding. Besides being a crane to remove damsels in distress from snowdrifts, I also double as a landing mat." He sat, then grimaced at his jeans. They'd ripped right at the crotch. It was definitely the worst day to have gone commando. "You don't have those sweatpants I loaned you handy, do you?"

Her eyes caught the rip in his pants, and she covered her mouth, laughing, her eyes darting away. "Oh my Go—Garrett!" She choked with laughter, a blush spreading on her face. "That's unfortunate."

Oh, come on. He stood, shifting the pants as well as he could to cover himself. "Let the record state I was not, under any circumstance, trying to expose my junk to you. And also, this water is freezing." He arched a brow, his face growing warm. "Not like we've never seen each other naked before."

Her eyes widened, and she gave him a mock glare. "We agreed to never speak about that again."

Talk about it, sure. Think about it, on the other hand . . . Only teenagers were dumb enough to think strip poker with their friends was a good idea. And luck had not been with Sam or Garrett. And *that* had fueled many fantasies and dreams on occasion because Sam had been hot. *That's one way to warm up.*

The last thing he needed was a hard-on while thinking about that situation. Not with the current state of his pants. "Why don't we drive on back?" Thank God he'd left his gym clothes in the truck. He had a shirt he could wear there.

They trudged their way out the door, both shivering. As he pulled the cabin door closed, Sam paused on the porch. Her expression sobered.

Garrett joined her. "Ready?"

She was silent. At last, she stuffed her hands in the pockets of her green puffer jacket. "I was thinking about how much I missed this view. I remember how we'd all come out here on school nights and find an empty cabin to use as our own personal hangout."

Also where strip poker had happened. "Bunch of naïve kids who didn't know much. Three of us escaped. At least for a bit, in my case."

She shook her head with a rueful laugh. "I was thinking more about how I could eat half a pizza and not want to spend the next day at the gym."

"Those were good times." Garrett inhaled deeply. He'd never get enough of the smell of the wood smoke from the cabins at this time of year. "You know, it took time to come around to the idea of living in Brandywood again too. I was determined not to come back here."

"So why did you?" She twisted her mouth. "Living here was as bad for you as it was for me. Look at how Dan Klein treated you last night. He practically said, 'well, you're a Doyle. I can treat you like shit, and no one will blink an eye.' He gets off on those power trips."

"I don't know." The top branches of the trees, bereft of leaves, swayed in the breeze. *Fuck, that wind's cold when you have icy water on your skin.* "I guess I figured it was better to have roots than not. Everywhere I went, people seemed to have family and a backstory. Being a stranger became exhausting. Everyone might think of me as a fuckup here—but hey, at least I don't have to explain it to anyone. And I don't have to watch the disappointment on their faces when they discover it."

Her lopsided, closed-mouthed grin had always been his favorite in grade school. His heart skipped a beat. "You're not a fuckup, Garrett. I'm going to go out on a limb and say you turned out okay." She leaned a little closer to him. "Just don't tell Katie I said so."

"Don't go holding me to too high of a standard yet." He winked. "There's plenty of time for me to prove you wrong."

CHAPTER EIGHT

SAM BURST into Laura's hospital room without bothering to knock. Laura sat in the bed nursing baby Charlotte. Mark occupied the chair across from her. Both lifted their heads in surprise.

"It's been a long day. Already." Sam smiled at her sister, coming toward her. "How's my new favorite niece?"

Mark laughed from the room's corner, standing. He pulled his baseball cap over his glossy black hair. "You know you already had a niece."

"Seriously. What's Bella? Chopped liver?" Laura patted the bedside, her expression turning more serious. "I've been dying to talk to you." She glanced at Mark. "You can go, babe."

Sam looked at her brother-in-law. "Actually, if it's about Mom, I think he should stay." Mark often played the role of referee between them, something she appreciated about him.

Mark hesitated, looking back at Laura for direction.

Laura nodded quickly. The gentle suckling of a newborn filled the space, an awkward silence descending. Sam met her sister's eyes and realized they were red-rimmed. Mom must have told her.

"We have to convince her to seek treatment." Sam broke the silence with a strained voice. "She can't give up without a fight—that's crazy. I've been reading and researching and there's a clinical trial going on in Minnesota at the Mayo Clinic we might be able to get her into. I called a friend of mine in New York whose father is on the board there."

Laura adjusted the baby, her gaze faltering. She gave Mark a glance and unlatched the baby, holding her out to him. "What type of trial?"

"It's for women with stage four ovarian cancer. Which— since they say Mom is terminal—she might qualify for. It starts in January." Sam twisted a ring on her ring finger—a delicate band of silver snowdrops Mom had given her as a teenager. She'd worn it every day since then.

"And what's the hope of the trial?" Laura's voice was quiet, without emotion.

Sam frowned, feeling as though she was being patronized. "The hope—" She scowled. "Obviously, to help give Mom a chance to beat this thing."

"So . . . lots of intensive treatment, which may or may not work, but might give her a reduced quality of life for a much longer time." Laura blinked back tears and took Sam's hand. "Sam, we have to respect her right to choose the death she wants. On her terms."

Pulling her hand back, Sam shook her head. "So that's it? We give up? Do nothing? There's also this injection that's on trial in Great Britain—"

"Not nothing." She and Mark exchanged looks again. "This head injury is going to make things tough, of course, but we have some time left with her. Time to make sure she does as much as she wants to—and can do—before she goes."

Mark came up beside Sam and put a hand on her shoulder. "For what it's worth, my reaction was the same as yours. But Laura talked some sense into me."

"It's not sense." Sam jerked away and scrambled to her feet. "Mom's too young to die. She's not ready for this. She's perfectly healthy in every other way."

Laura shook her head and wiped tears away. "But she's not. She's not healthy. The cancer has spread throughout her body and it's killing her. She may have been healthy before this, but not anymore."

Sam covered her face, anger bubbling up. She felt as though it would explode from her fingertips and in incomprehensible shouts. Sylvia had told her to count. She gasped for breath and her brain felt numb as the numbers formed shapes and colors in her mind.

At last, she felt a calm descend through the top of her skull. Enough to talk, at least. "I can't give up." Sam narrowed her gaze at Mark, unable to look at her sister as she said, "I won't."

Laura chewed on her lower lip. "I think right now, we have to take it a day at a time. Grief starts with denial, Sam. It's okay if you're not okay."

Spare me your armchair psychology. She tugged her sleeves into her palms, holding them tightly with her fingertips. "I'm still going to talk to her about these opportunities."

Laura nodded slowly. "In the meantime, have you given any thought to what you want to do?" Laura shifted, and pain crossed her face. "Mark said you were watching the cabins this morning?"

"Yeah." This didn't feel like the time to tell them about the disaster at cabin twelve. Though she'd have to file the insurance claim and get that going. Or Laura could handle that over the phone. A choked feeling overtook her.

She didn't want to be here, in Brandywood, handling the

cabins. Figuring out how to pretend to enjoy the last few months of her mother's life.

"Um, I have to be back in New York after Thanksgiving. My boss wasn't too happy when she heard I was here. So hopefully, we can figure something out in the next few days."

Disappointment filled Laura's face. "Oh, okay."

Sam's phone rang. "Speaking of which, it's my boss." She stood, avoiding looking at them. "I'm going to take this outside. Give you all some privacy."

"Sam. So glad I reached you." Maren sounded out of breath, as though she was leaving work and hurrying along the crowded city streets.

"I didn't think I would hear from you so soon." Sam pushed the button to the volume to the minimum, not wanting to be overheard.

"Well, I have news. Turns out you're free to stay home for a little while longer. I'm canceling the cookie thing."

No . . . Sam closed her eyes, hoping to keep her disappointment from her face. She ducked into the hallway and hurried away. *Where the heck am I going?* She reached a set of doors requiring some sort of key card and stopped. "Canceling?" she repeated dumbly.

"The test kitchen is pushing back against this one way too hard. They say they don't have enough time to prepare new and interesting recipes specific for the special. They're already booked solid with the rest of the Christmas agenda and, not to mention the space issues the crew is giving me."

"But, um—" Sam's mouth was dry. She'd fought so hard for this chance. And who knew when Maren would give it to her again? Most of the food shoots for the next several months were already booked with the contract photographer. "What about the advertising you've already done for the campaign?"

Sam turned aimlessly in the dead end, then moved toward

a large picture window by the waiting area of the maternity ward. From this vantage point at Brandywood General Hospital, the small town was picturesque, with buildings and houses tucked in among the winding hills and roads. Almost like you would picture a town in New England. Especially with the snow. She wished she had her camera.

"Better to lose that money than have this whole thing implode on me. I'm going to talk to the arts and crafts team. See if we can't change it to twelve Christmas crafts."

"But what if . . . ?" Sam's gaze drifted out the window again. "What about a location shoot?" *What the hell am I even saying?* A nugget of an idea had sprouted in her mind, raw and not fully formed.

"A location shoot? What are you talking about?"

"Well, um . . ." The faintest uptick of her pulse made Sam feel jittery. "What if-uh-what if, the crew came here? To Brandywood?"

"I'm listening."

Sam cleared her throat. "Well, I-I was telling you before about my mom and the cookie exchange. I know at least a dozen ladies that have unique family recipes they could share. What if it was . . . more like a home baker thing? With everyday women and home recipes? They're tested—they've been doing them for, well, some of them for generations—and, I can find a place to shoot it all too. Something with lots of natural light fitting the crew's specifications."

Silence crackled on the phone.

"Maren?"

"I'm thinking."

"I know how much you hate last-minute planning, but if you have to come up with something last minute anyway—"

"No, I love it."

Sam put a hand over her heart. *Oh, no, what did I do?*

Before Sam could say anything else, Maren went on blithely, "It completely solves everything. You can have twelve home bakers from your town present their best recipe. And the camera crew can film down there and have you on hand for photography. Then I don't have to redo all the plans, and we can give it an authentic country Christmas Americana feel."

Sam slumped against a wall and leaned her forehead against it. A scrub-wearing man passed her, giving her a worried look, and she straightened. She waved him off to show she was fine.

"You still there?" Maren's voice had taken an impatient sound.

"Yes—I'm—" . . . *processing* . . . "I'm thrilled." Hopefully, she sounded convincing.

"Perfect. Now, I know it involves additional coordination but we'll pay you extra. And this is what you've always wanted, isn't it? To coordinate an entire food shoot? It all works out."

Always wanted? Spun the way Maren wanted to view it, sure. But to say she'd always wanted to arrange a Christmas cookie shoot in her hometown with her mother's friends as home bakers on live-streamed video?

No. It sounded like an absolute nightmare. What the hell had she been thinking?

That you want to save your job. "Sounds great," Sam managed.

"Perfect. Send me your plans by Tuesday. We're all closing the day before Thanksgiving. Thanks, dear." Maren hung up without a goodbye.

Sam stared at the blinking digits on her phone. Less than two minutes.

That was all Maren needed to upend Sam's life. The thought of her New York life converging with life here made her nauseated.

How on earth would she pull any of this off? She needed to care for her sickly mother, handle the cabins, lodge an insurance claim, and now . . . manage and coordinate an entire social media campaign?

In a town that knew she'd disliked it so much she'd left? Even on her visits home, Sam had stayed away from Main Street. She didn't go to town unless she couldn't possibly avoid it. She hadn't even seen her mother's friends for years.

The last time she'd been anywhere close, she'd been on the porch of *The Dutchman* destroying her best friend's wedding.

Dan's words from the night before sounded in her brain. *"I thought you were too good for this town."*

Footsteps sounded behind her. She turned to find Mark, still holding Charlotte, who was swaddled and asleep. "It's a good thing you didn't leave the unit." He tilted his head toward the baby. "She's got an anklet off that will alert the SWAT team or something if she leaves the maternity ward."

Despite her affection for her brother-in-law, she didn't want to talk to him. "Mark, I need to be alone. I know you and Laura have the best of intentions, but I can't agree with you right now. Mom is not ready to die."

Mark's eyes were sympathetic. "Could it be you're not ready for her to die?"

Tears welled in her eyes. He didn't need to say it. That she'd be ready for Mom to be gone was ludicrous. "Of course, I'm not. But that's not what I mean."

"I know what you meant." Mark rocked the sleeping baby in his arms. Five years ago, when Bella had been born, Sam remembered how awkward he looked holding his newborn infant daughter. The awkwardness was long gone, replaced with the expertise of a father of three.

Deep within, her heart twinged. The pain pulsated out, reminding her of Eli. For a few months after their disastrous

February breakup, she'd mourned what she'd lost. When she'd gone to him at Valentine's Day, she'd had a picture in her mind of how it would go. *This time we'll make it work.* And the future would be filled with a destination wedding to St. Lucia, laughing as Eli—who wasn't exactly *Mr. Home Improvement*—assembled a crib. But as time passed, she realized slowly she hadn't lost this future of domestic bliss with Eli.

She had never had it. Her argument with Eli the day before only made it clearer.

She narrowed her gaze at Mark, feeling something snap within her. "If Laura had asked you to let her handle this emotional stuff we're going through with my mom—to go away and let her face it alone—would you have?"

"Is that what happened with Eli yesterday?" Mark scanned her eyes.

"Yeah, basically."

Understanding seemed to light in Mark's blue eyes. "No." He nestled his daughter closer. "But that doesn't mean Eli doesn't love you. I might be more of a stubborn blockhead than he is."

"Oh, he's a blockhead all right." At the end of the hallway, over an automatic door, an exit sign glared red and garishly. The word summarized all she was feeling, and she wished it could be a button she could push and find herself transported elsewhere.

She straightened, a heavy feeling tumbling from her shoulders. "Eli and I are finished. For good."

Mark looked skeptical. "You have a lot on your plate right now, Sam. Instead of visiting your mom this afternoon, consider taking a break. The past three days have been intense. Take some time for yourself. Get rid of some dead weight."

"I'm fine." Strangely, she felt better than she had five minutes earlier. Mark would never walk away from Laura because he'd committed to loving her forever. Eli and Sam had never made those specific vows, but what had hurt the most about Valentine's Day, was that if Eli had loved Sam, he wouldn't have been even considered going out and sleeping with another woman. And he wouldn't have driven away, leaving Sam alone. *We are finished.* "Actually, the truth is I am getting rid of dead weight."

She pulled her phone out and scrolled through her contacts. Finding Eli's name, she deleted him. The action was ceremonial in some ways—she knew his number by heart—but it still felt like relief. She quickly blocked him on social channels.

Mark observed her without speaking. When she looked up, he raised his brows. "Finished?"

"With Eli? Yes." Sam crossed her arms. "With everything I have going on, I don't need that. I don't need him. Our relationship might have seemed good a long time ago when we were dumb kids and didn't know any better, but I need something else right now. I can't keep looking back at the past and thinking either of us is going to magically change. It doesn't work. And it's never going to."

Mark's expression was sober. "Do you really think this is the time to be making big decisions?"

Like impulse decisions to pitch her boss with a shoot she wasn't sure she could pull off?

Maybe I'm not ready to leave Brandywood right now. Not while Mom was still lying in a hospital bed and Laura needed help.

In the distance, a bored voice sounded over an intercom. The noise brought Sam back to the conversation with Mark, and she shrugged. "People show you who they really are. If you don't listen to them when they show you, you're the idiot. And I'm tired of being the idiot."

Mark leaned over and gave her a one-armed hug. "Just promise me you'll go talk to someone else about it. I'm sure Katie would be up for hanging out later tonight after visiting hours end."

Hanging out. Where? On Main Street?

Sam shuddered.

But if she was going to do the job she'd offered to shoulder for Maren, she was going to have to get over herself. She was going to have to go back to the heart of Brandywood again.

CHAPTER NINE

GARRETT SAT in front of the Sanders's house, his truck idling as he waited for Luis to arrive. Being in the Army for so long, he'd formed the habit of arriving anywhere at least twenty minutes early. But that wasn't wise in this situation.

He checked his phone for traffic updates. Luis would be coming from Frederick today—he'd spent every weekend at his new girlfriend's place since September. However, that didn't account for Monday morning traffic. Or this being the week of Thanksgiving.

The weekend had been quiet. He'd given Sam a quick driving lesson on Saturday but she'd told him Katie was coming over, so he'd made himself scarce and promised to come back Monday around the same time. Sunday was his only day off and he didn't want to commit to anything. Even a driving lesson with Sam.

A tap on his window startled him, and he looked up from his phone. Trisha stood there. Thankfully, she was fully clothed this time in a tight spandex running outfit that hugged every curve.

He unrolled the window. "Morning. What're you doing out here?"

"I just dropped the kids off at the bus stop." She held a kid's squeezable yogurt tube in one hand. "Aren't you coming in?"

"Yeah, in a few. I have some calls to make first."

"Oh." Trisha pouted, her hand tightening on the yogurt tube. The tube squirted down the side of the plastic and onto her hand. She made a face. "I'm so dumb."

Garrett leaned toward his glove box. "Let me get you a napkin."

"It's fine." Trisha smiled brightly. She slowly licked the yogurt off her fingertips. "There's no need to waste good yogurt."

Her eyes locked with his as she traced her tongue up the yogurt tube and popped it into her mouth. "It's fantastic, actually." Her voice dropped.

Garrett clicked the glove box closed. *What in the hell am I supposed to say to that?*

Trisha laughed and put her hand on the window. Her eyes narrowed on Sam's jeans on his front seat. She'd left them in his truck and he'd brought them with him to return to her later. "I didn't know you have a girlfriend. What's her name?"

How she'd leaped to that conclusion, he didn't know. *Lady, you don't know anything about me.* "Uh, Sam," he lied with a tight smile. "I've known her since kindergarten, actually."

"That's fun. So much history together." Trisha licked her fingertip. "Joe and I met in college. I miss those days."

I bet. He imagined her immediately as one of those girls his buddies in the Army used to go to spring break in Mexico to meet. He'd never gone, because of Katie. Still, he didn't want to think about Trisha like that. "I should get back to those calls."

"All right." Trisha winked and started walking backward

toward the house. "See you in a few. Don't forget. You're mine when you're on the clock."

Garrett almost sank his face into his hands, but he got the feeling she might be watching him. From now on, he would listen to his gut and stay away from any jobs where he got even the slightest hint of red flags. No amount of money was worth the trouble this could cause in his life. Or his business.

He dialed Luis. "Where are you?"

"About five minutes away. So sorry, man. Traffic was killer getting out of Frederick this morning." Luis sounded settled and happy, though.

"You're not late yet." Garrett checked the clock. Still ten minutes before start time.

"I'm late in Doyle time." Luis laughed, his voice echoing and full of static. "When did you get there? Ten minutes ago?"

"Something like that." Garrett mumbled a goodbye. The curtain fluttered by the master bedroom and he dialed again, this time to Eli, who answered on the fifth ring.

"Everything okay?" Eli sounded out of breath, like he'd rushed from a meeting.

"Everything's fine. Did I interrupt you?"

"At the gym. When I saw a call from you so early, I thought it might have something to do with Sam."

Makes sense. Garrett cringed, leaning back in his seat. "Yeah, I think she's fine. I saw her Saturday. She was going out with Katie so I didn't hang around."

"She didn't mention me?" Eli's voice was unexpectedly hard. "Did she tell you why she blocked me across all social media?"

Sam had shown some level of comfort around him in recent days, but she hadn't shared that. "No, she didn't tell me. Since when?"

"Friday. I sent her a text when I found out, and she

ignored it." Eli sounded bitter. "As though I'm the bad guy in all this. I can't keep playing high school games. I went out on a date with a woman on Saturday. God, it was so nice to laugh and joke without the pressure of all that baggage hanging over me."

Garrett laughed. "That was quick. She blocks you on Friday and you're on a date on Saturday? Or was it the woman you started seeing in February?"

"No, I broke things off with her in March. But it's New York. A swipe right with a good match could get you a date in two hours," Eli sighed. "Just . . . let me know if she says anything. I know she needs space right now, but I'd like to end things properly. Not over the goddamned phone."

It surprised Garrett Sam had handled it that way. She hadn't talked about Eli much to him, but it seemed out of character. "You coming home for Thanksgiving? You could probably talk to her then."

"Nah. My parents' house is still out of commission and they're going to meet me in the Poconos at my uncle's instead. I'll be back in town around Christmas."

Eli seemed remarkably . . . detached. His and Sam's relationship had always been an odd one, but he would have thought Eli would be sadder to see it had ended. Maybe the fact Eli could simply swipe right because he was in New York, that he didn't have to work for a girl if he wanted one, had made him lazy. *But this is Sam he's letting go. Sam, whose mother is dying.*

Garrett cradled the phone on his shoulder and lifted his coffee. "Hey, did Sam tell you why her mom ended up in the hospital? I don't know if she'd want me to be the one telling you, but you probably oughta know."

Eli's silence was stony. At last, he answered, "No, she didn't tell me. She can tell me herself." Did he resent the fact Garrett knew and he didn't? "I should go, though. My trainer will wonder what happened. Talk to you soon, man."

Luis pulled up, followed shortly by Gus and Kevin. Garrett ended the call and headed out to join his crew, checking his watch.

Two hours. That was all he was staying this morning. He'd leave the guys to keep working, go do a driving lesson with Sam, and then he'd start the repair work on cabin twelve himself. He'd rather be there anyway.

"ALL RIGHT . . . foot on the clutch, slowly lifting. When you feel the engine engage, you drop your weight on the gas and lift the clutch." Garrett leaned back in his seat and popped open a can of energy drink.

Charlotte Redding's old truck lurched forward, the transmission grinding, sending a spray of the newly opened soda across his lap.

Sam grimaced at Garrett. "Sorry."

"I'm officially out of extra clothes in my truck so you better take it easy." Garrett chuckled and took a sip. "Of course, it's my fault for opening the can just then."

"Can't I learn an automatic?" Sam attempted to push the shifter into gear again and the engine screeched.

"If your mother drove automatic, yes. To be honest, she might be the last person left on earth that doesn't drive automatic." Garrett leaned back in his seat and crossed one foot over his knee.

"How'd you learn?"

Garrett threw her a cocky glance. "I know everything, Redding."

A smile hinted at her eyes. He had called her that nickname his whole life, but they hadn't really spent much time together since high school. She seemed to remember it with some level of fondness, if she was smiling. "You know"— Garrett set the drink in the holder and put his hand over hers before she tried to shift improperly again and ruined the truck —"I remembered earlier this morning that Eli once said he was going to teach you to drive."

"It didn't go so well. He wasn't exactly patient." Sam rolled her eyes. That was valid. Eli was not a patient man.

"I talked to him this morning. Apparently, you blocked him?" Eli's words had piqued his interest. Eli had been talking about Sam as though they were done for good. Did she feel the same way?

"Yup." She pulled her hand back from the shifter and set it on the wheel. "And Katie actually set me up a date this Saturday with some guy she knows. Mike Jarvis. I'm moving on."

Mike? The firefighter? He didn't know what surprised him more—Sam going on a date . . . or that she appeared to be planning to stay after Thanksgiving. "Are you staying in Brandywood?"

She grimaced. "For now."

"That doesn't sound like you're entirely convinced it's a good thing."

"I'm not sure it is. I sort of volunteered to do a big social campaign here. My boss wants me to find home bakers from Brandywood for it to feature classic Americana cookie recipes. Twelve of them. The cooks are supposed to make their recipes on a live feed and we'll feature pictures and recipes on our social channels."

"Sounds intense."

She covered her eyes with one hand, peeking through her open fingers. "I don't know what the heck I was thinking," Sam sighed. "So anyway, I'll be here at least until mid-December. Then we'll see how things go with my mom."

He approached the other bit of news more cautiously. "And the date?"

She smiled, her eyes sparkling with humor. "Someone Katie claims is 'perfect for me.' A firefighter—I think. We're going to Yardley's on Friday night." Then she added, "I mostly said yes to get Katie to stop pestering me."

Why do I feel relieved about that? He kept his face blank.

She drew a deep breath and looked out the windshield. "Ready?"

Garrett gave her a teasing look. "You should probably start the engine. It stalled after last time."

She turned the key sheepishly. "You know, I'm not the one who said I needed to drive. I was fine with rideshare."

"You won't be so fine with it if you're staying in Brandywood for a while. Those bills add up." Garrett stopped her again as she reached for the shifter. "Don't rush it. Push the clutch down, then shift, then worry about the pedal switch."

Sam stared at her feet. "Driving with two feet seems ridiculous. And then my hands are doing separate things too. How is anyone supposed to do four different things at the same time?"

"Ask a drummer. They're the masters of it." Garrett leaned back again, watching her. Something about her approach to the lessons put him in a good mood. It could be the furrow of concentration in her brow, or the way her lips drew tighter. When she'd been learning photography as a teenager, she'd often posed him and Katie for pictures. That same look of focus had been on her face.

The truck stalled again and he held back a laugh as she threw her hands up in the air and swore. "This is impossible."

"You know, when my dad taught me, he drove out to Murder Hill and put me at the bottom of it and then made me stop and start three times along the way to the top. Took me an hour to drive one-sixteenth of a mile. You haven't sweated until you've driven uphill in a manual for the first time."

"I'll take your word for it. Your father was an ass."

"Is an ass." Garrett didn't share the other side of the story. The cars honking, blaring past him, people cursing because he'd stopped in the middle of the road. His father's car rolling down the hill as he desperately crushed the clutch, the car stalling. His father's stupid belly laugh, breath reeking of Jameson.

He'd been fifteen years old but he'd gone home and cried.

Garrett's throat dried and he cleared it. "Why don't we do this? Shift it into neutral and turn it on. Then you can practice the pedal motion for a bit. No shifting for now."

Sam's cheeks were flushed. "Why do we need the car on for that?" Being as petite as she was, he'd always thought of her as a perfect combination of naturally pretty and cute. Especially with her snow hat with a pom on top. And when she blushed.

"Because it's freezing in here." Garrett increased the heat. "I'm used to my seat warmer on my truck."

"Okay. How do I do neutral again?" Sam looked sheepish.

Chuckling, Garrett nodded toward the clutch. "Push the clutch, then drop the shifter down. Here." He placed his hand over hers.

Her eyes darted to his. Her response to his touch was . . . surprising.

He moistened his lips, his throat feeling dry. "Uh—here—" With the palm of his hand still covering hers, he moved the shifter into neutral.

Her gaze focused on their hands, and she appeared to be concentrating.

Keeping his hand over hers, he felt a rush of blood to his

fingertips, making the backs of his knuckles and finger joints redder.

"So if you move your hand back and forth in the shifter like this"—he jiggled the shifter—"you can see how easy it is to move it around when it's in neutral. Whether you have the clutch in or not."

Her fingers spread and his fingers rested between them. This might be the sexiest driving lesson he'd ever given. He pulled his hand back.

Sam didn't seem to even notice the way she'd sent his pulse racing.

They practiced the motion for about ten minutes and then attempted to shift it into first gear a few more times. When she succeeded the last time, Garrett clapped. "Okay, now pull down the driveway and shift it into second when I tell you to. You're going to have to push the clutch down to shift gears, but it won't be as tough as first gear is."

Fortunately, the Reddings had a long driveway. David Redding had claimed in court he hadn't used any money he'd gotten from drug trafficking to buy the property—even though no one believed it—and by some miracle, Charlotte had gotten the property in the divorce. Garrett's mother had always said it was God's way of looking out for "those two beautiful little girls."

Sam drew closer to the end of the driveway, and Garrett checked quickly between Sam and where the street began. "Okay, start slowing down."

But they weren't slowing.

"Sam, stop—" Garrett began the warning but then caught sight of the car coming down the street. Even if she braked hard, she might end up halfway onto the street at this point.

Garrett dove across the middle of the truck and grabbed the hand brake. Jerking it up, the truck screeched as Sam slammed on the brake. They both tumbled toward the dash. Garrett braced himself with his forearms and felt Sam collide against him. The car on the street swerved, a long honk coming from the angry driver. Then the truck stalled.

Blinking, Garrett ignored the pain in his thigh where it'd hit the hand brake. That would leave a bruise later. He pulled away from Sam, who was trembling and pale.

"I can't believe that happened," she said.

Garrett caught his breath and pulled the keys from the ignition. "I hadn't had a single accident in seventeen years of driving. You come along and I'm in two of them in one week."

She glared and then burst into nervous laughter. "Please tell me there's somewhere around here that serves Bloody Marys at this hour."

"On a Monday?" Garrett dangled the keys. "No wonder you drive like a drunk. Slide over. I'll back up the driveway."

Once the truck was parked safely next to his in the parking pad, Garrett helped her out. His thigh ached and he rubbed his jeans over the sore spot with the flat of his palm. "Same time tomorrow?"

She rolled her eyes. "Only if you have a death wish."

"Obviously. Or I wouldn't have gotten in that car with you."

Her laugh carried into the gray days typical for this time of year. Every year, no sooner did the leaves fall from the trees than the days turned dreary and unmotivating. Somehow her laugh made it cheerier. "Care for some coffee? I have to do some work before I go to the hospital but I can probably afford to waste another couple of minutes."

"Sounds good." The truth was he was enjoying the time with Sam—more than he had thought he would. When Mrs. Redding had approached him in the grocery store earlier this year about doing work for her, he'd dreaded the thought of ever running into Sam again.

But he'd always had a soft spot for Mrs. Redding. She'd always been kind to him, even when she'd caught him sneaking into her house during one of Sam and Katie's sleepovers. It had been Katie's idea—she'd tell her mom she would sleep at Sam's house, and then he could sneak in. He'd been a dumb, horny teenager, but Mrs. Redding had done him the favor of not telling his parents.

She seemed to understand grounding didn't exist for him. Beatings, though . . .

Sam moved into the house ahead of him, and Garrett followed her. "So how is your mom? Is she coming home soon?"

"They're hoping they can release her tonight. So she'll be here for Thanksgiving." Sam unzipped her coat and hung it from the coatrack. Her tone made it clear she didn't want to talk about her mom. "Can I get you anything to eat? Jen Klein left muffins from Bunny's for me this morning in the guest lodge. And she told me to tell you she has a pumpkin pie with your name on it."

Curious as he was about Mrs. Redding, Garrett let the topic go and nodded at the news about the pie he'd ordered from Bunny's for Thanksgiving. He removed his jacket. "Ah, cool."

Sam smirked and flipped on the kitchen lights. "She was asking about you a lot, actually. She imitated the doe-eyed look Katie used to have in ninth grade. *Oh*"—she made her voice whispery and overly sweet—"*is Garrett coming with Eli today?*" Then she stuck a finger into her mouth and pretended to gag.

"Jen and I aren't even remotely interested in each other." He couldn't help but wonder if Sam was asking because she was genuinely curious about who he might be with. Although he'd take Jen over Trisha Sanders any day. He might never eat yogurt again in his life. Rolling the sleeves of his gray thermal Henley shirt up, he approached the sink and washed his hands. "A muffin sounds perfect, by the way."

Sam paused, her eyes flitting to the tattoos on his left forearm. "I should have known." She admired the design. "Celtic quarter sleeve? Impressive." She grinned. "Your mom must have freaked out."

Understatement.

"She did. Thus far I'm the only one of her seven children to get any ink. She's scared the other ones into not doing it." He dried his hands on a paper towel and tugged the sleeves back down. "According to her, it's a rule in the Catholic church you can't get a tattoo."

"You're the youngest. You can get away with it." She pulled a paper box of muffins from the top of the fridge. "Not to mention, you already broke most of the Catholic rules. Speaking of your mother . . . do you think she would be one of my home bakers for the magazine campaign? She makes the best Italian cookies around."

He couldn't imagine his mother tying a shoelace without bumbling it on a live stream.

"I can ask." He lifted a chocolate chip muffin from the box. "Who else you got? She might feel intimidated."

"Your mom. If you ask her." Sam gave a purposely exaggerated fake smile. "And I was going to ask Bunny today once I build up the nerve to go into town."

"Right. You haven't asked anyone. How many people do you have to have again?"

"Twelve." She started the coffee. "But . . . I haven't talked to anyone in years. I may as well be a stranger to them now. I'm trying to work up the courage."

Garrett took a bite of the muffin, the sweet flavor delicate in his mouth. Sam asking favors from the folks of Brandywood.

This must be killing her. "What you need is someone who is both a connoisseur of sugary treats, is charming, and well-liked with the ladies of Brandywood to go with you and ask."

Sam cut her eyes at him. "Too bad I don't know anyone like that."

"Fine. Then I'll leave you to it." He peeled the muffin liner off the bottom of his muffin. "Let me know how it goes."

"Doyle, I won't beg." She poured him a cup of coffee. "Sugar?"

"All of it." He dug through the fridge for creamer then held it out. "This too. When do you need people to get back to you with a yes?"

"How in the heck do you not have six cavities a year?" she asked as he spooned a few heaping tablespoons into his coffee. She took the creamer back from him, making a face. "By tomorrow. I have to submit my plans to my boss. And I'll need them to sign some paperwork."

"Okay, so we'll go tomorrow after your driving lesson. You'll have to ask them in person then." Garrett finished the muffin with two bites. "But I'll help. And you still didn't ask."

She looked as though she knew she'd skirted having to ask him for another favor.

"Thank you. You're a lifesaver." The way she said it, Garrett almost believed her. Could it be she'd asked him in to hint at this favor?

Not that he minded. At all. Because if one thing was certain, it was that he'd do almost anything for Sam Redding. *Always had.*

CHAPTER TEN

A BIKE HAD BEEN a bad idea. Not only because the old one Sam had found in Mom's shed looked like it hadn't been ridden since Sam was in high school. But the icy mountain air in her lungs?

She could barely breathe.

And Brandywood wasn't even at that high of an elevation. She slowed her bike, stopping on the side of the road as she struggled to catch her breath. A few cars roared past on her left-hand side. She had the feeling they'd been creeping along behind her, waiting for the road to widen enough to ride safely past.

She pressed her hand flat against her diaphragm, trying to rub out the spasm there. *Ouch.* Garrett's plan to have her driving seemed more appealing by the minute.

The winding road from the Redding Cabins into Main Street wasn't far. Only a few miles. She'd already missed the prettiest time of year for this ride—early in the fall when the forests were alive with foliage. But now, everything was brown.

The snow from last week had mostly melted away, leaving wet trails on the road.

As a kid, she'd felt she lived out in the sticks compared to everyone else. Most of her classmates seemed to walk into town or to school. Sam had been one of the few who had to take the bus.

She hopped back on the bike and pushed herself forward again, ignoring the cold whipping loose strands of hair against her cheeks. The temperatures here weren't any colder than they were in New York. And the ride was a lot less smelly. You never knew when you'd catch a whiff of something foul on a city street.

As the edge of Main Street came into view, Sam braced herself by holding her breath. She didn't need to be afraid of these people. She'd known them her whole life.

That's exactly why you're afraid.

She left her bike in the main parking lot at the top of the street. The street ran at a downward angle from here, giving her a good view of Main. She stretched, her legs feeling strangely wobbly.

Not much about Brandywood seemed to have changed. Bunny's and Yardley's still featured prominently on Main Street, a collection of cute shops in stone buildings along the street between them. Bunny's had frequently been a refuge to do her homework when she was in high school—they'd been one of the first places to offer Wi-Fi, which had been spotty at the cabins until recently.

Sam headed down the sidewalk, pausing by the brick façade of the first shop near the parking lot. *That's new.* A mural, saying *Welcome to Brandywood.* Whoever the artist was, they'd gone to great lengths to incorporate a lot about the town. Some of the Christmas traditions were depicted, including the street production of *A Christmas Carol* and the floating light festival over by the lake. The Fourth of July and St. Patrick's Day parades were also depicted, as well as the summer crab festival.

She had so many memories of all these events. A smile tipped at her mouth as she continued past the mural. It couldn't have all been so bad, could it?

"Sam!" Katie hurried toward her, the heels of her boots clacking. "I'm so sorry I'm late—" She caught Sam in a quick hug. "I swear I hit every stoplight between my house and here."

"No big deal. It gave me a chance to mentally prepare myself for Bunny's."

"I don't know what you're so afraid of. It's Bunny. She's like the sweetest person on the planet."

Easy for you to say. Far as Sam could remember, everyone had loved Katie. She had been effortlessly popular—the type of girl invited to everyone's parties and events.

"What are we having?" Katie asked as they slipped into a booth seat at Bunny's Café.

A few seconds later, Jen appeared at their table.

Sam peeked at the menu on the wall. She didn't have time for a long coffee date—she still needed to go to the hospital. At this rate, she'd have to stay up all night to do her actual job.

"Just the pita and hummus platter. I don't need anything else to drink. The water is fine." Jen scribbled the order down. She hesitated and looked between Katie and Sam. "Is that it?"

"Hot chocolate for me."

"Sounds good. I'll be out with that in a few," Jen said with a warm smile.

As Jen's figure receded into the kitchen, Katie leaned her elbows on the table and lowered her voice. "Watch out around that girl. She's a total whore. Got knocked up by some rando a couple of years ago. And now she and Garrett are secretly dating."

"Really?" Sam's gaze traveled in the direction that Jen had gone. She'd thought that might be the case but Garrett had adamantly denied it.

Katie snickered softly. "Can you imagine what Dan or Will would do if they found out? I'll have to let it slip in front of Dan. I know where his speed trap is."

Yes, I can imagine what Dan will do. Clearly. And the thought of it didn't thrill her in the very least, unlike what it seemed to do to Katie. Sam raised her glass of water. An uncomfortable feeling churned in her gut. Had Katie always been like this? Or had she grown up and away from the small-town gossip Katie seemed to relish so much? "Speaking of Garrett, how are you doing with him being back in town?"

"Oh, what do I care?" Katie made a face. She pulled off her winter hat and then combed her fingers through her red hair. "I've got a big weekend planned with that FBI guy I told you about. I'm going to his place in DC after Thanksgiving and we're doing all the touristy things. It should be fun."

Despite Katie's reassurances that she didn't care what Garrett did these days, Sam couldn't help but feel it wasn't true. All these years, Katie had carried on about him, despite her declaring her hatred for him after he'd left her at the altar. And when Sam considered Garrett had been in the military serving their country, when would Katie have seen him to be so bothered? He couldn't have done anything to her since their breakup. She didn't seem to let it go. *Why am I just realizing this?*

"Are you excited about the date with Mike?" Katie's shoulders wiggled. "I'm so thrilled you're finally going out with someone other than Eli."

"I've dated other men." And no—she was absolutely dreading the date. But she didn't want to hurt Katie's feelings by letting her know.

"Slept with other men, though?" Katie looked at her pointedly. "You need to go out there and have some completely casual, no-strings-attached sex with a hot guy. And Mike is *hot*. He was on the front cover for that calendar the Brandywood fire department does every year."

Sam squirmed. "There have been others." She looked around the café side of Bunny's bakery, hoping no one she knew was around. The last thing she wanted was for all of Brandywood to know about her sexual history.

Katie rolled her eyes. "Whatever. You need a good one-night stand. And if he ends up being great for you, awesome. I don't care who it is at this point—get back out there. On top preferably."

Grimacing, Sam shook her head. "You're ridiculous. You realize I'm not back in Brandywood to date, right?"

"Who cares? You can still get some while you're down here. What better way to relieve some of that stress you have going on with your family? If you do nothing but work and take care of your mom, you'll go nuts."

Jen returned to the table, balancing a platter. She set it in front of Sam and Sam's jaw dropped. A row of pita triangles filled one side of the platter, along with sliced peppers, cucumbers, alfalfa sprouts, and other veggies. A large bowl of hummus was in the center. "Oh my goodness, I had no idea it was so much. I can't imagine getting this much food at the place back home."

Jen looked serious, less friendly than before. *Odd.* "Bunny always makes huge portions."

"So, Jen, Garrett was telling Sam all about you the other day," Katie broke in.

Sam's heart sunk. A gleam shone in Katie's eyes

Jen didn't look at Katie. "Really?" Her voice was flat.

Sam shifted. Despite her age, Jen seemed to hold her own

against Katie. Sam cut in, "Garrett was just telling me how much you've helped my mom with the cabins."

"Oh—" Jen appeared less defensive. "Yeah. I'm so thankful to your mom. And Bunny. They're both the best bosses ever. I'll be at the cabins tomorrow night, actually. And on Thanksgiving."

"I volunteered to take a day shift next week on my day off from the salon," Katie said. "I'll stay a bit later that day and we can hang out. I'd love to find out how things are going with the Klein clan. I've been meaning to catch up with Dan too."

Jen shot her an incredulous look. "Sure."

As Jen left the table again, Sam frowned at Katie. "What was that all about?"

Katie sipped her drink. "She's a Klein. They're all racist jerks."

"I don't think she's like the rest of them." Katie's behavior was making Sam feel uncomfortable. "She seems to genuinely care about my mom."

"You might have forgotten the ethnic slurs Dan used to call you and your mom, but I haven't. Just because you've been gone doesn't mean much has changed."

Sam's interaction with Dan the other night gave her the same impression. Still, it wasn't fair to Jen to judge her by her brother. "They weren't *exactly* ethnic slurs, though."

"Humming the Mexican hat dance every time you walked into a room? Saying things like 'every night is taco Tuesday' at the Reddings' house?" Katie lifted her eyebrows incredulously. "I can't believe I'm having to remind you."

"No—no, I remember." *All too well.* Comments like those and the laughter they had elicited from their classmates made Sam want to forget she spoke Spanish. Brandywood wasn't exactly a bilingual town. She gritted her teeth. "But I would rather not discuss it."

"Sorry. Didn't mean to dredge it up." Katie hugged her mug with both hands. The grinding of the espresso machine overtook the noise in the café for a minute, the roasted aroma filling the air. "I'm so glad you're back in town for a bit. I wish it was forever. It feels like everything is right in my world when you're here."

"My mom and my sister probably feel the same way." Sam pushed the platter between them. "Share this with me."

"They do. But"—Katie scooped some hummus onto a pita triangle—"you seem to have a very full life in the city."

A full life.

Sam chewed a piece of pita, her eyes wandering the café. Truthfully, she wouldn't use that adjective to describe her life. She liked her job—but having a camera in her hands always made her happy. And she had friends but she didn't see them often these days.

She had a *busy* life.

Sam didn't want to dwell on it any longer. "So Mom comes home tonight."

Katie bit her lip. "I know. Are you ready?"

"Mostly overwhelmed. Because if I pull off this cookie campaign, I'm going to have to figure out a place to shoot everything by December seventh. There's no way I can ask people if a camera crew can invade their homes."

"Someone might be willing. Or you can always ask Bunny. I think it would be cute to do it here."

Sam raised her eyes to the silver-haired woman behind the counter. Outside of waving a hello when she'd arrived, Sam hadn't talked to Bunny. "God, it makes me so nervous to ask anyone from Brandywood for help."

Katie stood. "Time to face your fears. I'm going to ask Bunny to come over here. She's the nicest lady in this town besides your mom."

Sam fought the urge to hide under the table. Gratifying as it was to think people considered Mom so nice, if Bunny was as nice as her mom, it also meant Bunny had a side she didn't show to people. Mom had been strict and unyielding about a lot of things. Especially with her daughters.

Katie approached the counter, a wide smile on her face, and immediately engaged with Bunny. The noise in the café was loud enough that Sam couldn't entirely hear what was being said but Bunny looked over at Sam. She smiled, then nodded, coming out from behind the counter. She waddled every-so-slightly when she walked and Sam steeled herself for the encounter. Katie was right—if she couldn't face Bunny, she'd completely fail in this crazy scheme.

Bunny stopped at the table and Katie slid back into the booth. "Samantha! It's so lovely to see you in here again." A more somber expression crossed her face. "How's your mom? We missed her at church yesterday. It was a shock to us all."

"She comes home tonight." Sam hesitated, not knowing how much she should share about Mom's illness. Had her mother told anyone? Probably not. She wouldn't have wanted anyone to find out before her daughters.

"Oh, good. Tell her we're all praying for her. Can I drop a casserole off tomorrow? I won't stay."

"That would be great. And very appreciated. My mom probably doesn't want to eat anything I make." Sam grinned. "I can't remember the last time I cooked."

"Really?" Bunny lifted her gray brows, her round face registering genuine surprise. "And your mom is such a superb cook. I guess that didn't rub off, huh?"

She could cook—she chose not to, she wanted to say. But was that even true anymore? Takeout or prepped meals stocked her fridge. And she made a lot of protein smoothies.

Bunny looked back at the unattended counter and folded

her hands in front of her apron. "Katie says you have something you wanted to ask."

"Uh, yeah." Sam sat straighter. "I mean, yes. I work for *This Charmed Life* magazine as a staff photographer."

"I know. Your mother is so proud. We all got subscriptions from the magazine last Christmas." Bunny's blue eyes were warm, the corners of her eyes crinkling with the wrinkles of a lifetime of laughter.

Really? Sam was shocked at the level of interest the people in town seemed to have in her.

"Oh, that's nice." Sam struggled to spit the words out, her palms sweating. What if Bunny said no? Bunny was her best shot at a cordial reception. "Anyway, my Maren, I mean . . . my editor decided since I was going to be out of town for some time, we move our next big social campaign to Brandywood. It's twelve days of features of different Christmas cookies."

As she spoke, she eased into the familiar work world. "The aim is to have twelve different home bakers make a cookie recipe live on our social media channels. Then I'll style and photograph the finished cookies and we'll post them, together with the recipe, on our food blog."

Bunny nodded politely, but her face remained blank. "Oh, sounds exciting."

"I was hoping you could be one of the home bakers," Sam spat out. There. She'd done it.

A strange expression crossed Bunny's face. "I'm a bit more than a home baker, dear. I did study at l'Ecole Lenôtre in Paris."

Oh . . . shit. She'd insulted her. She felt the color drain from her face. "I'm so sorry. That's not what I meant."

"Well." Bunny smiled tightly. "It's true I didn't go on to fame and fortune, perhaps. So it's easy to forget," she sighed.

"Let me think about it. I should go back to the counter though. Don't want to leave it unattended for too long."

As Sam watched her waddle back to the counter, she pressed her hands to her flaming cheeks. She covered her mouth and looked back at Katie. "Oh my God, I'm such an ass."

Katie looked embarrassed for her. "That was painful to watch," she admitted. Then she looked at the hummus platter. "Should we take this to go?"

To-go had never sounded better.

CHAPTER ELEVEN

GARRETT AWOKE to the doorbell ringing. He lifted his head from his pillow, blinking blearily at his phone. Who the hell was here at six in the morning?

He threw the sheets off and stood, freezing in only his boxers. Searching the laundry basket, he grabbed a pair of sweatpants and a T-shirt and hurried down the stairs.

The doorbell rang again. "I'm coming already," Garrett called out. He glanced out into the sidelight. *Jen?*

Opening the door, he stepped back as she breezed past him, a paper shopping bag in tow. "What's up?"

She poked her head around. "Where's the kitchen? I figured if you won't come to see me at Bunny's, I'd bring Bunny's to you. Or breakfast, anyway."

Garrett pointed the way and then followed her. "And Colby?"

"He's still asleep. At my parents'." Jen's ponytail swished as she walked and then she stopped at the kitchen entrance. "Nice place," she said appreciatively. "Your kitchen is bigger than my entire apartment."

He'd bought the old farmhouse to flip and then liked it so much after he'd renovated it, he hadn't been able to part with it. He felt bad for not inviting her over before this, but he didn't invite anyone over, not with his work schedule.

"Thanks." He went to the island. "So what'd you bring me?" He still wasn't sure what she was doing here, but he didn't want to kick her out, either.

Jen removed a couple of cups of orange juice, a few slices of quiche, and two breakfast sandwiches from the bag. "I saw your old fiancée at Bunny's yesterday."

His eyebrows drew together. "And?"

"And . . ." Jen shifted. She pressed her lips together then looked back up at Garrett. "She's a bitch."

Garrett chuckled. "Very true."

"Yeah, well, she was joking with Sam Redding about how she's going to tell my brother all about our secret love life. My friend who works the counter at Bunny's heard her." A deep line furrowed between her brows.

His thoughts slogged through the morning brain fog. *Our secret love life?* "As in . . . you and me?"

"I know. It's ridiculous. But for whatever reason, Katie thought it would be a great joke. But if she goes running to Dan with lies—"

"Yeah, no, I get it." Garrett held up a hand. "Katie's a bit of a bloodhound. And if she heard you've been spending time with me, she won't be nice to you."

"But you've been spending a lot of time with her best friend," Jen said, crossing her arms. "Shouldn't that make you worried?"

"Sam?" Garrett combed his fingers through his hair. "That's not the same thing, though. And Sam's not like Katie."

Jen's glance was wary. "I don't know. They were cackling

together at Bunny's. I'm not saying Sam's the same but Katie's a bully. Birds of a feather and all."

Garrett stiffened. He'd expect this sort of talk from Luis, but Jen?

Jen watched him expectantly and then held out another warm paper cup. "Coffee? I made it taste as little as coffee as possible."

"This is . . . sweet of you, thanks." Total darkness continued outside the large picture window, dawn barely beginning. How early had she gotten up to do this?

She must be worried about this.

"Well, don't worry about Dan. Even if Katie says something to him, I can handle it. It'll be fine."

Jen didn't appear sure. "That's easy for you to say. Dan has single-handedly made it impossible for me to date in this town. You should be careful."

"I'll be fine." This probably wasn't the best time to mention Dan had been harassing him. *Poor kid.* The lengths her brother went to chase guys away really bothered her.

She sat on a stool at the island. "Who decorated for you? It's amazing," she observed, looking at the great room attached to the kitchen.

"My sister. Hannah." She'd staged the whole thing to sell it. When he'd kept the house, he'd bought all the furniture from her.

"Yeah, I was going to say it looks like there's been a woman's touch." Jen popped open one cup of orange juice and took a sip. "Eat." She pushed a sandwich across the counter. "It's maple bacon, an over-easy egg, and Vermont cheddar on a croissant. I made it myself."

Garrett unwrapped it from the parchment and took a bite. Breakfast was his favorite meal anyway but this was amazing. "Oh my God, this is good." He took another bite. "Sam should have you do a cookie for her social media thing. You're getting to be as good as Bunny."

Her eyes twinkled. "Don't tell Bunny. But I couldn't have asked for a better mentor." She unwrapped her own sandwich. "Speaking of Sam's thing . . . oh my gosh, she asked Bunny to participate yesterday."

"Oh, yeah?"

"Didn't go so well." She sipped her orange juice and swallowed a bite of sandwich. "Called Bunny a *home baker*."

Garrett winced. If there was one thing Bunny was proud of, it was her training in some fancy French school. What had Sam been thinking? "So what did Bunny say?"

Jen shrugged. "That she'd think about it." She popped open the plastic container to the quiche, and the container crinkled in response. "Can I borrow a fork?"

He fished one out of a drawer. "Poor Sam."

Jen lifted her brows. "Poor *Bunny*. This is what I'm trying to tell you. I think she's nice enough but everyone in town says Sam is a snob. She thinks she's above us all."

Garrett sighed. No, that wasn't really what Sam thought, but Jen didn't know Sam very well. It was sad that people considered her a snob. Garrett washed the last bit of sandwich down with some coffee. "It's not black and white. Sam had to deal with a lot when she was a kid. Especially from people like your brother."

"I know, but he regrets that. He's not the same anymore. Doesn't change that Sam started acting like she didn't know anyone from here a couple of years before she left. And then wouldn't deign herself to go into town until yesterday."

Garrett was far less convinced of Dan's sudden change of heart. After all, hadn't Jen come to warn him about Dan? "But why would she? No one ever apologized to her. Sam wasn't any more responsible for the things her father did than you are for the way your brothers treated people. I hardly think it's fair to say your brother is capable of change but Sam isn't."

Jen split her quiche with a fork. "True." She took a bite and gave him a puzzled look. "Are you all friends? I figured she hated you because of Katie."

"I didn't say we were friends." He had to be careful about what he said.

"Really?" She waved the fork in a small circle, pointing it. "Because it sounds like you're defending her."

"I—" Garrett ran his fingers through his hair. Finding it sticking up in places, he smoothed it flat. He must look ridiculous. "She's Sam. You know, Eli's girl. We've always been friendly. Mostly she drives me crazy. She's incredibly opinionated and stubborn . . . and ridiculously smart, which has always made fighting with her tough because I'm usually on the losing side."

Jen drew her chin back, her eyes widening. "Oh my God. You have feelings for her."

"No." Garrett stood straighter. He did *not* want to give that impression. Not to anyone. "No, no, no. Not at all."

She peered at him dubiously. "You sure?"

"Positive." He leaned forward and grabbed the other quiche.

Jen's expression was amused. "Be careful, Garrett. Even if you don't have feelings, you're right. She's Eli's girl. And you're Katie's ex. A bad situation if I've heard of one."

Garrett popped open the container for the quiche, wondering at the slight pinch in his chest from Jen's summation of the situation. *There isn't a situation, Doyle.* "When did you become a font of wisdom?"

"When I became a mom." She licked her fork clean. Like a normal person. *Not* at all the way Trisha had played with the damned yogurt. "They give you a certificate in the hospital when you leave with a baby."

Going over to the sink, she pumped some soap into a sponge and washed the fork. "Which is a problem when the small town you live in thinks of you as a kid." She shut the water off and turned toward him. She tilted her head to the side. "So what do you have going on today?"

"Leaving for work in about half an hour. I'm managing a job in town, so I have to show up for a few hours each morning to supervise how things are progressing. Then I'm going to the Reddings'. I need to fix the damage in cabin twelve." He didn't want to get into the driving lessons with Sam right now.

Yet he was still puzzled why Jen had felt it necessary to warn him about Dan. Was she worried? He frowned. "Much as I appreciate breakfast, you could have probably texted me about Dan."

"I sent you a few texts last night. Didn't hear back, so I was worried I'd freaked you out. Unfortunately, my hours to have conversations with people are not when normal people are available."

Why didn't I see the texts? He yawned, scratching at the scruff along his jawline. "I must have missed them. I had a few beers and passed out on the couch early last night. Sorry about that. I stayed late at the Reddings' as I'm trying to fit that repair job into my free time."

Her eyes clouded. "Drinking alone these nights?"

"Nah, just a couple of beers." He hadn't intended to imply he'd gotten drunk.

She scrunched her face. "I'm so sorry about cabin twelve, by the way. When Sam told me what happened, I felt awful. I should have told the guest that outside water was off for the year."

He let the comment about the drinking alone slide. Jen had

probably been too young to pay attention to the stories about his father at their height. "It wasn't your fault at all. I turned the water on. I should have made sure we turned it off. The Reddings have enough on their plate right now."

"Yeah, I know. Still. I felt bad when I heard."

That's because you're a good person.

Unlike the person who had caused the flood to happen. The more he'd seen of Katie's *true* personality since they'd broken up, the more he'd wondered how he'd been so blind to her faults as well. Had it been love or lust and a bit of juvenile satisfaction that the town's princess had loved him that had blinded him?

Jen threw the trash away and wiped the counter with a napkin. "I should get going. Thanks for not being mad at me."

Garrett chuckled, walking with her to the door. "For the texts I never saw or for waking me up at the ass crack of dawn?"

"Both." Jen threw him a grin.

As Garrett let her out, he leaned back against the front door pondering Jen's perceptions about Katie. Jen was right. Katie wasn't a nice person to hang around with. Perhaps not who Sam seemed to think she was, as well. But would Sam ever believe him if he suggested otherwise? *And would I ever want to do that?*

CHAPTER TWELVE

SAM POKED her head into Mom's bedroom. Mom sat in her bed in a nightgown, with the tray of breakfast beside her cleared. The morning news was on the TV, and Mom clicked it off when she saw Sam. "Need anything else?"

"No, I'm fine. Thank you for breakfast. It was delicious." Mom smiled, crumpling the paper napkin in her lap.

Delicious is probably a stretch. Sam had managed some eggs and toast with jelly. Nothing fancy. But then it was also seven in the morning. Her own breakfasts usually consisted of a sip of hot coffee and a protein bar if she was going to spin class.

"Are you ready for the holiday weekend?" Mom's expression grew sympathetic. "I'm sorry I can't help. It's a lot to have on your shoulders."

Thanksgivings were always crazy at the cabins. They booked a full year out for them. Some families had even made it a tradition to celebrate here in Brandywood.

Sam didn't care for the holiday. While others complained about whacky family members and overstuffing themselves, Sam only ever remembered a holiday weekend of making sure everyone else was having fun and collapsing into bed in exhaustion after helping Mom.

Family meals gathered around the table, turkey and cranberry sauce—that was for the guests in their cabins. Her mother had always made it part of the Thanksgiving bookings—a full meal inclusion the Reddings spent all day packaging for others to enjoy with their families. Still, who knew if she'd ever get to eat her mom's Thanksgiving Day meal again? Even if it was on her feet between deliveries. This year, Bunny had been generous enough to take an extra-large last-minute order of the to-go Thanksgiving feasts she advertised to customers at her café.

Sighing, Sam leaned her hip into the door frame. "How are you feeling this morning?"

"Good. I'm glad I'm home. I slept a lot better without someone coming into my room at all hours." Mom leaned against the pillows propped up on her headboard. "What time is Laura coming?"

"She said she'd be here at eleven. She was planning for eight, but Mark wanted her to rest."

Mom shook her head ruefully. "I don't know how she expects to take care of me. She should stay home. We both need nurses."

"I told her that, but she insisted. And you know Laura." Sam rubbed the sleep from her eyes, feeling like a frumpy mess. Had she even brushed her hair? After the incident with Bunny, she barely slept. How could she have been so thoughtless?

The light coming in from the slats in the blinds threw an interesting pattern of diagonal shadows across Mom's bed, and she studied it. The image would make a pretty documentary image. Mom, sitting in the bed, rimmed with the golden light beside her.

She should grab her camera and take some pictures before

Garrett got here. Having a camera in her hands might make her feel less frazzled.

Mom held out a hand. "Could you get me my medicine from the dresser before you go? I think I might need one."

Leaving her mom with her meds and a cell phone at arm's reach, Sam grabbed her camera from her room. As she made her way outside, the brisk morning air helped clear any additional fog from her mind. The day was gray, fog still draping the edges of the forest.

She paused and lifted her camera, adjusting her settings for the low light. She snapped a few shots, then forced herself to keep going. Thanks to digital cameras, she'd had to train herself to limit how many shots she took. Otherwise, she'd be stuck culling hundreds of pictures. Sometimes she used a film camera to challenge herself to take the time to compose her shots.

Letting the camera hang at her side, she started down the driveway toward the cabins, then slowed.

On a morning not too dissimilar to this, she'd watched red and blue lights bouncing into the fog. December. Right before Christmas. When other little girls were praying for Santa to bring Barbies and dress-up clothes, she'd ended up spending that Christmas season praying for her daddy to come back home.

A sharp pain throbbed through her heart.

"David Redding got what he deserved."

"My mommy says you can't play with us. Your daddy's in jail."

The voices filtered through her memory disembodied from their speakers. She couldn't remember who had said what to her anymore.

As an adult, sure, she could accept her father had been a horrible person. He'd ruined lives with his crimes. Even her mom had severed the connection. He never contacted Laura or Sam again.

But to a four-year-old girl who hadn't known any better? She had just missed her daddy.

She had never known David Redding, the narcotics trafficker, a man who'd exacerbated a small town's problem with drugs.

She'd only known the man who'd carried her on his shoulders. Bought her ice cream. Tucked her into bed and read her stories. The memories of him were so far away now, she could barely remember what he'd looked like. And he'd died in jail a few years earlier, so there would be no chance to reconnect someday and ask him the "why" weighing on her heart since childhood.

She swallowed the lump in her throat. Instead, the crimes he'd committed had weighed on her own shoulders, burning her with a sense of shame. One time in middle school, she'd been playing a game of *Monopoly* with some classmates, and she'd ended up with her token in jail. The kids she'd been playing with had snickered. *"Yeah, that's the perfect place for a Redding."*

She shook the thoughts away and lifted her camera again, aiming it toward the sign for the cabins. With the fog curling around it and the faint glimmer of the morning sun reflecting off the fog, the picture was pretty enough. But her mom had obviously taken the time to make a fall-like display near it. Hay bales, pumpkins, gourds. Cabbage flowers spilling out of a wheelbarrow on its side.

These cabins were her mom's dream. Her labor had kept them afloat. Every detail and decision about them resulted from her mom's hard work. *To hell with the memories of her father. And to hell with those people who had laughed at them.*

She wanted a memory of the Redding Cabins her mom had built.

Taking a few more shots, she smiled with satisfaction. She thumbed through the display, going through her images as she walked toward the guest cabins.

As much as she was dreading the Thanksgiving rush, she felt strangely energized. If Mom couldn't do the holiday her way this year, then Sam owed it to her to give it her best effort: give the guests the holiday Mom wanted them to have.

Garrett wasn't here for the driving lesson or to take her to talk to potential home bakers. *Thank goodness.* She went back up to the porch. She didn't have time to waste today. Not with that cookie project hanging over her head.

She opened the deck box. Getting a red and black buffalo checkered blanket, she unfolded it. The familiar scent of mothballs greeted her. Her mother kept them in there to keep the mice and bugs away. It was one of her favorite smells in the world—one that could transport her back in time to snuggles on star-filled nights. With her mom. With Laura. Later, with Eli.

Wrapping herself in the blanket, she sat on the swing on the porch and propped her feet up on the cushion.

When Garrett arrived minutes later, the bench's gentle sway had nearly lulled her to sleep. His boots sounded against the wooden slats of the porch, and he stopped at the door, ringing the bell.

"Over here," she said in a tired voice.

Garrett jumped. "Ah, you surprised me."

She mumbled an apology and sat, tucking her long dark hair behind her ear. "I didn't sleep too well last night."

"Scoot over." Garrett strode toward her and sat beside her. "Could that have anything to do with a certain home baker?"

She groaned. "How did you hear about that already?" She buried her face in her hands. "I'm so embarrassed."

"Jen stopped by this morning with breakfast. Told me all about it." Garrett tugged the blanket off one of her shoulders and put it over his own. "Mind if I share? It's freezing out here."

Jen had brought Garrett breakfast? That sounded . . . close. Maybe Katie was right about them. "I thought you said you weren't dating."

"We're not."

It's not any of your business, Sam.

His leg pressed against hers as though he'd scooted closer when he'd grabbed the blanket. For a reason she couldn't explain, she focused on the pressure of his thigh against hers, and her breath hitched. She didn't mind his closeness. If anything, she wanted to be closer.

Garrett pushed the swing back and then let go, sending them both into a rocking motion. "There's still hope with Bunny, don't worry. You just have to make her feel valued and appreciated for the brilliant pastry chef she is." He stopped the swing's rocking motion by flattening his feet.

Sam leaned against him. *Does he notice?* She chided herself. The flutters in her stomach were probably nerves about talking to the potential bakers. "Can I skip this day? Just wake me up when it's all over."

"That nervous?"

Nervous was putting it mildly. She wanted to throw up.

Garrett wrapped his arm around her shoulders. "You know, they're good people. All of them. Your mom's friends. Not the gossips from your childhood."

"You don't know." How could he possibly know that? There had been a time in her life when it seemed like everyone was talking about her family.

"Well, if they were, don't you think it's about time to let it go? You can't hold on to that hurt for the rest of your life."

"It's not just hurt." She swallowed a shaky breath. "It's fear."

"You know, someone once told me fear and worry don't stop the bad things from happening or give you extra time. The only thing they do is stop you from living the life you have today and steal your joy." Garrett's hand tightened on her shoulder.

She laid her head against his chest, her heart still feeling as though it would burst with nerves. "That's very profound. Are you quoting yourself by chance?"

Garrett's chuckle rumbled against her ear. "You would think that, wouldn't you?"

Goose bumps rose on her arms. He had to be doing it on purpose. Why would he be so close?

Stop it, Sam. He's not doing anything. You're being ridiculous. She'd never thought of him as remotely sexual. And even if she did, it was a natural response. He was an attractive man, after all. The physical barriers that existed with strangers weren't there.

She pulled away and stared at his profile. "Do you ever wonder why we weren't friends in school?"

"Are you telling me we weren't friends? I'm hurt." He smiled, the hint of a boyish dimple on his left cheek. She remembered those dimples—they'd faded into the leanness of his manly face. "I know the answer to that one. Four words."

"I know, I know. Katie MacKintosh and Eli Parker."

He tossed his shoulders in a shrug. "I was going to say *you were a snob.*" He held up four fingers as he spoke each word.

Just what she needed to hear. "Thanks a lot." The way he'd said it made her smile.

"I'm serious. Why would a gorgeous and talented woman like you look at oafish and perpetually-in-trouble and down-on-his-luck me and *want* to be friends with that train wreck? I was trouble by association, ask Eli. Pretty sure he ended up in more than one detention simply because I was sitting next to him. Not to mention, you were a goody two shoes." Garrett stood and extended his hand to her. "Ready to go stall a truck?"

Gorgeous and talented? Her heart skipped a beat.

His teasing had lightened her spirits without her even realizing it. "Do we have to do driving lessons today?" She took his hand and stood, pulling the blanket off. Folding it, she set it back on the swing.

"I don't have unlimited time to spare, Redding. If I'm here for a driving lesson, you're getting back up on that horse and giving it another go."

Chastened, she trudged toward the stairs. "Fine. But only twenty minutes. I need to get the plans to my editor by five, and so far, I have zero home bakers."

"You have one." Garrett jogged down the steps and turned with a grin. "My mom says she'll do it. For what it's worth, ask Jen too. She's turned into an amazing baker working for Bunny. And I doubt she'll say no."

"To you?" Sam gave him a knowing look. The idea of Garrett dating Jen troubled her, though.

"I meant to you." Garrett opened the passenger side door to her mother's truck and climbed in. "She likes you."

Had they been talking about her? Sam didn't like that idea, either. She didn't respond and climbed into the driver's seat. Her dislike for the idea must have shown on her face as she started the engine. "Don't worry," Garrett said with a wink. "I like you too."

"Oh, shut up." She laughed, then shook her head. She met his brown eyes. "But thank you. And for what it's worth, I like you too."

Something in his gaze flickered, a warm smile in his eyes. He looked away abruptly. "Well, it's about time. All this time and effort I've put into making you hate me had to backfire in my face eventually."

She rolled her eyes. Trust Garrett to be incapable of a heartfelt moment. "All right. How does this infernal contraption work again?"

THE DOOR CLICKED CLOSED, and Sam gripped the rail on the porch steps. She glanced at Garrett and let out a slow breath. "Now I know what Jehovah's Witnesses feel like."

Four straight noes. The women had been very polite and kind but not overly friendly. All of them sent good wishes to her family and inquired about her mother's health.

They all said no without hesitation.

Sam left Garrett on the steps and practically ran past his truck, humiliation burning inside her. Why had she thought this would go any differently? Having Garrett beside her made no difference. They all knew who they were doing the favor for. She crossed the street and kept going toward the elementary school playground. They'd updated all the equipment since she'd been a young girl there, and she didn't recognize it as the same place for a moment. Then she continued into the woods just beyond.

Garrett caught up with her. "Whoa, whoa, whoa." He held her by the elbow. "Where are you running off to?"

She faced him, anger bubbling inside her. "I'm done. I'm not asking another person in this goddamned town to help me."

"Yes, you are. You have to." Garrett dropped his hand. "They're being"—he looked back toward the house they'd left— "I don't know. Cautious?"

She yanked her hat from her head, her agitation building. "I can't do this. I can't come back to Brandywood and pretend I don't remember why I left. And for what? To watch my mom die? No, thank you. I didn't sign up for this."

Garrett pulled her into a tight hug. "Will you settle down?"

She stilled against him and pressed her forehead into his coat. "You know, you hug me a lot more than you used to." The snow from the previous week had almost all melted, leaving everything a sodden brown and gray. She preferred the snow.

"Because lately, you look like you need a hug." Garrett rested his chin on the top of her head. "Were you always this short, or did I just grow?"

Yes, the short jokes would definitely help. Her thoughts were as biting as she felt. "Maybe we should go back to you not hugging me."

"Not until you hug me back. Come on, Redding. A real hug."

She turned her face so her cheek was on his chest. "Has anyone ever told you how annoying you are?"

"Yeah, you."

Her arms remained stiffly at her sides. "If I hug you, will you let me go back home?"

"If that's what you want." His voice was more serious.

She snaked her arms around his waist. There wasn't any way she could reach around him, but her body rested against him comfortably. Too comfortably. *What in the heck is happening here?* Since when did Garrett's touch give her goose bumps?

He trailed his fingers against her lower back, rubbing her in what she imagined he intended to be a comforting movement. Except it was speeding her pulse.

Focus, Sam.

"It's what I want." The dull brick buildings of the elementary school swam in her vision, and she blinked. "Laura is probably over already. I haven't seen my niece and nephew since I got into town."

"And your job?"

"Screw it." What could she do? She didn't have home bakers. Her plan was barely a plan. "I don't have a place for them to bake, and I don't have bakers to do the baking."

"You could . . ." Garrett hesitated. "You could use my house. To film, anyway. My kitchen has great natural lighting. Lots of space."

She had given little thought to where Garrett lived now. Somehow, in her mind, she still pictured him living at his parents' house. But he was twenty-seven. With his own house. Like non-city people.

She probably paid more for rent on her one-bedroom apartment than he paid for his mortgage.

She shaded her eyes to the sun, peeking through the trees, and pulled away from Garrett. Cold air filled the space between them, leaving her with a dull feeling.

She wanted to be hugging him still.

Everything seemed upside down. As though the life she'd planned was slipping away from her. The job she'd worked so hard for. The future she'd thought she'd have with Eli. Her mother. "That's very generous of you, but it still doesn't solve the problem of the bakers."

"Do you have to give your editor a list of names today? If you have a place to film, can't you give her names later?"

"I don't know. But what difference does it make?" Sam sighed and stuffed her hands into her pockets. "It's hopeless. I'm never going to get people to accept me back into the fold."

Garrett crossed his arms. "You're talking to the man who left one of Brandywood's most beloved girls *at the altar*. You think coming back here was easy for me? If people talk to me and have accepted me, they'll do the same with you. Just give them some time."

Sam trudged back to Garrett's truck. "I'll see what I can do about my boss. I need to call my assistant, Rachel, and see if she'll come down here. God knows I could use someone familiar on my team."

"See that right there?" Garrett pointed a finger at her and then climbed into his seat. "That's exactly what you have to stop saying. I won't get offended but think about it. It makes it seem like this Rachel is your people. Stop thinking that way."

He had a point. She didn't know if it was entirely intentional, but she'd spent a long time thinking of everyone from Brandywood as being on one side of a line and her on the other. Then a more defensive voice reared inside her, and she leveled her chin. "But Rachel is my people. Why should I have to go backward? What's wrong with putting toxic things behind you and never looking back?"

"You didn't just leave toxic things behind, Sam. You left your family. Your friends. And, from the looks of it, you haven't put anything behind you. It's all still in front of you, eating you alive."

Her mouth tightened, her lips pursing. She was done discussing this with Garrett. As though he hadn't done the same thing she had. He'd signed up for the Army the day he'd turned eighteen.

They drove back in silence, with none of the banter or warm conversation they'd had recently filling the space. The engine thrummed, and the rush of churning heat from the heater flew past the vents. She pulled out her phone, typing an email to Rachel until her head spun with carsickness. The drive from the center of town to her mom's house was, fortunately, a short one—only about five minutes.

Slipping the phone away, she felt her heart lurch painfully

when the old sign for Redding Family Cabins came into view. What would happen to the cabins? Laura probably wanted to continue the business as she'd been working at it for years now. Even though Sam had only ever come home for holidays, the thought of coming back here and her mother not being here filled her with a deep, aching hollow in her chest.

She had wasted so much time, assuming it would always be there. So many times, her mother had called Sam, and she'd slid the decline button. Her mother would always leave a voice mail message. And she called her every day, even if just to say hello. Who else called her?

No one. Just work and occasionally Eli before this. Even Laura only called like once a month, usually with kids in the background interrupting every two minutes. Not that Sam begrudged her niece and nephew, but texting was easier.

Garrett pulled into the driveway and parked. He didn't turn the engine off, and Sam didn't feel like inviting him in anyway.

The front door to the house opened, and Sam frowned as Katie stepped out. She crossed her arms, her hands barely visible in her large tunic sweater. Katie scowled at them. Sam's eyes darted to Garrett.

The corners of Garrett's eyes narrowed. "Shit. I recognize that expression." He killed the engine.

Then Sam wasn't imagining Katie's anger.

Sam scrambled out of the passenger seat. "Hey, everything okay? I thought you would be up at the guest lodge."

"I was." Katie's voice was flat. She came down the stairs gracefully in her ballet flats. "Mrs. Herman called my mother and told her you all went to her house. And then left there and had some PDA-filled moment at the elementary school." Her eyes blazed at Sam, then Garrett. "What the hell is going on?"

Sam's jaw dropped. "PDA . . . what?" She exchanged a look

with Garrett who, true to form, began laughing. She could kill him. Him *and* Mrs. Herman.

Then again, Garrett didn't know how she'd felt about his hug. A flush of guilt crept into her chest.

"Katie, I don't know what Mrs. Herman was thinking. Other than being old and senile and a gossip. Will you stop?" she shot at Garrett.

Garrett sobered somewhat and smirked. He turned to Katie. "And here I was thinking no one would notice us making out at the elementary school. Sorry about that."

Now Sam was going to kill Garrett. Katie's eyes bulged.

"You're a dick," Katie spat, her hands fisting.

In the distance, a flock of geese started honking like they were part of the conversation. "There was no PDA-filled moment. Why on earth would I risk my oldest and closest friendship for—" Sam stopped short.

The words, despite being unintentionally hurtful, had found a mark. A subtle shift, a dark flash crossed Garrett's eyes. She locked eyes with him, her breath hitching before she continued, "Mrs. Herman upset me and Garrett hugged me. That's all."

A humorless smile pressed to Garrett's lips. "That's all," he affirmed. "Now if you'll excuse me, ladies, I have some work to get to. Cabin twelve won't fix itself."

He hopped back into his truck and was gone before Katie could say anything else. The gravel on the driveway crunched as Sam crossed it toward her friend. "Are you okay?"

Katie bit her lip. "He hasn't changed at all, has he? Still as annoying as always." She rolled her eyes. "Still as cute too."

Sam watched her, torn between hugging her and scolding her for believing Sam would betray their friendship with Garrett. She crossed her arms. "So . . . I take it you're not over Garrett, then?"

Katie sighed. "I'll never be over him. He was my first love. Like Eli and you."

Like Eli. The way Katie referred to first love made it sound like something sacred and wonderful. Yet when Sam thought of Eli, all she could think of was heartache.

Katie talked about still having feelings for Garrett, but if that was the case, why had she been so horrible toward him over the years? He'd been ASSHOLE on her phone because of what he'd done to Katie, but Sam questioned that now.

"You're dating someone else. And you're happy, aren't you? High school sweetheart or not, it's probably for the best you all didn't get married. Not if he wasn't ready to make that commitment."

A gasp sounded as Katie's jaw dropped open. "Are you defending what he did to me?"

"No—" Sam squirmed. *Yes.* She scrambled for a more precise way to put it. "Marrying your first love is great in the movies, but only if your first love is prepared to offer you the life you deserve. You've had a chance now to see there are a lot of other guys out there. Guys who might be much more compatible."

"Yeah, but—" Katie crossed her arms. "It hasn't worked out with those guys. I'm still alone. And part of it is probably because I keep measuring them all up to Garrett."

"Measuring up to a guy you've called the most miserable, selfish cretin to walk the face of this earth?" Sam set her hands on her hips. Katie's words weren't adding up. She complained about Garrett enough. That was true. But if she wasn't over him, then her complaints seemed to border more on some sort of obsession. An inability to move on from someone who clearly wasn't right for her.

Not that you have much room to talk. Eli's face flashed through her mind. Sam shifted uncomfortably.

Why was Katie still alone? She talked about going out a lot. But things didn't work out. Sam pursed her lips. And why *had* Garrett broken up with her? Sam had never asked.

"Look, if it bothers you, I'll talk to Garrett. Tell him I don't need his help after all. But you said you were fine with him helping me. And now that he's back living in town, you're going to have to make room in the sandbox." Sam couldn't help the odd feeling of defensiveness rising in her when she thought of Garrett. He was just as much from this town as Katie was. Maybe once upon a time, Sam would have thought Katie's jokes about making him a pariah humorous.

Not anymore. She knew what that felt like all too well. In a small town like Brandywood, innocuous situations or even traditions could hurt the most unsuspecting victim. She remembered sitting at home for father-daughter dances in school, feeling the eyes of her classmates on her when they talked about drugs in health class, as though she was responsible for her father's crimes.

"I *am* fine with him helping you. I don't know why but when my mom called me, it was like I was in high school again and this jealous green-eyed monster came over me. I'm sorry, Sam. Can you forget it ever happened? I'm an idiot. You don't need this right now." Katie approached and hugged her tightly.

Sam returned the hug, but her eyes followed the path Garrett's truck had taken toward the cabins. Garrett was over there working on fixing the cabin for her and her family. Garrett, who had offered her his house to use, who'd been a guardian angel the last week.

She couldn't just forget Katie's outburst. *Or the flash of disappointment and hurt in Garrett's eyes.*

For so long, Sam hadn't thought twice about what Katie said to her about Garrett.

But since she'd come back to Brandywood, Garrett had

been the guy she'd always known. Sarcastic and stand-offish, sure, but also sweet and thoughtful.

Though she wasn't sure if she'd ever thought of him as sexy before.

She bit her lip, pushing the thought away.

What else did Katie have wrong?

CHAPTER THIRTEEN

LUIS OPENED THE DOOR, and Garrett flashed the six-pack of beer in his hand. "Still playing?"

Chuckling, Luis checked his watch. "Nah. The other guys had to leave early. But come on in anyway. I've got the hockey game on."

"Sorry I'm so late." Garrett followed him into the living room. He'd stayed later than he'd expected at the cabin, losing himself in the familiar rhythm of work. He'd never intended nor wanted to go into home improvement like his father. But something about it set his mind at ease—being able to start with raw materials and end with something he'd imagined.

The scent of microwaved popcorn permeated the air and, sure enough, a large bowl was on the couch. Luis had once told him most nights popcorn was his dinner. The popcorn smell had seeped into the walls. One of their friends had brought over a candle one day for game night—sent by his wife in hopes he wouldn't come home smelling like popcorn. It hadn't helped.

"You've been walking around like you're carrying Godzilla

on your shoulders lately." Luis sat on his sofa and took a beer from Garrett. He popped open the tab and sat back, the low hum of the TV and the whistling of the crowd white noise. "You need to talk about it?"

Talk about how Sam had—without even blinking—acted as though he wasn't worth much?

"I'm good." Garrett sank beside Luis. "Things wrap up okay today at the Sanders'?"

"Yeah, real good. Gus did the skim coat on the attic walls. Mr. Sanders seemed pleased." Luis took a swig of his beer. "Hey, I meant to remind you. You know I can't be there on Saturday, right? I got a logging job."

Garrett opened a can of beer for himself. "Yeah, it's fine. I'm not too worried about Saturday. The husband and kids will be home." Luis was usually the only guy available on the weekends, though. Especially a big holiday weekend like after Thanksgiving.

Luis shook his head. "You with the ladies. Have you tried telling her you have a girlfriend?"

"Actually, I did—she saw my friend Sam's jeans sitting in the front seat of my work truck. So I told her Sam was my girlfriend."

Luis didn't look away from the TV. "Isn't Sam your friend Eli's girlfriend?"

"Used to be. They're split now." Garrett's fingers tightened on the can, leaving an indent. "She's also my ex-fiancée's best friend."

That was enough to get Luis's attention away from the TV. He lifted his brows in an exaggerated manner. "Your best friend's ex-girlfriend and your ex-fiancée's best friend. Holy shit. What're you doing with her pants in your truck?"

"She's Mrs. Redding's daughter. I drove her home after the hospital the other day and . . ." The explanation now seemed too ludicrous to describe it. He smiled at the memory of Sam practically waist-deep in a snowbank. The circumstances—her distress, the large dent on his truck, Dan's harassment—had made it less amusing. But that image of her would stay with him for life.

"I see that look on your face. She lost her pants in your truck?" Luis started laughing. "Yeah, happens to me all the time." He leaned over and grabbed a handful of popcorn. "Sounds like you've been playing with fire."

"Nah, it wasn't like that." He fidgeted with the tab on his beer can, wiggling it back and forth. *Am I, though?* When he'd sat with her on the front porch and hugged her at the school, something about it had felt different.

He'd been turned on by her before, but that wasn't it. There was something there, simmering, like electricity. *And the weird thing is, you were pretty sure she felt it too. Moron.* She'd set him straight as soon as Katie had shown up. *That's why it hurt.* "Eli asked me to spend some time with her while her mother is sick. As a favor to him. So I've been helping where and when I can."

"Does Sam know? I don't know a lot about women, but that could get you in trouble. Especially if she likes you." Luis made a face, then spat a popcorn kernel into his palm. "Mrs. Redding's a nice lady, though. I hope she gets better. Reminds me of my mom. Only person in town I've met that can make a decent arroz con pollo."

"She came home from the hospital yesterday." He'd been tempted to pop his head in at the main house when he'd left this evening, but Laura's minivan was in the driveway. He imagined all of them were at the house. Between Laura's C-section, a newborn, and Mrs. Redding's injury, they didn't need him intruding.

And the thought of seeing Sam right now made the knots in

his shoulders feel tighter. All damn day, he'd thought about returning to the house and confronting her about the way she'd reacted to Katie's ridiculous behavior. She was better than that —wasn't she? Jen hadn't been so negative about Sam in the past. What had Jen seen in Sam and Katie's interaction at Bunny's that put her off?

"She's not my type. A little too uptight. Slave to work and doesn't know how to let her hair down and relax." He threw back a swallow of his beer and then drew the can down slowly, realizing Luis hadn't been asking about that.

"Mrs. Redding? Or Sam?" Luis gave him a knowing, amused look. "Oh, you poor bastard. You've gone and fallen for your best friend's girl, haven't you?"

His best friend's girl. Eli's girl. That was what everyone had always thought of Sam as.

Everyone except him.

He finished his beer, then grabbed his coat and dug out his flask. Unscrewing the lid, he took a sip, the smoky flavor of bourbon burning the back of his throat.

Luis raised his eyebrows. "Hey, man. Slow down there. There's no last call at this establishment."

Garrett smirked. "This conversation needs more than light beer." He took another swig. Thoughts of Sam had a way of making him feel like the floor was falling through, and he couldn't catch a grip.

"You getting mad? It's because I'm right. I know how you get with women when you're interested. And look, you may be getting to finally know this girl, but it's still not a good idea."

His jaw clenched, and he looked away from Luis, the truth of his feelings choking him. "I've known her since kinder-garten." His voice was quiet.

"Hell, man. I don't care if you were born in the same hospital at the same time. She's still your best friend's girl. The bro code is the bro code." Luis lifted the remote and paused the game. Turning toward him, he frowned. "Forget about what Eli asked you. You spend any more time on this girl, and you won't have a best friend. Unless you think she's worth it. Or she's good in bed."

Enough already. "Don't be an asshole." Angry or not with her, this was someone he'd cared about his whole life. Luis might not be as familiar with Garrett's history with her, but he'd shut up about it if Garrett drew the boundary. Garrett nodded toward the TV. "You can put it back on again."

Luis arched a thick dark brow. "Look, you know I'm only busting your balls. We've been through some shit together. I gotta look out for you." Then he shrugged and unpaused the game.

Garrett didn't respond, still thinking about Sam. Had he let himself dream about her more than usual? Luis would be the best one to call him out on something like this. Besides Eli, he was probably the friend who knew him best. *Hell, he probably knows me better than Eli at this point.* They were close enough that Luis had moved to Brandywood when he'd left the Army two months after Garrett even though he was from San Antonio.

After a few beats, Luis asked, "You given any thought to joining the timeshare? There's good money to be made in those logging runs."

"I don't know." Garrett hesitated, leaning back in his seat. "I probably missed the golden opportunity. Should have done it before I invested all the money into the house. You getting more jobs, though?" Out of all his Army buddies, Luis seemed to have struggled to find his footing out of the service. He worked with Garrett and had joined a timeshare for a helicopter with some friends.

"Yeah, some good ones. It's a shame the chopper sits over at

Ben's farm most of the time though. It'd be good to pick up some more work for it. Hell, I'd even settle for helping with rescue jobs on the Appalachian Trail."

"Private helicopter pilots never seem to occur to people to hire right off the bat, but the work is there. Give it some time. Getting in with some of those logging companies seems to be progress. Why don't you reach out to some land survey companies? They might be looking for people."

"Sure I can't tempt you to buy in? You're the one with a good head for business."

Garrett smirked. "Nah. What can I say? My days flying choppers are in the past. I can barely find the time to maintain currency." The idea didn't bother him as much as it used to. He sipped at his flask again and stood. "I should probably get going. Early start tomorrow. See you then."

Luis nodded a goodbye, flipping the TV back on as Garrett let himself out. As Garrett approached his truck, the large dent in the front bumper caught his eye. He hadn't had time to get an estimate for the bodywork. He'd been running circles around helping Sam in his spare time.

All for what? The door slammed behind him as he sat in his truck. He started driving. Fog had crept in, covering the road with a dense haziness reflected from his headlights.

For a woman everyone said he could never love freely and who'd never appreciate him anyway.

Seeing Katie on that porch today had taken him back. Everyone, including Sam, had always assumed he'd left Brandywood as a teenager to get away from his father.

He'd left to get away from the feelings he couldn't control.

He slammed his open palm against the steering wheel. What would it take to get Sam out of his system?

Why was it always like this?

He felt like a love-obsessed idiot who couldn't learn his

lesson. And he expected nothing to come from it. He never had. But damn if it didn't make breathing hard.

He regretted offering his house to Sam to use for her work. He needed to spend less time with her, not more. He would have to tell her after Thanksgiving that it wouldn't work after all. And then, hopefully, she'd go back to New York soon. She didn't have any intention of living in Brandywood again. And she couldn't stay too long if she hoped to keep her job.

He turned onto his street, and the flash of red and blue lights behind him made him groan.

He should have expected this tonight too.

Dan climbed out of his police cruiser and sauntered up to Garrett's window, his face hard to see in the fog. "License and registration."

Anger flared like a coal stove filled with one too many hot embers. "Who the fuck are you kidding, man? You know why you pulled me over. You're twenty feet from my driveway."

Dan narrowed his gaze. "You been drinking, Doyle?"

"I had one beer. You want to arrest me? Go ahead. I'm sure the judge would love to hear how many times you've pulled me over this year. And that you basically sit at my driveway trying to entrap me."

A flashlight shone into Garrett's face. "Why don't you get out of the truck?"

Garrett's hand curled into a fist. This was not the night to go to jail for beating Dan senseless. Garrett had a few friends in Brandywood's police department. If this continued, he'd have to reach out to them.

He climbed out. No sooner was he out than Dan grabbed him by the scruff of his coat collar and pushed him, face first, against the back door. Garrett's cheek hit the cold, moisture-laden window. The two men were close in size, though Garrett had about an inch on Dan.

Dan leaned in, twisting Garrett's collar. "I hear my sister paid you a visit this morning."

How the hell did he know that? He should have sold the damn farmhouse and bought farther out of town. Closer to the woods, like the Reddings. Even with two acres, he still had neighbors close enough to see his comings and goings. The way news traveled in town, he wondered if his closest neighbors stayed plastered to their windows with their phones in hand.

"Nothing happened, Klein. She brought me breakfast."

"You fucking my sister?" Dan's grip was so tight that the front of Garrett's collar dug against his throat.

And this was exactly why he would never consider being interested in Jen. And Jen was still too torn up by the guy who'd gotten her pregnant and then skipped town at the news. Garrett gritted his teeth. Dan pulled back on his collar, forcing Garrett's face off the glass by about an inch, then he slammed him back against the hard surface. "Not a chance."

"Stay away from my sister. Or I'll tell everyone about how I found you fucking Sam Redding on the side of the road the other night." Dan let go of Garrett's coat, his teeth bared as he stepped back.

Garrett wiped his cheek with the back of his hand, straightening. "Right. Actually, I've already told Jen the snowbank story so you're a little late."

"Not how I remember it."

"Is that what this is all about? Sam comes into town, and suddenly, that old demon comes out to play? Don't you think the chip-on-your-shoulder routine is getting old? Even your mother moved on—"

Dan glared. "Don't talk about my mother. Or my sister."

Garrett couldn't help himself. He knew better, but he was in the mood to piss off Dan right now. Dan, who had always taken it upon himself to hate Garrett because he'd defended Sam as a kid. Fuck him. He crossed his arms. "Which one?"

Even in the low light of the evening, Dan's face appeared red. "Get the fuck out of here before I embed this flashlight into the back of your head."

Garrett had spent too long in the Army, maybe, but the threat made him laugh. Fate had thrown a whole new twist on their dynamic when Garrett had gone from the scrawny kid to both bigger and taller than Dan. "Jen can figure out for herself what—and who—she wants. And as for everything else, let it go already. You're not the only one who had to suffer things because of your dad's stupid decisions."

The rage in Dan's eyes seemed to bubble, nearing a boiling point. Then his fist connected with Garrett's jaw, sending spots flying in his vision as Dan placed him in a chokehold. His jaw throbbed, and blood dripped onto his chin, his lip split. Garrett spat at the metallic taste, and Dan gave him one last shove.

He directed the flashlight toward his door. "You remember what I told you. Don't talk to Jen. Don't look at her. And if I ever find out you as much as laid a finger on her, I swear to God, I'll destroy you."

Garrett wiped his mouth with the back of his hand. "Fuck you." He climbed back into his truck. As Dan's police car roared past him, he settled both hands on the steering wheel, his nerves shaken.

Garrett was sure Dan had turned off the police cruiser's dash cam and didn't catch what was most definitely police harassment.

Another fight with Dan? He could practically hear his mother's sighs each time he'd come home looking like this.

But they were way past childish spats.

And what the hell had it ever gotten him? Nothing from Sam, that's for sure.

He pulled into his driveway and briefly contemplated putting up an electric fence around the perimeter. And a gate. Keep everyone out. He scanned the exterior of his house, feeling like it could be booby-trapped somehow.

His phone buzzed in the cupholder beside the shifter. Digging it out, his heart skipped a beat at the notification on the home screen. *Sam.*

Sam: *Hey, you okay?*

His eyes narrowed at the screen. Admitting to Sam—or himself—that she'd hurt him was deeper than he wanted to go right now. Especially after she'd dismissed him so easily.

His thumbs hovered over his screen, then he answered.

Garrett: *Yup. You?*

Sam: *Yeah, I didn't have time to thank you for your help today.*

Garrett: *No problem.*

Three dots appeared beside her name for nearly a full minute as though she was typing a paragraph. He stared at it, tempted to put the phone away. Curiosity—and hope—got the better of him. Then at last, another message popped up.

Sam: *My boss is giving me more time to find bakers. Thanks for offering your place.*

He shouldn't read into her not offering an apology. She was Katie's best friend. Always had been. What was it Jen had said? *Birds of a feather?*

Things like that were what drove him crazy about home. Everywhere the Army had schlepped him, he'd always seen as temporary. He liked the familiarity of Brandywood. The sense of belonging. Here he had friends from childhood and family.

But small towns had a darker side. People like Katie and Dan. And feelings for Sam that didn't want to seem to quit, no matter who he'd dated over the years.

Maybe Sam was right to leave. Maybe Brandywood could all go to hell.

CHAPTER FOURTEEN

GARRETT'S FINGERS tightened around the handle of the six-pack in his hands as he paused by the picket fence in front of his parents' house. The paint on it was peeling badly, the front gate still broken. Years ago, his father had removed the gate, promising he'd replace it the next day. It didn't appear to have budged since then. The withered leaves of a poison ivy vine wove through the slats.

I should replace the damn thing myself.

He'd had the thought before. But it would mean being there for more than just an afternoon with the buffer of his siblings. Because it wouldn't just be replacing the gate. It'd be fixing the whole fence. And painting. Hell, the fence probably needed replacing too. The last time any of it had seen attention was when he was in high school.

His mom deserved a new fence. His jaw set tight.

The soft fall of a footstep behind him caught his attention. His brother, Scott, approached with a football in one hand and a casserole pan in the other. He grinned, threatening to toss the ball toward him, and Garrett raised the beer bottles. "Only if you want to lose the sole source of sanity tonight."

Scott grimaced. "You know better than to bring that inside, Gar."

As the eldest, Scott seemed to fall into that Type A, strait-laced role he'd been born into perfectly. Garrett rolled his eyes. "Don't worry, it wasn't my idea. Mom asked me to bring it. Said Dad doesn't want the rest of us to have to suffer for his sake."

Scott stopped on the sidewalk beside him. He tugged at the buffalo checkered scarf around his neck. "You think Shae's husband will go on about the school board again?"

"God, I hope not. But that's why I have the beer." Jimmy had a way of droning on about the most boring topics imaginable. "Ready?"

With an eleven-year gap between them, Garrett still hadn't gotten used to being the "bigger" brother. He'd grown four inches taller than Scott after he'd left for the Army.

They'd never been especially close, but since Garrett had moved home, he'd gotten more comfortable seeing Scott as a friend. Their other brother, Cormac, rarely made it home from Nashville, leaving them alone to fend with a group of loud sisters Scott affectionately called a gaggle.

Noise streamed from inside. Shae and Bridget's kids didn't help the matter. Garrett exchanged a look with Scott, then pushed the front door open.

"Attack!" Two of Bridget's kids were standing near the stairs with Nerf guns in hand. Blue and orange darts flew toward Garrett and Scott.

Scott held the casserole dish out toward Garrett. A smile gleamed in his eyes. "Take the sweet potatoes. I'm going to deal with these little punks. You better watch out." He tore after them as they screamed delightedly.

Garrett shook his head. *Better him than me.* Closing the

door with his foot, he took in the dated salmon-colored carpet on the stairs. Hannah seemed to materialize from thin air and was at his side. "Oh, thank God. Uncle of the year is here." She took the casserole dish from Garrett, tossing back face-framing highlighted dark hair from her face.

"Trust Scott to take one for the team." Garrett smiled in the living room's direction. Already, Scott had tied his scarf around his head Rambo-style.

Hannah scanned Garrett's face. "You look . . . tired. What happened to your lip?"

"Thanks, sis. You look like shit too. Happy Thanksgiving." The ribbing was an easy enough way to avoid answering her question. He hadn't slept well the past two nights. Trust Hannah to notice with the skill of a bloodhound. She knew him better than almost anyone. But they were the closest in age.

She cackled. "All right, I deserved that. Come on in. Mom's busy freaking out that her cranberries didn't set. And Mandy brought Brussels sprouts instead of green beans."

Garrett made a face. "She trying to kill us?" He followed her to the kitchen, where his mom was standing at the sink, her silver-streaked black hair swept up with a clip. Garrett came up behind her and set the beer on the counter. "Need anything?"

Mom's blue eyes darted toward the beer. She smiled tightly. "Sure. You want to go help your dad? He's smoking the turkey outside."

Garrett squinted out the kitchen window. Sure enough, his father was out there standing beside a smoker, his hands stuffed deep into his pockets. If he knew Shae and Bridget's husbands, they were watching the Cowboys game. Baltimore was playing them today and his father was a big fan. Why wasn't he a zombie in front of the TV with the other men?

His mom turned back to her disastrous cranberries, scooping them into the mold with a red-stained spoon. Garrett stared at her profile, but her eyebrows furrowed in concentration. Mom was many things, but not subtle.

Sighing, Garrett grabbed a beer bottle. He twisted the cap off and made his way back outside. At least he hadn't taken his coat off.

Smoke filled the chilly air and billowed out the smoker's sides. His father was bent over a bowl of wood chips, which he had soaking in water.

Dad looked up as Garrett stepped out onto the moss-coated paver stones of the patio. He straightened and smiled, his dark eyes bright. "Hey, you made it." Then he chuckled. "I guess that's a stupid thing to say. I got used to you and Cormac being absent for the holidays. Mom's sure glad we're almost all together."

Garrett took a swig from his bottle and nodded. "Yup." He stuffed one hand into his pocket. Mom kept insisting. *"Talk to your father. Give him a chance."*

"A chance, Mom? Like the two hundred you gave him? He had more than enough chances, don't you think?"

"He's worked so hard, Garrett. I know it's hard to forgive him. Believe me. I know it. And I don't expect you to forget any of it. But he's a totally different person now that he's sober."

Garrett took another swig from his bottle. His father didn't look any different. Just older. And what had changed? Mom had always made excuses for him. And excuses for why she'd stayed. Seven kids, keeping the family together, child care costing more money than she could have ever made on her own.

Mom loved the man she knew Dad could be.

All valid reasons.

He *got* all of it. He'd heard the reasons, the stories about how his grandfather had been a drunk and beaten his father too. Patterns of behavior. Whether in the blood or in the waters of abuse they'd all been baptized in, the result was the same, though.

He drew his mouth to a line. But it was Thanksgiving. And he was more grumpy than usual, thanks to Sam. His mom wanted him to try for her sake. He managed a slight smile. "I'm surprised you're not in there watching the game."

His father made a face. "I was. It's a bloodbath. Second quarter and the Ravens are already down by twenty-one."

Garrett grunted. "No wonder you're out here." He edged closer. "I hear you're in charge of the turkey this year. That explains why I missed the smell of Mom's bird."

"Yeah, we went to the Turkey Festival over at the high school three weeks ago. Mom fell in love with the smoked turkey. And I had this old contraption I got years ago. Figured I should put it to good use."

Lips twitching in a smile, Garrett shook his head. "You and your junk collecting." For as long as he could remember, his father had the habit of bringing home "deals" and "great finds" he'd either picked up from flea markets, yard sales, or the dumpsters of his home improvement clients.

"This one's not junk. Eight-hundred-dollar smoker when new." His father shrugged. "But I am thinking of selling some things from my shed. You know anything about how to load things on eBay?"

Garrett dipped his chin, a tight feeling spreading across his chest. *More help I don't have time for.* "Selling things?" His father was notoriously terrible at letting anything go.

"I want to see if I can get enough money together to take your mom to Italy for our anniversary in March. She's always wanted to go see the Vatican and all."

Exhaling, some of the tension in his chest and shoulders released. Mom would love that. Garrett nodded. "I'll see what I can do."

The back door opened, and Hannah came out, wrapped in a chunky sweater. She'd grabbed a beer too and winked at Garrett. That was their pact. *Leave no man behind with Dad.* "How's it going out here?" Hannah sidled up to Garrett. "You hear Mom's left us all to Dad's culinary prowess?"

Dad wiped his eyes as though the smoke was stinging them and laughed. "I may or may not have one of Bunny's turkeys shoved in the garage fridge. Just in case."

Hannah wagged a finger at their dad. "You're not inspiring any faith in this meal." She turned toward Garrett. "Speaking of Bunny, I heard from your ex that Sam Redding is back in town for a while." She gave Garrett a knowing look.

Hannah was one of the few people he'd ever talked to about Sam. Garrett blinked at her quizzically. "What does that have to do with Bunny?"

"Katie said something about a cookie show and Bunny practically kicking her out of the café for implying she was some backwoods cook."

That wasn't the most accurate description of the situation. Garrett threw back another swallow of beer. "You'd think by now you would have been able to find a new hairdresser."

Hannah cut him with a sharp glare. "First, ouch. And second, this is Brandywood, Gar, not some giant metropolis. My choices are Blush Salon where Katie works, the barbershop, or the place where all the town grandmothers go. If I were to switch stylists, Katie would see and frankly, she scares me too much for me to let that happen."

He couldn't form an argument to that. Still, Katie's distortion of what happened to Sam bothered him.

Dad poked at the coals and added a few more wood chips. "Been a long time since I've seen Sam. How's she doing?"

"Ask Garrett." Hannah's mouth twitched. "I bet he's seen her."

"You know she's back in town because her mom is dying of cancer, right?" Garrett didn't understand what Hannah was playing at. Teasing him about Sam was one thing. Doing it in front of Dad was another. "She's not planning on staying."

"Yeah, I heard. That's a shame. Charlotte Redding is a wonderful lady. I'm sure her girls are devastated. Are Sam and Eli still together? She could probably use a friend. You should invite her to dinner here sometime."

Dinner? With you, Dad? Then again, Sam might be the only woman he wouldn't be embarrassed to bring over here. She'd been to his house before plenty of times. The thought of her coming here didn't fill him with the anxiety—unlike when other women he'd dated had suggested he should take them back to Brandywood to meet his parents.

He checked himself, startled by the direction of his thoughts. *You're not dating Sam.*

Dad wiped his hands on his jeans, then pulled out a pair of gloves from his jacket pocket. They were old leather work gloves, not ones meant for cold.

The sight of Dad's gloves reminded Garrett of time spent together in his dad's workshop. Dad had taught him the basics of woodworking as a boy. How to use power tools. And he didn't wear gloves often. Garrett could practically visualize his father's dry, callused hands holding a brush loaded with varnish. Teaching him how to keep it bubble-free.

A lump formed in his throat, and he cleared it, refocusing his mind on his father's question. Hannah was giving him a questioning look.

What had his father asked? Oh, right. *Sam and Eli.* Garrett shook his head. "No, they're done."

"About damn time." Dad winked. "She's a pretty girl, Garrett. Maybe what she needs is a reason to stay in Brandywood."

If things had been different, Garrett wouldn't have minded their curious looks. Or Hannah's, at least. Garrett looked from his father to Hannah. "Don't think she wants to come back, Dad. Not all of us can forget what our dads put us through as kids." Avoiding his father's gaze, Garrett left them on the patio and headed inside.

As he did, he felt the weight of his phone in the back pocket of his jeans. His last texts with Sam weighed on him. He should wish her a good Thanksgiving. The holiday gave him an excuse to contact her, make things go back to some feeling of friendship between them.

The screen door banged as Hannah followed him. She caught him in the kitchen. "What was that all about?"

Mom was in the kitchen alone, peeling potatoes. She lifted her head to look at Hannah. "What was what about?"

"Garrett being rude to Dad when Dad was trying to be friendly." Hannah put her hand on Garrett's elbow, coming closer to him. "What's going on with you? You look totally miserable."

"I'm fine." Garrett glanced hesitantly at Mom. Her expression was unreadable. He didn't want to talk about his dad or Sam with his mom and sister. Much as he loved them, they'd always seen him as the screwup with a temper that impeded good things. He took off his coat and hung it over the back of a chair at the kitchen table. Rolling his sleeves, he walked over to a drawer. He fished out another potato peeler and then grabbed a potato from the pile in front of Mom.

Hannah wasn't the type to let things go, though. She loomed at his side, leaning against the counter. "This is about Sam being in town, isn't it?"

He gave her a hard look to silence her. "So, Mom, I was thinking of coming by next week sometime and fixing the gate in the front. You still want the fence to be white?"

"You can't keep self-sabotaging, Garrett. Ever think about giving yourself a shot with someone who makes you happy instead of one of these women who treats you like dirt?"

"Oh my God, let it go already, won't you?" Garrett gripped the potato in his hand so tightly that he set it down, relaxing his hand.

Mom smiled sympathetically at Garrett. "Why don't you let my baby boy and me peel potatoes in peace, Hannah? It's Thanksgiving. I'm glad he's here this time."

Hannah rolled her eyes. "Always Mom's favorite." She sauntered away, shaking her head at Garrett.

Mom thankfully said nothing. They stood side by side, peeling the potatoes, the soft clinking of the peelers and the whir of the refrigerator the only noise. Garrett released a tense breath, relaxing with the repetitive work.

He'd spent more time in this kitchen than most places in the house. The exposed-brick backsplash and chestnut-stained cabinets had long since gone out of style—if they'd ever been in style—along with the plaid wallpaper. No stainless steel here. White appliances, about twenty years old. Even the floral swag above the doorway to the dining room had long since lost its vibrant pink and yellow hues and faded like an old photograph.

He'd shared a bedroom with his older brothers who had frequently banished him from the room. And other than Hannah, his sisters had seen playing with him as a chore. He was the youngest, after all. So he'd come to the kitchen and followed his mom around. Learned to cook from her. Mom didn't bug him. She was content to let him be as quiet as he wanted or answer questions when he felt like asking.

He eyed a few pies on the stove. "What'd you make?"

"Bridget made those. Apple and pumpkin." Her eyes twinkled. "Don't worry, your beloved pecan pie is in the fridge. I made it last night."

Garrett grinned. She knew him well. "Speaking of cooking, Sam wants to know if you'll make some Italian cookies on a live-filmed special for her magazine. They're filming it at my house, actually."

Mom cringed. "Oh, Garrett, I don't know. I'd be so embarrassed. I'm terrible in front of people."

Garrett took her hand. "Would it help if I told you I already told Sam you'd do it and I don't want to tell her I lied?"

With a snicker, Mom shook her head, then pulled her hand away to swat him. "You want me to cover for your lies? Why would you tell her that?"

"She was down about not having anyone to help her with the assignment. She needs twelve home bakers from Brandywood for twelve days of filming. I promised to help her find them."

Mom pushed a salt-and-pepper strand of hair from her forehead. "I don't know I'm that good of a baker."

"You make the best damn Italian cookies in town. Probably better than the ones from Italy too." Garrett squeezed her shoulder. *Please say yes*. He wasn't sure what he'd tell Sam if she refused.

She gave an exaggerated sigh, a smile creasing the lines around her eyes. "All right. For you. But you should be careful, sweetheart. That's all I'll say. When you're ready to talk about anything, though, I'll be here."

CHAPTER FIFTEEN

"ARE YOU GOING OUT?" Laura looked up from the dinner table, where she was attempting to feed Carson spaghetti. Carson's entire face, his hairline, and his naked chest were covered in the sauce.

Sam laughed, then sat at the table to pull her high heels on. "Where are his clothes?"

Laura cut a few noodles with the side of her fork. "We call these his spaghetti clothes. Someday when you have kids, you'll get it. It's so not even worth attempting to get spaghetti stains out of clothes."

"Not worth getting stains out of diaper-exploded onesies, either," Mark said, coming in from the living room holding Charlotte. "I threw that one straight in the trash."

"Mark!" Laura shot him a wide-eyed look, then laughed. "Ouch, don't make my stitches hurt." She turned her attention back to Sam's shoes and pointed with a fork. "So you didn't answer my question."

"Yeah." Sam finished buckling the strap of her other heel. "Katie set me up on a blind date." She smoothed the front of her sweater. "Unfortunately, my wardrobe options are limited until Rachel comes. I don't think I've worn this dress since college."

"Sweater dresses never go out of style." Laura's expression became more serious. "But should you be going out right now? I mean, you're not planning to be here long, and you should attempt to spend some more time with Mom. Start putting up some Christmas decorations."

"I can do decorations tomorrow night." Sam stood. "Mom's busy with Bella anyway." She moved to the side to look in the kitchen doorway where Mom and Bella stood at the counter, making chocolate chip cookies. "Should she be doing that?" Mom still wore gauze on her head.

"She was lying down most of the day," Laura assured her. "She wanted to."

Sam set her hand on the back of Carson's high chair. She'd spent the last three days manning the cabins. With Jen working the night shift tonight, she finally had time to breathe. Laura's refusal to acknowledge how much she'd given to the family over the past thirty-six hours was maddening. She turned her attention back to Laura's awaiting stare, reading the simmer of her frustration with Sam. "I'll spend some time with Mom once we get through the weekend. I'm stuck here until after this cookie campaign is done anyway."

Fortunately, Maren had agreed to give Sam more time to find bakers because they had a shooting location. The entire project was a disaster in the making, and Sam didn't want to think about it right now.

"Stuck here. Nice attitude." Laura grabbed a napkin and wiped Carson's face.

From where he stood in the room's corner, Mark looked between the two sisters, studying their faces. Was he trying to figure out if he should intervene or leave?

"I am stuck here." Sam kept her voice low, not wanting Mom to overhear. "Nothing has changed, Laura. Brandywood is still the same, and I feel completely helpless here. I know you can't work right now, and Mom needs my help, but this isn't my home anymore."

Laura stood and popped the tray off the high chair. She set the tray on the table and gathered spaghetti from Carson's lap. Even his diaper was stained an orange-red. "If that's how you feel, can you tell Mom? Because we were talking about her will today, and she's planning on leaving you half of this place. If you want nothing to do with this, she can probably leave you her savings instead."

Sam stared at her. Laura's words stabbed Sam in the gut. "Are you serious right now? That's what you're worried about? Who will get the cabins? Mom isn't even dead yet. You're so unbelievably selfish."

Mark winced, giving his wife a look as though she should stay silent.

Laura's jaw dropped open. "I'm selfish? I've been holding down the fort for *years* while you've waltzed in and out of here like some princess who doesn't even care enough about her family to come home more than four times a year. So you helped at Thanksgiving. Congratulations. That's the bare minimum."

Mom approached from the kitchen, Bella's hand in hers. She smiled at her five-year-old granddaughter. "Mark, why don't you take Bella and Carson upstairs for a bath?"

A thankful expression crossed Mark's face and he nodded. "Sounds good." He handed Charlotte to Laura, took Carson from the high chair, and practically fled up the stairs.

"If you two are going to argue," Mom said, shuffling toward the table. "No peleen enfrente de los niños." *Don't fight in front of the kids*. She sat.

Sam's phone buzzed in her purse. She checked it. "My ride is here."

"Don't you dare walk out in the middle of this conversation." Laura glared at her.

Sighing, Sam sent the driver a message she would be out soon. She tucked the phone back in her purse. "What do you want from me, Laura? To pretend I'm happy to be here? You think Mom wants that?"

Mom flinched. "I don't want you to pretend anything."

Laura threw up her hands. "She wants you to want to be here. But you don't want to be here. You don't care about this place at all."

And that was a good enough reason to disinherit her? "It's not this place. It's not you. I love you all. But Brandywood—"

"Oh, for God's sake, will you get over yourself already? You think you were the only person they were talking about? You weren't. They were talking about me. They were talking about Mom. And you know what, by the time you got to high school, those people you hate so much were all saying what a great job Mom had done. How impressive it was that you were valedictorian. How fortunate we were despite our dad being who he was. So you had some bullies in your class. So what? You're twenty-seven years old, Sam. It's time to move on."

Mom sat quietly during Laura's tirade, sadness in her eyes. "I don't want you two to fight."

Hurt and angry, Sam grabbed her jacket from the coatrack. "Why don't you tell that to your favorite daughter? I'll always be the villain here anyway. I'm late for a date."

She stormed out the door, immediately regretting her words. *Go back and apologize to your family. Cancel the stupid date.* She didn't even want to go. But she greeted the rideshare driver, who opened the door for her. She climbed into the back seat and slammed the door.

She'd never felt like a screwup more in her life than right now. This wasn't what she wanted. She wanted to support her family. Regretting the last few days or weeks or whatever time Mom had left would be horrible.

A fresh flush of anger coursed through her. If only Mom would get treatment. She wouldn't have to be thinking about weeks or months. Then there would be time to plan. Mom had always wanted to go to Europe and Laura had talked about going, just the three of them, when the kids got older. And Mom had finally put away enough money to retire in a few years and have Laura take over the cabins.

Sam held back a sob. Mom had scrimped and scraped and struggled to live a little more comfortably. Mom had little in the way of a pension. And now she would never get to enjoy what she had worked so hard for. How could Laura be so at peace with that?

She caught the driver peeking at her through the rearview mirror. Sam looked away and pulled out a tissue. At this rate, she was going to arrive at her date with running makeup.

The car pulled in front of Yardley's within a few minutes and Sam got out. She stared at the old pub, dread building. Mike agreed to meet her at the bar. *Please don't let me run into anyone.*

She stole a few moments to gather her composure, then pushed past the door. Funny how as a teen they'd talked about coming out here someday. Then she'd left and the only time she'd ever visited Yardley's actual bar was for a last-minute night out that one of Katie's other bridesmaids had arranged two nights before the wedding.

Sam blinked in the pub's darkness, trying to get her bearings. Come to think of it, it was almost five years ago to the day she had been in this bar. Garrett and Katie's wedding date had been scheduled for the day after Thanksgiving. The date itself might be off by a few numbers, but its significance was still striking.

She found her way to the bar, the long wood-top weathered. The wall perpendicular to the bar was littered with coasters stuck into it with pushpins. Over the years, locals had written notes or signed their names and tacked them to the wall. Somewhere up there was a coaster with Eli's and her names on it. The visceral feeling of embarrassment as Eli had crossed from the dining room after junior prom and tacked it to the wall was as vivid as it had been back then.

The expectation was if a guy tacked your name up on Yardley's wall, you were an official item. Despite that, Eli hadn't pressured her into sex. They'd been seventeen when they started dating officially. They hadn't ended up sleeping together until college when he visited her in her freshman year.

The old man was still here too. Peter Yardley noticed her from behind the bar and his grizzled head nodded.

She pulled her gaze from Peter, looking for Mike. Katie had been sure to show her Mike's picture a few times, but she didn't see him. Instead, Garrett sat at the bar, staring at his phone.

Son of a bitch. She'd told him she had a date here tonight. She stalked up to him and crossed her arms. "Stalking me?"

Garrett drew his head back, a look of surprise in his eyes. "Stalking—" A cursory glance down her length dissolved the puzzlement from his features. "Oh, your date. I completely forgot."

What the hell?

He looked terrible. His eyes appeared red. Glassy. An ugly yellow and black bruise colored the left side of his jaw. He was clearly drunk. She'd been worried about him since Tuesday, and he'd barely responded to her texts. Could something else be wrong?

The seat beside him was open and she took it. "You okay?"

"Just fine." Garrett didn't look at her while he spoke, a glass of what appeared to be whiskey in his hand. He slung his drink back and then motioned for Peter to provide him with another one.

"Okay, now I'm worried." She put her hand on his forearm. "What's going on? Sitting here getting drunk on your own. What happened?" She hesitated. Did Garrett have a girlfriend? Or someone in his life? He'd never said.

Garrett scowled. "You're right, Redding. I'm here on my own. Not looking for company tonight but thanks. You wouldn't want it to get back to Katie anyway."

Ouch. She slid off the stool. Guilt throbbed through her. She'd never apologized for the comment she'd made in front of Katie—but then again, it had only been a passing comment. Not an excuse for him being an ass to her. And she had tried to send him a message.

Without responding to him, she moved to the far side of the bar, furious. She didn't see Mike, so she searched for an open spot at the bar with two seats. She found one and put her jacket on the second chair, to save it.

When she'd first seen Garrett, she'd initially paid attention to the annoyance. But seeing him had also given her a strange sense of relief. His rudeness, though, had provoked a choked, crushing feeling of loneliness.

She checked her phone. Mike had said seven and she had been a few minutes late. Had he left? It was almost ten minutes after seven. Opening her texts, she found his name.

Sam: *At the bar. You here?*

The message read seen, then the ellipses showed the other person was typing. After about a minute, it disappeared. No message.

She put her phone down and ordered a gin and tonic.

Her drink came, but still no sign of Mike. Or a reply to her text.

A growing feeling of awfulness washed over her. Why was she even here? Laura wasn't completely wrong. She was home to spend time with her family. This date had been Katie's idea, not at all how Sam would have approached trying to deal with her feelings for Eli. She twirled the ice cubes in her drink around with the cocktail straw.

Thirty minutes. Another drink. Still no response to her text.

Mike wasn't coming.

Fuck this place.

She kept her focus on her phone, determined not to sit there looking pathetic as she waited. She might have to kill Katie for this, though. Sam had been on a fair number of bad dates in the past but had never been stood up.

The chair beside her bumped. A skinny guy with long, greasy dyed black hair swept into a ponytail, pulled it back and sat.

"Hey, I'm saving that seat." Sam pointed at her jacket. "That's mine."

The guy looked skeptical. "For who? I've been standing at the bar for the last twenty minutes. Bar's crowded. You can't hold a chair." He yanked her jacket off. "Here."

Normally, she would have let the chair go. But Sam was angry, humiliated, and did *not* feel like dealing with another jerk. Especially one who didn't even look like he could shave yet. She grabbed the chair. "I said, I'm saving the seat. And don't touch my jacket. The guy I'm waiting for is running late."

The guy's dark eyes flashed. "Look, this isn't kindergarten. You can't save seats."

Sam stood and faced him, her jaw clenched. Just then, an arm slid on her shoulder. "Hey, honey, sorry I'm late."

Garrett stood beside her, a smile pasted on his face. He squeezed her shoulder and then looked at the guy. "This guy bothering you?"

Count. Sylvia's training came to her mind as white spots of anger danced in her vision. *You don't want to make a scene at Yardley's.*

That would be all she needed. Yet another reason for anyone to start a rumor.

Of course, if Katie heard Garrett was seen at Yardley's on a date with her, a different rumor would start, but she could at least explain that one to Katie.

Her smile toward Garrett was equally fake. "Hi, honey. Everything is under control."

The guy's eyes widened at Garrett and then he slunk away.

Sam let out a slow, restrained breath. "You didn't have to do that. I can handle myself."

"I'm not questioning that." Garrett dropped his hand. "But you're welcome anyway. How's the date going?"

Jerk. He must have noticed she'd been stood up. She crossed her arms. "So now you can talk to me?"

"I could always talk to you. I just didn't want to." He stumbled and steadied himself on the bar.

He *was* drunk. "And why not? Is this about what happened with Katie? Because I'm sorry. But what was I supposed to say? That I'd risk my friendship with her to mess around with you?"

"I think you said enough." Garrett straightened and squinted with one eye. "And since I've served of no purpose here, I'm going to get going. Night."

She watched him slip into the crowd and sighed. She didn't want to go back to a contentious relationship with Garrett. Not after everything he'd done for her. She threw some money on the bar and grabbed her jacket. Following him, the frosty night air hit her cheeks hard.

He was already halfway to the parking lot.

She ran up behind him. "You planning on driving tonight?"

"I'm not an idiot. Grabbing my garage door opener from my truck. I gave Eli my house key from my key ring, so I have to go in through the garage." Garrett turned and faced her. "What's it to you anyway?"

"Well, for one, I would lose every ounce of respect and admiration I have for you if you drove drunk." She set her hands on her hips.

"Admiration?" Garrett laughed sardonically then opened the door to his truck. He yanked the garage door opener from his visor. "There's a good one, Redding." He traded his baseball cap for a winter hat and slammed his truck door again.

"Will you stop with that last name crap? I'm not one of your Army buddies." She followed him as he made his way down the sidewalk. "What are you going to do—just walk the whole way?"

"Unless you magic up a license, yup." Garrett stuffed his hands in the pockets of his jacket. "It's only like a ten-minute walk."

She fell into step beside him. "I think I could manage an automatic."

"Maybe. But if Dan Klein is hanging out at the bottom of my driveway, I don't need you getting pulled over for driving without a license." Garrett didn't slow. "Hell, even if you did, you were pounding drinks too. Two drinks in a girl your size is probably enough to put you over the legal limit."

Was he counting my drinks?

She couldn't figure out if that annoyed her or not.

His long strides were hard to keep up with, especially in heels. Her feet were freezing. She should have worn boots instead. And a warmer coat than a leather jacket. She grabbed his elbow. "Will you just slow down?"

Garrett stopped and looked back at her. "I'm tired. I want to go to bed."

"You're drunk." She stepped closer to him, squeezing her hands to stay warm. Why hadn't she brought gloves? She had left the house in too much of a rush. "Is that why you're drinking tonight? Because Dan Klein is harassing you?"

Garrett leaned back against a utility pole. Staples from old flyers covered the pole's length—it didn't look the least bit comfortable. Garrett assessed her. "Dan can go fuck himself. I'm not wasting my thoughts on him."

"Then what?" Her shivering had grown stronger.

Garrett nodded toward Yardley's. "You should go back. Mr. December might show up eventually, and from what I've heard from the women at Bunny's, you don't want to miss a date with him."

Fresh embarrassment prickled her cheeks. He must know about the firefighter calendar Katie had been going on about. "I'm actually glad he didn't show up."

Garrett gave her an odd look then understanding dawned on him. He started walking again. "Because you're not ready to move on from Eli. I get it."

Eli? Huh. No, that had been the furthest thought from her mind. She practically had to trot to keep up with him. "Please slow down. It's pretty much impossible for me to keep up with you and I don't want to walk you to your place in a broken heel."

Garrett laughed. "You don't have to walk me to my place."

"Well, maybe I could use some company tonight." Her breath crystalized and fogged in front of her. "It's been a really shitty night."

"Because of Mr. December?" Garrett looked over his shoulder at her, then seeming to notice the pace he was setting for her, he stopped again.

She caught up to him, her heart racing from exertion. "Why don't you let me call you a car?"

"It's a ten-minute walk, Redding. I'd already be halfway there if it wasn't for you. I'm not from New York, like you."

From New York. She lifted her brows. "How am I from New York?"

"You're impractically dressed for a night at the end of November in the mountains." Garrett smiled tightly. "And encouraging me to do rideshare. Go home. And I don't mean to your mom's. You don't want to be here anyway."

"Why are you acting like this? I thought we were—" She stopped, her shoulders falling. That feeling of closeness with Garrett over the last week . . . had it all been one-sided?

His face darkened. "You thought we were what?"

"Nothing." Sam turned and looked back up the street, half-tempted to just walk away and call a car. Garrett awaited an answer. "I don't know. Friends? You've been nice to me, Garrett, even when most everyone else has been making me feel like I'm this awful human being."

Whatever anger Garrett seemed to hold toward her seemed to thaw and his mouth pursed. Unzipping his coat, he took it off and handed it to her. "I know. You don't need my help, but if you're going to walk me back to my house, you should probably have it. I'd offer you my shoes, but I don't think they'll fit."

She laughed lightly and put the coat over her shoulders.

Garrett's warmth radiated from the coat. And his scent. Raw and masculine, with a hint of something smoky and sweet. Almost the way the pipe tobacco from the old cigar shop in town used to smell. She'd stopped in there occasionally as a kid, just to fill her lungs with it.

Addictive.

Something in the scent and the warmth of his body made her legs tingle, her nerves lurch.

"Thank you." She willed her feet into motion and continued at his side. "Now are you going to tell me what's wrong?"

"Nope." Garrett put his hands in his pockets. He gave her a sidelong glance. "So are you going to patch things up with Eli then?"

"No. If being back has taught me anything, it's that Eli is part of my past. We keep trying to make it work, but I think it's mostly because we were always good friends and neither of us wanted to hurt the other by letting go." Her gaze moved to the picture windows of the shops lining Main Street. Overnight, Christmas decorations and lights had gone up. "And in the end, we probably hurt each other more than we would have if we'd just had the courage to let go."

"Then why were you glad Mr. December didn't show up?"

She pulled his coat tighter around her. Why had she? Because she had only agreed to do this for Katie's sake. *And because* . . . she blinked. "I don't know. It was just a dumb blind date. I would rather spend time with someone I care about. Like you. So it all worked out."

Garrett froze, swiveling on one foot to face her. He caught her by the wrist and opened his mouth, but no words came out.

Then his thumb brushed across the soft skin right near her palm.

Gentle, but deliberate. A caress so thoughtless she shouldn't have noticed. But she did. She noticed.

And goose bumps rose under his grip, her fingertips buzzing into their own strange life, aching to reach his fingers and brush against them.

Her breath caught and her eyes flew to him, her breath slowing as he scanned her gaze. Then his gaze closed off and he let go of her wrist. "Well, I'm glad it worked out too."

What the hell was that?

The sensual tug wasn't unfamiliar, but it had never been so strong, never so intense. Garrett had touched her before. But something just then had been different.

"Yeah, sure." They started back down the sidewalk once again and she followed him as he turned down a side street. "Truth be told, I got into a huge fight with Laura tonight and I'm not in a hurry to go home in case they haven't left yet. Laura and Mark have spent every day at my mom's house until like nine at night."

"She probably just wants to spend as much time with your mom as possible." Garrett's eyes moved skyward. "It smells like snow to me tonight. What do you think?"

The moon wasn't in sight, as the sky was thick with clouds. "You know they make a great app for your phone to find out." She grinned then relented, diving back into the topic she'd rather ignore. "I know that's why Laura's there. And she wants me to be there too. But I don't know. I just can't figure out how to act as though everything is perfectly normal and we should celebrate Thanksgiving and happily decorate for Christmas while my mom is choosing to give up on life. They want me to get a Christmas tree. What the hell for?"

"Acting normal isn't always as easy as it looks, Sam. My guess is your mom is probably more afraid than she lets on. But if this is her way of conquering that, go along a bit. For her sake."

His words struck her with unexpected sadness. Was Mom afraid? She'd seemed so calm, so rational about it all.

Sam hadn't thought about her mother's fears. *You selfish brat.*

"You know I can take you to the tree farm tomorrow afternoon. You can't exactly drag one to your house without a car and I'll have more time to help you tomorrow than I will during the week."

A Christmas tree. His words about going along with things pushed her toward a nod. And it was true. Getting a Christmas tree would be tough without help. "All right. What time?"

The front of one of Garrett's boots hit a section of sidewalk lifted by the roots of a nearby tree and he stumbled forward. Sam grabbed him by the arm to stabilize him. "Whoa there."

Garrett caught his balance and then looked at her hand. "You know, if I'd fallen, I probably would have just taken you with me. You're five foot nothing and in heels."

"Can't blame a girl for trying to help. Even a giant oaf like you." Sam dragged his arm over her shoulder. "But maybe I should help you walk. You're not walking so well tonight, you drunk." She cringed at her own words. What if he thought she was comparing him to his father?

He didn't miss a beat. "Don't worry. The drunk comments sort of roll off me. There's a big difference between occasionally getting drunk and doing it nightly and then beating your wife and kids."

"Yeah, but what led you to drink tonight? Girl problems?"

"You might say that." Garrett gave her a long, hard look. "But I'd rather not talk about it. Really."

She had to drop it. He'd made his wishes clear about four times now. Her curiosity was piqued though. In a lot of ways, Garrett was a stranger to her now. She hadn't spent time with him in years. And never in this one-on-one context. What did she know of him besides what he'd told her recently?

"So how's your cookie campaign coming along?" Garrett dragged his feet as he walked, as though the slow pace was tedious to him.

"It's coming. My mom wants to share a recipe. And Katie asked her mom for me. So that's three." He looked cold and she peeled the coat away. "Here, take this. I don't want you to freeze."

"I'm fine. The cold is nice. Besides, the alcohol takes the chill away."

That much she could remember from being drunk, though it had been a while. "Oh, I also asked Jen. So four. Thanks for the tip."

They made it to Garrett's house within a few minutes. As they ambled up the driveway, Sam scanned for any nearby cars. Whatever Garrett's fears of Dan were, they didn't appear to be valid tonight.

Garrett's house. *Wow.*

She'd forgotten how other people who didn't live in Manhattan dwelt. He was only a few months older than her and . . .

All this space.

The night couldn't do the house's exterior justice but he'd done a good job with exterior lighting. The wide, wraparound front porch was inviting and outfitted for gorgeous evenings outside in any season, a glass of wine in hand.

She smiled at the swing seat. "I would be out here every day if I lived here."

Garrett's gaze swiveled in the direction she stared. He shrugged. "I can't remember the last time I sat out there."

Did she imagine it, or was there something *wistful* in his voice?

Garrett pushed the button for the garage door and it gave a mechanical, metallic shake before creaking upward. Sam raised a brow. "That thing sounds ancient."

His laugh carried the potent scent of whiskey. "It's about the only damned thing I haven't replaced in this house. Eventually. But I was thinking of putting barn-style doors in."

"I'm impressed with your creativity. I never knew you were into this sort of thing." She pulled Garrett's arm away and stepped back, feeling the emptiness of the space between them.

He seemed to hesitate and then tilted his head toward the door. "You want to look around inside?"

She did. Yet something about his words made her heart skip a beat.

He's Garrett, not a guy asking you into his house for drinks and sex.

She nodded.

He closed the garage door and then flipped on a light switch in the hall. She followed him and a few more overhead lights flipped on.

Holy shit.

"Your house looks like it belongs in a magazine," she breathed appreciatively, wishing she had her camera with her. She didn't need it with her to know the way the light would come in the windows, though. She could see the mountains from the large picture window between the great room and the kitchen, which apparently was right off the garage.

He was right. The house would be perfect for the cookie campaign. "I can't wait to take pictures here." She ran her fingertips over the stone of the massive fireplace by the great room's main wall. The textures in the house were incredible. Even in the kitchen, he'd mixed the stark white of the marble counters with a few areas of dark-stained butcher block. "This is like a photographer's dream. I would give anything to have a space half this nice for my product photos."

Garrett stood off to the side, watching her quietly, his face a total mask. He didn't smile but came closer to her, crossing the space between them. She peeled his coat away and laid it on the arm of a sofa. "I'm so impressed with you," Sam whispered. She hoped Garrett didn't hear her as she wasn't sure how he'd perceive that comment.

He stood beside her and touched the mantel. "This came from a tree that fell beside your mom's house, actually."

Her eyes darted to the smooth, beautifully varnished wood. "Really?"

He lifted her hand. Guiding her hand to a hidden place on the side, he touched her fingers to the wood. "Remember that tree where we all carved our names as kids? This was it. If you feel right here, you can feel the indents of your name."

Her breath caught. Not because it was weirdly fascinating and touching how he'd repurposed something with so much sentimental value. But because of his proximity. *He is so close. So warm. He wants me to know that he kept this. Something with my name on it.*

All the things about him she'd tried to pretend not to notice —his raw, masculine scent, the way his nearness made her skin feel on fire, how much she wanted to touch him—pulsed in her mind. Her lungs ached, her chest squeezing at the fact that Garrett's hand hadn't pulled away. It remained on hers.

God, he was so close behind her. That pull, that deep, sensual longing flared back.

Maybe she had drunk more than she realized.

She didn't lower her hand and neither did he. In fact, his index finger glided down the back of hers, so gently, she almost groaned. Her fingers curled in response.

Whether she'd meant it as encouragement, he was close enough now that his other hand grazed her left hip.

He was doing it *on purpose.*

Her body seemed to respond faster than her head, a deep pulse, warm, wet forming between her legs.

They were friends. She almost said it out loud. Friends and nothing more.

But his fingers had splayed against her hip now, and she was deeply aware of the weight of his hand against her hip. With his other hand still connected to hers, his fingers dug between hers, interlacing them and spreading them as his palm dwarfed the back of her hand, his hand enclosing hers as he lowered their hands.

He brought both of their hands around her waist, pulling her so her back rested against him.

Garrett was hard. *For her*.

His breath was on her neck, gentle, laden with whiskey. He hadn't as much kissed her cheek, yet this felt more intimate than anything she'd experienced . . . *ever*.

What the hell was happening? She wanted it to continue. Her body throbbed for him.

His left hand continued to stroke her hip, but just barely, his touch featherlight. What would it feel like to have his hand glide over the naked skin there? Possessively, as he was doing right now?

Her nipples hardened in response. She let out a slow, shattered breath.

As though impatient for overthinking everything, her body responded. She backed closer toward him. His hardness against her was undeniable now. Neither of them spoke. They didn't need to. They communicated in some other language, primal but just as loud and demanding as a shout.

His lips were on her neck now, smoothing up the curve of her jaw, right near her earlobe. The stubble of his chin was rough against her cheek.

Seeking.

Garrett was making her nervous.

A bundle of sexually charged, fluttering nerves that didn't seem to want to quit firing.

She turned her face toward him, and their eyes met.

His gaze was dark and heady and . . . *burning*.

Kiss me. His focus dropped to her mouth, a question written in his eyes.

His lips brushed hers gently, and she moaned in response.

Then his warm breath was on her mouth, his lips against hers, soft. As though somehow terrified of giving in completely.

But then again, no kiss had ever been this hot. They breathed against each other's mouths, her heart pounding in her ears. Nothing had ever felt this delicious. His lips were against hers, coaxing, gently, then more firmly, molding against hers. Perfectly.

She needed air. To breathe. *Had she been breathing?*

This feeling of needing everything.

She needed everything.

A tether to hold her to the earth.

Garrett's hand on her hip flattened against her curves, drifting onto her thigh, skimming the hem of her short skirt.

She pulled away abruptly, her hands shaking. "I'm so sorry —" She gasped. *What the hell, what the hell?* Her body screamed at her to go back, go back to the magic. But the spell was broken, and badly.

Garrett steadied himself against the mantel. Without her hand in his, this time. He said nothing, his eyes closed.

"I . . ." Sam scrambled for some sort of excuse to explain what had occurred between them. He was drunk. She had more to drink than she'd understood. "I should go home." Her cheeks flamed, and she turned. She didn't know the way out except through the garage door she'd come from.

She pulled out her phone and slid up to the home screen, looking for the rideshare app.

Garrett straightened and then lifted his chin. She couldn't look him in the eye. Not a chance. If she did, she might end up right back in his arms.

Instead, she fled.

CHAPTER SIXTEEN

GARRETT. A poor waste of a man.

A poor waste of a man, with *hope*, he added, easing his foot onto the gas after a stoplight. The truck rolled forward. His internal monologue sounded like the start of a movie trailer in his head. He shook his head, feeling idiotic and terrible at once.

And . . . happy?

Moron.

Damn headache. He'd nursed it all morning with aspirin and sleep. The headache reminded him there was nothing to be happy about. He'd been so drunk last night that he'd gotten sick after Sam had left. So drunk he'd tried to kiss her. *Really* kiss her.

Bella Dawson was riding her bike in the Reddings' driveway. The sky was liquid gold and pink, silhouetting Bella like it was a postcard for the cabins or something. Slowing, he pulled his truck off to the side. Mark waved from two feet behind his daughter. Two-year-old Carson was in his other arm.

Garrett climbed out. "It's amazing how much Bella

reminds me of Laura as a kid." Garrett smiled at the little girl. She stuck her tongue out and tore off on her bike.

Mark chuckled. "Don't take it personally. She's getting increasingly sassy as she gets older."

Garrett closed the door to the truck. "If there's anything I've learned through the years is how to deal with the Redding sass. Though I'm sure I don't have to tell you about it."

Mark rolled his eyes. "Laura and Sam were at it all last night before we left and then again this morning. This situation isn't bringing out the love, that's for sure."

Garrett started up to the house, then paused. "Can I ask you a question?"

Setting Carson on the gravel, Mark looked over. "What's up?"

Was Sam in the house or still at the guest lodge? Garrett checked his watch. It was nearing five. Tough call. He inched closer to Mark. "How's Sam really doing with her breakup with Eli? She's barely mentioned him to me—and I'm not sure if that's just because of my friendship with Eli or if she just doesn't talk about it."

The porch creaked, and Garrett lifted his head sharply. Mrs. Redding was sitting on the swing, and she'd stood. Relieved it wasn't Sam, Garrett waved. "Evening, Mrs. Redding."

"It's good to see you." Her accented voice was quiet but warm. She approached and leaned on a pillar by the steps.

Mark looked at his mother-in-law, then back at Garrett. His expression was thoughtful. "She's . . . I think she's doing all right. To be honest, I haven't heard her mention him."

Mrs. Redding cut in from her place on the porch. "That's not a bad thing, is it, Garrett?" She leveled her dark gaze at him, a smile at the corner of her mouth.

As strange as it was, Mrs. Redding seemed to strip away that protective, hidden layer where Garrett had buried his feelings for Sam long ago. Her eyes were intuitive, her face compassionate. *How long has she known?*

Especially given that Garrett had barely started to admit the fact to himself.

Until Thanksgiving, when he'd watched his brothers and sisters and their families after dinner. His parents looked happy —something he wasn't used to. And all he could think about was Sam. He could imagine her among them, teasing his sisters, playing with his nieces and nephews, and cuddling with him by the fire. It had been so, so vivid. She'd blocked Eli's number because she couldn't see why she should keep it anymore. *She's finally single. It's possible she could be mine.*

So he'd gone home and picked up the phone to call Eli, then chickened out.

What was he going to say? *Hey, Eli. You know how you asked me to be there for Sam? Did you mean date her by chance?*

Instead, he'd drunk himself to sleep.

He'd gone out to Yardley's last night to continue the marathon. The last time he'd realized he was still in love with Sam, it had nearly destroyed his life.

And then she'd shown up beside him, looking beautiful and dressed for a date with that idiot firefighter Mike Jarvis, whom Garrett was certain he'd punch in the face when he saw. His jealousy had made him slip up more than once last night.

The front door to the house creaked as it opened. Sam stepped out, wearing jeans and a sweater. This time she looked dressed for the weather. Garrett's heart picked up in pace.

"Hey." She came up beside her mother. "Garrett has promised to take me for a good old-fashioned Christmas tree cutting experience."

"Sounds fun." Mrs. Redding leaned over and kissed Sam on

the cheek. "We'll leave dinner for you. Helen Morello brought over a lasagna, so it should be a good one."

They said their goodbyes to Sam's family and were on their way within minutes. "Your mom looked good," Garrett said, pulling onto the main road. His interaction with Mrs. Redding had unsettled him. She'd said nothing, but still—the look she'd given him was clear enough. She understood his feelings toward her daughter. Didn't mean he knew what she thought.

Would Sam bring up the kiss?

"She's trying. At least to look good. Puts on makeup. Gets dressed better than I do. I feel like a *shlub* in my jeans and ancient sweaters. But then again, I don't have any of my normal wardrobe here."

"That's impressive that you fit in your clothes from when you lived here." The casual conversation helped distract from the heavier thoughts from earlier in the day, and he tried to keep his tone cheerful, despite his headache. "If I tried to put on a pair of pants or sweater from high school? Well, let's just say the clothes would laugh in my face."

She tilted the angle of her seat, relaxing back. "Trust me when I tell you there are not many options there. I'm just lucky I liked oversized sweaters so much back then. Fortunately, my assistant, Rachel, is coming next Tuesday. She's going to help me set up for the social campaign and bring me my staging props, gear, and—more importantly—clothes."

Then they both seemed to run out of words. Chitchat was something he could only maintain for so long and only with a few select people.

Tension descended between them. He had to address what had happened the previous night. Apologize for it, even. "Sam—"

"Hey, listen—"

They made eye contact, and both smiled. "Go ahead," she said.

"I was . . . pretty damn drunk last night. I got a little carried away and"—he drew a sharp breath—"sorry about what happened." He took his eyes from the road to glance at her.

I don't regret a single bit about it.

She didn't answer for a few heartbeats, and he looked back at the road, the yellow, broken lines gleaming in the fading light.

"We both probably drank more than we should have." She smiled tightly. "But it's water under the bridge. I think our friendship can handle a few drunken kisses. I'm surprised it never happened before."

It was an odd thing to say. They hadn't seen each other for most of their drinking years, and in high school, she'd been too strait-laced to drink, even when she'd joined them in acts of teenage rebellion. And when she was in college . . .

Eli and Katie.

"For what it's worth"—Sam fidgeted with the hem of her coat—"I've really enjoyed the last couple of weeks getting to be friends outside of everything that happened when we were younger. I've known you my whole life. You've known me. But our friendship sort of took a back seat to the other people we were involved with. Which wasn't really fair . . . to either of us."

"I was also an idiot for a long time." Garrett grinned.

Her laughter was a balm to his headache. Lightness to the pressure in his chest. "I can't argue with that."

They pulled into the tree farm. Garrett got out of the truck and grabbed a backpack he'd shoved a power saw into before leaving his house.

"How on earth are we going to see a Christmas tree? Will they even let us out into the field?" Sam squinted into the dark rows of trees beyond the bright lights of the large red barn housing garlands and wreaths.

"It'll be fine. Who needs a perfect Christmas tree anyway? Maybe we'll get the poor Christmas tree that keeps getting bypassed and just wants a happy home." Garrett paused before the barn. "But either way, I think we should start with hot chocolate."

"You're making me want to grab an artificial tree from Target with all that happy home talk." Sam glanced around. "I'm going to hop in line for the port-a-pots if you want to grab the hot chocolate."

They separated, and Garrett moved to the line for the food truck. With the sun having set, the families and couples at the tree farm were partaking in the holiday activities by the barn—or buying from the pre-cut lot. Part of the barn housed a train setup, and close to the entrance was a spot to pose for pictures with Santa.

Garrett stuck his hand into his coat pocket, his hand brushing against the flask of whiskey he'd packed earlier in the evening. His fingers curled around it, and the pounding of his head seemed to increase. Pulling it out, he uncapped it and took a quick swig. The familiar flavor was warm and heady, stinging the back of his throat as he swallowed.

I would lose every ounce of respect and admiration I have for you if you drove drunk.

He released a breath and moved up in line to the front window. He ordered and paid, searching the area beside the barn for Sam. She stood over by a stand of wreaths, examining the prices. When his order was up, he grabbed the cups and took a sip.

The hot chocolate singed his lip, and he spat it out. "Motherfucker." He carefully wiped his mouth with the back of his hand and approached Sam, his lip aching.

Garrett held the paper cup of hot chocolate out toward Sam. "It's practically at napalm levels, so I'd give it a minute."

Sam laughed and pulled the lid off. Steam billowed from her cup. "And you know from experience?"

"Yes, ma'am. Burned the roof right off my mouth. I'm not sure if I'll ever be able to taste anything again." Garrett winced and frowned, then tossed his cup in the nearby trash can. It wasn't worth the trouble. He held his hand past the twinkling globe lights strung near the barn. "Shall we get on with it? Many more adventures on this ill-advised old-fashioned family Christmas activity await us."

They'd just started past the pre-cut trees toward the field when Garrett nearly stopped in his tracks. Just ahead, Trisha and her husband and children were posing for pictures with Santa. Hoping he could slip past without notice, he steered Sam the other way, but Trisha looked up.

Maybe what Trisha needs is proof. Proof of his lack of interest. Garrett turned his head toward Sam, his lips grazing her ear. "You know how I just apologized for kissing you?"

"Yeah?"

"Can I kiss you again? As a favor?"

Sam furrowed her brow. "W-why?"

"I'll explain later."

"What type of kiss are we talking about here?" She pursed her lips. "A peck on the cheek?"

Even though he didn't look at her, Garrett could feel Trisha's stony stare. *Please, for once, Sam, go easy on me.* He smiled and said through gritted teeth. "Let's just say it's the type of kiss that will help me. *Honey.*"

The gentle reminder he'd helped her the previous night at Yardley's seemed to work. Sam bit her lip. "All right. I'm assuming this is for show." She wrapped her arms around his neck, and hot chocolate splashed onto his coat, running a rivulet down his chest. "Oops. Sorry." She set the cup of hot chocolate on the ground.

Despite the initial impulse, Garrett hesitated for a split second. His lips had been so numb from alcohol last night that he'd barely been able to remember the feel of her kiss this morning. Last night the whiskey had been braver than he was. But it was now or never. He grinned, then lowered his lips to Sam's, kissing her deeply.

CHAPTER SEVENTEEN

WITH GARRETT'S lips on hers, it was as though a thunderclap had sounded. The moment was charged, electric, and any ounce of resistance and hesitation she'd had melted away.

God, he was a good kisser.

Garrett's lips shouldn't feel this good.

This wasn't like the previous night, which had been raw and sexual. But it was still wonderful. And she'd been dreaming about kissing him again. If he'd told her in the truck he'd regretted the kiss, she would have been mortified. *And disappointed.*

Her pulse raced, and as he pulled away, she struggled to catch her breath. He scanned her eyes, a hint of a smile in his, then darted a look at a family sitting with Santa.

The woman in the family was looking at them as though she'd just taken a swig of coffee and found grounds in her cup.

Sam grinned, then pressed another quick kiss to his mouth for good measure.

Linking arms with him, they started back toward the Christmas tree fields. She gave him a sidelong glance when they were sufficiently out of earshot. "Care to explain?"

Garrett shook his head. "Not really."

As though she was going to let him get away with kissing her and then not telling her why. "Well, you promised you would. So out with it. I'm guessing it had something to do with that pretty woman on Santa's lap?"

"Nope, I'm good." Garrett's jaw tightened.

Sam gasped. *Could it be . . .?* She stopped and crossed her arms. "Garrett Doyle. Are you having an affair with a married woman?"

Garrett hesitated.

Her eyes widened. "You are!" Disappointment curdled in her throat.

"No." Garrett cocked a brow at her. "Maybe I just wanted an excuse to kiss you." Then he turned and continued between the row of trees.

She peered at him, his words making her stomach flutter. Chasing after him, she grabbed him by the elbow. "Wait—"

He stopped, and he chuckled humorlessly. "Her name is Trisha. I'm currently doing a job for her and her husband. A big one." He stuffed his hands in his pockets. "And every time she can corner me, she comes onto me. I might have told her I have a girlfriend named Sam—so . . ."

Her lips parted. Garrett being hit on by married women at work didn't entirely surprise her—though his confession about lying about a relationship with her did.

Sam edged closer to him. "Can I confess something too?" *Shut up, Sam. Don't say it . . .*

Garrett lifted his chin. "What's that?"

She moistened her lips with the tip of her tongue. "I've

been thinking about that kiss in your house all day." Her words seemed to hang in the frozen puffs of air between them.

He scanned her eyes, a smile twitching at his lips. "You too?"

Maybe it was the hot chocolate or the pale sliver of moonlight or the scent of Christmas trees, but being here with him felt . . . strangely like home. They came together magnetically, and Garrett's mouth descended on hers.

His hand cradled the back of her head, the other drawing her in by the waist. Her heart slammed against her chest as their tongues collided.

I'm making out with Garrett.

Her arms intertwined around his neck as he pushed her toward the trees. The needles poked her back, but she didn't care. She wanted this.

She wanted him.

This wasn't a kiss between friends—*nope.*

When he pulled away, he dipped his forehead against hers, struggling for breath. "I'm sorry—"

"Why are you apologizing?" She laughed lightly, then stood on her tiptoes, catching his lower lip against hers. He responded to her kiss with one of his own, and they were kissing again, their lips molding perfectly together.

"God, Garrett," she murmured between a kiss. "If I'd known how good of a kisser you were, I would have kissed you long ago."

He pulled back, just slightly, then scanned her eyes. Saying nothing, he released her. "We shouldn't be doing this. This is— this is not a good idea."

She blinked hard, then nodded. *No, right. Right. Because of Katie. And Eli.*

And . . . oh, crap . . .

Now she understood his apology better.

His hands curled into fists at his sides then he stalked a few feet away. Turning, he returned toward her, pulling her into his arms. He kissed her again, as though he didn't want to stay away, then let go just as abruptly. He sank between the row of Christmas trees. "God, I need a drink."

He removed a flask from his pocket, and her stomach sunk as she watched him open it and take a swig.

Was this why he had been drinking?

Was Garrett . . . interested in her?

She sat across from him. *Bad idea.* Moisture from the ground seeped in through her jeans into her underwear. She grimaced. "You could have at least warned me I'd get a wet ass if I'd do this."

He chuckled and took another sip from his flask. "Yeah, it's pretty miserable." Then he drew in a deep breath and pulled his knees up, looking uncomfortable because of his long legs. "To be fair, though, you were born here too."

She chuckled.

Garrett paused and looked around to be sure he wouldn't be overheard. The fields weren't lit well enough to see the trees, and they were relatively alone. "Eli would never forgive me."

"I don't belong to him, you know. We're not together anymore." She tried to say the words with as much confidence as she could.

"And I haven't been with Katie for five years, but do you think that will make a damn bit of difference to her? When I moved back to Brandywood, she literally found me to tell me I needed to stay away from any of her 'places' in town or she'd make my life miserable. As though I didn't take enough risk of being miserable just by coming back here."

She crossed the space and sat beside Garrett. The sarcasm and jokes belied his true nature. He was sensitive, and he'd been hurt repeatedly.

She'd let Katie's feelings toward him blind her—for how long? How often had she listened as Katie droned on about what a jerk Garrett was? In high school, she'd taken advantage of him, demanding to be spoiled with things he couldn't afford to buy her. Making fun of his less-than-stellar car and wardrobe.

Of course, Garrett had been hurt. His father had been abusive his whole childhood. He'd been made fun of for his shabby appearance and family's low income.

In high school, Sam had been so busy being embarrassed for her own circumstances that she hadn't seen the kid in the class who had it worse than she did. Even though she'd known all of this.

He'd been right in front of her the whole time.

Her father went to jail, at least. Garrett's beatings—they'd continued.

What if Garrett finds out my anger can be equally explosive? Would he hate her for it?

She leaned back, closed her eyes, and breathed in the fresh scent of pine and the wood smoke from the barn's firepits.

"How did I not realize what a bully Katie was?" Sam asked, furrowing her brow.

"Because she's your best friend. She doesn't treat you the same way she treats everyone else." Garrett extended one leg out in front of him. "You want my opinion?"

The answer to that question was increasingly a *yes*.

"People in Brandywood have been nicer to me than I thought they would be. The MacKintosh clan, though? There's not too much anyone will do to challenge their position in town. Not with Katie's dad being who he is. Half the people in this town go to his church." Garrett rubbed the back of his neck. "But that doesn't mean they all haven't noticed Katie's behavior. The wariness you may have felt all your life might not have been directed so much at you as the company you kept."

Sam blinked, watching the gentle sway of the wind on the pine trees.

Could Garrett be right?

But what on earth was she supposed to do? She loved Katie. They'd been friends their whole lives. Sam couldn't just turn on her because she'd discovered her ugly side. If she was honest, hadn't she always known Katie could be cruel when she wanted to be? Wasn't it her duty to stick by her friends and possibly help them?

Whatever her duty to Katie was, she doubted it included kissing Garrett Doyle.

"I'll never be over him. He was my first love." Did Sam want to continue kissing Garrett? Yes. But was it how they should move forward? Probably not right now.

Wiping her hands on her pants, Sam struggled to her feet. "Come on. Let's go be the soggy-assed twins who cut down a Charlie Brown tree because we can't see anything." She stomped her foot, the backs of her thighs feeling frozen. "This is like a rite of passage in every Christmas movie, right? Cut the tree, wear flannel, bake cookies?"

"Yeah, but that would make us the couple." Garrett smirked. "Not to mention, you'd need some corporate boyfriend to show up and ruin things between us."

Sam chuckled because Eli fit that part. *But Garrett and I are not a couple.* And truth be told, they might never be. They weren't teenagers. They could handle being friends who had kissed. *You can be sexually attracted to someone and have nothing ever come from it.*

And, anyway, Garrett hadn't exactly suggested he wanted something more from their friendship. It wasn't like he was trying to take things any further.

Garrett stood. "You know, that sort of makes me think, though. There might be a way to win over some of those frosty Brandywoodians who think you're like Katie."

Sam crossed her arms. "Yeah? What's that?"

Reaching into his backpack, Garrett pulled out the saw. "How do you feel about cutting twelve Christmas trees?"

CHAPTER EIGHTEEN

"YOU AND GARRETT seem to spend a lot of time together."

Sam looked out from the tree, pulling her scratched arms out. She lifted another section of lights and avoided looking at Mom, who sat on the sofa unwrapping Christmas ornaments from tissue paper.

She held back a smile, thinking of the Christmas trees they'd delivered around town a few nights earlier—and the complete line-up she now had for the Christmas cookie special. "Yeah, he's been helpful lately."

"I've always liked him." Mom lifted the ornament she'd unwrapped. A black construction paper sheep with its body wrapped in white yarn. Sam had made it in kindergarten. "This is one of my favorites. Reminds me of when you learned to sing 'Away in a Manger' and wouldn't stop singing it for months." She placed the ornament carefully on the table.

Sam smiled. "I like that one too." For the first time in a week, Laura and Mark hadn't come over. It had given Sam and her mother time to decorate the tree, which had stood undecorated for two days in the living room.

Mom's mention of Garrett had brought a sudden gloom to her spirits. She hadn't seen or heard from him since Saturday night.

He'd even skipped a driving lesson with her today. Her thumb had hovered over their text thread, and she'd typed out a message.

Until it occurred to her that he hadn't really said he was coming. Since her mom had come back home, it was as though he'd silently excused himself from that chore. It was fine. He'd taught her enough that she could practice on the back road between the house and the cabins.

But it hurt.

Those damned kisses. *What was I thinking?* Why couldn't she stop thinking about it now, either? Each time she did, though, it felt like forbidden fruit.

Katie would be so hurt. One day, she seemed to be happily buzzing about her new boyfriend. The next, she'd been standing on the front porch crying because someone had spread a rumor about Sam and Garrett.

Was it possible some people just couldn't move on?

"Mom?" Sam wrapped a branch with lights carefully. "Why didn't you ever get remarried?"

Mom's smile froze, momentarily, but enough that Sam caught it. Mom lifted another ornament from the plastic storage bin, lowering her gaze. "You know, it's occurred to me recently that I'm running out of time to tell you some things you should probably know." She placed a few wrapped ornaments on her lap. "I think that's the part of this I'm the most grateful for. I know my expiration date is approaching, so I have time to remedy some mistakes."

Sam's throat tightened. "Mom, don't talk like that." The casual way Mom mentioned death made her want to scream.

"It's true." Mom unwrapped an ornament. She set it down,

and it wobbled before coming to a stop on the table. "I think the thing is, Sam, I felt like I got what I deserved by marrying your father."

Why was Mom being like this? Sam put the lights down and came closer. She squatted next to the couch beside her. "Mom, look, I don't know how fate and life work, but that's ridiculous—"

"Your father was married when I met him. I had an affair with him."

Sam caught herself on the couch, her shock so visceral it spread from her torso, tingling up her spine to the top of her head. She blinked at Mom several times. "What?"

Mom stared at her hands. "Your father was married to another woman here in Brandywood. I started working for him as his bookkeeper, and we had an affair. I got pregnant with Laura, and he left his wife for me." When she looked up, her face was red. "I've been ashamed since then. I never wanted you to know because—well, it was a horrible thing I did."

Sam covered her mouth, feeling sick. A hundred questions popped into her mind. Her mother . . . her church-going, sweet, conservative, rule-following, strict mother . . . *had been a home-wrecker?*

She sat back on the floor, trying to think clearly. "Is that why Dad's family never wanted to have anything to do with us?"

Tears rolled down Mom's cheeks. "Yes. And, I thought, why your father got into the drugs. The guilt ate him alive." Mom moistened her lips and put the ornaments on the seat beside her. "Your father's first wife . . ." Her gaze dropped to the floor once more. "They had two sons. One who's three years older than Laura. The other was born two months after Laura. He should have been a year above you in school, but they held him back a year, and he ended up in your class."

Nausea pressed further up her throat. She had half-brothers? *Who?*

And I went to school with one of them?

Her mother had been pregnant at the same time as her father's first wife. And he'd left the other woman. Pregnant. With a three-year-old.

Her mother had destroyed a *family*.

"Oh my God." Sam scrambled to her feet. Digging her hands into her scalp, she gripped her hair by the roots, tucking her face into her curled arms. What the hell? She struggled to get her composure, the room around her spinning.

The whispers. The looks of judgment. "Does everyone in town know about this?"

Mom nodded, wiping her red eyes. The flowing tears had turned into an expression of pain and regret. "For years, people didn't want to have much to do with me. It wasn't until your father went to jail and people saw me struggling with two little girls that they took pity on me. But"—she swallowed—"I'd deserved it, Sam. I brought it upon myself. And you girls. Even my family wanted nothing to do with me. Why do you think we made such infrequent trips back to Venezuela?"

She took in a broken breath. "That was the worst part of it." She wiped her eyes with the back of her hand. "What happened to you two girls because of what I had done. My transgression. You were beautiful and perfect and blameless, yet I'd brought you into this world covered in a blanket of shame."

A piece of Sam's heart shattered, hearing her mother's guilt and shame. But how could she have never told them something so important? *Unless* . . . she looked at her mother sharply. "Does Laura know?"

Mom nodded slowly. "Someone in middle school told her.

Called her a bastard, and she came crying to me. I had to tell her the truth."

What the hell? That had to be over fifteen years ago. *Why the hell did no one tell me?*

"So I'm the only one—the only idiot—who didn't know about this?" She dropped back, taking a step away from her mother, uncertain if she really wanted to know the answer to her next question. "Who are they, Mom?"

Mom looked confused. "Who are who?"

"My half-brothers." Her voice trembled with anger. "Who are they? You said one of them was in my class."

Blanching, Mom cowed in her seat. "Warren and Dan Klein."

Dan Klein.

A montage of his angry looks, his ugly words came hurling back toward Sam with lightning speed. "But . . ." Her words sounded pathetic, even to her. "He's a Klein."

"Betty Klein got remarried. Her husband adopted both boys, and then Betty and her husband had their own daughter, Jen."

"And you let her work for you?" The words exploded from Sam's mouth.

Standing, her mom scratched at the bandage on her head. "A few months after your father was arrested, I finally found the courage to send Betty a letter, begging her for forgiveness. She didn't respond for several months. Then she called me and asked to come over. We'll never be friends, but she forgave me. We've been cordial ever since. It was Betty Klein who helped us keep this house. Betty's forgiveness paved the path to others helping me as time went on."

Sam could picture Dan's mother, but just barely. She'd hated his mother. Dan had come from her. Therefore, she'd believed she had to be just as bad as he was.

"You don't deserve forgiveness," Sam spat, her fingers curled into such tight fists her nails dug into her palms. Her own harsh words made her wince, but she wasn't about to take them back. "Do you have any idea how Dan has treated me all my life? And not just me, Mom—anyone associated with me. He made Eli's and Garrett's life hell too. And no wonder I barely had any friends in school. It's a miracle that anyone let their children be friends with me."

"I know." The depth of sadness in Mom's eyes seemed limitless. "I know, Samantha. It's all my fault." She wiped her eyes with a tissue, then blew her nose. "And I owe you an apology. I should have told you. I shouldn't have done what I did—but . . . at the same time, God gave me you and Laura. Something I didn't deserve. He gave me so many things I didn't deserve."

This was too much to handle.

She turned in a circle looking at the house she'd grown up in. The bed of lies she'd been raised in.

She ran for the door, grabbing her jacket. "Sam!" Mom called behind her, but she didn't stop.

She didn't even have her phone in her pocket to call a goddamned ride, but there was no way she was going back into her house.

Pulling her jacket on, Sam hurled herself from the porch steps onto the gravel and started running. Her boots weighed heavily, the late afternoon sun cold and too bright. She hadn't gone to the gym once since coming home, but she found her stride quickly, even wearing jeans and boots.

Blood pumped through her broken heart, her sobs coming from someplace deep, forlorn, and inconsolable.

"Your mom is a stupid bitch."

Dan's face swam in her tears. His angry eyes. His hateful looks.

One time in fourth grade, her class had been playing musical chairs at a school function. Sam had won. As the teacher had silenced the class to hand out the prize, Dan had blurted, "*What a surprise. A Redding is good at winning the game where they have to steal something. Sam the Swindler.*"

Her classmates had laughed, and the nickname continued that year anytime Sam earned anything, even things like the honor roll or the award for the highest average in English. As though she didn't deserve to win. She hadn't understood the joke—her father was in jail, but not for being a thief.

Now it makes sense.

All this time, she'd thought he was just cruel and a bully. And he had been.

But he had also been an abandoned little boy, staring at the girl his father had chosen instead of him.

She did *not* want to have any sympathy for the bully who had tormented her. *Fuck him.*

Her head pounded like a spike had been driven into her temples, the pressure of her bubbling emotions cresting and escaping in ragged breaths.

The icy wind cut across her face. *Where was she even going?*

She couldn't go to the guest lodge. Jen was working already, and there was no way she could face her.

But the weather was cold, with an inch of snow on the ground from the short-lived storm from the day before.

She kept running. Her hands shook, and her hair tumbled around her face. Stopping, she broke down, covering her face and crying out.

All this time, she'd thought there could be no justification for the way her childhood had been. Only to find out her beloved mother had caused so much of the pain she'd known. She'd known her father had been despicable, but even this seemed like a new low for him. Her entire existence seemed dirty and horrible. How could she ever look at anyone the same way again?

Consumed by the awfulness and horror of this new reality, she broke into a sprint once more. Up ahead, the woods and fields that made the cabins so appealing to guests came into view. Quaint wood cabins of varying levels of sizes and luxury. Most were outfitted with Adirondack chairs and firepits—sufficiently far enough from one another to allow privacy but close enough to give a sense of community. A few were duet cabins—right beside another one—so families of any size could come and have enough space to share.

Her mother had always treasured the community that Brandywood offered.

Family.

Fucking hypocrite.

Sick to her stomach, Sam sank beside a tree, her side cramped from running, her lungs burning from sucking in the cold air.

The cabins could offer shelter for now, but they were still at capacity because of the holiday.

All except one.

"I THOUGHT I'd find you here."

Startled by Garrett's voice, Sam looked up at the doorway of cabin twelve. She scrambled from the blanket she'd spread to sit on the floor in front of the fireplace. Most of the room was closed up in tented plastic, but she'd pulled the tape away to get the blanket and supplies she needed. The bed was too laden with the furniture on the other side of the room, though. She'd sleep on the floor tonight.

"Go away, Garrett. I don't want to talk to you."

He shut the door, leaving them with only the glow from the fireplace. "Still making fires like an expert girl scout, I see." He joined her beside the fire. "Mind if I stand here? It's warmer."

She crossed her arms. "I told you—"

"Yeah, I heard what you said." He didn't leave and crossed his arms as he looked at her. "Your mom is worried sick about you. She called me looking for you. I drove to her house and found your phone in your room."

"Does she know you came here to look for me?"

"No, I didn't tell her where I was going."

"Good." A petty feeling of satisfaction simmered in her gut. Her mom could be worried for one night because she wasn't going back to the house tonight. She sighed. "Did she tell you why I ran off?" Was it possible that people like Garrett and Katie could know the truth?

Garrett grabbed her hand. "Look—"

Her jaw opened. *He knows.* "Why didn't you ever tell me?"

"I didn't find out about it until a couple of years ago. It's not like we ever talked until recently. And it's not exactly something I can bring up in casual conversation, especially given I didn't even know you didn't know."

She glared, feeling even more idiotic and duped. "And Eli? Katie?"

Garrett lifted his hands. "It's not exactly a secret, Sam."

"Except to me. Everyone knew but me." A horrifying thought occurred to her. What if the whole reason she'd been stood up by that firefighter was that he'd known and chickened out on having dinner with the daughter of Brandywood's own Hester Prynne? She had been living her own version of *The Scarlet Letter* her whole life.

Oh, for fuck's sake.

Garrett held her shoulders. "You did nothing wrong. You know that, right?"

Her shoulder tingled at his touch, the same tight pressure she'd felt earlier when he'd touched her. She met his gaze. "My entire existence has been called into question, and that's all you can give me? Everyone in this town only ever looked at me with disgust."

"That's not true. Not everyone." Garrett's eyes narrowed. "Not me." Then after a moment, he added. "Or Eli. Or Katie. Actually, I can think of a good twenty people I know never once would have been anything less than kind to you."

She dodged his touch and tore past him and outside. "Well, you can all just go to hell. *Someone* should have told me."

Garrett stalked behind her. "Someone? Who exactly? You've been running away from here for years, Sam. You think your family wanted to give you one more excuse to never come back?"

Snow, which fell in thick flakes, landed on her face, but if she was going to have a heated discussion with Garrett, she didn't want it to be in the cabin. Cabin eleven was a duet cabin and right beside them. And occupied. The last thing she wanted was people overhearing. Even if they were strangers.

Once she was sufficiently into the woods, she whirled around to face him. "And I'm supposed to want to come back here? What the hell for?" She extended her hands. "Look around me, Garrett. Where are all those wonderful people I'm supposed to return for?"

Snow gathered on the top of Garrett's hat. Given the amount, he'd been walking for a while. The stubble on his face was also thicker—as though he hadn't shaved for several days. His shoulders were raised and radiated tension. Then he pulled out a flask and uncapped it. "Sam, you couldn't see what's in front of you if it hit you right between the eyeballs. While blowing on a trumpet. With a flashing sign." He took an angry swig, looking away.

What the hell is that supposed to mean? And why the hell did Garrett have a flask in his pocket again?

Seeing him standing there, flask in hand, made something snap in her. She'd never realized how much Garrett had grown up to look like his father. And the flask—made it hurt. A deep pressure came from her solar plexus. Was this how his father had started? A drink here and there to take the edge off?

She stalked up to him and grabbed the flask out of his hand. "Is this why I haven't heard from you? Because you're still drinking yourself to a stupor?" Fuck Sylvia's exercises. She was angry, and throwing something would feel good.

She hurled Garrett's flask into the woods. The dull sound of it clunking against a tree trunk followed, then a soft thud.

Then silence.

Soft, shimmering snow falling, falling, falling.

Just the two of them, their breaths fogging the frozen air in front of them.

Garrett stared at her as though she'd lost her mind, his eyes narrowing. "I'm not drunk. And what do you care?" He took a step toward her. "No, really. What the fuck does it matter to you, Sam? You're not even planning on being here after a few weeks. Don't come in here after years and act like you give two shits about what happens to me after you're gone. You never even thought of us as friends."

She gasped, his words striking her hard and painfully, her breath feeling choked. "I can't believe I ever thought you'd changed. Why are you even here? I'm sorry you can't handle someone who cares about you—and yes, I care, I'm not ashamed of it—tell you I'm worried about your drinking."

"Why?" Garrett's eyes flashed, and he came closer.

She took a step back, struggling to understand his sudden surge of anger. "Why what?"

"Why do you care?" He stepped closer still.

"I-I don't know. I just do. I've always cared."

"Bullshit." Garrett shook his head and then turned, walking between the trees. "You have never given me a second thought. Never once looked at me the way I looked at you. Now I have to go find my flask. Thanks for that, by the way. My grandfather gave it to me when I joined the Army."

The way he'd looked at me? A stupefied, tingling pressure filled her chest. She chased him. "What the hell are you talking about?"

"Forget it." Garrett took his cell phone out and put the flashlight mode on.

"No, I won't forget it." She blocked his path, her breath coming in short, angry bursts. But she had to know what he was talking about. "What the hell do you mean?"

"I mean—" Garrett fidgeted with his hat as though struggling to keep the words in. Then he dropped his hand. "I mean that from the moment I saw you as a kid in kindergarten . . . on that fucking porch of The Dutchman . . . watching you jump feet first into a snowbank . . . every single time I looked at you, for forever, I didn't think about what an annoying pain in the ass you were—which you *are*, by the way. I thought about how in love I was with you. All this time."

Sam stared in stunned silence.

Garrett loved her?

She shoved him. "Don't you dare." She shoved again. "Don't you dare tell me you broke up with Katie because of me. I mean, I always knew what I said had something to do with it but—"

"It wasn't what you said. It was you! How could I marry her when I loved you?" Garrett roared, his shoulders heaving.

"I know. I know. I'm not allowed to, *supposed* to love you, Sam. And I swear to God, I have *tried*. You think I want to love someone who I have absolutely no hope of ever being anything other than a piss-poor friend to?"

Her heart hadn't stopped racing, her ears ringing so loudly she could barely hear him or think straight. "But Eli—" Snow clung to her lashes.

Garrett's voice dropped several degrees. "Yeah, I know."

All those teasing, sarcastic comments. The bafflement she'd felt with his warmth one moment and then standoffish behavior the next.

"And Katie—" Her own voice trembled. Katie would hate her for life if she found out.

"Yup." He covered his eyes with his hand, rubbing his forehead.

Yet.

The idea excited her. Made her feel warmer and more alive than she'd felt in ages.

She took a hard look at him, standing there, the tall, masculine figure, broad-shouldered and strong. Had she ever paid attention to him? He was objectively handsome, not in a way she'd ever truly realized. Maybe it had been because Katie had simpered for so long about "how hot he was." But the stray thought had passed her mind that he was good-looking if you could get past the lack of depth and constant derision.

She wasn't sure how the conversation had gone so astray from her mother's shocking revelation . . . to this.

Another revelation.

But was it really?

Garrett stood there, a defeated slump to his shoulders.

She wished she hadn't thrown his damned flask. She could use a drink herself.

The world always seemed to still as the snow fell. When

she'd first moved to the city, she'd missed the noises outside her window at night. The woods were anything but quiet. Sometimes the tree frogs had been so loud she'd used ear plugs. And even in the winter, you'd hear the owls, the bleating grunts of mule deer.

But now. Silence.

The snow crunched, and she stopped within Garrett's reach.

"Sam, you couldn't see what's in front of you if it hit you right between the eyeballs. While blowing on a trumpet. With a flashing sign."

And despite everything, laughter bubbled in her throat.

He lifted his gaze at her laughter, and the anger and frustration in his face thawed. "I shouldn't have said anyt—"

She placed her fingertips on his lips, silencing him. The instant she touched him, her body seemed to sizzle with life.

Garrett thrust his phone into his pocket, then cupped her face with both hands. He drew closer to her, one hand shifting to the base of her neck, his fingers digging into the strands of her hair. "I'm going to kiss you. Unless you say no. And if you don't say anything, I'm going to assume it's a yes, okay?"

Her heart pounded. "Kiss me, Garrett." Garrett searched her gaze and then lowered his lips to hers softly.

It wasn't the slow, sizzling touch from the night after Yardley's or the Christmas tree farm. The kiss unleashed something else, washing over her.

The cold seeped into her skin at that moment, whether it was because her nerves were firing in ways her body didn't understand or not—she wasn't sure. His lips were soft and warm. Despite the cold, his breath was smooth against her mouth. His lips fitted hers perfectly. The magnetism between them was undeniable, the rising heat like a tidal wave about to break, taking her out with it.

His hands rounded the curve of her spine and lower, onto her backside, gripping her as he lifted her. Her arms wrapped around his neck, her legs around his waist, and he carried her through the snow back toward the cabin.

The door slammed, and her back was against it.

With her legs around his waist, he pulled one hand from her backside and dug it into the hair at the nape of her neck. His tongue slid across her lips, and she opened her mouth to his. As his tongue dipped into her mouth, their tongues collided, tasting, and claiming.

His kiss. His lips. His mouth.

A deep longing broke inside her as he pulled back, and she yanked the coat from him. Her hips dropped lower on his, and he was long and hard against her. The soft, sensual swell of her own sex against him.

She tilted her head, the kiss frantic, their mouths exploring, their tongues demanding. He pushed her sweater over her head, the air cold against her flat stomach. Then his fell away, so his chest was bare, their skin touching.

The hardened muscles of his chest were smooth and well-sculpted. His tattoos ran up from his mid-forearm on the left up to his shoulder. She ran her hands over his chest and back around his neck.

She took it back. Garrett wasn't just handsome. *He is gorgeous.* She kissed him once again.

Though never in her wildest dreams had she expected this tonight, she didn't want to stop. Didn't want to question anything. He wanted her as much as she wanted him, and that was enough.

A finger slid along to the back of her bra, unhooking it.

When it was on the floor, Garrett's hands were on her breasts, his thumbs encircling her hardened nipples. He squeezed and then pinched them sharply, and she bowled over with the pleasure. His touch was electric, her desire for him growing.

"Garrett—" She gasped.

Why does this feel so perfect?

His mouth continued demanding from hers.

As the kiss deepened, he pinned her hard against the wall and then lowered her legs from his waist. Her feet hit the floor, her knees wobbly as his fingers deftly unbuttoned her jeans. His hands slid inside, pushing her jeans away from her hips, then curved over her hips, smooth on her skin, fingers pushing into the elastic of her underwear.

Underwear. Not a thong. Not lace panties. Nothing cute. She hadn't dressed for sex and didn't even have makeup on.

She wasn't sure when she had last shaved her legs. Oh, yes, Friday. For the date.

Sex.

I want to have sex with Garrett.

She tried to step out of her pants, but they stayed stuck on her boots. Garrett paused, glancing down. Then he lowered himself to his knees, bending over to unlace them. Her cheeks burned, her fingers grazing the top of his hair, then playing with the soft brown waves. "Stupid boots." She laughed, and he grinned up at her as he pulled them off, along with her thick wool socks.

Her feet hit the cold floor, and goose bumps rose on them— no . . . that was the feeling of Garrett running his hands up the backs of her legs. She shook, steadying herself on him. He stopped, eye level with her hips, and his hands ran back around her backside again.

Her skin was on fire.

He dipped a kiss to her belly button and moved lower, pushing the underwear from her hips, exposing her to his view.

Thank God I got waxed before leaving New York.

He breathed out slowly, raggedly, and his eyes lifted to hers. "You're beautiful." Then his hands were on her hips once more. "God, Sam—" He moistened his lips with his tongue. "I want to taste you."

A choked yes strangled in her throat, and she breathed shallow breaths as his fingers moved between her legs. "You're so wet." One finger dipped inside her. Then two. And his fingers touched her expertly.

She moaned as he lifted one leg over his shoulder and buried his face between her legs. Then he was kissing her, his tongue probing as she pulsed against his fingers, his tongue, her desire rising.

Her face was flushed with heat, her head against the back of the door. She couldn't stand if he continued like this.

He pulled away and hooked one arm under her knees. Lifting her, he carried her to the blanket she'd laid in front of the fireplace. He laid her down, then returned his mouth and hands between her legs, holding her tight to his mouth as her hips rose in response.

The man wouldn't let her go, thank *godddddd*. Swirls of heat and pink and white and, pleasure . . . she crested higher, floating in the air.

She wanted to feel him inside her. Not just his fingers and tongue, but all of him. Dizzy with desire, Sam groaned. "Garrett, please—" She gasped as he suckled her again. "Please fuck me."

Garrett lifted his head, his eyes like liquid lava scorching her. "Are you sure? I didn't expect this to happen."

She searched his eyes. "I'm positive."

"I don't have a condom."

"I'm on the pill. And I'm healthy." She watched his breath rise and fall, the hard, tense muscles of his shoulders.

"I am too."

Then what the hell are you waiting for? She was completely naked, and he was still wearing pants, but she strangely didn't feel exposed. She just wanted him to be inside her. *Now.* "Unless you don't want to."

Garrett laughed and stood. "If I haven't made what I want clear, I'm not sure how else to do it."

She sat up and grabbed at his belt. "You could start by taking off your pants."

He gave her a lusty gaze. Pulling away, he unlaced his boots, then took off his socks and jeans.

She tugged at the waistband of his boxers. "These too."

As his boxers dropped away, she stared at his hardened length appreciatively. He crawled back to her, but she laid him down on his back. When she straddled him, she guided him inside her, slowly, gasping at the feel of him inside her.

"Ohhh, wow," she managed, then lowered herself farther so that he was fully, deeply planted within her. "I'm about to come already."

"I want you to come." Garrett took her breasts in his hands, letting her take the lead as she rocked against him. "I don't think I'll last too long either."

She laughed, her heels rocking back as she found a rhythm. "Then we can do it again. I'm not really interested in sleeping tonight."

"You. Are. Incredible." His hips lifted to meet her motion. As though desperate, their movements became feverish, harder and harder until she was moaning at full volume, her cries seeming to echo against the plastic on the one wall.

Why did I wait so long to do this?

It had been so long since she'd had sex, and everything with him was too new, too sensual for her senses. A slow, hot-boiling climax built inside her, her body rocking harder against him.

Then she was moaning so loudly she could hardly restrain

it. Her thighs squeezed, not wanting to let go, her pleasure only increasing with each thrust. Garrett's hands were on her breasts, squeezing. "You're so goddamn perfect, Sam."

His own pulsating response followed, pouring deep with her. They both moaned with pleasure then she collapsed on top of his chest, her entire body sizzling and tingling.

He ran his hands over the curves of her naked body before coming to rest on her lower back. With her ear pressed to his chest, she could hear his heart pounding, feel it against her cheek.

She closed her eyes, a strange feeling of peace settling deep into the recesses of her bruised and battered heart.

Because Garrett Doyle just made love to me.

CHAPTER NINETEEN

GARRETT WOKE BEFORE SAM DID, the first streams of sunlight coming into the cabin window. He leaned over and pulled the sheet over her shoulder. Her skin was like ice. The fire had gone out long ago, and they'd been too busy having sex during the night to replace the damned logs.

He had rug burn on his knees, and his back would probably ache for days.

But . . . damn . . .

He'd spent the night with Sam.

He swallowed, his mouth dry and his lips chapped. His truck was still parked outside Mrs. Redding's house. The poor woman must be worried sick.

Softly, he ran a hand down the length of her arm, tucking her closer against his chest. In the night, he'd promised to kiss every square inch of her body. He'd done his best to meet that goal too.

They'd grabbed all the pillows and bedding from the mattress in the room and made a makeshift bed on the floor.

Garrett checked his watch. He would be late for work if he

didn't get up soon, but how could he leave now? He had the woman he'd wanted for so long in his arms, and she was more vulnerable than ever. How she hadn't known the truth about her parents was shocking. He had the utmost respect for her mom, but it was awful that this had been hidden from Sam. No wonder she'd run.

And then there was the other truth.

Eli was going to kill him.

He had never been one for rules except one: you don't sleep with your best friend's ex.

Or your ex-fiancée's best friend.

He was a terrible, terrible friend.

He would do it all over again in a heartbeat.

Sam stirred and turned into him, blinking sleepily against his shoulder. "How is it morning already?" she mumbled.

He suppressed the whispering voice of his guilty conscience and glanced out the window. "Damn, the sun didn't want to give us more time."

She glided her hand down his torso from where it had rested. He was already hard, but the wicked gleam in her eye only increased that effect. Her hand was on him. "I'm not going to be able to walk today." He chuckled into the top of her head.

"Mmm . . . what? I'm not doing anything." Her smile was falsely innocent. And she looked happy.

Happy to be with *him*.

Not that he could think straight with what she was doing.

His phone rang, and Garrett squinted one eye open, scanning the floor for his phone. It was all the way over on the other side of the cabin in his jeans. He almost ignored it, but the image of Luis or one of the other guys sitting alone at the Sanders's house filled him with discomfort.

He pulled away from Sam and crossed the room. Fumbling for his phone, he rubbed the sleep away from his eyes.

Mrs. Redding. "It's your mom," he whispered, answering the call. "Hello?"

"Garrett." Mrs. Redding released a sigh. "I've been so worried. Did you find Sam? I tried to get through earlier, and your phone went to voice mail."

"Yeah, no, I found her." *He should have at least sent a text to let her know.* Acid clawed at his throat. Instead, he'd spent the night with Sam and hadn't thought of how sick Mrs. Redding was or how this might affect her.

"*Ay, gracias a Dios.*" *Thank God.*

Sam sat up, wrapping herself in a sheet. Her expression was unreadable, but she came up behind him, wrapping her arms around him.

Hell, I can't think straight with her doing that, either.

An awkward pause followed, then Mrs. Redding asked, "Is she there with you?"

The volume must have been loud enough for Sam to hear because she came around in front where he could see her and shook her head vigorously. "Nope. No, ma'am. But I'm sure she'll turn up when she's ready to talk to you."

"Oh, I just thought maybe. Because your truck is here."

Shit. How was he supposed to explain that one?

"Yeah, I'll pick it up soon. And I'm sure Sam will show up home at some point today." Making another quick excuse, he got off the phone, then lifted his jeans. He pulled them on, the tickle of irritation creeping into the taut muscles of his shoulders.

Had Sam wanted him to lie to her mother because she didn't want to deal with her mom right now . . . *or because she doesn't want her mom to know about me?*

Maybe both.

"Feel like talking about it?" Garrett asked, buttoning his

waistband. It felt easier to face her with some pants on—no matter what they'd done last night.

"No." Sam wrapped the sheet tighter around her and sat.

Silence engulfed them. A powerful gust of wind sounded outside the window, rattling the Christmas wreaths Sam must have hung on the cabins' windows while decorating. Each cabin was also outfitted with a Christmas tree after Thanksgiving too.

Wind traveled down the chimney's flue, the scent of smoke and dust lifting into the air. The promising start to the morning had flatlined, and Garrett's head ached. His gut twisted, remembering his flask. No way to find it now. It would be buried under the snow—God knew where. When it melted, he could come out here and do a better search.

He had to go to work too, and the thought of leaving Sam tore him up.

Sam played with the fringe on the blanket. "I'm sorry for making you lie, Garrett. But I just don't—I don't feel like talking to her. I know I have to. I'm just not ready." She pulled her bra on. Turning her sweater inside out, she pulled it over her head and slipped her arms through the sleeves.

She still looked gorgeous, sitting there in nothing but a sweater, her dark hair messed up but tumbling over her shoulders. Garrett closed the space between them and squatted, then kissed her. "You know I'm on your side, right? I just want to make sure this is about your mom and not because you regret what happened with us."

Sam returned the kiss, then scooted closer to him. She rested her forearms on his shoulders, her eyes warm. "I don't regret what happened last night. Not for one second."

He smiled, her proximity enough to make him forget the phone call. How could he regret the best night of sex he'd ever had with the woman he'd always wanted? Being with her had been better than any fantasy he could have imagined. "Me neither."

She stood and pulled her pants on. "Good. Because I'm coming over to your place tonight." The windows rattled again, and she grabbed the blankets and folded them. "I'm going to go tidy up in the bathroom." She closed the door behind her.

Tonight. The thought of Sam in his bed made him want to pull her back down on top of him. Garrett resisted the temptation and stretched. After he'd finished dressing, he looked around the half-finished space. He grimaced, not relishing the thought of facing Mrs. Redding if she suspected he'd slept with her daughter.

He lifted his head as Sam exited the bathroom. She'd pulled her hair back into a ponytail. He smiled. She was beautiful.

Sam stirred the embers in the fireplace to ensure they were extinguished and turned down the heater. "Should we get going?"

They stepped outside. The morning was a dull gray, but the guests at the cabins were rousing. A woman at the closest one sat on the front porch, drinking a cup of coffee while sitting on the porch swing. She ignored their presence.

Garrett groaned at the empty parking pad beside the cabin. "My truck is at your mom's." He checked his watch again. He'd definitely be late to the Sanders's.

"Why don't you grab a UTV from the guest lodge? I have to take over for Jen anyway. I'll grab you a key." Sam stuffed her hands into her coat pockets.

"Don't you think you should go talk to your mom? She's obviously distraught, Sam."

Sam's gaze traveled to the smoke billowing from the chimney of another cabin. "She's lied to me my whole life. So has Laura. I don't want to talk to either of them." She shot him a stern look. "You're lucky I'm not mad at you for not telling me. You only get a pass because we hadn't talked to each other in years, and you didn't know the truth back when we did."

Garrett's eyes drifted over the snow-covered hills. "You might want to know who told me."

Sam made a face. "Eli? Yeah, I'm going to have some serious words with him. I don't forgive him, either."

"It was Katie." Garrett cleared his throat. He remembered the conversation well enough because it had been one of those rare occasions when he'd come home and run into her. "She was over at Yardley's at the same time as Eli and I were out. And drunk. She came over and started talking to Eli—going on about the moment her daddy told her she'd needed to be friends with Sam Redding because she needed a good friend. I'm not saying she didn't end up becoming a genuine friend to you. But I thought you might want to know."

Sam's jaw dropped open. "Her daddy?" Her eyes flashed. "Like I was some sort of charity case for friendship?"

Walking toward the guest lodge beside her, Garrett said, "Look, you know how Katie is. When she loves you, it's easy to ignore that mean streak she has. She's fun and generous—easy to get along with. But, uh . . . I don't know. Once that façade disappeared for me, I just couldn't ignore the other stuff. And if she finds out about us . . ."

Sam shrugged. "So what? Anyway, it's about time she and everyone else let go of this goody-two-shoes, 'Eli's girl,' 'Katie's guy' bullshit."

Garrett scanned her face. While he'd thought Sam was finally feeling something for him—the possibility existed that last night had been revenge sex too.

The idea disconcerted him. The night hadn't included bold declarations or even whispers of love. She'd been passionate and into it, but what did that really mean?

As they drew closer to the guest lodge, Sam sighed. "I have to go back to my house soon anyway. I need to make some phone calls. Rachel is supposed to be coming from New York today with all my stuff for the campaign. Are we still on for driving lessons later?"

Garrett nodded. "I wouldn't miss it." He slowed as the guest lodge came into view. A silver Jeep Cherokee was pulling up to the guest lodge. He stiffened and glanced at Sam. "What's Katie doing here?"

Sam paled. "Shit." She stumbled a bit, then glanced furtively. "I totally forgot she's helping me cover the guest service desk so I can get some of my work done. Ah, crap." She pasted a smile on her face. "She's probably seen us by now. You don't think she'll be suspicious, do you?"

"Didn't you just say so what if she finds out?" Garrett winked at her. It was easy enough to make a joke out of, even if he couldn't help but feel a twinge of disappointment at her words. "Here's your big chance."

Sam's cheeks flushed, words seeming to catch in her throat as she opened her mouth, then closed it again.

Garrett slid his hands into his pockets. "Then again, it's easy enough to explain. I came to show you the progress on the cabin before I go into work."

She released a deep breath, relief in her eyes. "Yeah." She nodded quickly. "Yeah, that's true."

So much for "so what."

Katie was getting out of her car, a paper cup of coffee in hand as she waved to them. "Oh, hey, you two. Didn't expect to see you both up so bright and early."

Her overly sweet tone was a sign she was trying too hard. Garrett hid a smile. She was likely trying to hide her annoyance at seeing Sam talking to him. *To make up for her outburst last time?*

Sam had put a little more distance between them as they walked. He studied her profile. Given what he'd just told her about Katie revealing to him about Sam's parents' affair, she was doing a pretty good job keeping her expression unreadable. If Sam truly was angry with her, she hadn't shown it.

She hadn't afforded her mother that much grace. Or him, even.

Could it be possible Sam was less confident in her ability to speak openly with Katie than she let on? Or was she feeling too guilty because she'd hooked up with him last night to be confrontational?

She smiled at Katie. "Hey, I forgot you were helping today. Thanks so much for getting here early."

Katie shrugged and sipped her drink. "I wanted to get an early start because of the snow. If I'd known you would be here this early, I would have grabbed you a coffee."

They entered the guest lodge, stomping their feet on the front rug. Jen was behind the desk, a man standing in front of her. ". . . it was loud. Too loud, and not at all what we paid for. One of our kids woke up and was asking what the hell was going on." The man's face was red.

Jen eyed Sam, then Garrett. She looked back at the unhappy guest. "But, sir . . . I'm not sure what you were hearing. There's no one in the cabin beside yours. It's closed for repairs."

"Don't you have security cameras around here? Take a look," the guest said, crossing his arms.

Garrett and Sam exchanged a glance. Had they been loud? "I can take over for you, Jen," Katie offered, setting her drink on the counter.

Garrett's fingers curled in his jeans pockets. *Goddammit.* The security footage would be damning if Katie looked at it.

A flustered Jen stepped back, her cheeks red. "Um, the

cameras are broken. I noticed it last night and was going to report it today."

"Hey . . . I'm the owner." Sam slid in behind the desk beside Jen. She looked at Jen. "Why don't you go off shift? I can handle this while Katie settles in." Sam pulled out a set of keys from a drawer. "These are for the UTV." She set them on the counter for Garrett and turned back to the man, her entire demeanor shifting.

Katie said nothing as she pulled her coat off and hung it from the rack. Her gaze flicked over at Garrett and her lips pursed in a tiny smile. As though she was pleased to find him watching her. *Fantastic.*

Does it make me a bad person that I'm not worried about what she feels if she finds out about Sam and me?

Jen headed into the back room and exited a few minutes later, carrying a sleepy Colby, who carried a wooden toy train. Just as Jen stepped past the desk, Colby dropped the train, which slid behind the main desk. He extended his hand with a cry.

Sam picked up the train and returned it to Colby with a smile. "Don't worry, bud. Got it right here."

"Thanks." Jen's smile didn't quite make it to her eyes. "He's obsessed with trains right now."

"Choo choo tun-nel." Colby grinned, holding the train with both hands.

Jen's posture relaxed somewhat, beaming at her son. "That's right. Pop-pop got you a new train tunnel for your birthday. He's been playing with it nonstop."

Garrett held the door for her, giving Sam one last glance. She didn't look at him, her attention directed entirely at the customer. Katie joined her behind the counter, but she watched Garrett closely as he left with Jen.

"Thanks," Jen mumbled, snuggling Colby against her

shoulder. She hurried out into the parking area, her gaze averted from Garrett.

He wasn't the most intuitive with women, but her demeanor seemed off. Could it be what the client had said? She couldn't suspect it had been him and Sam, could she? But the way she rushed toward her car made him think otherwise. She opened the back door and put Colby in his car seat.

"See you later." He headed toward the UTV.

"You're going to get hurt, Garrett."

Garrett turned. Jen had closed the door and started her truck with the remote start. Leaning against the door, she dug something from her diaper bag, a somber expression on her pretty face.

Garrett snuck a glance toward the guest lodge and inched closer to Jen. "What are you talking about?"

Jen's eyes narrowed. "I know. I saw you two go into cabin twelve in the security cameras last night." Her face reddened. She held out a thumb drive. "Here's the footage from last night's cameras. I pulled it from the computer from the back on my way out, so there's no chance Katie will see it."

A half dozen curse words streamed through Garrett's head at once. He breathed out slowly, stuffing the thumb drive in his coat pocket. Thank goodness she'd taken it. "Jen, please don't tell anyone."

"It's not any of my business." She looked away from him again. "But I really don't want to be caught in the middle of this. Or lying to Katie for you. I've had Dan breathing down my neck because she told him we were dating. She's not a nice person, Garrett, and she can make all of our lives miserable if she wants to."

"That won't happen." Garrett's attempt at reassurance sounded less confident in his mind than it did in his tone.

"You sure?" Jen crossed her arms. "How do you know Sam

won't tell her? I know we haven't been friends for long, Garrett, but you're going to get hurt." Her chin jutted upward. "Just . . . I don't need to be on Katie MacKintosh's shit list. I've got enough problems of my own."

She reached for the car door handle.

Upset with himself for putting her in this position, Garrett scrambled for the right words. He had to make this right. Or better. Something. Garrett put out a hand to stop her. "Wait, Jen. I didn't mean to cause you—"

"Yeah, I know. But what are friends for?" She grinned wryly and played with the hem of her plaid shirt. "If I'm honest, though, I worry about Sam because even though you and her family all seem to see a different side to her, I've also heard from my brothers how she treated them. And I worry about what she's really after here with you."

"Sam—" Garrett's hand dropped to his side, his voice lowering. As though Katie could hear from this distance. "I love her."

Jen raised a brow, unamused. "Well, she doesn't love you. She loves Eli. It's always been him, Garrett. It always will be him. Everyone in town knows that."

Why did he feel the need to fix this? With every word Jen said, he only felt worse. "She just found out about Dan and Warren yesterday, and she was distraught. I—"

A bitter, angry laugh left her. "And you think last night was anything other than an attempt to make herself feel better? Congratulations, Garrett. You were her scratching post. I don't know what you see in her, but I promise you, she will break your heart. Then you'll just be the poor dumb fuck who was too blind to see her for what she really was. And lost everything over it. Just look who she's friends with and how good she is at pretending you don't matter to her."

She skirted away from him and climbed into her truck. She

drove away, leaving him standing in the cold, with the croak of a grackle for company.

The worst part was that she had just spoken his deepest fears out loud.

———

A TEXT MESSAGE popped up on Garrett's phone as he navigated the streets of Brandywood.

Sam.

The hair on the back of his neck stood.

As he was only a block away from his parents' house, he continued toward it. It'd be a convenient place to pull over and see Sam's message. Once he'd stopped, he lifted his phone.

Sam: *Wishing I was still back in cabin twelve with you . . .*

A smile curled on his lips. He'd been half-expecting her to tell him she'd changed her mind about him after hanging out with Katie.

Garrett: *Oh, yeah?*

Sam: *Very. Hurry and do your work stuff so we can do that "driving lesson" . . .*

He laughed out loud. He liked this eager side of her.

Garrett: *I will.*

Daydreaming about her and ignoring how they'd left things was too convenient. He couldn't help to be curious about how things had gone with Katie.

Garrett: *Everything okay in the guest service cabin?*

Sam: *I left already, grabbed my phone from home. Obviously. Didn't really feel like hanging out with Katie. For lots of reasons. Going to the library.*

Before Garrett could respond, there was a tap at his window. He startled, then looked up.

His dad was standing beside the passenger side window. He smiled.

Garrett set his phone on the console beside him and opened the window. "Hey."

"I saw you pull up. Figured I'd come out to say hello, but you were staring at your phone with a goofy grin on your face and didn't even notice me." His father's eyes glinted. "Who are you talking to?"

It bothered Garrett that since his father had gotten sober, he'd made persistent attempts to have a normal father-son relationship. *"Turning over a new leaf"* didn't erase the years of terrible memories.

Garrett cleared his throat. "Just a friend. Sorry, I didn't see you."

His father patted the window frame. "Well, you coming on in?"

He checked the time. He was already late for his job, but Luis was there. Popping in for five minutes wouldn't make him on time at this point. And he wasn't quick enough on his feet to think of an excuse to say no. "Yeah, but just for a minute. I wanted to get some measurements for the fence in the front. See about replacing it when this snow melts."

Dad grimaced. "I can help you out. I've been meaning to do that project for a while. You're better at finishing what you start than I ever was. But it was always hard to come home and pick up my tools again too. You know, cobbler's children go barefoot and all."

The door to his truck slammed as Garrett moved toward the fence. Even if he hadn't planned on squeezing this project in right now, he might as well get the measurements. "I can take over some things on your list. I'm sure Mom would be happy to have them done. I'll call her and ask what she'd like to see fixed first."

He began counting the fence posts. "What're you doing?" his dad asked, seeming surprised.

"Counting the posts. They're eight feet apart." He could sense what was coming, and his chest tightened.

Dad shook his head. "Hold on. I have my tape measure right inside. I'll get it. I'm sure it's probably more accurate."

As his dad went inside, Garrett resisted the urge to roll his eyes. He already had everything measured when Dad returned, paint-splattered silver tape measure in hand. "Here you go."

"I already got it, Dad." Garrett typed in a few notes into his cell phone. "I'm writing the numbers down right now. I don't need the exact distance."

"Always a good idea to double-check your numbers." Dad started pulling out the tape measure, the metal wobbling in the air, sounding as though it was slicing it. He made his way to the gate.

"Dad, I got it." Garrett's voice was firmer this time. He didn't have time to waste on this level of unnecessary precision.

His father dusted the snow from the gate. As though that would make a difference. "I just don't want you to buy anything you don't need. I want to pay for this—"

Garrett gritted his teeth. This was the exact opposite of what he'd intended for the fence. "Dad, you had over ten years to do this goddamned project if you were so interested in it. How about you let me take it over now?"

Dad stiffened. Straightening, he slid the measuring tape away with a click. His lips pressed to a line, and he nodded tautly. "You're right." He stuffed the measure away into his pocket. "Of course, you're right. I'm sorry for interfering."

Rubbing his eyes, Garrett sucked in a breath. He had even been in a great mood this morning. *This isn't what you want, either.* "I'm sorry, I just—"

"No, you're right, Gar. I should have done it a long time

ago." He stuffed both hands into his pockets, his shoulders hunched. "I should have done a lot of things a long time ago. And I don't know how to fix things now. What I did to you, your mom, and your siblings is unforgivable. I-I don't blame you for not forgiving me. Cormac doesn't come home because of it. And Bridget and Shae will only let the kids come over when Mom and I are both here." He held out a hand. "A-and I'm not saying I blame them. I really don't. I deserve that and more. I'm the one who's sorry, Garrett. I really am." His eyes looked unusually bright, the rims red.

Open conversations with his father were something he didn't know if he could get used to. Garrett swallowed a tight lump in the back of his throat. His phone buzzed in his hand, and he didn't look at it, shoving it into his back pocket instead. "Dad . . ." *I don't know what the hell to say to that.* He sighed and looked back at his truck. "I should get going. I have a job to get to."

That doesn't feel right either. But what was done was done. He didn't know how to talk to his father about the past or pretend it hadn't happened.

"Yeah, me too. I'll clear your mom's car so she can get to work." Dad started back toward Garrett's truck with him.

The idea of his mom working was just as odd as the concept of his father now being a handyman for the high school. But when the secretary at church had retired, the priest had offered Mom the job. "They didn't close schools with the snow?"

"Maybe, I don't know. I usually go in anyway, just to check on things." Dad smiled tightly at Garrett as he climbed back into the truck. "I'll see you around, Gar."

As Dad shuffled through the snow back toward the house, Garrett gripped the steering wheel tightly. He wanted to be proud of the hard work his father had done in bettering himself.

The last thing his mom needed was someone dragging out the wounds from the past. And this wasn't the first time Dad had apologized, either. He'd written letters as part of AA and sat the whole family down after getting sober to make apologies in person.

He'd watched buddies from the Army spiral. Seen humanity at its worst.

At least his father was trying.

But why couldn't he get the feeling of *"too little too late"* out of his heart?

He turned on the radio, then pulled out his phone again.

Sam: *Thanks for being there for me last night, by the way. You don't know how much I needed it.*

Garrett smiled at the memory of her, checking his other notifications. He'd also missed a phone call from Eli.

He set his phone down, then pulled the shifter into drive.

One thing at a time, Doyle. You're sure as hell not perfect either.

CHAPTER TWENTY

THE HINGE on the front door squeaked as Sam opened it, and she grimaced. So much for coming in quietly.

As she slipped inside her house, the creak of a floorboard told her the door's opening had been noticed. Laura peeked down from the top of the stairs. She glanced back toward Mom's room, then tiptoed down the stairs.

Mom must be sleeping.

"Where the hell have you been?" Laura's hand rested on the handrail.

Sam narrowed her gaze at her. "Library. I had to get work done."

"And last night?" Laura came to the bottom step, closer to Sam.

"I was with Garrett." Sam took her coat off and hung it on the rack. Breezing past Laura, she moved into the kitchen. "Where are the kids?"

Laura followed her. "The baby is upstairs, and Mark took the other two sledding." She came to the side of the fridge as Sam opened it. Sam pulled out a carton of orange juice, ignoring Laura, and grabbed a glass from the cupboard. She poured herself a glass.

"So that's it?" Laura asked, frowning. "You spent the night at Garrett's house? Why was his truck here?"

Sam smiled to herself, thinking of how their driving lesson had turned into a quickie in the library parking lot. The plan had been to teach her parallel parking . . .

She sipped her orange juice, hiding her smile with her glass.

Laura's brows furrowed. She stepped closer. "What's that expression supposed to mean? Oh my God. Sam, did you—?"

"Sleep with him? Yup. Turns out, we're into each other. But not really your business, Laura." Sam drained her glass, then set it on the counter with a clink. She turned her back to the counter. "I'm not interested in talking to you. Or Mom. I'm here. That's more than enough of an effort on my part right now. Sorry, but it's going to take over twenty-four hours for me to wrap my head around the fact that my family spent my whole life lying to me."

Laura's mouth dropped open. Normally, the revelation she was sleeping with Garrett wouldn't have been something Sam would just drop like a bomb. Part of their sisterhood was sharing details like that—and knowing the other wouldn't say anything to anyone. Fortunately, Laura seemed to know to let that topic go and just shook her head.

"Mom's a wreck, Sam. Considering how sick she is, don't you think you could find it in you to talk to her for a minute at least?" Laura's expression softened. "I'm sorry, Sam. I feel horrible that you had to find out this way, and I wish Mom had told me she was going to tell you so I could have been here."

Sam took the glass to the sink and washed it. "Do you really think that would have made a difference?"

"No, but—"

"Laura." Sam shut off the faucet and turned to face her. "Let's not talk about it. I'm not ready. Before Rachel arrives, I have to shower and throw in a load of laundry. She's supposed to be here in like ten minutes."

"Rachel, your assistant from New York? Are you sure this is a good time?"

Sam nodded. "Yup. She's coming to help me with my work assignment." She opened the door to the basement and descended the stairs. Hopefully, Laura wouldn't follow her.

Flipping on the light at the bottom of the steps, she paused, more shaken than she'd let Laura know. Mom not telling her was one thing—parents sometimes hid things like that, right? Adoptions, former hippie days.

But her sister?

Her sister was only a year older than her, not the typical proverbial "older sibling." They'd grown up more like twins and had been friends through middle school. Sure, in high school, Laura had wanted to shrug off her little sister in front of her friends, but that hadn't bothered Sam too much because they were still close at home. It wasn't until college that their lives had gone in two totally different directions.

Laura had plenty of time to tell her the truth and no reason not to.

A mildew smell came from the laundry room, and Sam groaned as she approached the washing machine. She'd done it again. Put her laundry into the washer a couple of days ago and forgot about it. *Crap.* She'd have to start the laundry by rewashing the load she thought was already done.

Fortunately, she had some clean clothes in the basket here. She grabbed a flannel shirt and a pair of jeans and underwear. She'd take a quick shower in the basement bathroom before starting the washer. The water pressure from the well didn't allow the shower and washing machine to run simultaneously.

And getting dressed here meant she didn't have to go to the second floor and past Mom's room.

She showered quickly and dressed, towel drying her hair as she walked back to the laundry room. She found a hair clip in the basket labeled *"Things Lost in the Dryer"* and twisted her hair up. *Good enough.* She could grab her makeup bag before going out. Fortunately, she'd left it in the living room.

Opening the lid to the washer, she wrinkled her nose. This was going to need some bleach. She checked in the cabinet for the bottle of bleach and carried it over to the washer. Uncapping it, the smell stung her nostrils as she poured it into the bleach dispenser.

"Sam?" Mom's voice came unexpectedly.

Sam's hand slipped, and she drew the bottle back quickly. Bleach splashed out onto the flannel top she wore. "Shit." She dabbed at her shirt with a cloth. "Sorry."

Mom only wore a nightgown and had dark circles under her eyes. *You shouldn't have made someone so sick come to the basement to see you.*

The sight of her was enough to make that horrible ache in her heart come rushing back. She couldn't do this right now. Rachel might already be here. "Sam, I was so worried about you."

"I came back this morning for my phone. You were asleep. I didn't want to wake you up." The washing machine lid banged shut, and she turned the washer on. She couldn't meet Mom's eyes. "I'm sorry for worrying you."

Her mother came closer. "*Mi amor,* I'm so sorry—"

"Mom, please. I promise. We'll talk. But I need some time." Sam blinked away a few tears. She looked up, catching the stricken expression on Mom's face. *Does she get a pass because she's sick? Am I being a jerk for not giving it to her?*

"*Está bien.*" *Okay.* Mom looked like she might cry.

This wasn't fair. *It's my turn to receive sympathy. Isn't it?* God, she hated how much that made her sound like a whiny toddler.

Laura's voice interrupted the soft whir of water flowing into the washing machine. "Sam, your friend Rachel just pulled up," she called from upstairs.

Thank God. "I have to go. I'm going to Garrett's tonight, so I'll see you tomorrow, okay?"

Mom nodded, her face drawn and pale.

"Let me help you up the stairs," Sam said, sighing. She set a hand on Mom's elbow, leading her through the basement. They took the stairs slowly, and the sweet scent of her Mom's shampooed hair floated toward her. She'd always loved coconut-scented everything. The thought made her heart feel even heavier.

Leaving Mom with Laura, Sam headed outside. Rachel was climbing out of her car onto the gravel parking lot. She wobbled in her high-heeled boots. "Rachel Avery, you are a sight for sore eyes, and please, never leave me again."

Rachel pushed a strand of her jet-black bangs, streaked with pink, out of her eyes and laughed. "Two weeks in the country and you're practically Laura Ingalls Wilder." She scanned Sam's outfit. "Even with the flannel. And bleach stains, apparently? You look all *home-ecy*. Oy vey. Also—you left me."

"There are pictures of me wearing overalls as a kid. The bleach is new for me, though—I knocked a container over while doing the laundry. Just happened." A blast of wind froze the tips of Sam's ears, making her eyes water. She'd come out of the house without a coat or hat. The sun had already set, though, and the closer they drew to winter, the chillier the temperatures dropped. "How was the drive?"

"All right. I hit some traffic outside of Philly." Rachel

scanned the vicinity. "I never knew this place was so quaint. Great glamping place."

"My family was pushing glamping on people before glamping was a thing." Considering her mother's revelations the previous day, everything about her childhood felt tainted now, though. "I snagged you a cabin. Easier than you staying at a hotel."

"Maybe for you. I'm all about the room service. Is there skiing nearby? It felt like I drove up a mountain to get here."

"Not too far—about twenty minutes?" She crossed toward Rachel's car and peeked into the back seat. The tiny hatchback was stuffed with so many things there was no way Rachel could have seen out the rearview mirror. "Wow. I made you pack half of my apartment."

"Basically." Rachel smirked. "I'm billing you time and a half. What is it with this assignment anyway?"

"I told you I was trying to position myself to do more food photography work. Maren was about to kill the entire project, so I threw a Hail Mary, hoping to save my chance." Sam's voice was wry. The passenger side door was just as packed as the back. "I'm going to grab the UTV I drove up here earlier. I need to return it to the guest service lodge. Why don't you follow me to your cabin?"

"Now you're using football references and—wait. I thought you hated all forms of driving. Who *are* you?" Rachel looked puzzled.

"I'm learning. My friend, Garrett, is teaching me." He'd shown up for their lesson today, but instead of driving, they hadn't been able to keep their hands off each other. Sam smiled to herself, thinking of the way the lesson had ended instead.

"What's that look all about?" Rachel's eyes widened. "Did you finally get laid? You did, didn't you? I can see it in your eyes. Tell me everything. But first, I need to pee. I've been on the road for seven hours. And food. I need food. The greasier and more country-style, the better. Butter wrapped in bacon, preferably. Then you tell me."

Sam laughed and glanced back toward the house. Hopefully, her family couldn't hear. Having Rachel here was wonderful. Someone who knew her as she was now and with whom she could talk about Garrett without bias. "All right. We'll drop off the car, give you a chance to put your stuff in the cabin, and go out. Let me just grab a few things from my house."

Within forty minutes, they were sliding into a booth at Yardley's. "Is this place always so packed? It's a Tuesday at six."

"It's one of the most popular pubs around here." Rachel wasn't kidding. They'd had to wait twenty minutes for a table—at the bar, where there was open seating. The dining room had a forty-minute wait.

"We didn't have to visit the most popular place straight off the bat." Rachel scanned a menu.

"You forget I don't live here anymore. I don't know all the restaurants in town."

"You've been here long enough to get some," Rachel answered pointedly.

"True." Trust Rachel not to forget to bring that up, either.

The bar server arrived to take their drink orders. As he was leaving, a familiar voice came up behind Sam. Cold hands covered her eyes. "Guess who?" Katie asked. Her arms dropped lower, around Sam's neck, as she hugged her from behind. "I didn't know you were coming out tonight. You should have told me earlier."

A knot formed in the pit of Sam's stomach. *I avoided you earlier.*

Katie came to the side of the table with a wide grin. "Hey, Rachel, good to see you again." They'd met one time Katie had spent a week with Sam in New York, but Sam hadn't counted on Katie remembering Rachel.

Rachel gave Katie a blank look for a split second, and her eyes darted to Sam questioningly. "Kate . . . right?"

"Katie." Her smile didn't falter. Far as Sam could remember, the only person who had ever gotten away with calling Katie by the shorter form of her name was Garrett.

Rachel nodded distractedly. "Good to see you too." She pointed at the menu to Sam. "Is crab dip good here?"

"Oh, it's the best." Katie nodded enthusiastically. "Not as good as Bunny's, but you can't grab a drink there." She turned back to Sam. "By the way, I recruited another person to bake for you if you still need people. Do you remember the librarian from the high school? She's still there, still making the best cookies for the students. Anyway, she remembered you and said yes."

Sam could read in Rachel's expression that Katie's overly enthusiastic, bubbly way of talking was the complete antithesis of what she wanted after a long day of driving. But she didn't want to send Katie away rudely, either.

The knot in Sam's stomach tightened. "Actually, I think I'm full up on baking slots."

Confusion flickered in Katie's eyes. "You recruited twelve people?"

As though she didn't expect me to do it without her help. Sam wasn't sure if her resentment was from what Garrett had told her earlier about Katie knowing about Mom. Or was it something else? Growing up? *Guilt?* "Yeah, Garrett helped me, actually. Turns out, when you give someone a free Christmas tree while asking, they're more likely to say yes."

"So you bribed them," Rachel observed dryly, leaning back as the server arrived with their drinks.

He slid a beer in front of Rachel and a gin and tonic in

front of Sam. He turned to Katie. "Sorry, I didn't get your order. You want me to grab you a chair?"

Katie looked from Rachel to Sam, her green eyes hesitant. "If you all don't mind me joining you. I just came to happy hour with some friends from the salon, but I see them every day."

Of all the days Sam didn't want Katie to join her, today topped the list. She'd expected guilt to be twisting and slithering up from her gut. The muscles in her thighs were aching from the night she'd had with Garrett. *You should feel guilty.* She visualized Garrett between her legs, and it took every ounce of effort not to grab the table.

One night and she was a goner.

Totally addicted to sex with Garrett.

Had sex been that good before? Or had she just forgotten?

No, not a chance. She couldn't have forgotten.

She offered a smile she wasn't positive looked genuine. Thank God no one could read her thoughts. Her dirty thoughts. *Of Garrett . . .*

But Sam didn't have an ounce of guilt. Katie didn't own Garrett. "Of course," she managed.

The server returned with a chair for Katie and she sat at the table and ordered a drink. Rachel quirked a well-defined microbladed eyebrow at Sam, eyeing her suspiciously. She leaned forward on the table on her elbows. "All right. I want to hear all about this Garrett guy. Spare no detail. I want to hear everything about him."

Shit.

Even though the noise level didn't change, the volume in Sam's head seemed to drop to a din, as though her focus had become laser sharp. Katie blanched. Sam kicked Rachel in the shin under the table as discreetly as she could, giving her a hard stare.

As much as Sam was angry with Katie, the last thing she wanted was to have her find out about Garrett like this.

"Garrett?" Katie repeated. She glanced at Sam uncertainly. "What's she talking about?"

Sam's heart pounded, and she smiled, fumbling for words. "Oh . . . uh . . . Rachel met Garrett leaving the cabins. Thought he was cute. Funny thing, Rach. Katie and Garrett were engaged once upon a time."

Rachel looked like a deer in headlights. She sipped her drink, then answered cautiously, "Oh, um. I didn't know." The look she gave Sam made it clear she wanted answers, and now, and might just kill Sam for throwing the situation to her to fix. "I'm sorry. I didn't realize that. He was just . . . uh, really hot."

"Oh . . ." Katie blinked a few times. "I mean, how could you know? I'm sorry, I just. Sore subject. My advice would be to stay far away. Looks are totally deceiving in that case. He dumped me the night before our wedding."

Rachel's jaw dropped, and she gave Sam a look as if to say, *and that's the guy you're sleeping with?*

Defensiveness uncurled in Sam's chest. This was not going well. Neither with Rachel nor with Katie. She prayed Rachel wouldn't give away anything else. "It was five years ago. They were both young."

"Not *that* young." Katie scooted back as the server brought her a cosmo. The glass clinked against the table. "And we dated since sophomore year of high school. Anyway, any relationship with him can only end with him taking a torpedo to things. He has a terrible reputation with women."

Sam had heard it all before—though she'd appreciated the absence of a Garrett-the-asshole rant recently. But given what had happened with Garrett, Katie's words took on a new life. One that poked holes into the light-hearted feeling she'd been carrying all day when she thought of Garrett.

"Wow, that's really shitty." Rachel swigged her drink, the corners of her eyes narrowing perceptibly. "I think I've lost all respect for this Garrett guy. Too bad."

Katie's face had reddened. She shook her head and swallowed. "I'm sorry. I didn't mean to cut in and go on like that." She bit her lip. "It was just so embarrassing, you know? To show up at the church to get ready for our wedding and find a letter telling me he wasn't coming? We couldn't even get the word out to all our guests. And all the money we'd spent."

Sam furrowed her brow, feeling sick with the way Katie was twisting Garrett's image to Rachel. "I thought you said Garrett eventually paid your parents back."

"He did, but still—" Katie stood. "I'm gonna go to the ladies' room. Get a grip on myself. If the server comes back, could you order me Old Bay wings? I want six."

Rachel closed her menu. "Those sound amazing."

Katie smiled warmly at her and left the table.

Great. Now Rachel and Katie are on the same team.

As soon as she was out of earshot, Rachel leaned even closer. "Tell me you're not fucking your best friend's ex."

Feeling the blood drain from her face, a bitter feeling stung the back of Sam's throat. "It's not that simple—"

"Oh my God. Sam. Have I taught you nothing?" Rachel pushed her bangs out of her face. "You've got to be kidding me."

"It just happened last night. And honestly, he's not the person I thought he was. Or I never saw him for the person he was. Katie's trashing him unfairly. But either way, he's been there for me with everything I've had going on." She dropped her voice, nervous that Katie would return at any second. "And he told me he's always been in love with me, Rach. That the reason he didn't marry Katie was because he realized he was in love with me."

Rachel covered her mouth. Then she propped her elbow on the table and shifted her hand under her chin. "I don't think you know how bad that sounds. Because from this side, I'm wondering what the hell you're thinking."

Sam's shoulders dropped. "Please don't judge me."

"I'm not judging you." Rachel's eyes widened. Her hands moved faster the more she talked. "I'm *worried* about you. Your mom gets terminal cancer, you're in constant fights with your sister, and you decide to stay in the hometown you've told me a billion times how much you hate. Those are all big things. And now this?"

Rachel's gaze cut right through her. "Sam, what is going on with you? Is this worth the stress it will cause you in the long run?"

Sam's appetite was fading fast. "*This* thing with Garrett is the best thing that has happened to me in a long time. Yes, the other stuff is all true. And I know. The relationship is messy and complicated, and I don't know how the hell I'm going to tell Katie or Eli, but it's the one thing bringing me actual happiness right now."

"Eli?" Rachel's face was quizzical. "What does Eli have to do with this? Didn't you two break up this summer?"

Sam watched the bubbles of tonic fizzle up the side of her glass. "Garrett is Eli's best friend."

Rachel was silent, her eyes searching Sam's face. She bobbed her head as though processing. "Sam? Do you have any idea how fucked up this all is?"

"Don't you think it's antiquated to act like all that possessive crap matters?" Sam had enough. "We're not doing anything wrong."

"Yeah, you are. Do you know why? Because you haven't told either of them. And let's say in a perfect world, even if it was okay to sleep with your friend's exes like it won't affect your friendship—which it totally will—the minimum courtesy you should show them is to be honest with them about it."

"So I should leave whether I get to be happy in their hands?" Sam pierced the lime in her drink with the cocktail straw and fished it out. Rachel was speaking to her own guilty thoughts, but it also wasn't fair. "If Garrett and I make each other happy, why shouldn't we get to be together? It isn't as though Katie or Eli wants either of us."

"No. That's not what I'm saying. I'm saying"—Rachel shook her head—"I . . . I don't even know what I'm saying anymore. You're confusing me." She took a pull from her drink. "Holy mother. I'm going to need another drink."

Rachel lowered her voice once again. "Just do me a favor. Figure out if this friendship with Katie is something you really want in your life. Or if it's worth saving. Because I'm telling you right now. That girl won't be okay with you sleeping with her ex. So she either needs to never find out you hooked up with him or he better be worth losing your friend over."

Sam silenced her with a look, seeing Katie approaching from the bathroom. They talked on the phone and texted regularly, but their friendship had changed since Sam had left Brandywood. But it was still hard to reconcile that Katie had known the truth about her parents and had *never* mentioned it. Surely, she'd known Sam hadn't been told. *Did best friends hold on to something so crippling?* Had she just been a charity case for Katie?

"Did the server come back for our order?" Katie asked, sitting. When they shook their heads, she checked her watch. "I'm going to grab him by the collar and drag him back here. I bet you anything he's hanging out by the kitchen trying to avoid last-minute happy hour orders. It ends in ten minutes."

"I think he's a couple of tables over." Sam tilted her head toward the table a few seats down.

"Oh, good." Katie turned her gaze back to Sam. "Speaking of awful guys, I went to the firehouse today. Gave Mike Jarvis a piece of my mind. He feels awful about standing you up. He was called to work and totally dropped the ball on everything. Anyway, get this. He wanted me to apologize and see if you'd want to go out this weekend."

Sam laughed sarcastically. "He has my phone number, Katie. He can send me a message if he's sorry—which he hasn't. Or ask me out again himself. To which the answer is hell no, never."

"I know. I'm just telling you what happened. Don't worry, I have your back with everything. I told him to go to hel—" Katie broke off, her eyes widening as she stared toward the door.

Sam frowned and looked over her shoulder, following the direction of Katie's gaze.

Eli had just walked in.

CHAPTER TWENTY-ONE

GARRETT CHECKED his phone once more and paced in his living room.

Almost midnight and still no sign of Sam.

Laughter came from the television, the comedy series doing nothing to stop his thoughts. She had said she'd turn up, and that was enough to be disappointed over. But the complete silence in response to his texts?

What. The. Hell.

He stalked to his kitchen and grabbed another beer from the fridge. Three empties hung out by the sink, but he twisted the cap off and flipped it into the trash. Taking a long pull from the beer, he caught his reflection across the open space in the picture window.

You drunk.

He heard it in Sam's voice, but it wasn't that which bothered him.

But there was a difference. Unlike his father, he didn't need it. And thanks to his father, even the scent of alcohol was a comfort, reminding him of the closet where he'd hidden when his parents argued when he was very young. He must have been only five or six to have fit in that old pantry where Mom kept the recycling bin. But he'd thought it was perfect. He could grab a snack, and as long as he didn't have to go to the bathroom, he could stay in there for hours.

But the scent of alcohol might bother Sam, considering she'd commented on his drinking the day before. He didn't want to do anything to ruin things now. If she was even still coming. He'd stopped at Bunny's and grabbed some slices of chocolate cake, which were on the counter. Popping a container open, he broke off a piece and ate it, avoiding looking at the clock.

Sam had texted him all day. Practically nonstop. She'd said she was taking Rachel out to Yardley's. And he hadn't heard from her since.

"You're obsessed," he muttered to himself and flopped down on the couch.

Was he? Could you love someone your whole life without being obsessed?

Until she'd come back into town, he'd convinced himself he'd done a good job of moving on.

He wanted to think of last night the way he'd thought about nights with other women. *Sex—and we'll see how it goes.* After the debacle with Katie, he'd been cautious to talk about futures. Not that he'd ever met anyone he'd wanted to date for longer than a handful of months, at the longest.

But Sam?

She will break your heart.

Sam, the one woman he'd especially never let himself think of a future with?

And last night had been about sex—at least, for her. Not about futures. She was going back to New York eventually. The way things seemed to be going with her family, it might be sooner than later.

He checked his phone again. Still nothing.

A flush of anger rose within him, and he slammed the phone onto the coffee table.

The softest of knocks on his front door caught his attention. Garrett sprang to his feet and strode across the living room and kitchen into the foyer. He opened the door.

Sam stood there, looking cold. She breezed past him as he held it for her. "I had Rachel drop me off a couple of blocks away. It's freezing out here." She pulled her coat off and stomped her boots on the front mat.

Garrett closed the door, and she snuck behind him, slipping her hands under his shirt. As her frozen hands flattened against his stomach, he jumped. "What are you trying to do to me?"

She chuckled, her grip tight. "Warm my hands up."

That laugh. It was enough to melt the frostiness and frustration from earlier. She was here now, which was all that mattered.

He took her hands and turned around, interlacing his fingers with hers. "Do I look like a fireplace to you?"

"You look pretty hot to me." She winked, then attempted, once again, to pull her hands away and touch the skin under his shirt.

His grip remained tight as he laughed, wrestling her back. "You stay off me. Devil woman."

They were both laughing now, and he let go and made a run for the kitchen.

She caught up with him as he swept her into his arms, trying to catch her hands. She slid them under his shirt, onto his back. "Ahhh—" She nestled against him as he twitched with cold. "See, that's all I wanted."

Digging his hands into her hair, he drew her head back. His

mouth descended on hers. The laughter and chasing had spiked his adrenaline, and he wanted her. All of her. *Now.*

Something soft landed against his cheek, and he drew his head back, puzzled.

Chocolate icing was on the tips of Sam's fingers. The chocolate cake was on the nearby counter. She had a playful gleam in her eyes. "Oh, no." Her tongue flicked against his cheek. "Mmm . . . you taste good."

He groaned. "God, I want you." His lips returned to hers, parting hers as his tongue tasted her own.

The kiss turned wild, and he peeled her flannel shirt from her shoulders and the undershirt over her head. Her boots had been left at the front door, so she easily pushed her jeans off her hips. Since it was so late, he'd changed into sweatpants and a hoodie, and they came off easily. His tongue lashed into her mouth as he unhooked her bra, pushing it off and away from her perfect breasts.

He had every intention of worshipping those fantastic breasts. Her hands cupped them, and she moaned when he rolled her hard nipples between his fingers.

Then he flipped her, his hands still on her breasts, and leaned her over the counter. She reached out, gripping the sides as he thrust inside her.

Warm, tight, so wet.

His.

THEY'D MADE it from the counter to the couch, then the stairs—which he'd never thought about christening before but turned out to be perfect for burying his head between her legs. Now they lay in his bed in the middle of the night.

The lights were still on. Maybe his neighbors would think he'd gone out of town and left a light on.

Sam was nestled in his arms, her eyes closed. He'd always thought she was beautiful, but *God* . . . her face was flushed pink from sex, and there was something so both heartwarming and sexy at the same time about it.

"Are you asleep?" Garrett smoothed his hand over her shoulder.

"Getting there." She opened one eye. "I haven't ever had so much . . . exhausting activity . . . in one day."

He kissed the top of her head, not wanting to think about her past. Instead, he pulled a blanket over them. They hadn't discussed whether she planned to spend the night here, but she seemed to want to stay. He should grab his phone, send a message to Luis, and ask him to handle the Sanders tomorrow. But his phone was downstairs on the table where he'd left it before Sam had arrived.

Sam rolled onto her side, propping her head up as she stared at him. She traced a fingertip over his chest and played with the sprinkling of curly dark hair there. A ring graced her finger, a circlet of silver snowdrops. For as long as Garrett could remember, she'd worn it on her left hand. She had a habit of twisting it when she was nervous, like she stopped to do as she lay back once again.

Something seemed to be on her mind, but her dark eyes gave little away. She sucked in a deep breath. "So . . . Eli showed up at Yardley's tonight."

Garrett stiffened. Eli was in town?

He'd received a call from him the previous evening, but he'd been busy searching for Sam and hung up after a minute. He hadn't called him back.

Taking her hand, he kept his breath at an even pace, not

wanting to jump to conclusions. After all, Sam had seen Eli and still come here. That counted for something. She wanted to be with him, not Eli.

"Oh, yeah?" he managed. His voice sounded as casual as he'd attempted. "What's he doing back in town?"

Sam's fingers tightened against his, and she rubbed her thumb over the fleshy part of his palm. Her hand looked small compared to his. "He wanted to talk to me." She continued staring at their hands as though mesmerized by them. Or she was avoiding his gaze. "I've been avoiding his calls, and I guess he heard about that thing with Mom somehow."

Probably his fault. And he'd avoided Eli's call today too.

"So he took some days off work and came here." Her thumb stopped its movement, and she added, "He says he wants to get back together with me. That being apart has made him realize how much he misses me."

Garrett had to bite his tongue. Eli had missed Sam so much he'd been out on a date with someone new within days of leaving Brandywood. Sam's breath caught, and she turned to face him. She still couldn't meet his gaze, and now the flush on her cheeks was spreading to her chest, a full, hot blush.

"Garrett, he proposed."

Proposed.

The word pierced like a quiver of burning arrows unleashed straight into his heart.

"What the fuck?" Now Garrett couldn't control his reaction. He pulled away from her, his eyes narrowing. "Eli proposed to you?" His mind tried to unscramble her words and the meaning behind them. His voice sounded gruff and thick. "What did . . . what did you tell him?"

His eyes pleaded with hers. *Please tell me you said no.*

Sam drew in a shaky breath and sat up, covering herself

with the blanket. "Well, he proposed in front of the entire bar. I, uh . . ."

Jealous, disgusted nausea rose in his chest. "You said yes?" He stood, feeling unsteady, and crossed the room toward his dresser for a pair of boxers. Standing naked in front of her didn't feel right now.

"No—" She scrambled from the bed, dragging the sheet with her. "No, no, I didn't say yes. I said I would think about it." She swallowed, her eyes shiny with tears. "I didn't want to embarrass him in front of everyone there, and I didn't know what to do. I couldn't tell him about us." She came toward him. "But I'm going to tell him no. I don't want to marry him."

Garrett grabbed a T-shirt for himself out of a drawer. He tossed her another one. "Here." Her clothes were downstairs. And he couldn't have this conversation while she stood there like that. He turned his face while she pulled it on.

His hands fisted, and he stalked toward the windows. The curtains covered them, but he felt the need to check them out, ensure no one was outside, as a slick sweat broke out on the back of his neck.

"Garrett—please. Say something." Sam had pulled on the shirt now, and she came up behind him.

He tugged at the hair on the top of his head, trying to think clearly. "Let me get this straight. Eli shows up and proposes. You tell him you'll think about it and then come here . . . and we fuck before you tell me." Anger curled at the ends of his fingertips, writhing its way up into the stiff, taut muscles of his neck. "What am I supposed to say? Do you have any idea what sort of position that puts me in?"

She touched his forearm. "But nothing's changed. Eli coming in at the eleventh hour and throwing a proposal into the mix changes nothing."

He let out a sardonic laugh devoid of any humor. "Are you kidding me? My best friend asked you to be his *wife*, and you're saying it changes nothing?"

Sam flinched. "But you already knew how Eli felt about me when we started this."

"What I knew was Eli said you two were done. That he just wanted you to be happy and he hoped I could be there for you in the meantime. I never would have even considered being with you if I knew how he felt—"

Her brow furrowed. "What?" Her eyes blazed. She stepped away from him as though he had struck her. "When?"

Garrett scowled. "What are you talking about?"

She glared. "When did you make this little arrangement? What was it—step in as my boyfriend while he figured out if he wanted to be with me? Was it just friendship? Sex?"

She tore off across the room. "I-I can't believe this. I thought you gave a damn."

Unable to help himself, Garrett followed. "It wasn't like that. I did—do give a damn. I told you that last night." He caught her by the arm, spinning her around to face him. "I love you, Sam. I didn't tell Eli I would help you for his sake. I did it for yours." He continued, his voice biting, "I'm sorry if I'm a little thrown off because Eli just proposed to you, and you didn't bother to tell him no or tell me about it. I thought you would have the decency to tell me something of that magnitude."

She pulled her arm back, lifting her chin. "Sorry to disappoint you, Garrett. Guess I'm just as shitty as everyone thinks." She stormed down the stairs, her footsteps pounding on the wooden slats. Hard to believe that just an hour earlier, they'd been sprawled on those stairs making love.

He sank onto the top step, holding his head in his hands.

He listened as she went to the kitchen, gathering her things. He couldn't let her go like this.

Yet how could he continue things now?

Eli coming back wasn't some sort of symbolic gesture. He'd come back and basically announced to everyone in town that he and Sam were still very much together—that he loved her.

If Garrett didn't let her go now, he would be the world's worst friend. A traitor and a liar.

A crushing feeling pushed in on his ribs as her footsteps announced her return to the foyer.

She'd dressed. Her hair was back in a messy bun at the top of her head, her coat open at the front. Chocolate stained her shirt from the cake they'd devoured after having sex. She laid his T-shirt on the railing. "I called a ride. It'll be another ten minutes." She stared at her phone.

He was going to lose her.

Fight for her.

Such a ridiculous phrase. Fight? For what? Love shouldn't be something that was fought for. Relationships, sure they took work and growing . . . but love was there, or it wasn't. And in her case, it wasn't.

He stood, gripping the rail as he stared at her. "Tell me one thing. Did you tell Eli you'd think about it because you didn't want to embarrass him? Or was it something else? Do you want to think about it? Was it, by any chance, that you couldn't bear to tell the love of your life anything other than yes?"

She sat on the bottom step, not facing him. Several seconds ticked by, the stale, dull silence of the night overwhelming him.

She leaned against the wall, swinging her legs around so her feet were on the bottom step, and hugged her knees. "About a year ago, at Christmas, Eli and I spent a weekend together, then broke up again. But I wanted to fight for us, which Eli said I wasn't willing to do."

She twisted the ring on her finger again.

"So I flew out to LA to be with Eli around Valentine's Day. I asked him to get back together. He said yes. Then he went out and slept with another woman."

Garrett gripped the rail. He'd honestly thought Eli had been a dick to sleep with another woman when he'd seen Sam. But to know that he'd agreed to become a couple again and then slept with someone else? That was hugely different.

"So we got into a huge, explosive fight, and I left. I threw things at him—really lost it. I was so enraged that I just . . . couldn't keep it in . . . ." She trailed off and bit her lip.

Wiping her eyes, she stood. "It destroyed my relationship with Eli." She cleared her throat. "Ten years of pretending he loved me only for him to cheat on me. And I shouldn't have lost it the way I did, I know. I started therapy for my anger. But that's the type of person I am, Garrett. An angry, explosive person who probably isn't good for you. And I know how you grew up—and the things you faced with your dad and his anger. Who knows—I might be the same way.

"And, for what it's worth, Eli's not the love of my life. Because he wouldn't have done that to me if he was." She headed for the door. "I'll just wait on your front porch."

Garrett struggled to breathe. He clamored down the stairs behind her.

He didn't know what to say. How to fix a situation that seemed so hopeless? So irrevocably broken and twisted.

She turned her face toward him, and he searched her eyes.

She also doesn't know what the hell she's talking about.

He slipped his hand into hers, then shook it. "Hi, I'm Garrett."

Her eyebrows came together quizzically, her hand limp in his.

"I dated a girl I didn't really care about for years. Told her I loved her. After leading her on for a while, I realized I was in love with her best friend and dumped her at the altar."

She let out a broken, surprised cry, her eyes welling with tears as he held her shoulders. "I also slept with the girl my best friend has loved since grade school . . . a few hours after he proposed to her. Apparently." His thumb and forefinger grasped her chin gently, and he lifted her face toward his. "We all make mistakes, Sam. Big ones. What defines us is whether we allow ourselves to be defined by those mistakes."

"But I did a horrible thing to Eli—"

He set his hands on her shoulders. "You're nothing like my father, so don't let me catch you comparing yourself to him again. I'm not making excuses, but you've recognized that you crossed the line with your anger, and that takes a lot, Sam. Having the courage to face your demons is a big step. And I promise you—no one in town thinks you're a shitty person. You may not see or know the way people around here admire you, but I promise you they do."

Sam covered her mouth with her palm, her eyes squeezed shut as though struggling for composure. When she opened her eyes, she said, "Even if that's true, I don't know how to do the right thing. Being with you *feels* right, Garrett, but when I think about Eli, that makes me feel horrible. Don't you see? I have to go."

"No." He squeezed her shoulders gently. "No, Sam. Don't run from me. From us. Whatever happens with Eli, we can face it together. Don't run away because you're scared. I'm right here. Right beside you."

She wiped her eyes and smiled sadly. Standing on her tiptoes, she pressed a soft kiss to his lips. "I wish you'd told me a long time ago how you felt." She unlocked the front door. As she did, her phone beeped, alerting her that her driver had arrived. Headlights shone into his driveway as a car pulled in. Sam sighed and stepped out.

Don't let her go, you idiot. But she was walking away. Even after he'd tried to come after her.

Garrett watched her get into the car and reeled backward, away from the door, feeling as though the walls of the house might collapse on top of him. No, that was him. He was collapsing.

She was walking away.

Numb and shaking, he climbed the stairs. His eyes fell on the unmade bed. The sheet she'd been wrapped in was dropped on the floor. Gathering the sheet, he held it against his face. Her scent lingered on the soft fabric. Tossing it across the room, he sank against the bed, head in his hands.

Eli had already told Garrett some of what happened that night, but he hadn't known Sam's intention. Sam's violence wasn't like his father's. Sam had lashed out *in* her hurt. His father had lashed out *to* hurt. Completely different.

The look of haunted regret on her face, though . . . had he lost her now? She had enough going on in her life. Why would she want him when it just meant more stress and drama?

How could he live without her, now that he'd gotten a glimpse of what he could feel with her?

And then there's Eli. Garrett had kept his distance from Sam for so long because of Eli. He'd respected his friend. But Eli had let her go. Repeatedly. Sam had blocked him and made it clear that in her mind, they were done. But Garrett didn't want Sam for only one day. He wanted forever. First, he'd beg her to be with him.

Eli would never forgive him if he knew the truth, and pretending the last day hadn't happened was impossible. *If only—*

His bedroom door opened, startling him from his thoughts.

Sam stood there with her face streaked with tears. Her eyes were red, her face splotchy. She shrugged and let out a broken sob. "I'm sorry."

She came back to him.

He folded her into his arms. Cupping her face, he kissed her swollen lips, forfeit to the only thing he knew how to do: love her anyway.

CHAPTER TWENTY-TWO

SAM WOKE to the smell of coffee, and she stretched, rolling over in Garrett's bed. Garrett was sitting on a loveseat in his room, staring at a laptop. A mug steamed on the nightstand beside her.

He glanced over the screen. After a few clicks, he closed the screen. "Morning, beautiful."

She threw him her best smile and held out a hand toward him. She'd never been much of a morning person, but after the previous two nights, she was especially exhausted. Garrett joined her on the bed, sitting beside her as he took her hand. "You're wearing too many clothes." She tugged at the waistband of his sweatpants.

He laughed. "I don't normally walk around my house naked. Especially to make coffee." He leaned forward and kissed her gently. "Has anyone ever told you how gorgeous you are when you wake up in the morning?"

Right. She was probably disheveled. She wrinkled her nose. "You don't have to try that hard to get in my pants again. Though you might be late for work."

Garrett took her other hand, then pushed her onto her back. Leaning over her, he dipped his mouth to hers. "I already texted my homeowner that I won't be there today. So I'm yours as long as you're available."

"Yes, please." She returned his kiss, trying to avoid thoughts about the day ahead of her. She needed to get every detail of this shoot down. Or Eli.

Not going to think about that right now.

Garrett. He was the man she wanted. She'd gotten in that car the night before, and Garrett's words echoed in her mind. *Don't run from me.*

So she'd made the driver stop only a block away and return. All she'd known was, for once, she didn't want to run. How many times had she run from Eli? And even when Mom told her the truth a couple of days earlier—she'd run.

She knew what was on the other side of running away from the people she cared about. And even though staying terrified her, running scared her more this time.

But how to tell Eli she'd fallen for his best friend? That she couldn't marry him because she wanted Garrett? She had no idea.

She wrapped her arms around Garrett's neck as he pushed the blanket aside and took his pants off.

"I feel like we should be exploring other rooms or something." She tugged at his earlobe with her teeth. "We could make a checklist of all the rooms in your house. Find a new position for each one." He'd reached down and was torturing her with his fingers. She moaned.

He teased her with a few more electrifying strokes, then pulled his hand away. She gasped at the void. "Your wish is my command. Of course." He swung her into his arms, carrying her out of his room over his shoulder. "Pick a spot."

Laughing, she wiggled her feet. "Put me down, you crazy

man. I was just kidding. You're taking me far away from my coffee." Somehow Garrett made her feel sexier than she ever had, though he couldn't get enough of being with her.

"In the hallway at the top of the stairs, it is." Garrett set her down. "Though I can't say it's the most original of locations. And I'm insulted. Coffee over sex?"

She steadied herself on his chest. Finding her footing, she gave him a teasing glance, hoping her expression made her look sultry. "Just so happens I've had a lot more sex than coffee recently."

The scrape of a key in the front door lock made them both freeze, but just momentarily. They sprang away from each other as the front door opened.

Eli.

He stood at the open doorway, stiff with shock, staring at them. An icy draft churned its way up the stairs from outside.

Oh. Shit.

Sam hid behind Garrett. Bolting back into Garrett's room, she searched for her clothes but didn't see them anywhere. She settled for a T-shirt and a pair of boxers as she heard the door slam.

Male voices—arguing—came from the hallway.

Her face burned.

Think.

But what could she say? Eli had seen them. There couldn't be any denying it.

Much as she wanted to hide back in Garrett's room, she couldn't leave him to face Eli alone. Especially not naked. She grabbed Garrett's sweatpants and hurried toward the door.

Garrett met her at the doorway. She held the sweatpants out and met his gaze. His eyes weren't completely readable, but he was upset.

He pulled on the sweatpants, then dragged her into his arms for a hug. "I can handle this."

She shook her head. "No, not without me." She lowered her voice even further. "How did he have a key?" She had a faint memory of Garrett saying something about it when she'd walked him home from the bar.

"I had lent it to him."

She followed him back to the stairs. Eli wasn't at the door anymore. Had he left? "Where is he?" she whispered.

Garrett didn't answer. As her feet hit the hardwood floors at the bottom of the stairs, she wished she'd asked Garrett for socks. The downstairs was brutally cold, and somehow, that felt like a disadvantage right now. The muscles in Garrett's back were taut, his posture rigid.

Never, ever would she have picked this scenario to be the one to expose to Eli what had happened with Garrett. The word *expose* stuck in her brain and produced a giggle. Garrett threw her a look over his shoulder as though she'd completely lost it. She touched his back, trying to center herself, then Eli came into view in the kitchen.

He still wore his coat, his hands shoved into his pockets. He stared out the picture window at the early morning sun, which glinted softly off the snow. The snow seemed to throw extra, diffused light into the kitchen. Eli's sandy-blond hair was tousled, his face haggard, as though he hadn't slept.

Garrett stopped a few feet away, and Sam came up beside him. Eli looked at her first, his blue eyes narrowing as he took in her clothes. "So what is it, Sam?" His voice wobbled as though he did everything he could to show restraint. "You're fuck buddies with Garrett now?"

"No!" Her voice was sharper than she'd intended. The shame pressing in was strange, lined with self-defense. "No, it's not like that."

"What in the hell is it? Revenge? You get mad at me, so you decide to sleep with my best friend? Because from where I'm standing, I can't really comprehend how two people who barely tolerated each other a few weeks ago are now standing across from me acting like they've been playing house behind my back."

"I wouldn't say I barely tolerat—"

"I don't want to hear it, Gar." Eli pointed a finger at him. "Shut the fuck up!" He slapped his hand against the counter in front of him, his face going a shade redder.

"It just . . . happened, Eli. This just started. It had nothing to do with you." Sam crossed her arms, trying not to appear cold.

Eli blanched. "So last night when I—" He struggled with the words. "Wow. That must have been a good laugh for you. 'I'll think about it.' What you meant was, let me go back and fuck Garrett first."

She flinched each time he swore. The way Eli said it, it sounded so ugly and degrading.

Garrett left her side and crossed the room. He returned with the hoodie and socks he'd discarded the previous night and handed them to her. As his hand connected with her, he searched her gaze. "You're shaking," he said.

Eli watched them intently. She gave Garrett a tight smile. "Just cold. Thanks." She pulled the clothes he'd given her on, but a chill had seeped through to her core.

Garrett nodded, then turned to face Eli. "Look, I pursued her. I love her, Eli. I've been in love with her for a long time. She did nothing wrong."

"Spare me the *falling on your heroic sword* bullshit. She knew. She knew exactly what she was doing. You think she loves you?" Eli laughed, crossing his arms. "I know this woman. Ask her what your name is in her phone. You might be blinded by infatuation and lust, but I *know* her better than anyone." He turned his gaze back to Sam. "Tell him the truth, Sam. Do you love him?"

Garrett and Eli were both looking at her now. She steadied herself on the smooth surface of the butcher block. Last night Garrett had bent her over this counter.

She squeezed her eyes shut, her traitorous memories making it impossible to think. Love. Did she love Garrett? Their relationship was so new that she had barely gotten beyond want. She wasn't ready to tell Garrett she loved him. Not when she knew how he felt about her. It wouldn't be fair to him, even if it hurt him now.

She didn't want to hurt either of them.

She lifted her chin. "I need him, Eli."

Watching two men she cared about flinch at her words felt like an out-of-body experience. Despite her best efforts, she could read it clearly enough: she'd hurt them both. Garrett did a better job of hiding his hurt. But he had years of practice with hiding his emotions.

Eli took a step back. His eyes darkened with pain. "You knew I loved her."

Garrett cleared his throat. "You said you wanted her to be happy."

"I didn't mean with you!" Eli exploded. He was the shorter man, but he stepped forward menacingly. "And don't you dare take what I said to you in confidence, because of our friendship, as a good excuse to stab me in the back."

When neither of them responded, Eli ran his hand through his hair. "Even if . . . even if you somehow thought I was completely done, that should have been enough to stop things last night when I returned and pro—" He choked on the word and covered his mouth as though it made him ill to think about it.

It would have been easier to defend . . . if Garrett hadn't said the same thing last night. They had crossed that line when they'd first slept together at the cabin, but last night . . . even after she'd told Garrett. . . even after he'd told her what a horrible position it put him in, they'd let it happen.

She'd been angry with Eli for so long that it had been difficult to think of him without resentment. But she'd also loved him for most of her adult life.

Before Rachel had dropped her off the night before, she'd cautioned Sam, told her not to come. But Sam had been determined. When Eli had proposed, the only thing she could think about was Garrett. She wanted to tell him, wanted him to tell her it would be all right.

But he hadn't done that.

Because it wasn't all right. It would *never* be all right.

No matter how much they wanted to be together, Garrett was the one person it would never be all right for her to be with. And now she'd blown up his friendship with Eli. None of them would ever recover what they'd had before this.

Sam's throat went dry. She approached Garrett and tugged at his fingers. He gave her a sidelong glance, his jaw clenched, his eyes flat. "Can you show me where the dryer is?"

Garrett held her gaze. His eyes darted to Eli, and he nodded. "This way."

As they walked through the kitchen, Sam saw a bowl of pancake batter mixed by the stove. A carton of eggs was open beside it. Things that Eli must have noticed. Her heart squeezed. No wonder Eli had said they were playing house.

Garrett opened the door to the laundry room, and she followed him in, then shut the door. *What can I possibly say to Garrett to make this hurt less?* To make him hurt less. Because on the inside, Sam was in agony.

He stopped the dryer and pulled her clothes out, handing

them to her. When Garrett finished, he turned and leaned back against the dryer, his hands on the flat top. "It's all over with us, isn't it?"

The truth hurt more than she even understood, but she nodded. *Why does this hurt ten times more than when I found out Eli went on that date with another woman? How am I once again alone?*

Holding back tears, she leaned forward and slid her arms around his waist. She rested her cheek on his chest, squeezing her eyes shut. No matter how much she wanted to stay, she had to force herself to walk through that door.

Garrett cradled the back of her head, the other hand resting on her upper back. Tears burned in her eyes and slipped onto his skin. The soapy scent of laundry detergent and dryer sheets hung in the air—a scent she decided she'd probably hate in the future. She listened to his quiet, steady heartbeat for a moment longer, then pulled back and wiped her eyes. "I'm sorry, Garrett," she whispered.

His eyes were red, his jaw clenched. He closed his eyes and rubbed them, then met her gaze again. "I may be an idiot for saying this, but the last day with you . . . was the best day of my life. And if I had to do it all again for one day, knowing what I know now, I would do it all over again. Please, Sam. You don't have to leave. I know you're scared, but you don't have to be. I'm right here."

She stared at the clothing in her hands. She couldn't let him hope. Couldn't leave things unfinished. He'd been better to her than she could ever possibly be to him. "I'm not coming back this time."

"I thought you might say that." He straightened. "Listen, for what it's worth, you can still use my house for the shoot. I know it might be awkward but keeping your job is more important. I'll just make myself scarce on the days you're shooting."

Regret consumed her, her heart and body both at desperate war with her mind. *Don't go.* But she couldn't stay. "I can't do that. I don't deserve that much from you."

Garrett cupped her face, then kissed her forehead with a kiss so gentle and feather-soft that it must have taken every ounce of his restraint to make it so. "You deserve *everything* good. But you're going to have to choose it." His hands dropped to his sides, he stepped away and left her there. Alone.

Bracing her hands against the cold, hard metal of the washing machine, tears fell down her cheeks, and her body trembled. *Please come back.* She stared at the closed door. Garrett was right there, just like he'd said.

But so was Eli.

And there was no way to love one without hurting the other.

CHAPTER TWENTY-THREE

THE GENTLE TAP on the door to Sam's bedroom preceded the squeak of the hinge. She rolled over in the bed as Laura popped her head in. "Can I come in?"

Sam curled her knees up and replaced the blanket she'd been wearing. The chill she'd been walking around with didn't seem to want to leave her, no matter how many layers she wore.

Even though she hadn't answered, Laura came in, closing the door with a soft click. "Where's Charlotte?" Sam asked. She'd gotten used to seeing Laura with the infant in her ring sling.

"Downstairs with Mom." Laura sat on the foot of Sam's bed. "You planning on getting up soon? I feel bad for Rachel. She's doing her best to field phone calls from your boss and handle everything, but she's clearly stressed."

Sam closed her eyes. The numbness enclosing her was beginning to fray with every word Laura spoke. "It's been two days, Sam. You can't stay here forever. Not to mention, Mom thinks it's her fault. She doesn't deserve that."

Two days. Two days of lying in bed. It felt like two lifetimes—the longest days of her life. She'd cried and slept and cried some more. Scrolled mindlessly through her phone on do not disturb mode. Ignored every message except Rachel's. And that was only because it was unfair to Rachel. She'd left her stuck in her mother's house and her terrible hometown and hadn't looked back.

Selfish. That was what she was, right? Self-righteous. Hypocritical. Hypercritical.

She'd even tried to do an online meeting with Sylvia. Sylvia had gotten three minutes in before Sam couldn't take it anymore. She'd left the meeting and blocked future calls.

Face pressed to her pillow, she ignored Laura's question and stared at the wall. Her mother had never changed her room since college, but she'd never let her decorate it the way most teenagers did. Her posters were of incredible landscapes and wildlife. Another dream she'd burned to the ground.

Laura ran her hands over the floral quilt that served as the bedspread in the room. "Do you want to talk about it?"

"Not really." Not with Laura, anyway.

"Katie's popped in like four times. Want me to call her to come over? Talk to someone."

A bitter laugh left her. "Talk to Katie about Garrett? You must be joking." She didn't know what made her feel worse: that her best friend cared enough to come and check on her even when Sam had ignored her messages or that what she was upset about would hurt Katie badly if she knew.

"Yeah, well, she thinks this is all about Eli's proposal. He's still in town. Everyone knows about that part of it. Katie keeps texting me, but I haven't answered."

She had no idea how to face Katie. If Katie was still talking to her, it meant Eli hadn't said anything. *Thank God for that.* And she had to tell Katie. This wasn't something she could hide and hope to keep her friendship with Katie. Katie deserved to know the truth. She'd been a good friend to Sam over the years.

Laura pressed her lips together. She lay back, staring at the ceiling. "Are you in love with him?"

"Eli?"

"No. Garrett."

Sam rubbed her eyelids and propped herself up on one elbow. Her head was throbbing with a headache, the base of her skull feeling as though something grasped it in a tight vise. "What difference does it make? We can't be together."

Laura didn't answer. She rubbed her midsection as though the incision hurt, then dropped her hand to the quilt. "Sam, let things go. You're not the only one in life who has made mistakes. And definitely not the only one who questions whether you're where you should be. You think I've never wondered what my life would have been like if I had left Brandywood and gone out exploring my dreams?"

Sam's throat tightened, feeling raw. "But you have Mark. And three kids. That was your dream."

"One of them. Not all of them." Laura sat and faced her. Sighing, she took Sam's hand. "I've been hard on you a lot. But there's a part of me that always wished I had the chance to see life the way you did. And in the end, it's sort of like that butterfly effect. If I had changed one thing, I might not have had my family. So I have to accept I made the best decisions with the knowledge I had—and the things I have in my life now make those decisions worth it, even if I lost out on other things I'll never know about."

"I'm sure your family would love to know they're a great consolation prize."

Laura's eyes darkened. "You see? That's the problem. You always choose the worst way to think about it. It's like the whole thing with Mom. Rather than listening to her and understanding that her mistakes, however terrible they were, still gave her a life she wouldn't trade, you just focused on how those mistakes made your life harder. How she ruined things for you. But guess what, Sam? You wouldn't even be here if she hadn't made those mistakes."

Sam purposely kept her gaze even, her expression blank. Laura had always thought the worst of her, probably more than most. How dare she try now to act like she cared?

Laura sighed and stood. "I don't know why I ever try with you. You will always just think about how things are affecting you." She turned to go.

Self-saboteur. Why did she keep lying to herself? She didn't want Laura to go. She wanted Laura to care.

Sam sat up in the bed. "Why didn't you ever tell me about Dan and Warren?"

Laura crossed her arms. "Because you weren't ready to hear it. I'm still not sure you should have been told. Look how you reacted."

"You should have told me." Sam tugged at the knots in her hair, then wrinkled her nose. She needed a shower.

Laura let out a slow, exaggerated sigh. "Yes, because you've handled it so well. You ran out on your dying mom and refused to talk to her, then you decided to sleep with your boyfriend's best friend. When that blows up, you stay in bed ignoring everyone and everything, including the job you've coveted for so long above everything else."

If Laura was trying to make her feel better, she was failing miserably. She had the right to be angry with Sam. Laura would never choose to sugarcoat anything. She'd had this conversation with Sylvia a dozen times, who had coached her on strategies to deal with her family when they criticized her for valid points.

"He's not my boyfriend—"

"For all intents and purposes." Laura rolled her eyes. "Don't worry, I'm not just blaming you. Garrett should have stayed far, far away. But that's beside the point. Sam, can you imagine if you'd heard about it before? You never would have come back home. Ever. Believe it or not, many people in this town care about you. And not just Mom and me. Wherever I go, people ask me how you're doing. When you're coming home."

"None of that is an excuse, though, Laura. You *should* have told me. I had a right to know about Dad. About Dan and Warren. Do you have any idea how much it changes everything?"

Laura's face twisted, tears brimming in her eyes. "Maybe you're right. But neither Mom nor I wanted to lose you. Push you further away. It's been hard enough feeling like you never wanted to be here. It's also not the easiest thing to know when to tell someone, you know? I found out in middle school, and it damn near crushed me. I wanted to protect you from what I felt —and the years kept passing, and it went from when to tell you to, oh crap, is it too late to tell her?"

Sam got up. "Well, it doesn't matter anymore. Me finding out the way I did was a day late and a dollar short—or whatever the saying is."

Frustration crossed Laura's face. "We're all people, Sam. People who make mistakes. You don't have it right about Mom or me or anyone, really. Case in point. Until recently, didn't you think Garrett was an asshole? You all were barely friends. You were wrong about him, weren't you? Don't you think there's a chance you could be wrong about everyone else?"

Laura's comment made Sam's lips curl with nervous laughter. "I don't think everyone else wants to sleep with me."

Laura smirked, and the tension between them eased. "You

never know. All this time, the whole town has just been in love with you."

Sam held the sleeves of her sweater between her palms and her fingers. Laura had a point, though. She'd been so wrong about a lot of things, including her own family history.

She sat back on her heels in the middle of the floor on a small rug she'd woven on a kid's loom as a child. Covering her face, she struggled for composure. Her head pounded. She needed a painkiller. Or food. Or water. And absolutely, definitely coffee. Her headache was probably mostly because of caffeine withdrawal. "I miss him," she whispered.

Laura shuffled over and stood in front of her. "I can't bend over and give you the hug you need because it's not good for my incision. Can you meet me halfway?"

Sam laughed lightly again and stood, hugging her sister. *Her big sister.* Laura never seemed to need her as a kid. But she'd been more aware of everything. She'd gone through the same things, maybe even more painfully. The way she'd found out about their parents had been far worse.

She wanted to stay mad at Laura for not telling her, but Laura had suffered just as much as she had.

Sam wiped her eyes and stepped back. "You know what the truth is? With all the crap I've been dealing with, I feel it could have been a lot easier if things hadn't blown up with Garrett. I know it's stupid, given we were barely together."

"It's not stupid. Well"—Laura shook her head with a sarcastic laugh—"it's a little stupid. Not for you to miss him. But to think there wouldn't be any consequences. Have you talked to Eli? At all?"

"No, but I know I have to. I just have some things to tell him that won't be easy. I can't go backward. Not with Eli. I've known for a while that things weren't working with him. They were never going to work." Sam fidgeted with her ring. "I never told you, but I tried to get back together with Eli in February. But he cheated on me, and we got into a huge fight."

Laura stared at Sam quietly. Her eyes took on a shiny appearance, and she blinked tears away. "Sam, you should have told me. God . . . I'm so sorry."

Her sympathy took her by surprise. "I didn't want you to hate him for it in case we ever got back together. Because even after that, I still wasn't ready to let go."

"No, I get it, but this is the sort of thing you tell the people who love you. Especially so they stop pushing you toward a cheating bastard."

Sam smiled tearfully and hugged her again. Sharing that part of her life with Laura felt freeing. "And thank you."

"For what? Making you feel like crap?" Laura raised her brows. "I'm the one that should be apologizing."

Sam sniffed. "No, for being understanding about everything. I was so embarrassed to tell you about Eli. You probably think I'm an idiot for not cutting him off completely after that."

"Oh, honey." Laura held her shoulders. "If you think you're the only person in the wrong relationship, you are quite wrong. In fact, it might be a good starting point for you to talk to Mom." Laura squinted and made a face. "And, unlucky for Mom, Dad married her. Though, as I said, if he hadn't, I wouldn't have a sister, so I can't exactly hate him."

Unlucky indeed. Mom and Laura would probably have been better off if her father had stayed with Betty Klein. Sam wrinkled her nose. "It's so weird for me to think of us having brothers. Have . . . have you ever talked to either of them about it?"

"Actually, yes. Warren Klein and his wife are nice to me. Their son is in Bella's kindergarten class, so earlier this year, Warren called us over for dinner. He said he wanted to introduce the kids to each other as cousins. Start on a better path." Laura toyed with an earring. "Dan is another matter, though."

"Dan always was the worse brother." Across from them, the floor-length oval mirror showed their reflections. "Funny how neither of us really look like them."

Laura shrugged. "Not that weird. We're half-Venezuelan. And their mom is so blond." Reaching over, Laura took Sam's hand. "But are you ready to talk to Mom about it? I think there's a lot Mom would like to tell you."

No. Sam drew a deep breath. "I'm pretty mad at her, Laura."

"I get it. And you have a right to be. But, Sam, she's dying. She doesn't have long. And even though you're angry, there's no way to make up with her once she's gone. I just don't want to see you live with regret. Talking to her might give you a chance to ask some questions. Questions you probably want to be answered before it's not a possibility."

Sam stared at the floorboards.

Sylvia's smoky voice sounded in her ears, and Sam closed her eyes, reliving the moment in her office. *"Do you want to know what anger is?"*

"What?" Sam set her hand on the flat space below her belly button. *She was angry. Angry with Eli.*

Angry with herself.

She'd stayed with a guy all this time, for what?

To have him toss her to the side?

"Anger is an acid that can do more harm to the vessel in which it is stored than to anything on which it is poured." Sylvia pointed at a framed quote beside her couch. *"Mark Twain."*

Sam swallowed the lump in her throat, then looked at Laura, who stood there quietly. Sylvia was right. Anger was eating at her heart, destroying her.

She didn't want to be angry anymore.

She didn't want to lose the last few months with Mom. Tears rolled down her cheeks. "She's really dying, isn't she?"

Laura nodded, her own eyes reddening. "She's really dying."

"I know I've been wrapped up in my own things, and I'm sorry. You all are important to me. I love you so much."

"I know you do." Laura wrapped her arm around her shoulder. "It's about time you just let us love you the way we all want to, Sam. We don't bite. Well, maybe Carson. But the rest of us. Not so much."

Sam pushed a strand of hair behind her ear. "I know."

They left the room together and headed downstairs. No sooner had they reached the bottom than Rachel poked her head in from the kitchen. "Oh, thank God. You've left the bedroom." She scrambled over, holding a laptop and a phone. "Maren will have my head if I don't give her a schedule for this thing. Your head, actually. But I told her your head is busy getting everything ready at the location, and it has terrible cell service, so you'll have to call her back."

"I'm the worst." Sam gave her a one-eyed squint, feeling as though she'd just woken up and her eyes were too sensitive to the light. She shifted. "Problem is, I still don't have a schedule."

Rachel blanched. "Doesn't the shoot start in a couple of days?"

"Yeah, I've been just putting things off and . . ." Sam pulled a hair elastic from her wrist and threw her hair into a messy ponytail. She straightened, watching Laura as she continued toward the living room. Bella and Carson watched cartoons on the television there while Charlotte snuggled in Mom's arms.

Sam swallowed, looking at the quiet scene. She'd been here for weeks, but how often had she stopped to play with her niece or nephew? Or sit and have breakfast with Mom?

Or just talk on the couch?

When had she become so self-absorbed?

Sure, she'd helped at the cabins, but out of obligation, not love. And she'd ignored her family. *How do I make this better?*

Squaring her shoulders, Sam looked back at Rachel, who still awaited a response. "Let's face the facts, Rach: I've failed. I can't get this thing together."

Rachel scanned her face, her eyes darting back and forth wildly. "Sam, you'll lose your job. I'll probably lose my job. Neither of us can afford to be out of a job at Christmas."

"Maren will know you had nothing to do with it. I'll make sure of it." Still, the panic on Rachel's face made her cringe.

"I-if you don't feel like shooting, I can try." Rachel looked like she was going to cry.

Sam looked across the room again and caught Mom and Laura sneaking a look. Her stomach soured, a combination of stress and hunger making her feel sick. "I don't know what I'm doing. Or how to get it together right now."

"I can call a few of my friends," Mom said. She approached, resting the baby against her shoulder. "See who can pitch in to help. What do you need?"

"Everything." The pain in Mom's voice twisted her gut. Sam met her mother's gaze, feeling awful that she hadn't talked to her until now. "I need a schedule, and I need to buy ingredients. To store ingredients. There's no way everything we need will fit in Garrett's fridge. Lodging for the crew. Make sure the Wi-Fi at Garrett's can handle everything."

Laura joined them. "Most of my friends are fellow moms who will tell you they want to do something with lots of enthusiasm but then secretly hope a blizzard comes through that day so they can cancel. But they have good hearts and will pull through when you need them. They'll help."

Rachel laughed. "That's not just moms. Introverts are

united on that one. I have a complete list of pre-made excuses for why I have to cancel plans."

The four women stood there with silence between them.

"Didn't your friend Katie say she was going to ask that Bunny lady about borrowing her fridge?" Rachel asked hopefully. She fished her phone out. "I'll call her. She texted me her number. See if she's made any progress." Rachel darted back to the kitchen.

Sam watched her. "Is it bad of me to feel some relief if this whole project falls apart?" she asked Mom quietly. "A new job wouldn't be the worst thing on the planet."

"Is that what you want?" Mom pressed a kiss to Charlotte's cheek.

Charlotte slumbered peacefully, her pink eyelids firmly closed, her little mouth open.

Sam's throat hurt without warning and caught her off guard. She covered her mouth with her palm, then leaned back against the wall. *Breathe.*

"What I want is—" Tears poured from Sam's eyes. "What . . . I-I want, if I have kids someday, is for them to have a grandmother. I don't want pictures. I don't want just stories. I want you, Mom. To be here. I want you to fight." *Mom, I don't want to lose you. How can I fathom a world you're not in? Please don't leave me.*

Laura whisked Charlotte from Mom's arms. Mom turned to Sam, slipping her arms around her as Sam wept brokenly.

For the past few weeks, she'd done her best to put these thoughts far from her mind.

Focusing on Eli and Garrett and even the stress of her goddamn job had been so much easier than this.

Her mother was dying. She had . . . what? Weeks? Months? A year?

And then what? Would she be able to walk in the end?

How would it go?

She reached through the darkness of her mind, groping for something to hold on to. Mom's arms only drew tighter.

Sam cried on the shoulder Charlotte had just occupied. The scent of new baby and warmth lingered there. *Life.* "Pp-please tell me you're not choosing this path because you still think you deserve punishment." Sam lifted her face, searching Mom's peaceful face. Mom's eyes held sadness, but not the desperation Sam felt.

She knew she was dying.

And she had accepted it. The look in Mom's eyes told Sam she didn't want to die. She loved them. Loved her grandkids.

"Of course not, sweetheart. Of course not. I just—" Mom pressed a kiss to her forehead. "The things from my past were things I wanted you to hear from me. But this is a separate issue. I'm just too sick. There's no cure, only treatment. And I'm going to do some of it. But I don't know how long I can take it. Right now, the pain is sometimes so bad I can barely sleep. The worse it gets, the more it consumes me. Who knows how I'll be? I don't want that to be all you remember about me. *Una muerte miserable.* That's not the way I want things to be."

It would be a miserable death. *God, this is so unfair.*

Sam gripped her hands. "But if you had more time . . . if I had more time with you. We could see all the places you've always wanted to go to. I thought I'd have more time with you, Mom."

"We've had all the time we were meant to have. Let's not waste any more of it, okay?" She dipped her forehead against Sam's.

With her forehead still touching her mother's, Sam nodded tearfully.

"Good. Now let's figure out how to keep your job. Because

I don't want you losing the things you've worked so hard to build."

Rachel came running from the hallway again. "Katie has news. She says Bunny might help with the kitchen for a mention on social feeds. She's talking to her."

Laura shot Sam a look. "You know, if you get Bunny on board, there's a good chance you can get other people to help with this thing. Particularly Peter Yardley. He'll want the same sort of exposure for his business as Bunny gets."

Sam dried her eyes with the backs of her hands. "Do you really think people will help me? I've been such a snob for so long."

Mom put her hands on her hips. Sam tried not to focus on the odd pear shape her slender mother had taken on recently in her abdomen. "Get your coat. It sounds like it's about time for you to go back into town." She grinned at Sam wryly. "Hope you like feathers."

"Feathers?" Sam glanced at her reflection in the hallway mirror. She looked like an absolute wreck. No way she could go into town like this. "I need a shower first."

"Sometimes, the only way to get that pesky past to leave you alone is to eat some crow." Mom pinched her cheek in the way she would do with Bella or Carson. "Go take that shower quick, and then we'll go. I'll be right there with you. And, *mi hijita*—you're going to be just fine. Because you're not alone. And you never have been. It's time you let the town of Brandywood prove it to you."

CHAPTER TWENTY-FOUR

"I'M DONE with the wiring on that TV unit. Did you have time to see it? It's pretty cool."

Luis's voice sounded distant, and Garrett blinked, his brain feeling like it slogged to catch up. Squeezing his eyes shut, he heard his pulse in his ears. That headache. *Christ.*

"You okay, man?"

Garrett stumbled back. *Where the hell had Luis come from?* He stood beside Garrett, only a few feet away, a divot between his thick eyebrows. Garrett shook his head as though to clear it. "Yeah. Headache."

Luis's frown only deepened. "That woman really messed you up, didn't she?"

"It's fine." He didn't want to talk about her. Didn't want to think about her. As it was, he'd been thinking about her without pause since she'd walked out of his house. Her assistant had called to plan to use his house as the shooting location tomorrow. And now he dreaded the prospect.

What had Luis said before? An eyelash was stuck between

his lower lid and the corner of his eye. The drinking in the morning was a development. And for the first time, he barely felt the effect of the alcohol. "What were you telling me?"

The look Luis gave him made it clear he was worried. Still, he pulled his phone from his back pocket. "Follow me to the living room. The TV, it's pretty cool."

Garrett wiped the paint from his hands with a rag. The attic room was almost done—he just needed to paint the trim. Luis wasn't the best detail painter, so he'd had him doing odd jobs while Dean and Gus finished the master bathroom. Even when this happened with other jobs, though, Luis rarely turned up so often to chat. Garrett couldn't help thinking Luis was checking up on him.

A sharp, incessant noise rang in his eardrums as he made his way down the stairs, gripping the rails of the attic stairs. He didn't feel steady, but Luis didn't need to know.

They went down another flight of stairs into the living room. Luis picked up the remote for the TV he'd just hung on the wall. "Check it out. When you're not watching it—it looks like a framed piece of art." He flipped through the images on the home screen and settled on one of a tree. The television screen took on a matte appearance, adjusting to the ambient light.

Garrett lifted a brow at Luis, who looked at the television with a big grin. He rolled his eyes and pulled out his cell phone. "Check it out. I have a five-inch device in my hands that can access the world's collection of music, books, movies, and works as a flashlight and tape measure."

"Man, nothing impresses you." Luis pursed his lips. "You disappoint me."

Garrett laughed and glanced at his phone. "That's because I've known about TVs like that forever. You need to get out more often. And look"—he pressed the screen mirroring button on his phone. It connected to the television immediately—"now my device can control yours."

"Oh, piss off."

Garrett disconnected his phone and walked off with a chuckle when the front door to the house opened. Trisha and Joe entered with their children in tow. Garrett had kept his head down and gone out of his way to never be alone with her, but his eyes darted to her briefly now. She was wearing actual clothes this time.

Trisha flinched. Not a trace of flirtation or sultriness. *But some sadness?*

"Hey, Mr. Sanders. I got your television working. Come look at this." Luis waved him over.

The kids immediately started hopping around Luis and their father, asking to watch television. "Hold on now. Let me see how this thing works," Joe told his kids.

Then Garrett was out of earshot. He started up the stairs when he heard footsteps behind him. Trisha tugged him into the mudroom, right off the main stairwell, and shut the door.

"Why have you been avoiding me?" Trisha's voice was an anxious whisper.

Garrett's gaze drifted through the small, brightly lit room. A glass outside door highlighted the cubbies set up for Trisha's grade school children. Beside them, the washer and dryer looked sparkling clean, as though she had never even used them. The entire house was picture perfect.

A bored housewife who didn't seem to realize how good she had it.

Garrett's gaze narrowed at the laundry machines and something about them made his heart squeeze so tight in his chest he could barely breathe. He swallowed, the lingering taste of beer in his mouth bitter.

Sam had dumped him in the laundry room of his own house.

That was what he got from her. A two-minute conversation and an "I'm sorry." No explanation. For all he knew, she was out there now, holding hands with Eli and telling the world about their engagement.

As though everything between them meant nothing to her.

"Garrett? Please say something." Trisha touched his arm. Her eyes were wide and . . . *damn* . . . innocent? Was she really playing innocent right now? While her husband showed the kids the new television just a few feet away? She took advantage of the distraction and excitement to use it for her own game.

All the anger he'd been holding back, all the fury rose like a snarling beast inside him. He wanted to punish her. Prove he could best her at this ridiculous game for once and for all. Take control.

He turned a few steps away toward the door, taking the phone out of his pocket. Pressing the screen mirroring button, he watched the icon turn, then turned on the screen recorder. He slipped the phone back into the front pocket of his jeans, far enough down so it wasn't obviously sticking out of his pants, but so the camera was uncovered.

He faced Trisha once more. "What is it you want me to say?"

She crossed her arms. "You've been avoiding me all week."

She didn't seem to notice his phone. *Good.* "Avoiding you? Excuse me? You mean, getting my work done. The work you hired me for. I'm not interested in whatever you're offering here if you need me to be clearer."

Her eyes narrowed. "You're not interested in sex?"

Despite everything, his heart was pounding in his chest. "Not with you, no, thank you, ma'am."

She snorted. "Yeah. Right. I saw the way you kissed that woman at the tree farm. Your message was loud and clear."

Garrett blinked rapidly. *If the message you got was that I wanted you, it was obviously anything but clear.* He picked his words as carefully as he could. "Trisha, no matter how many times you throw yourself at me, I won't sleep with you."

Her lower lip pouted. "I can't believe you'd reject me like this. No one has ever turned me down be—"

The words didn't finish coming out of her mouth. Joe Sanders threw open the door to the mudroom, his face purple with rage. "What the fuck have you been up to, Trisha?" He grabbed her by the collar, twisting her shirt.

Joe slammed Trisha against the washing machine, and she cried out as her pearl necklace broke. Pearls scattered onto the floor, clinking and rolling. Tears streaked her face, and her eyes filled with fear as Joe lifted his hand to slap her.

Garrett caught his hand. "Settle down," he warned, digging his fingers into Joe's wrist. Trisha dove behind Garrett, and he felt as though he was falling.

"Get the hell out of my house." Joe spat in Garrett's face, and it landed on his cheek, dripping slowly onto Garrett's shirt. He stepped forward menacingly. "Before I beat your ass. And hers."

His threat only made Garrett step closer, his chest heaving. "Luis," he called out. "Call the cops!"

"No! Stop!" Trisha pushed between the two men. She turned pleading eyes toward Garrett. "No. No . . . don't call the cops. Please don't. He's sorry. He just lost his temper. It's my fault. I shouldn't have." She turned and hugged her husband, tears on her face. "I'm so sorry, baby. I'm so sorry. It's all my fault. You didn't hurt me."

"Get out of my house," Joe said to Garrett again, his eyes still blazing with fury, his hand wrapped tightly around his wife's neck.

Fuck. Me.

For the first time, Garrett really noticed Trisha. The faint bruises on her arms, on her cheek—covered by makeup. "Do you want me to leave you with him?" Garrett asked.

"Yes, please. Leave. And don't call the cops. I'll tell them nothing happened. It's a waste of time to involve them." Trisha wiped her face and turned back to Joe, running her fingers over his face soothingly. "I'm so sorry. I didn't mean to make you so angry."

Garrett turned the screen mirroring function off.

Luis was in the doorway now. Garrett filed past Joe and Trisha. "I'm calling the police," he said to Luis. "Don't you dare leave this woman alone with that man. I'll be outside in the truck waiting for the cops to show up."

He moved into the living room. Two of the children watched television calmly as though nothing had happened. The third, a little boy about five years old, hid behind the couch, his head buried in his arms.

Garrett stared at them. He wanted to feel nothing. He wanted to feel everything.

But he was numb.

Ordering his legs back into motion, he moved out into the cold, out into the truck. The soft clink of glass greeted his ears, and he glanced at the door. A few empty beer bottles sat there.

When had he started accumulating these in his truck?

He sank into his seat. His hands covered his face. The little boy, hiding behind the couch. The other two kids.

So used to it they didn't even blink.

I'll tell them nothing happened. Trisha's voice echoed in his mind, his pulse loud in his ears. He squeezed his eyes shut.

"You stupid, lazy bitch. You think I deserve a burned dinner? I work hard, bitch. Is it too much to ask for a good dinner when I get home?"

"Honey, I didn't do it on purpose. That oven thermostat has been off, I've been telling you—"

"Now it's my fault? When the fuck am I supposed to have the time for it, Becky? You sit all day at home on your ass. I'd like to see you spending a day carrying bags of concrete like I did today. When's my break?" The lasagna pan crashed into the sink, the sound of glass breaking.

Slap.

Garrett scrambled from the pantry, where he'd been hiding, his hand in a fist. He slammed it against his father's thigh. *"Don't hit Mommy!"*

"Fuck the hell off, Garrett." His father grabbed him by the collar and slammed him into the nearest cabinet. The room spun.

"Bruce, no. Don't touch him." His mother dove for him, but his father pushed her away.

His father loomed over him, his eyes blazing.

"He's my son. He needs to show some respect. Tough guy, huh? You're a fucking coward, Garrett. Not brave enough, not strong enough, and sure as hell not smart enough. Weak. Just like your stupid mother."

Slap.

How many times would he see those reminders of what his mother had endured because of alcohol? How many times had he wished his mother had fought for her safety and that of her children?

You're not strong enough.

Garrett shuddered. But Mom hadn't been a coward. Because his father had been a monster. Dad was the coward.

You're such a fucking coward, Garrett. You couldn't have told me to my face? Instead, you just walked out on me. Left me to handle all the humiliation.

He couldn't remember every text Katie had sent after he'd broken up with her. But he remembered that one.

You coward, Garrett.

When things got tough, you couldn't fight for Sam. She's terrified. She runs. And you just let her walk right out that door.

Cowards come in many forms, Doyle.

He pulled out his phone and stared at the screen. The day after Sam had left, he'd gotten so drunk he'd woken up in the shower lying in his vomit. The screen of his phone was cracked from slamming it at some point that day.

Nothing happened.

How much had he had to drink today?

Nothing.

Not nothing.

He couldn't remember.

He was in control. He could control this. Just like he could control . . .

Nothing. You can't control anything, Garrett. Especially not how you feel about Sam. Or how she feels about you.

He rubbed his jaw with his open palm, his skull pounding. That trick with the screen mirroring. Impressive. "You're so fucking brilliant." The scornfulness of his words dripped as he slammed his hand into the steering wheel.

His hands shook. He stared at them, turning them over until they were palm up. Not steady. Not collected. Not in control.

Shaking.

He called the cops. She might say Joe had done nothing, but maybe she wouldn't. Perhaps she'd find her voice.

He knew the chances were slim.

He knew.

The beer. The whiskey. The headache. *The pain.*

And nothing was numbing it.

He picked up the phone and dialed.

"Mom?" He closed his eyes, slumping back against his seat. He bowed his head.

"I need some help."

CHAPTER TWENTY-FIVE

"... and then I take the cookie and roll it in the egg white, like this..."

Sam stood in the corner of Garrett's kitchen, watching as Mom baked her favorite cookie recipe—raspberry thumbprints—in front of the camera crew. How many memories did she have of baking these with her mom in high school? She'd never come back home to bake Christmas cookies since then.

"Your mom is a natural," Maren whispered beside Sam, breaking the spell.

Sam nodded without taking her eyes off her mom as she rolled the cookie in chopped walnuts. One crew member turned and threw Maren a warning glare, and Maren shrugged her shoulders apologetically with a smirk.

Maren had flown down the day before to host the campaign and play the role of sidekick. Without camera experience, the home bakers needed the guidance of someone with as much camera experience as Maren had. Her timing in delaying her arrival had been fortunate, though—Sam had just settled the line-up for the campaign. Laura had been right: once Bunny had agreed to it, the whole town came together in force to help her. There even seemed to be excitement in the town for the project. Garrett's house had become an unofficial center of activity, with people milling around.

Some people in town even sat in the living room to watch the filming—including Eli. While Sam hadn't been paying attention, he'd slipped in earlier with a bouquet of red roses in his hands.

His presence weighed heavily on Sam's mind. He sat in the living room with the other people who'd chosen to stay, silent and attentive. But each time she looked at him, she couldn't help thinking about the last time they'd talked, in this very kitchen.

Memories of Garrett were impossible to escape here. Rachel had done her the favor of handling all the arrangements with him, but part of her still hoped he'd turn up at some point. Not while Eli was around, though. She didn't need a repeat of the last time.

As though that was even a possibility. That would involve her being here with Garrett first. And being happy. The memory of how he'd thrown her over his shoulder was a bitter-sweet one.

God, she missed him.

A lump formed in her throat, and she mouthed, "Excuse me," to Maren. Maren nodded firmly and continued watching. Sam's part wouldn't really come until everything was baked anyway. That was when she'd finally get a camera in her hands for what seemed like the first time in forever.

Tiptoeing from the kitchen, Sam went into the living room. Her movement wasn't unnoticed. Eli lifted a brow at her.

Giving him a tense smile, she continued past the living

room to the garage door. The garage itself was open, and Peter Yardley had taken it upon himself to bring a keg of hard cider and cream of crab soup for the crew, setting up a lunch station there. Bunny would turn up with treats for them all when she found out.

Peter's wrinkled face broke into a smile under his wool hat. "Cider?" he asked, his voice booming.

Sam gritted her teeth, closing the door quickly behind her, and lifted a finger to her lips. "They're still filming," she whispered. She came closer to him. "I'm all right for now. But I will take you up on that crab soup. I'm going for a walk. Get to know the outside of Garrett's house a bit."

"You know, I was talking with Walter Baxter next door." Peter nodded toward the neighbor's house. "He seems to think you might already be acquainted with Garrett's house. Says there was a lot of yelling going on over here a few mornings ago."

Sam felt the color drain from her face. She looked to see who might be milling about, but no one else was outside with them. *Thank God.* "I don't know what you're talking about," she managed, stepping closer to him.

Peter gave a loud, rousing laugh, then ducked his red face as he realized his volume. "Don't worry, girlie, I won't tell anyone. I told Walter to put a lid on it too. But I must admit, I'm disappointed you picked the Hollywood kid over Doyle."

She set her hands on her hips. "Who says I picked anyone?"

Peter ladled a paper cup of cream of crab soup for her, then wiped his hand on his apron. He came out from behind the table and handed it to her with a plastic spoon. "Says the poor sap who's been drowning his sorrows at my bar—or at least, was. Didn't see him last night."

Sam thanked him for the soup and took it. It steamed in the

frosty air but warmed her hands through the cup. "Garrett's been drinking again?" The thought made her stomach churn.

"Worries me too. Kid looks so much like his dad used to—it's like a bad flashback." Peter shook his head. "I cut him off occasionally, but I have never seen him like this. That boy has always had a thing for you, you know." He sank into a camping chair in the garage, the seat squeaking, the canvas stretching under his weight.

Sam sat in the empty seat beside him. "I know. He told me." She took a spoonful of soup and closed her eyes, relishing the soft hint of sherry. She could get many good things in New York, but no place in the world knew crab like Maryland.

Studying her profile, Peter nodded slowly. "Good for him. He finally did it, eh? I was hoping he would get around to it. That's why I sent Mike Jarvis packing that one night."

Sam's jaw dropped. She inspected Peter's sparkling blue eyes and his round face. "Sent Mike Jarvis packing?"

Peter grinned widely. "Yeah, sorry about that. I saw Garrett at the bar that night, and then who should show up to make him even more miserable than the girl of his dreams to go on a date with Mr. December? I cut Mike off at the door and told him to go home. Leave you alone."

She continued to stare with an open mouth. "You . . . Peter. I felt horrible at being stood up."

"Did you?" Peter's eyes glinted. "Heard you walked Garrett home that night."

"But I didn't stay—" She didn't know what was more absurd. That she should be talking about her love life with an eighty-year-old man or that he was interfering in it. She swallowed a few more spoonfuls. "Does anyone else know?"

"A few of the fellows at the lodge. Garrett has done a lot of handiwork for us as we've all gotten too old to climb ladders. They're all rooting for him. Don't worry, we're trying to keep it from spreading too far. Had to make Brian not breathe a word of it to his wife. If that woman finds out, everyone in town will."

Sam felt the urge to find whoever "Brian" was and shake him by the shoulders until he promised her as well. Mom always said that gossipy old men could spread news faster than a group of middle school girls. *Turns out she was correct.*

Before she could stress to Peter just how important it was for him to keep silent, the garage door opened again.

"Hard cider?" Peter perked his head up, nearly shouting. The words echoed from the garage walls.

Eli slipped out and closed the door as quickly. "You may need to end up having to make this a closed set," he told Sam with a laugh. He took a red plastic cup from the table and filled it with cider from the keg. "Thanks, Peter."

The older man nodded and stood. "Say hello to your father for me, will you? Didn't see him at the bull roast this year."

"Sure thing. I think he was on a business trip, but you'll probably catch him at the next one." Eli tilted his head toward the driveway. "Can we talk?" he asked Sam.

Sam finished her soup and tossed it in an open trash can. "Sure." She turned to say goodbye to Peter, but he'd already busied himself pulling more food from a warmer bag behind the table.

She trudged from the garage beside Eli. Her conversation with Peter had been unexpected and revealing. Over the past few weeks, the times she'd spent with Garrett had been fairly isolated. But he was a part of this town. And it sounded like Garrett had worked his way back into the good graces of many. Sam hadn't missed Peter's preference for Garrett over Eli. And that his friends were rooting for Garrett. *For me, though? Or for him to find love?*

She shoved her hands into her pockets and looked at Eli.

"Do you ever feel like we made a mistake by leaving Brandywood so young?"

Eli shrugged. "Neither of us was ever going to accomplish our goals here. I miss aspects of small-town life. But everything always stays the same here."

"Does it really, though?" Sam glanced at Garrett's beautiful home. She barely remembered the old farmhouse now. "I always felt that way. Like I was changing, and home was just . . . static. But I think I misjudged everything."

"Is that why you were so quick to run to Garrett?" Eli's voice had a hard tone to it. "Because you think he's changed? That he's not the same sarcastic asshole that left your best friend devastated in the worst way possible? He had his reasons, and they were valid, but it was still a dick move."

Sam stared at her feet. *She* knew why Garrett had put a stop to the wedding and had thought Eli would have applauded his best friend for not leading Katie into an unhappy marriage, even if Eli hadn't known to the full extent.

But she doubted Eli was in the mood to give Garrett credit for anything right now. "You and I both know there are worse ways to be devastated."

Eli's face reddened. "I didn't mean—"

Sam paused, watching the breeze drifting through the brown blades of grass in Garrett's yard. A feeling of desolation seemed to penetrate the gray wintry day. "I'm not trying to bring things down from the shelf. We've both hurt each other over the years, and mostly because neither of us had the courage to look each other in the eye and say it was really, truly over."

Eli turned back to her and gripped her hands. "But I don't want it to be over. It may have taken a lot for me to get here, but I know what I want now, Sam. A future without you would be the worst thing imaginable. I hate that I pushed you so far that you felt like you needed to turn to Garrett, and it's going to take some time to work through that, but I know we can get over this together."

Did he really believe that?

She considered his words. The fights, the aching loneliness, the moments of rage. She'd spiraled into depression and anger that Sylvia had helped her work her way through—but nothing had ever made their relationship work again. Even the change in career had done wonders for her outlook, but not for the way she and Eli functioned together.

She squeezed his hands and let go. "I realized after last Valentine's Day that we would never work, Eli. And not just because you cheated on me. That was a symptom of the fact that we didn't work—not the cause. When I said 'maybe someday' in the summer, what I should have said was no. I knew we were done."

"You . . ." Eli shuffled one foot, kicking a rock from the driveway into the grass. "You didn't think you could tell me?"

"I didn't know how to tell you. How to let go. Not without risking losing everything I thought we had."

Eli's face darkened. "What you thought we had?"

She nodded, knowing her words had cut him.

Eli pointed back at Garrett's house. "And you have that with him?"

Her face flushed. "I-I don't know." She bit her lip. "But it doesn't matter, Eli. Whatever Garrett and I had, it's over. I care about him, and I care about you. But it's not about *who* I care about. It's about the fact that right now, the stress this is bringing me isn't something I need in my life."

"But if we just try—"

She wrapped her arms around his neck, cutting him off. She'd loved Eli most of her life. Not having him there to talk to would be so strange. He knew her better than anyone. "Don't you think ten years is a hell of a lot of trying, Eli? We don't work. I think we both know that. And we've known for a while. It's hard to think of a world where other people are more important, but that's the future."

He stiffened, and she hugged him for a moment longer. Letting him go, she wiped her eyes with the corner of her sleeve sticking out from her coat. A streak of mascara stayed behind on the fabric.

He cleared his throat. "I guess I have a ring to return."

She didn't want to dip into a topic that might bring out more anger, but her guilt pushed her toward it. "Eli, I just want you to know that Garrett didn't pursue me. It just sort of happened. I don't know what it will take for you to forgive him, but I don't want you to lose your friendship because of me."

A tinge of red spread across Eli's neck. "I'm never going to forgive him, Sam. I can't get that image out of my mind—of the two of you together."

"He thought you were over me. And you were willing to forgive me."

"That's different. You're the love of my life. I never should have let you convince me to leave while you were going through all of this. I thought he was my friend—but he's not. Simple as that."

"It's not that simple—"

"It *is*, though. He doesn't get to take advantage of the girl I love while she's upset and vulnerable and betray me like that. He and I can never come back from that. I don't trust him."

A car made its way down the street in front of Garrett's house, the sound of the tires on the asphalt carrying like a crashing wave on the shore. As it continued past and was replaced with silence, a cold void seeped through her skin. "But he—"

"Ask Garrett if he knew the risk of losing our friendship

when he started things with you. Ask him. Because I guarantee you, he did. And he did it anyway, Sam. I don't blame him for thinking the reward was worth it. I think you're worth it too. But am I glad everything blew up in his face and he gets nothing in the end? I sure am. He deserves it. And he will never, ever deserve you."

CHAPTER TWENTY-SIX

THE PLATE CLINKED on the table in front of Garrett, and he looked up. Jen leaned into the table, wearing her uniform. "You looked too sad and lonely over here, so I brought you a brownie sundae. It's on the house."

Garrett rubbed his burning eyelids and thanked her. "Haven't seen you for a bit."

"I was avoiding you. Dan's been bugging me ever since Katie lied to him, and it just seemed better not to give him any more reason to harass you." Jen fidgeted with her nametag. "But you look like hell. And, anyway, I figured you could use a friend right now."

The café was relatively empty of patrons for this time in the afternoon. Just a woman writing on a laptop in the corner and a dad with his two children getting cookies. He gestured to the empty booth in front of him. "Want to sit?"

Jen shrugged and slid into the booth. "Place is dead today. Bunny is over at your house, ironically."

"I know. That's why I'm avoiding it." Garrett lifted the

spoon beside the sundae. He dipped it into the fudge dripping down the side of the whipped cream.

Quirking an eyebrow, Jen's voice was flat. "I would have thought I'd see you at Yardley's."

Garrett licked the fudge from the spoon. "I did sort of the worst thing I've ever done in my life the other day—and I'm taking a break from Yardley's. Or alcohol, anyway. Probably for life."

She tilted her head. "I don't think getting involved with Sam is quite at that level. But we don't have to talk about it if you don't want."

He sighed, tapping the spoon against the plate. "Yeah, I don't mean that." The sweet taste in his mouth had a bitter tinge to it. "I was drinking at work—outed the wife's attempts to start an affair with me to her husband. Husband turned out to be an abusive asshole. Probably scarred her children for life. The good news is she ended up telling the cops the truth, and I hear she's left him."

Jen's teeth showed as she grimaced widely. "That's a mixed bag. Both bad and good."

"I guess." The brownie had lost its appeal, but he didn't want Jen to know that. He cut into it with the side of his spoon, the ice cream running a river into the warm center. He left the spoon sitting there. "So I went to AA for the first time last night."

Jen studied his face. Without asking, she stole the spoon and took a mouthful. "You're a good person, Garrett, you know that, right?"

"Am I?" He squinted at her. "I'm not sure what your definition of a good person includes."

"Yeah, you just have shitty luck. And you're not the best judge of character." She grinned. "Maybe that's why I always felt like I could talk to you. I empathize with that."

"Hey. I consider myself an exceptional judge of character."

She shook her head and asked, "Then what the hell are you doing with Sam?" She put her hand out. "Stop, don't answer that. Forget I asked. It's none of my business."

"Dan tormented that girl in school. It sure as hell wasn't the other way around. You know how many times I heard her say anything back to him? And it wasn't only him. She just kept her head down, did her work, always came out on top." Garrett let out a long sigh. "I don't know—she seemed special. When everyone else was spending holidays thinking about what they were going to do and where they were going to ski or whatever —she was the one who stayed behind, working to help her family."

Jen bit her lip as though processing the new perspective. "But she left. Let her family handle everything."

Garrett shrugged again. "They didn't need her as much. Hell, I left too. So do lots of people. What's so bad about leaving? There's a lot more to the world than Brandywood. Not everyone comes back. Despite feeling as though everyone hated her here, she never stopped coming back, even if it wasn't as long as her family wanted."

"I don't know—" Jen took another bite of the brownie. "I'm probably not the most unbiased person with this. Her mom has been slowing down for the last few months, and it's killing me that no one noticed her deteriorating. But I guess I didn't either. Anyway," she sighed. "I worked hard making that sundae for you, and you're clearly not going to eat it. I hear that chocolate is a wonderful way to deal with your sorrows."

Garrett drummed his finger against the table. "Until recently, my coping mechanism of choice was Jameson."

She regarded him. "Did I ever tell you Colby's dad was a recovering drug addict? Addiction doesn't discriminate between good people and bad people. And it doesn't make you one or the other. I'm proud of you for making that first move toward sobriety. It's difficult to recognize you can't control something everyone else seems to handle just fine."

Sobriety. The shame during that first meeting was something he didn't want to dwell on. How he'd ever let it become a problem in the first place, he didn't know. He'd been so smug. So sure he didn't have any issue. He would never be like his father.

He'd never hit anyone while drinking. But the lack of control—he'd let alcohol take that from him for a while. *Liquid courage*, some of his buddies in the Army called it. But it hadn't been courage. And he couldn't forget how weak it really made him. He couldn't afford to.

The door to the café opened, and Betty Klein came in carrying Colby. Jen stood, wiping her hands on her apron. "Hey, Mom."

Betty brought Colby over to his mom. Jen swooped him into her arms and hugged him fiercely. "Hey, bud, have fun with Mom-Mom? I bet you're ready to go home."

Colby nodded and hugged Jen tightly.

Betty greeted Garrett, then turned toward her daughter again. "Bad news, honey, I can't watch Colby tomorrow. They called me in to cover a last-minute shift at the hospital. They're really short on nurses right now."

"Tomorrow?" Jen blanched. "Tomorrow's the day I'm supposed to help Sam Redding with that live baking demo."

Betty winced. "Honey, there's nothing I can do. Women are going to have babies whether we plan on it. They need someone there."

"What about Dad?" Jen asked hopefully. "When does he come home from Toronto?"

"Not until next Saturday." Betty touched her slender fingertips to her throat. "I'm so sorry."

Garrett sat straighter. "I can do it." The words were out of his mouth before he had thought it through. He'd never changed a diaper before, let alone babysat a kid. But he owed Jen. A lot, actually.

Both women looked at him with surprise. "You'd do that?" Jen asked.

"As long as you're all right with him eating ice cream all day." Garrett winked. "Just kidding. I think I can boil a hot dog or two."

Betty looked pleasantly surprised. "Why, that's lovely of you to offer, Garrett."

Jen hugged him, squishing Colby between them. "See? You're a good person."

A good person. Garrett tried not to roll his eyes and lifted his hands in mock defeat. He checked his wristwatch. Almost four. "Speaking of which, there's something I have to do. Nice seeing you, ladies."

He headed out of Bunny's, zipping his jacket as he walked toward his truck. Jen's pep talk had strangely helped. For someone who had never left Brandywood and was still pretty young, she seemed to have life experience in spades.

He hopped in his truck, a jittery feeling creeping up his stomach. He'd been avoiding this talk for too long.

The drive to his parents' house didn't take long. His parents were only a few streets away from Main. For most of his childhood, he'd biked up and down the historic streets of Brandywood—past the expensive houses—to get to the quiet neighborhoods behind them where the ranchers and Cape Cods were shabbier.

He sighed as he pulled onto his parents' street. His father's truck was parked on the street. Mom had told him last night Dad would get home around now.

Sure enough, Dad was getting down from his truck. He

wore faded jeans, the edges of his long flannel shirt sticking out of an old corduroy jacket. On his head was a baseball cap, which wasn't unusual for Dad.

Dad noticed him immediately. He squinted toward Garrett's truck, then rubbed the back of his neck and made his way over as Garrett turned off the engine.

He released a slow breath. *Now, Garrett. Not later. Not anymore.*

Opening the door, he nodded a greeting toward his father. "How are you doing?"

Dad lumbered toward him. Garrett didn't remember when he'd outgrown him. Eighth grade? That was around the time when his father had quit trying to hit him. *It's a lot harder to smack someone who's towering over you.*

"Hey, Gar." Dad set his hand on the truck. "How are you, son?"

Mom had talked to him, and the idea unnerved Garrett. Made it hard to look his father in the eye. Garrett cleared his throat. "I'm okay, Dad." He cleared his throat. "Do you have a minute to talk?"

Dad pulled off his baseball cap, showing his matted hair. He looked around. "You want to go inside?"

Garrett crossed his arms, leaning against the door. "Nah, right here's fine. I'm not trying to ambush you. I just—"

"Mom told me about taking you to AA last night." Dad's face reddened, then he nodded stiffly. "A-and . . . I'm proud of you."

He thinks I want affirmation? I don't want to have this in common with you.

Garrett stared into his father's eyes. For so long, his inner voice held so much scorn for his father. His humanity had disappeared because he was the horrible son of a bitch who had made his and his family's life hell.

But could he ever be anything other than that?

"Dad, I . . ." Words failed him. Anything he'd thought to say last night blanked out of his brain. *Gone.*

His father drew in a sharp breath. "Did Mom ever tell you that she packed her things the day after you left for basic training and moved in with Shae?"

Garrett drew his head back. "What?"

With a mirthless chuckle, Dad said, "Apparently, Shae had been asking her to while you were in high school, but you know, Shae was living in Frederick. Mom didn't want to move you out of Brandywood and miss that time with your friends."

Mom had actually moved out? Garrett's expression must have relayed shock. "Why didn't I hear about it?"

"She came back. After about a month. Said if I was going to be the asshole who made her miserable, I should be the one to move." This time, his father laughed for real, his eyes twinkling. "Your mom. She's always had a fire in her, that's for sure."

Unsure of this conversation's direction, Garrett listened to the engine ticking as it cooled. "But you didn't move out. Or get sober for a few more years."

"No." He cleared his throat. "I didn't. And I wish I had. That month without her was pure hell. But I wasn't drinking nearly as much as I had in my heyday, and we were comfortable together. At least for a few years. Then I binged again, and Mom told me to sober up or get out. No more chances." He bowed his head. "It shouldn't have taken that much. And I'll keep asking for your forgiveness, Garrett. For everyone's. I'm not a brave man. Not like you. But I will never stop trying to earn your forgiveness."

A brave man?

Garrett stared at his boots, his lips pressing to a line. *Far from.*

He scanned his father's age-lined face. "Dad, it's not about forgiveness. I forgave you a while ago. Don't think I would've been able to look at you again if I hadn't. And I don't know if I even realized it." He shifted his weight to his back leg, slipping his thumbs into the belt loops of his jeans. "It's that I haven't been sure how to forget what happened. I don't think I can. The trust . . . it may never be there. But that's why I'm here."

He placed his hand on his dad's shoulder. "I forgive you, Dad, and I hope I can learn from your mistakes, not make them myself. But how we move forward . . . well, that's not something I know how to do on my own. And you're going to have to be patient with me. Took almost my entire lifetime for me to see you one way . . . I don't know how long it will be for me to see you another. But I promise to be fair to you and do the damn work I have to do as long as you keep doing the hard work you're doing. Because I am proud of you for it, and I hope you can accept that."

Dad's eyes filled with tears, and he wiped them with the back of his hand. "Thank you, Garrett. Thank you." He sniffled, then reached out toward him. "Mind if I shake your hand?"

Seeing his father crying made Garrett's heart throb painfully. *You got to start somewhere.* "You're my dad, so I think I can manage a hug." He pulled his father into a bear hug, then clapped him on the back.

Releasing him, Garrett stepped back, then stuffed his hands in his pockets. *Why do I feel like a kid right now?*

His father wiped his eyes again. "So I hear Sam Redding may have led you on a downward spiral?"

How the hell did he hear that? "From who?"

"Peter Yardley. At least, that was his guess when he called me to tell me he was worried about you." His father took out a pack of tissues from his pocket and wiped his nose. "You want to know what I think?"

Drinking at Yardley's had probably been a mistake. Who knew what he'd told the old man? He snapped his brows together. "What do you think?"

"I think you should keep trying. Don't give up on that girl—she's special."

His heart had been pushing him in the same direction. "She's leaving. Going back to New York soon."

"Then ask her to stay." Dad shrugged, lifting his hands up. "You don't know what she'll say if you don't. Make a grand gesture. Just don't let her go without trying."

Stop running, Sam. Stay with me.

But as Sam had once said, Brandywood would never be her home again. And Garrett doubted she'd ever change her mind about that. Especially with her mom dying and . . . well, with whatever they'd had finished as well.

Garrett had some work to do anyway. Now wasn't the time to dwell on how special Sam was.

One step at a time.

"We'll see. Come on," Garrett said, tilting his head back toward the back of his truck. "I have something for you."

"Oh, yeah?"

Garrett lowered the tailgate, then nodded toward the fencing lying in the back. "Yeah. A project for us to work on together. It's about damned time *we* fixed this fence."

CHAPTER TWENTY-SEVEN

SAM STUDIED the last shot she'd taken on the screen of her camera, then peeked through the viewfinder. She spun the front dial, narrowing her aperture. "Tilt that reflector, slowly," she instructed Rachel. Some of the light was fading now that the sun had shifted.

Rachel did as she asked until bright light filled the shadowed side of the plated cookies. "Perfect. Right there." Sam snapped a few more shots, a smile spreading to her lips. The smile was involuntary, even though she was completely aware of it. Being behind a camera made her smile, especially when a shot worked out exactly like she saw it coming together in her head.

She'd been practicing food photography at home but still couldn't keep the flutter from her gut. The gear was familiar, of course, but the techniques were completely different. She'd enrolled in a few courses, bought twenty different subscriptions to food magazines, and studied images on social media. And even though she hadn't intended originally to be a food photographer, the idea thrilled her.

The joy she felt behind the camera, though, never changed. No matter what type of mood she was in.

She took one last shot and straightened as she examined it on the screen. "Love it." She grinned at Rachel. "Pack it up. We have what we need." Behind Rachel, the camera crew was still moving their equipment to one side to leave the room semi-functional for Garrett.

Bunny remained in the kitchen, along with Maren and Katie. She'd insisted on cleaning up the mess she'd made in the kitchen, even though Maren had assured her they'd hired people to do it. Sam lifted a Linzer cookie Bunny had made from the plate she'd photographed. "Mind if I have one of these, Bunny?"

"Enjoy it!" Bunny smiled broadly, crumpling a sheet of used parchment paper from the cookie sheet. "In fact, I think we should all go back to my café. I can show these out-of-towners what Brandywood food should taste like." She winked at Maren. "Except it'll have to be BYOB. That damned Yardley man bought up all the extra liquor licenses in town and won't let me have one."

Maren smoothed her fingers over her silver pixie cut—as though there was anything to smooth back into place. She'd gone gray early and had been a quick adoptee of renouncing color treatments, favoring her natural color instead. Sam had never seen her in anything less than designer clothes and always perfectly styled. "Oh, ah, is Brandywood known for its cuisine?" Her expression was doubtful, despite how earnestly she appeared to ask it.

Rachel rolled her eyes at Sam. The day before, when they'd settled Maren into a cabin for the next two weeks, she'd been walking around with her arms wrapped around herself as though she was practicing not hyperventilating. Sam had assured her about twenty times that any remaining "bugs" were probably dead or dormant with the approaching winter. Finally, Maren relaxed when Sam suggested she take Laura's old bedroom in the main house.

"We have everything here," Bunny said cheerfully. She wiped the counter. "Even a new pho place on Main Street. Very popular with the young kids, though I don't know what the fuss about noodle soup is all about. Too much cilantro. Give me a good vichyssoise or a gazpacho."

Maren's face brightened. "Ah, you like the cold soups?"

"I like anything . . . as long as it's good." Bunny winked again.

Maren laughed. "That sounds like my motto."

Rachel ducked next to Sam, taking a Linzer cookie for herself. "Sounds like Maren might have found someone in town she can be friends with after all." She bit into the cookie, and her eyes widened. "Man, these are good."

"Bunny's pretty amazing." Sam removed her lens from the camera and searched her bag for the lens cap. "Though I should check with Mom to see if she's feeling up to going out. It's been a long day."

"She's been over at that coffee table writing for hours." Rachel nodded at Sam's mom. "She writing a book or something?"

A book? Sam lifted herself to see over the back of a couch. A stack of cards lay beside her mother. "No, she's a compulsive thank-you note writer." Sam shrugged. "Probably writing them to everyone who has been dropping off casseroles."

Sam finished packing her camera bag and threw the strap over her shoulder. She approached her mother, who scooted some cards to the side, setting her hand over them. "Feeling like going to Bunny's tonight?" Sam asked.

Mom rested back against the cushion. "That sounds nice. I want to spend as much time out enjoying myself." She smiled broadly, though her face was wan. "Garrett's house is lovely. He's a good man to allow his entire house to be thrown into chaos for a few weeks."

"Hmm . . ." Sam sat beside her. "He has good taste in decorating." Sitting here, in the house he'd taken the time to restore, made her long to see him again. To ask all the questions that she'd never gotten around to in the brief time they'd spent together. Garrett didn't open up easily, and now it seemed they'd mostly talked about her problems, her life.

"His sister Hannah is an interior designer," Mom said with a knowing look. "I'm willing to bet she had a hand in it. You open that fridge, though, and you can tell a man lives here alone. Nothing but frozen pizzas and hot dogs. I had to store one of my medicines in there."

They shared a laugh, and Sam took Mom's hand as Katie approached. She sat across from them and had been clearly listening to their conversation. "Hannah is by far my favorite Doyle." Katie ran her hands over the fabric of the couch and sighed. "We still grab lunch occasionally, and she's one of my clients. I just saw her a couple of weeks ago. She thinks he's completely hung up on someone." She lifted her oversized purse. "And look what I found in his bedroom closet—" She pulled a woman's faded flannel shirt from it. "Clearly a woman's."

Sam's flannel shirt. She hadn't even remembered leaving it here, but . . . she *had* worn it over here. The night Rachel had come into town. "Why the heck were you in Garrett's closet?" Sam kept her voice even, despite her irritation.

She resisted the urge to reach for it, though Mom stiffened beside her. Sam had worn the shirt since high school, and Laura before that. The pattern was unremarkable enough that Katie probably wouldn't even recognize it. Sam hadn't taken her coat off at Yardley's because she'd been cold. But the bleach stain on the lower part of the shirt—the one Sam had given it while doing laundry—Mom had seen that.

Katie shrugged. "I was just looking around. Don't worry, I'm going to put it back. I just wanted to show you."

"Garrett trusted me with the keys to his home so I could do this shoot, not so I could make it an open house for people to poke around his things." She crossed her arms. "Come on, Katie. Don't put me in a bad position. Just go put it back." Sam avoided looking at her mother, who watched her thoughtfully.

Katie pouted, then stood. "Fine. But I just had a look around. It's not like Garrett's ever going to invite me over here. I was curious to see. You could just let me have my fun."

As she plodded away, Sam stared at her. *She's unbelievable.*

"You handled that well." Mom's voice was dry.

"Do you think she recognized it?" Sam met Mom's gaze.

"No. Though if she did, I suppose you could tell her you left it here the other day—if you want to continue lying to her about Garrett."

"Mom!" Sam looked around to see if anyone else had heard, but they were relatively alone in the living room. She didn't want to know what Mom knew of her relationship with Garrett —or what Laura had told her. Sex was something she had never discussed with her, and she wasn't about to. "I'm not lying."

"Omitting the truth is lying. Trust me, I know all about it." Mom's look was pointed as she put her writing materials into a canvas bag. "And I don't think Katie would see it that way."

Now Mom sounded like Rachel. "I think it would be better for everyone if she never finds out. Especially now that things with Garrett and I are over."

"Are they?" Mom looked deeply into her eyes. "I'll be the first to tell you that love is not an excuse for behaving however you want. But, Sam"—Mom gathered the letters beside her— "Garrett was young when he broke up with Katie. And yes, it was messy. But he also did them both a favor. A divorce is much messier, even now. What's the statute of limitations on Katie having a claim to him? Is he never allowed to be happy again? You'd know better than anyone the number of relationships she's had since then."

"It's not just that, Mom. There's Eli too—"

Mom scrunched her nose. "I have tolerated that man because you care about him, but the time has long since passed that he should have been able to commit to you. You're my daughter. It's hard to look at a man who has broken your heart as often as Eli has and think too kindly about him."

Was her mother giving her a blessing to go after Garrett?

The moment of hope vanished as Katie's footsteps sounded in the room. She popped her head in. "I think we're all about to head to Bunny's? You ready?"

Sam stood, the gentle tug of pressure at her heart reminding her of the guilt she'd been living with for days. What was the statute of limitations?

With Katie in the picture? Probably forever.

"Yeah, I think we're ready." Sam held out her hands for Mom to help her stand.

"I can drive you two," Katie offered, pulling the zipper up on her coat. "It's too cold to walk today. I hear we're supposed to get snow over the next few days."

"Actually." Mom gripped Sam's forearm and stood. She beamed at Sam. "Sam drove us here. She learned to drive the past couple of weeks, and Mark took her to get her permit yesterday."

"Really?" Katie gaped at her and hugged her. "Took you long enough! I'm so proud of you. I should go grab some champagne to celebrate."

"It's not a big deal," Sam said with a shrug.

"It's fantastic." Katie gathered her hair over one shoulder, then pulled a wool hat over her head. "Now we can take a road trip, and you and I can split the driving duties. Like Thelma and Louise or something. Maybe this summer?"

Katie had talked about doing something like that before. *If you're still talking to me.* Sam nodded, trying to look as enthusiastic as Katie appeared. "Sounds great."

"Perfect. We can start planning it after Christmas. I'm going to go see if anyone else needs a ride."

As Katie stepped outside, the smile vanished from Sam's lips. She stared at the door, feeling gross. "I have to tell her the truth." *Tonight, if possible.*

Mom gathered her things. "Eso es lo que te estaba diciendo." *That's what I was telling you.*

"Do you think she'll forgive me?" Sam gave her an anxious look.

Mom fidgeted with the letters in her hand. "I don't know, Sam. Forgiveness is a tough thing sometimes. But I think we all have to hope for forgiveness, even when it's frightening, don't you?"

Mom was clearly speaking from experience.
Probably with me.

Sam played with the snowdrop ring on her hand, unable to meet Mom's eyes. It couldn't have been easy for Mom to tell her the truth about her affair with Dad. *And my reaction probably didn't make it any better.* She'd told her mother she didn't *deserve* forgiveness.

Sam, you hypocrite.

Sinking beside her mother, Sam touched her forearm gently. "Mom, about the whole thing with Dad. I want you to know I forgive you. It was . . . really *hard* finding out so late about something that would have changed my perspective on a lot of my life. And I wish you would have told me before. But, I know telling me must have been tough."

Mom's eyes looked misty. "You have no idea, Sam. I don't want to lose you. I didn't know how to tell you." She straightened and held out the stack of letters and cards to Sam. "Speaking of things I want to tell you, I was going to give you these originally as a Christmas present, and I decided I don't want us to be sad on Christmas."

Sam eyed the letters. "What are they?" As she took them, she noticed her name and dates on the outside of the envelopes. *"For your wedding day." "For when you have children." "For when you have your first married fight."*

Sam froze and looked up at her mother, her heartbeat slowing. "Mom, what are these?"

Mom sighed. "I know I won't be here for everything I want to be here for, but one of the gifts I have been given is knowing I have some time before my expiration date. I wrote a few letters for you to open on special occasions. And birthday cards. So you'll know I'm thinking of you and love you."

Tears escaped Sam's eyes, and she hugged the letters closer. "I don't know what to say to this."

"I know it's sad." Mom leaned forward and hugged her. "And you don't have to open them. But in case you ever wish you could talk to me again, think of this as one way you can."

"How are you so thoughtful?" Sam hugged her back tightly. She didn't want to let go.

Mom kissed her cheek. "I had a lot of years of practice not being thoughtful. And I decided I could do better. We can always do better, Sam."

SAM PARKED her mother's truck in a small parking lot at the end of Main Street and shifted the car into neutral. She'd dropped her mother over by Bunny's Café so she wouldn't have to walk the extra way. Smiling as she shut off the engine, she remembered Garrett's patient instructions as she'd ground the clutch and slammed on the brakes.

She closed the door to the truck. A light flurry of snowflakes had fallen on the drive over. Katie was right. The night smelled of coming snow.

She started toward Bunny's, then stopped. Garrett was crossing the parking lot, keys in his hand. He slowed, looking right at her.

The gravity drawing her toward him hadn't decreased, that was for sure. The two nights they'd spent together had only made her want more. She'd walked out on him . . . would it be fair for her to walk up to him now? If only to say hello?

His expression gave little away, but he checked over his shoulder, then walked toward her cautiously. He stopped a few feet from her. "I was hoping I might see you here. I just saw your mom going into Bunny's."

"Oh, yeah?" The part of the town on the hillsides beside Main Street seemed to twinkle with Christmas lights and decorations. Through the branches of trees, front porch lights took on their own pulse, throbbing like hers. She edged closer but kept her distance. "It's been . . . your house has been perfect for the filming. Thanks for being so accommodating."

Stiff silence hung between them. A flash of hurt crossed his eyes as he realized this was it. This was how things were going to be now between them. Awkward. Tense. Unfulfilled.

He swallowed a breath. "No problem. I should let you go." He started toward his truck.

She should let *him* go.

Let him keep walking toward that truck, then go to Bunny's, where she'd spend the rest of the night pretending the only man she wanted to be near was the one she couldn't have.

He left a trail of footsteps in the snow that had accumulated on the parking lot. The words she shouldn't tell him came out. "I told Eli I wouldn't marry him."

He stopped. His warm breath fogged the air in front of his lips. "For now?"

"No, I mean never. We're done. For good." Offering Garrett any sort of hope was wrong, wasn't it? But she couldn't seem to help herself. She approached him. "He showed up when we were filming and brought an enormous bouquet of roses. We talked, and I just . . . he and I don't make sense anymore. And maybe we never did."

Garrett stared, unblinking, at his truck. He turned and gave one firm nod. "Good for you. I'm not sure if it makes me worse of a person to say it or not, but Eli hasn't been worthy of your love for a long time."

She held her breath, hoping he'd say more, but he didn't. She couldn't expect him to. He'd put so much on the line for her.

A sad smile hinted at his lips. "Speaking of roses, I have something for you. Saw them today while walking through Main. I figured I'd leave them with a note for you in the house for tomorrow. You know—as congrats on that campaign coming together." He took the last few steps toward his truck, which beeped as he unlocked it. Opening the back door, he pulled out a snow globe.

Filled with snowdrops.

Her favorite flower. She closed the space between them, her eyes wide. "You remembered?"

His hand settled gently into the small of her back, without pressure, drawing her closer to him. His lips were close to her ear. "I've always remembered you, Sam. I always will." She shivered.

Pulling back from him, her gaze was fixed on his lips. None of this was fair. Closing her eyes, she pressed a sweet kiss to his mouth. She wanted everything with him, yet she had to tell him goodbye again. His arm encircled her waist, and he returned her kiss as though it took all his restraint not to take it further.

But Sam wanted more. She wanted to be enveloped in Garrett's arms because those arms felt right. *He* felt right. She could feel the beat of his heart, even through his jacket and hers. Or maybe that was wishful thinking. As was wishing there were no clothes between them at all and they were at his house, in his bed—

A door slammed.

Sam and Garrett sprang apart as Katie climbed out of her car a few rows down from them.

Oh my God.

She didn't look at them, adjusting her purse on her shoulder, as she turned and headed toward Main Street.

Maybe she hadn't seen.

"I have to go—" She dashed away from him, and he grabbed her hand.

"She's just baiting you. Let her have some time to cool down. Katie always reacts better once she's had time to cool down."

"But what if she didn't see—"

As though she could hear, Katie stopped at the top of the parking lot and looked over her shoulder. Right at them. Then she kept going.

She had absolutely seen. Sam's knees felt weak as she steadied herself from Garrett's grip. "I have to explain." She put the snow globe in her purse.

Garrett released her hand. "I won't keep apologizing for loving you, but if that's what you want to keep doing—apologize—go right ahead. Every time something scares you, you just keep running away."

Giving him a scalding look, she turned from him and ran.

"Katie!" Sam's boots slid as she ran toward Main Street on the slippery asphalt. Katie didn't slow or stop. At least with Eli, she and Garrett had both had something to lose. Having him at her side, however humiliating the circumstances, had been comforting.

She somehow caught Katie right before she went into Bunny's. Grabbing her by the elbow, she breathed, "Wait, please."

Katie whirled around, then slapped her across the face, the sound ringing in Sam's ears. Sam reeled back, holding her cheek, stunned.

Her eyes flashing, Katie took a step toward her. "How dare you pretend to be my friend?"

"I wasn't pretending. I am your friend." Sam lifted a shaking hand away from her cheek, the skin feeling raw and hot. "Katie—"

"Are you sleeping with him?"

Sam swallowed hard. By now, the door to Bunny's Café had opened. Bunny and Maren stood there, and her mother was only steps away. On the sidewalk, some people had stopped to watch them amid the busy Christmas season.

Katie, as though emboldened by the audience, took another step. "Are you sleeping with Garrett, Sam?"

"It wasn't—" Sam kept her voice low. Of all the ways she'd envisioned talking to Katie about this, she'd never imagined doing it in front of so many people. The experience felt like a nightmare where she was walking around naked in the middle of town.

"You're unbelievable." Katie's eyes narrowed. "You're sleeping with *my* ex-fiancé. He's mine, Sam—"

"Oh, come off it. We haven't been together in five years." Garrett's voice rang through the night air, dulled by the snow.

Sam choked back a cry. Garrett approached. *He didn't let me face this on my own.*

But there must be twenty people watching.

Katie's face drained of color, and she crossed her arms. "I went to bat for you, Sam. Spent my whole life telling everyone you deserved their kindness and sympathy. Helped you make sure you could do this project." She turned with blazing eyes to Maren. "That's right. She had no plan for this cookie thing until I stepped in. She told me all about how her assistant found a billion excuses to keep you out of the loop."

Oh, God. This is much worse. She couldn't meet Maren in the eye to gauge her reaction.

The only thing worse than standing naked in the middle of town might be having the person who knows every one of your secrets spouting them off. Sam's head buzzed.

". . . and the whole town knows you just got engaged to Eli . . ." Katie was saying. The more she spoke, the louder and calmer she seemed to get. "Now you're sleeping with his best friend? Cheating on him?"

What. The. Hell. Katie knew she'd told Eli no, even if it wasn't common knowledge.

"No, that's not true—"

"You didn't just betray me. You betrayed everyone, didn't you? Eli, your mom, Laura—have you told her how much you hate Brandywood and plan on selling the cabins the minute she dies?"

Sam gasped. "What are you talking about?" But Sam also knew exactly what Katie was doing. She wanted as many people to hate Sam as she did right now.

"You're a liar, Sam. You told me what your plans for those cabins were—"

"Katie, stop." Garrett walked closer to her, reaching a hand out.

She laughed in his face. "Don't even start, Garrett. I'm sure Sam would be interested to know how Joe Sanders caught you having an affair with his wife. That she left him for you. You destroyed a family, Garrett. Joe told me himself." She leveled her gaze with Sam. "I bet you didn't know he was having sex with another woman, did you?"

That can't be true. Katie's words made Sam sick, though.

Garrett stared at Katie as though he didn't know where to begin answering her.

"Did I ever tell you how Eli asked me out in sophomore year of high school, Sam?" Katie's lips curled. "That's right. Your soul mate—he wanted me, not you. But you know what I did? Because I was your friend? I pushed him away so that you would have someone to take pity on you."

Everything else Katie had been saying was a lie. She had to be lying about that too. Sam finally found her voice. "Katie, you've said enough."

Katie took a few steps away as though sensing she needed to leave. "Don't worry, Sam. This whole town? They love me. They're *my* friends. And as soon as I finish telling them what an asshole you are, they will all turn against you. Again! Congratulations, bitch. Hope you enjoy a poor excuse for a fuck."

Turning on her heel, she stormed past them both and back toward the parking lot.

Garrett was at her side. "Sam, don't listen to her—"

"Stop. Just stop." Humiliation washed over her. She closed her eyes. This was her worst nightmare come to life.

"Katie's lying, and you know it. Look at me." Garrett put his hands on her shoulders. "I didn't have an affair with Trisha. She left Joe, yes, but because Joe was abusive."

Did she even want to know?

"People are staring at me," she whispered. Her fingertips

shook. "Wondering if what Katie said was true. I can't do this right now."

Shaken, Sam kept her gaze down, unable to look at anyone there. Not Maren, who would probably fire her. Not Mom, who might believe Sam, but she was too embarrassed to face.

Run.

CHAPTER TWENTY-EIGHT

THE BELL on the door to the fudge shop jingled. Garrett ducked through the low entrance, carrying Colby back outside. He tightened Colby's jacket around him. The snow was falling heavily, but the fudge shop was the only place in town selling ice cream cones this time of year, which was the only thing Colby had wanted when Garrett had offered him a snack.

"We'll be back in the truck in four seconds," Garrett said. Colby grinned, his cheeks red. He didn't seem to mind the snow much and held his hand out toward the large flakes.

Opening the door to the back seat, Garrett popped Colby into the car seat Jen had installed in a rush this morning. She'd done him the favor of not bringing up the gossip that had raged through the town the previous night. The bombs Katie had hurled into the air must have reached Jen. Late the night before, Jen had sent him a text message letting him know she would still help Sam. *Still* meant someone must have tried to put a stop to it.

He pulled his truck into the street, windshield wipers pushing the snow away almost as quickly as it fell. Keeping his gaze focused forward, he crawled down Main Street and headed toward the Reddings' house. With the snow falling as quickly as it was, Jen had wanted Garrett to take Colby to the guest lodge there, instead of staying at her apartment. She lived on the far side of the town.

"You doing all right back there?" The rear-facing car seat thing was disorienting. How did parents not constantly worry about their kids when they couldn't see them? Garrett flipped the rearview mirror downward, trying to angle it so he could see Colby.

Colby didn't answer, but his legs shifted in his seat. He was still fine, right? He'd just keep the mirror down this way to check on him.

The trip to the Reddings' took twice as long as it usually would, and by the time Garrett pulled into the driveway, snow covered his mirrors and the back window. He continued past the Reddings' house toward the guest lodge.

Parking his truck, he turned it off and opened the door.

A flash of red and blue against the snow made his shoulders tense.

Dan was already out of his police car, his face red. "Why the hell didn't you stop?" he demanded. "I've been following you since you pulled out on Main."

"I didn't—" Garrett paused. Giving Dan a reasonable excuse didn't make a damn bit of difference. He had no reason to pull him over, like usual.

"Get back in your car," Dan demanded.

As Garrett complied, Dan yanked open the back seat.

"What the hell do you think you're doing?" Garrett snapped.

Dan had already unbuckled Colby from the seat. He lifted him out. "Taking my nephew away from you."

"Dan, your sister asked me to watch him. You don't have any authority here."

Without responding, Dan set Colby on his waist and carried him across the snow-covered gravel parking lot to his police cruiser. He opened the passenger side door and set Colby down. "Wait here for Uncle Danny," he said, closing the door.

Garrett's fingers curled around the steering wheel. He scanned his console for his phone. Jen would be furious if she knew Dan was doing this—but would he even be able to get in touch with her right now? She was probably in the middle of live filming.

Dan strode back to the truck with his shoulders thrown back like the arrogant asshole he was. It occurred to Garrett that Dan probably had more in common with his biological father than he would ever want to admit. Ironic.

Garrett turned his truck back on so he could roll down the window. "You know the routine by now," Dan said, drawling in mockery as he stood beside Garrett.

Lifting his phone, Garrett waved it. "Here's what's going to happen. Suppose you don't bring Colby over here. In that case, I will call the dispatcher and tell them you're kidnapping your nephew without your sister's permission. Or, you can make your own life easy and bring him back, then creep back into whatever shithole you came from."

Dan's eyes narrowed. His hand shot into the car, and he tried to snatch the phone from Garrett, but Garrett's reflexes were faster. Dan swung for Garrett once more, then yanked the door open.

"Get the hell out of my car." Garrett's temper flared as Dan pushed him to the limit of his patience.

Dan grabbed Garrett by the jacket and tried to wrest him from the seat. "I told you to stay away from Jen. That sure as hell involves staying away from my nephew." Dan's eyes cut at Garrett. "I've heard all about how you've been fucking Sam Redding while you were making a play for Jen."

For most of his life, Garrett's comebacks had gotten him into more trouble than it was worth. However, knowing how infuriated he could make Dan right now was irresistible. He chuckled. "Can I help it if your sisters seem to like what I offer?"

Gathering every ounce of his strength, Dan yanked Garrett out of the car. The two men tumbled, and Garrett's face connected painfully with the gravel parking lot. The snow protected him somewhat, but the sting of deep scratches and bloodstains on the snow told him he'd made contact on a few places.

Garrett pushed Dan off him with his legs and rolled away as Dan came at him again.

Grabbing a fistful of snow, Garrett shoved it into Dan's face.

The two men struggled, seemingly equally matched in strength and size. At last, they both lay side by side, panting from the effort of fighting in the snow. The ridiculousness of it struck Garrett with an odd sense of hilarity, adrenaline, and fury pumping through his veins.

He sat up, searching for his phone, which he'd dropped in the struggle. He didn't see it anywhere. *Fantastic.*

"The next time you come near my sister . . . hell, the next time you call that other whore my sister . . . I'll kill you." Dan stood, wiping blood from his lip.

Good. He'd wounded the son of a bitch.

"You realize she never had a dad either, right?" Garrett narrowed his gaze. "You hated her for taking your father . . . but what sort of father did he turn out to be? And you've let the stupidity of one person turn you into a hateful, pathetic human piece of garbage." He wiped a drop of blood making its way down from his temple.

Dan didn't answer. His whole body went rigid.

Garrett turned to see what he was looking at. The police cruiser sat there, lights still bouncing into the snowflakes falling around it.

The passenger door was open. Garrett's heart thumped painfully.

Both men bolted toward the cruiser.

A light set of footprints, barely visible with the rapid rate of snowfall, went a few feet from the cruiser toward the woods.

Garrett cupped his hands around his mouth. "Colby!"

Dan's shout followed.

The woods on the other side of the police cruiser were a steep drop-off—and the footprints ended at the top. At the end of the steep hill was a ravine.

Garrett scanned the woods. He didn't see Colby anywhere.

Panic filled Dan's face. "What color was his jacket?" he demanded.

"Uh . . . gray, I think." Not the most useful color in a situation like this. "Colby!" Garrett called again. He continued calling, his throat hurting from the strain. He started down the hill. If something happened to Colby . . .

Calm was key. The kid just had to be hiding somewhere. Maybe around the other side of the police cruiser.

Dan continued searching up by the cars and the guest lodge, the two combing the immediate area as quickly as they could.

After several minutes and still no sight of him, Garrett found Dan. "One of us should stay and keep looking. The other one can go get more help. And tell Jen."

"I'm staying." Dan's eyes were red, terrified. He appeared to be shaking. "He's my nephew."

Much as he didn't want to leave Dan here, Garrett nodded. He reached for his phone, then realized it was lost in the snow somewhere. "Can you call my phone?" He gave Dan his number.

Nothing. Cold weather and phone batteries didn't exactly play nicely together. His phone was probably dead by now. "Fuck."

GARRETT SLIPPED into his house through the garage, noticing the absence of fanfare from the last few days. No one from town had been hanging around his house or garage when he'd left early in the morning. He doubted the snow held them back.

Jen was in the middle of baking, but fortunately, Sam and Rachel were off to the side, close to the garage door.

Garrett met Sam's eyes and waved her toward the door.

She frowned, her gaze zeroing in on the cuts on his face. Without hesitating, she grabbed her coat from a chair and followed him outside.

"There's a problem," Garrett said. Somehow, he was relying on his Army training to sound calm.

"What is it?" Sam's face wore a tired expression, as though she hadn't slept well.

"Colby is missing."

"What?"

"Dan took him out of my truck and sat him in the cruiser. We got into a stupid fight—*again*—and then discovered Colby had disappeared from the cruiser."

"Oh, God." *She sounds as terrified as I am.*

"My phone is under a few inches of snow by the guest lodge. I need to get back."

Sam breathed out. "Okay. I'm going to head to my house. Hopefully, I won't get stopped since I'm not officially licensed yet. I'll take my phone with me and give Rachel an update when I get there."

"And Jen?" Garrett searched her gaze. "We need to tell her."

"Agreed. But wait until I get back to the house and call with an update. For all we know, Dan's already found him. I don't want to freak her out if we don't have to yet." Sam found her keys in her pocket. "I'll call you in ten minutes. And, Garrett?" She started toward Mom's truck.

He lifted his chin expectantly. Her ability to stay calm under pressure was admirable.

"Thanks for teaching me to drive. It comes in handy."

CHAPTER TWENTY-NINE

THE UTV FLEW over the snow-covered trails, and Sam swerved to avoid a tree.

Still no sign of Colby. Or Dan.

She arrived at the guest lodge before any first responders. Dan wasn't there, though his police cruiser remained on, the lights still flashing. She'd called Rachel, who confirmed Dan hadn't been heard from, then grabbed the keys to the UTV from the lodge. She knew these woods better than anyone—she'd spent her childhood in them.

Unfortunately, the part of the woods Colby appeared to have gone into backed up to the state park. Which meant there wasn't any sort of neighborhood nearby to provide hope of someone else finding a wandering toddler. The state park had always been a blessing for the Reddings with guest bookings. Now, that area offered a foreboding curse.

She stopped the UTV by the ravine. She would have grabbed a pair of galoshes if she'd thought about it more before going out. They had some spare ones in the guest lodge. At least she'd worn her snow boots over to Garrett's house earlier.

Climbing out of the UTV, she balanced herself against the frame.

Thick, thorny brush littered the sides of the ravine. Could Colby have even made it over this amount of brush? If he'd lost his footing and rolled from the top, like Garrett believed, he might have gone through an area with less brush.

The immediate area didn't reveal signs of anyone—not even Dan. Hopping back into the vehicle, Sam pulled back onto the trail, riding along the side of the ravine slowly. She kept her eyes on the banks, then crossed into a shallow area. The other side wasn't nearly as steep and easier to navigate with the UTV.

She tried to focus, to keep her mind off the problems swirling at the edges of her thoughts. Katie had made good on her promise. Outside of Jen and Peter, everyone else had called Rachel to cancel their participation in the campaign. Tears of grief and anger had fallen when Rachel delivered that message.

She hadn't believed everyone would once again turn against her, but at least it revealed that Brandywood would never again be her home. She felt so broken by how hard and quick Katie had turned on her too. Peter would do his shoot tomorrow, and the campaign would have to wrap up—a humiliating defeat. Sam had given Maren a letter of resignation this morning.

It was time to move forward.

Once she could find a missing little boy.

A flash of color caught her attention, and she slowed the vehicle to a stop.

Dan Klein sat in the snow on the bank, holding his head in his hands.

Sam jumped from the UTV, her heart in her throat. *Please don't let it be Colby.*

But there was no trace of the little boy.

Squatting beside Dan, she placed a hand on his shoulder. Tears ran down his smooth-shaven cheeks, his shoulders shaking with sobs.

He didn't look at her.

He didn't have gloves on. Didn't really have any proper snow gear—he was still wearing his uniform, including his shoes, and a fairly lightweight jacket. No hat.

"Dan." She shook his shoulder.

Wiping his nose with the back of his hand, he cried in a broken voice, "How could a two-year-old just vanish? There's nowhere to hide!"

She reached for his hands. They were red. He was in danger of frostbite out here like this. "Dan, you need to go back."

"Not without Colby." Dan shook his head and fumbled for the nonexistent hat on his head. He put one unsteady knee up. "I'm not going back without him. It's my fault he's gone."

She gripped his jacket lapel. The snow was falling faster now. "You are going to get frostbite out here at a minimum. And if you don't go back, they're going to have to make this a search for two people instead of one. Do you really want to divert the efforts from trying to find Colby?"

Dan blinked at her as though struggling to comprehend her words. His eyes met hers. Saliva collected at the corners of his red, torn lips. "You know, I saw him once."

She furrowed her brow. Was he delirious? "Colby?"

"No. Your dad." He wiped his mouth. "I was doing a prison transport. And guess who it was?" He released a slow breath. "The whole time, all I wanted to ask him was why. Why he pretended my family never existed. Instead, all I could do was look at the son of a bitch and hate him even more."

Dropping her hands to her sides, Sam searched his forlorn face. She didn't want to make him feel better, but this whole thing had grown and festered. And Laura was right . . . it was up to all of them to put the future onto a brighter path.

"What's your last name?"

Dan wiped his eyes. "Klein."

"Right. You're a Klein. Your father, Bob Klein, adopted you and has loved you for over twenty years as his son. The man who shares our blood was a poor excuse for a father, and in the end, he left us both, Dan. *Your* father is not that bastard you picked up for a prison transport one day. We're all a lot more than blood and genes. That's the best part of being human—we get to choose who we're going to be."

"You deserve everything good. But you're going to have to choose it." Garrett's voice flooded her memory.

"Come on." Sam reached out a hand to Dan. "I've got to get you back. You are not in great shape."

He shook his head. "I can't go back without him."

"I'm going to keep looking. Let me drive you part of the way, at least. I'm not comfortable leaving you out here. It's sundown. And seriously, Dan, they don't need someone else to search for. You know this. Go back for Colby's sake."

At last, Dan nodded. He followed Sam back to the UTV, crawling into the passenger side. "My phone died," he admitted as Sam zipped up the plastic canopy. The UTV wasn't warm by any means, but it kept the snow from continuing to accumulate on top of them.

"Battery life doesn't last long in the cold." She fished hers from her bra, returning her hand to the wheel as quickly as possible. "Take this. Put it next to your body. When I drop you off, I want you to call 911 and keep walking. In case you need to use it, the passcode is 11888. Repeat it back to me."

After he did, Dan sat in silence, staring at her. After some time, he said, "I've always been a jerk to you."

"Yeah, you have." She shrugged. "I won't say it doesn't

matter, Dan. It wasn't the easiest to deal with, and we don't have to be friends. But it will only keep hurting us if we don't fix it."

"For what it's worth, I regret it. I am sorry. What's broken has nothing to do with you. It's the mess inside me that needs fixing. I thought I had moved on and gotten better about the whole thing. Then Jen got knocked up and was left to handle everything on her own, and it all returned to haunt me. And now . . . *oh, God.*" Dan looked like he might be sick. "Colby. I love that kid so much. Like he was my son."

Sam's heart ached. She couldn't imagine how she'd feel if this was Bella, Carson, or Charlotte.

Sam found where she'd crossed the ravine, slowed, and stopped. "I'm going to keep looking until I find him." She helped Dan out. "Don't forget to call." Pointing to the side of the ravine. "Follow the tracks. But hurry. This snow is falling so fast that they won't be visible for long. Only use the phone if you need it."

Saying a prayer she hadn't booted Dan out to his death, Sam climbed back in and turned around. She'd done what she could for Dan. Colby was just as vulnerable.

She raced through the woods, trying to make up for the time she'd lost with Dan. Passing the spot where she'd found him, she continued along the side of the ravine. Had the water dragged Colby this far, was there even any chance he was alive?

Of course, she could be completely wrong. Maybe he hadn't gone into the stream at all. Maybe he'd gone the opposite way, climbing through the woods, trying to get back up to the top. But how could he get so far so fast? Dan was right—there weren't many places to hide that would make him invisible.

Her gaze narrowed at the swiftly moving stream. The amount of snow they'd gotten so early in the season had raised the water level, making the stream deeper than usual. If Colby had been carried out by the stream, he probably wouldn't have gone any farther than those shallow areas she'd crossed in the UTV. They hadn't been deep enough.

A child vanishing into the woods so quickly, without a trace, was hard to imagine . . . if she couldn't remember someone else who used to vanish in these same woods.

Over twenty-five years ago, her father had built a tunnel he'd used for his operations. She could still picture the detectives in the woods, hauling evidence from the exit closest to the guest lodge, where the tunnel started. Mom had never filled the tunnel, and to the average viewer, it just looked like a culvert pipe to divert a stream. The cost of filling it was more than her mother could afford. Eventually, Sam had taken to playing in it.

For a child who loved tunnels, it was a perfect place to play.

The exit to the tunnel was closer to where she was now, near an old wooden bridge.

Once she found the bridge and parked the UTV beside it, she grabbed a flashlight from the tackle box where they kept emergency supplies and headed back out into the snow. The exit to the old pipe was still there, a trickle of water running through it and into the stream. She turned on the flashlight and shone it inside.

Even though she'd been inside the tunnel before, it had been years. And even then, snakeskins, mice, and animal skeletons had been everywhere. She shuddered and climbed in. "Colby," she called. Her voice echoed in the tight space.

As a girl, when she crawled through, she'd been able to crouch while walking. Now she had to go on her hands and knees. "Colby!"

Was this futile?

Colby could be anywhere. And what made her think she

was going to find him, anyway? She was a photographer. Not particularly skilled or brave when it came to something like this.

You know this land better than anyone.

She crawled forward, her arms feeling wobbly as she crawled. Maybe, once, she'd known this land better than others. But she and Brandywood . . . they'd rejected each other, hadn't they?

Colby's safety had nothing to do with that because *he* wasn't a part of all that. She called out for him again, feeling strangely desperate. This wouldn't have happened without her coming back to town, though. Dan's harassment of Garrett had gotten worse since she'd arrived, hadn't it? And Jen wouldn't have needed babysitting if not for her.

She had to find him. Had to make this right. "Colby!"

Then—a voice. Muffled. Distant, but not too far.

Crawling faster, she pushed onward, grateful for her gloves as she set her hands down without looking to see what she was touching. The hint of uneven pressure under her hands was enough to remind her of how gross it was in here. She called his name once again.

You know this land better than anyone, Sam. You can find Colby because this land . . . it's a part of you.

"Mama." The voice was tiny.

Hearing his voice, her heart started pumping faster. She moved faster still, grateful for the flashlight in the dark space.

At last, she reached him. He blinked in the light of the flashlight and then burst into tears as Sam gathered him in her arms. She held him tightly, soothing him. "It's all right, Colby." She fought the urge to cry, knowing right now he needed comfort and strength, not to be frightened by this stranger he barely knew.

She shone the flashlight toward the other exit. There wasn't any light coming from that direction. How far had she crawled? She'd been going uphill on her hands and knees. It made more sense that he'd continued moving once he'd crawled in here, and they'd found each other somewhere in the middle of this damned tunnel.

His clothes were soaked and filthy, and cobwebs hung from his hair. Tucking the flashlight into the top of her wool hat, she paused, trying to think of the best way to get him out of here. She couldn't carry him very well. Slinging him over her shoulders and onto her back, she flattened his torso against her back. She gripped his arms around her neck, settling his head into her shoulder. "Keep your head down," she told him, starting forward.

The crawl back down the tunnel was considerably slower, and she arched her back, trying to keep him from bumping the top. His hands weren't covered with gloves and felt icy against her neck.

Whatever instinct had brought him into the culvert pipe had probably saved his life. The space had served like a snow cave.

When they reached the exit, she shifted him off her back and set him down. She clamored out and lifted him snugly in her arms, continuing to soothe him as best she could. The snow hadn't slowed, and the UTV blended with the surroundings. She shook the snow from the top and unzipped it, catching sight of her gloves. Normally gray, they were nearly black on the palms and fingers.

She strapped Colby in, tightening the straps as far as they would go. She strapped herself in, then started forward. They lurched on the snow and zipped across the stream. *Come on. Come on. Get us home.*

With the rate of snowfall, Sam could barely see from the windshield, but she pushed on, determined. Colby's booted feet barely made it to the edge of his seat, and on any other day, it would have been comical, but not today. The tears had dried, but streaks remained on his face. *The poor baby*.

They had barely gone a few feet when a loud, metallic screech reverberated through the UTV. The vehicle jolted, the moment so fast, so shocking, that Sam barely knew what was happening. A loud crash followed, a blur of white and twisting, cracking, sinewy metal and bone and splintered wood.

Then . . . the soft vision of snow, drifting, spinning . . . silence.

"Colby!"

She recognized the sound of her own voice, but it felt far away.

He was wailing in his seat, dangling.

Unbearable pain throbbed in Sam's leg, near her knee. Her hands hadn't stopped shaking. Dragging herself out from her seat, she crawled across her seat to get to him.

With one arm, she held him as she popped open the latch for the seat belt. It freed him, and he tumbled into her arms, clinging to her neck.

"It's all right, buddy." She rubbed his back.

But nothing was all right. The UTV was on its side, and—even if her leg wasn't broken—there was no way she could roll this thing over. They were stuck here indefinitely.

And she didn't have her phone.

The engine continued to run, but on its side like this, it seemed dangerous to keep it that way. If the exhaust pipe filled with snow, carbon monoxide could be a problem, not to mention that she wasn't sure how damaged the vehicle was. The last thing she needed was for it to catch on fire. She turned it off and looked at Colby, who shook with cold. He couldn't stay in his soaking wet clothes. She had to change him. Now.

Gritting her teeth, she set him down on her lap and

peeled his wet clothes away. He cried, wiggling against her. "Colby, listen. I don't want you to be wet. Do you want to be wet?"

He shook his head, blue eyes wide with tears. She pulled the shirt off, then the pants. His diaper was a problem she couldn't solve with efficiency. It was wet, which kept him cold, but if he peed without it, he'd start the problem all over again. Still, she had to hope someone would find them soon.

She took the diaper off. Then she unzipped her thick coat and wrapped it around his shoulders. She tucked his arms and legs into it, zipped it, then tied the sleeves together around the bottom, making it like a sleeping bag. Covering his head with the hood, she tugged the top down so his face could peek out better.

"Warmer?" She wrapped him in her arms again. Without a coat, her teeth chattered, her own shivering taking on sudden intensity.

He nodded.

She flipped onto her back, feeling around for the tackle box of emergency supplies. Finding it, she dragged it toward herself, wanting to move as little as possible. Each movement made her cry out in pain.

She opened the kit. There wasn't much in there. A bungee cord, a few hand warmers, and a first aid kit. She tore a hand warmer package open with her teeth and shook it. Once it warmed, she slipped it into the jacket with Colby.

"Hold on to this, okay? It will help."

For now, they would stay in the UTV. With the rate of snowfall, it provided them with better shelter than they would have otherwise. And anyone looking for them could see the UTV better. If it got bad enough, she would drag them back to the tunnel—no matter how much it hurt.

Lying back, she kept herself as still as she could, her brain firing pain signals that made her want to scream. She gripped the steering wheel and closed her eyes.

The cracked windshield was slowly getting covered with snow. The sun was going down.

Someone had to find them soon.

But what if they didn't?

CHAPTER THIRTY

GARRETT SLAMMED THE PHONE. His shoulders radiated tension, and he took a slow, practiced breath.

Beside him, Jen continued to cry quietly, but she glanced at him hopefully. Laura gripped her hand.

He shook his head. "They say the state troopers can't get a helicopter out there in these conditions."

Jen buried her face in her hands, and Laura pulled her into a tight embrace.

Garrett stood, leaving the two women at the Reddings' kitchen table. He made his way out to the hallway, feeling helpless and angry. First Colby, then Sam.

How could they just disappear? How could an entire UTV disappear?

Mrs. Redding was out on her front porch, despite the cold. The porch heater was on, and she stood near it, staring off into the darkness surrounding the house. Garrett joined her. He'd searched for hours, and Mark had found him at last, convinced him to take a break. People were still searching, but the snow was making everything more difficult. They had to go in shifts and stay close to each other.

"We're going to find them." Garrett sounded more confident than he felt.

He was terrified.

Mrs. Redding nodded. She met his gaze. "Can you make me a promise?"

He drew a deep breath. "What's that?"

"This time, promise me you won't let her go when she comes back." Mrs. Redding gripped his hand. "What can I say—mothers always want the best for their daughters."

Garrett's throat tightened, and at last, he squeezed her hand. His voice sounded hoarse when he answered, "I won't."

He stared at the flashlights flickering through the woods.

What they needed was a damned searchlight.

He needed a damn helicopter.

Even if he had to fly it himself.

He released Mrs. Redding's hand and went back inside for his coat. "Can I borrow your cell phone?" he asked Laura.

Laura nodded and handed it to him. Throwing his coat hastily over his shoulders as he walked back out, he headed toward his truck, dialing. Luis picked up. "Who's this?"

"Hey, man, it's Garrett." He slammed the door to the truck. "I need you to meet me at Ben's farm. I have to borrow your helicopter."

After giving Luis the details, he slammed the shifter down, backing up with an ease and fluidity that came only because of his Army training. At times like this, he was thankful he'd joined and learned skills for dealing with intense situations. He might have drunk too much and seen things he couldn't forget. Still, the military had helped him channel some of the destructive behavior from his youth into a discipline. On a good day, he could control things better.

He flew over the snow down the back roads. When a friend from grade school—Ben Pearson—had approached him last summer about joining a timeshare for a helicopter, Garrett had opted out and given Luis the information instead. Doing logging runs and taking part in emergency services weren't things he wanted to do. Who knew he would need a helicopter again so soon?

He tried not to think of the worst-case scenario, and the snowfall reflecting against his headlights made it difficult to see. *Concentrate.* He slowed, adrenaline and anger pumping through him. *Goddamn, Dan.* This time he'd gone too far.

Please let her be safe.

He couldn't think about that.

Please let her . . .

He released a slow breath, his lips puffing as he did, his breath frosting. The heat had barely kicked on yet. If he was cold and he'd just come from inside, what about Sam and Colby?

God. *Jen.* This had to be a parent's worst nightmare.

Hell, this is my worst nightmare.

With the snow, he almost missed the poorly marked entrance to Ben's farm. He turned in, and the tire tracks up ahead told him Luis had beat him there. Thank God. By the time he pulled up to the barn Ben had converted to house the chopper, the lights were already burning brightly, Luis and Ben were waiting for him, the engine intake of the helicopter installed with a filter to protect it from the snow.

He was up in the air within minutes, Luis with him. Garrett handled the controls. "Visibility is bad, man," Luis said, peering from the windows.

It was bad. And flying in the mountains during a snowfall was even more dangerous. "Thanks for coming," Garrett said through his headset. They could both be in danger during conditions like this.

Luis's voice had that tin can sound that came through the headset. "It wasn't a question. You're up here, then so am I."

Orienting himself was difficult, and Garrett had to rely on every tool at his disposal. He squinted into the night-vision goggles. Thank God Luis had done this. He also brought to it so many of the unique advantages they'd had in the military.

Luis turned on the floodlights as they flew closer to the lands near the Reddings' house. Garrett's heart thumped faster in his chest.

Where are you, Sam?

The movement of the blades sent a spray of snow off the tree tops, and they flew closer to the ground. He should have let Luis take the controls.

Trust Luis.

Garrett's breath was tight in his chest as they circled the area. He mapped out a pattern of the most likely regions of his mind.

Come on, Sam.

After what seemed like forever, Luis's voice crackled over the headset. "I think I see something. Three o'clock. Looks like a tire."

His heart was pounding so hard he could barely think straight. He circled the space, trying to see what Luis had seen. Sure enough, there appeared to be a large object buried in the snow, a tire just barely visible. If it was the UTV Sam had taken, it was upside down.

Shit, shit.

He looked for an open place to land. Any place.

The top of what appeared to be a cliff ledge might work. He'd have to find a path down from there, but it was the closest he could find. He brought the helicopter down, snow filling the surrounding air like fog. They couldn't risk leaving the helicopter out there with no cover—too much risk of ice and the intake filter getting covered.

"I'm going out there," he told Luis over the headset. "Take over the controls and get back up in the air. I'll try to signal to you if I find her, but don't hang around if the weather gets any worse. The last thing I need is for one more person to disappear out here."

"I ain't going nowhere."

Garrett grabbed a flashlight and a rope before he clamored out. The snow was already about two feet deep. *No wonder the search teams had scaled back.* This would be rough going.

He tied the rope around a solid tree at the top and then started down the cliff's side. One of the less sophisticated ways to go down a forty-foot drop, but the adrenaline pumping through the fibers of his muscles seemed to have taken over. When he got to the bottom, he remembered the balaclava mask he'd been wearing earlier while searching for Sam. He yanked it out of his coat pocket, then pulled it on.

He wanted to sprint to the area where they'd seen that tire. But the snow drift made it impossible to run. His quads burned as he drew closer, his chest heaving.

Flipping the flashlight on, he oriented himself and kept going. In snow like this, the landscape appeared too similar. No doubt that had been part of why Sam had gotten lost.

Then he was there, and the tire was unmistakable. A UTV tire.

He dove toward the wreck, setting his flashlight down on a nearby log. He cleared off the snow, trying to see in.

Sam's dark hair.

And beside her, Colby.

His heart was in his throat, which felt thick and lined with saliva. "Sam!"

He reached for her. Her eyes were closed—and she appeared to be sleeping.

But not sleeping.

She hadn't responded to his shout. Or the movement.

No. No. No.

Colby's eyes blinked open.

Oh my God.

He pulled off his glove and shoved a shaking hand into the UTV, reaching for Sam. Her head lolled to the side as his fingertips grazed the soft spot on her neck where her pulse should be.

Holding his breath, he stared at her face, her serene expression. He couldn't lose her. Not now.

Not ever.

A soft, faint pulse throbbed under his fingertips.

Oh, thank God. Thank God.

Colby was crying, reaching for him. "Let's get you both out of here."

WHAT A TIME TO *decide to get sober.*

The phrase had repeated itself through Garrett's mind more than once tonight. While he drove to Ben's farm.

While he flew over the Reddings' land.

When they caught sight of the flipped UTV.

What a time to get sober.

When he'd gathered Colby into his arms.

When they'd flown him and Sam straight to the hospital.

The hospital where he'd seen her for the first time in five years almost a month ago.

Where she'd flown back into his life like an unextinguishable flame. Where he'd realized that all this time, he'd been trying to find his way back to her.

What a time . . .

She shifted in the bed, and Garrett touched her hand. He loved this woman. He would always love this woman.

And he didn't care what he had to lose to love this woman. He'd traveled the whole damn world and found nothing, no one who made him feel what she made him feel. Without her, he'd been lost. He wouldn't lose her again.

A SOFT KNOCK at the door stirred Garrett from his sleep. His legs stretched out, and his knees locked. He gripped the arms of the chair and lifted his chin.

Eli stood there, the unshaven stubble of several days on his face.

Garrett's head still felt thick with sleep, but the sun was up.

He checked his watch. Six in the morning. Before the shift change. No wonder Eli had woken him.

Eli came in and stood at the foot of the bed, gazing at Sam. Thick, warming blankets still layered her. "She looks peaceful."

Garrett wiped his mouth and stood, coming to stand beside Eli. "She broke her ankle so they had to reset it. Gave her some pain meds, so she'll probably sleep for a while." The rawness of what he'd gone through felt like an open wound that wouldn't heal for a while. He didn't want it to heal. *Don't forget how much you love her.* "When I found her unconscious, I thought she was dead. Thought I had lost her. I can honestly say that was the closest I've ever experienced to pure hell."

Eli, his friend, his rival. Eli, who hated him now. Garrett didn't know where to start with him.

The two men stood side by side, not speaking for several

minutes. At last, Eli turned. "You know we can never be friends the same way we were." He looked down, his blue eyes veined with red. "But I had my chance with her, and I really screwed it all up. She deserves to be happy."

When Eli looked up, he met Garrett's eyes, his gaze locking with him. "She deserves a man that will commandeer a freaking helicopter in the middle of a snowstorm to find her. Just take care of her." He chuckled sardonically. "And not in the way I asked a month ago. But don't let me hear about you leaving her at the altar. Or else our friendship will really be over."

What?

Garrett blinked at Eli, unsure if he'd heard him right. "I don't know that I've earned your forgiveness."

"Think of it as starting a new friendship. One where she's free." Eli clapped him on the shoulder, then let go, stepping back. "Where we're all free." Dipping his chin in a goodbye, Eli gave a small wave and left.

CHAPTER THIRTY-ONE

THE SMELL of freshly baked cookies permeated the air.

Sam drew a sharp breath, her eyes opening. She squinted, then took in her surroundings. She was in a hospital. Or what appeared to be a hospital, if not for the unusual décor.

The room was bursting with flowers and trays of cookies wrapped in cellophane. Tins of cookies were stacked on the sparse furniture.

Everywhere.

And in the lone chair beside her—Garrett.

She tried to draw her knees up, then stopped, pain throbbing up her leg. Closing her eyes, she remembered the crash. The snow.

"Colby?" she asked.

"He's fine. He's out of the hospital. You not only saved his life, but he barely needed treatment." Garrett crossed his arms. "That was quite a stunt you pulled, Redding."

"I don't remember . . ." She moistened her lips. Garrett lifted a Styrofoam cup for her with ice water and offered it. She sipped from the straw.

"You had hypothermia and lost consciousness. Fortunately, your boyfriend spent a few years flying helicopters for the Army, so he found you." Garrett then sat on the side of the bed.

God, he was sexy. Even in the middle of the hospital in these settings, she couldn't help the flutters he gave her. She laughed lightly. "Boyfriend? I must have missed a lot."

"It's a temporary arrangement." Garrett reached for her hand.

Yup. His touch is enough to make my nerves tingle.

She shifted again, but her leg felt . . . weird. Stiffening, she pushed the sheets to the side to find her ankle in a cast. *Oh, no.* "What'd I do?"

"Broke your ankle, but you'll be okay after six weeks in a boot. Crutches. Mark may not be so all right since your mom and Laura are expecting him to take over care of all the Redding women."

She winced. *Shit.* Just what her family needed. One more of them laid up. "Poor Mark."

"Well, luckily for you—and Mark—I've just cleared my schedule for the next month. You know, it being the holidays and all, I figured I would take it easy, go on vacation—"

"How nice for you." She glared, laughing.

Garrett leaned forward and dropped a kiss on her lips. "Actually, I plan on being a pain in your ass as much as possible."

The thought of Garrett taking care of her, of being with her . . . *Am I asleep?* She shouldn't get to be this happy, should she? She looked down at the stiff hospital blanket, folding it between her fingertips. "What about Eli? And Katie? And the whole town hating me?"

"First of all, the whole town doesn't hate you. People were a bit concerned to hear that you might be selling the beloved Redding Cabins, but Laura and your mom stopped those rumors. And then Trisha Sanders set the record straight about the lies Katie had spread about her. Once those lies were exposed, everyone took your side. I hear Katie's gone to live with her grandmother in Baltimore for a while."

Wow. All that had happened while she'd been unconscious? She couldn't help but feel sad about Katie, though. They'd been friends for so long. Was this how it would end?

"As for Eli, he came by to see you. Told me if I ever leave you at the altar, he'd kill me. Or something." Garrett raised a brow. "Which frankly I find insulting. As though someone could ever accuse me of being less than reliable with my devotion to you."

Sam grinned, her heart skipping. Was it possible? *Did Eli really say that?* "Eli forgave you?"

Could they be together?

Katie and Eli felt like less of an obstacle somehow now anyway. After what Katie had done, Sam wasn't interested in tiptoeing around her feelings. And she'd always love Eli but not the way she loved Garrett. Garrett felt more than right. He felt like home.

Garrett nodded and squeezed her hand. "Which got me thinking. This assumption we'd get married. It hinges a lot on a certain woman I'm in love with deciding if she loves me. I mean, it's obvious to me, of course, but it'd be nice to—"

"I love you, Garrett." She interlaced her fingers with his. "You arrogant, ridiculous man. You're wonderful, and I'm sorry I wasn't ready to tell you before. I knew I loved you. I—"

He silenced her with another kiss, then grinned. "Good. Because actually, I'm not interested in being your boyfriend." Reaching into his pocket, he pulled a ring box out and flipped it open. "I have something more forever in mind."

Her jaw dropped. *He's proposing?*

"I—" The diamond sparkled against the garish fluorescent

light overhead. "When did you buy a ring?" she managed. She was stalling and hoped he wouldn't be hurt. But she needed a moment.

"Found it at the bottom of my cereal box this morning." Garrett dipped his lips to hers. "So what do you think? You? Me? Maybe a couple of rug rats, eventually?"

She closed her eyes and returned a quick kiss, a grin on her face. "This may be the worst proposal I've ever heard. Not to mention, we just started dating. Or something. I—"

He laughed, then slid off the bed, getting to one knee. "Redding, I've loved you my whole life. And it might be crazy to propose when you're just waking up after almost freezing to death, and we've barely been together, but I've been waiting a lot longer than that. When I realized that losing you just wasn't an option anymore, I also realized I wanted our lives together to start today. And the next day. Forever."

He held the ring box toward her again and peeked out from behind it. "Now, will you marry me?"

Happy tears misted her eyes. *I love Garrett.* She nodded through her tears. "Yes. I love you, you crazy, crazy man." Had she ever even told him before?

He slid the ring from the box onto her finger. "Crazy about you." He kissed her with the sort of kiss that made her want to yank him down on top of her, despite her broken ankle.

A few excited squeaks came from the door, and Sam disentangled herself from Garrett enough to see her mother and Laura standing in the doorway. She buried her face in Garrett's shoulders, her cheeks growing warm as they approached. "You heard?"

"We were outside listening." Laura rolled her eyes. Mom took the chair, her face beaming. "Looks like you two have enough cookies to last you for the rest of your lives too."

Sam stared at the containers of cookies. "Yeah, what's that about?"

"When the people in town heard about how you saved Dan and Colby, everyone stepped up. Everyone that called out of the shoot came back. Rachel's been handling all the shooting for your cookie campaign, and they have more people trying to help now than they need," Laura answered. She grabbed a tin, peeking into it. "Oh—snowballs. These are some of my favorites." She pulled out a powdered sugar-covered cookie ball.

Rachel? A peaceful feeling settled in Sam's chest. As it should be. Rachel was a talented photographer, and she'd worked harder on this campaign than anyone. "Hopefully, Maren will see how good Rachel is and give her my job."

"Maren ripped up your letter of resignation." Garrett sat at the foot of the bed. "So your job is still yours if you want it. She did, however, fly back to New York. Peter has replaced her as the host. His cookie episode went viral, and viewers demanded more of him. Much to Bunny's . . . disappointment. But Maren offered Bunny a monthly column in the magazine, so she's pretty happy about that."

Sam raised her brows. "Peter?"

"The man made chocolate chip cookies." Mom shook her head. "I don't know that those even qualify as Christmas cookies." She took Sam's hand and stared at the diamond gracing her ring finger. "You two better get married soon. I want to be at that wedding."

Soon. The gentle heartbreak, the painful reminder Mom only had *soon* left put a sad note on the moment . . . but Garrett took her other hand. He squeezed it.

Sam met Garrett's gaze. She wanted forever to start today too. She smiled once again. "How about a Christmas wedding?"

THE FOOTRESTS on the wheelchair wobbled as the nurse pushed Sam out of the hospital. She stopped at the curb, where Garrett had pulled up to wait for her. He came around the front of the truck and handed her crutches as she got up from the chair.

"All set?" Garrett placed one hand on the small of her back, guiding her toward the passenger side.

She hated the crutches, and not just because it meant she would have to be limping around everywhere. They dug under her arms painfully. But it was hard to feel like complaining about something like that when she was finally going home. The word struck her with a strange intensity.

Home.

Brandywood?

Or New York?

"I'm ready," Sam said, then slid into the seat. Garrett took the crutches from her and put them in the bed of his truck. Closing the door, he went around to the driver's side. As he pulled away from the curb, she glanced back at the hospital. If someone had told her almost a month ago when she'd shown up to visit Laura that she'd still be here, she would have laughed.

"You know what we haven't talked about?" She folded her hands in her lap, the diamond on her ring finger sparkling in the sun. She still hadn't gotten used to looking at it. Her snow-drop ring had been moved to the other hand, where it would live from now on.

The turn signal sounded as Garrett drew closer to the exit. "What's that?"

"Where we're going to live," she sighed, studying his profile. "I know you have a house here, and Brandywood is home to you, but—"

"You're not sure you want to be back here?" Garrett asked.

She glanced out the window. Being home had been an interesting experience. For the first time, her childhood made sense to her. And that had been painful. Being here to take care of a dying mother was no less painful.

But Garrett had helped her heart to feel whole. As though it could heal. "I'm not sure what I want," she admitted.

"I will follow you to the moon without questions, Sam. But we can talk about it . . . you've got to be kidding me," Garrett muttered, his gaze going to the rearview mirror.

Sam looked over her shoulder. Police lights flashed from the cruiser behind them. *It can't be . . .*

Garrett pulled over, and sure enough, Dan stood from the driver's seat. He adjusted his hat and made his way over, but this time to the passenger side. He tapped on the window.

"Doyle." Dan nodded as a greeting. "Sorry to pull you over." His gaze went to Sam. "You mind if I talk to . . . um, my sister?"

Sam lifted her brows.

Sister?

Garrett rested his hands on the steering wheel. "If you're asking me to get out of the truck—"

"No, nothing like that." Dan's face looked haggard, his eyes tired. "I got my pay and rank reduced for what I did to you. I told my lieutenant the whole thing—about how I'd been harassing you. I'm sorry about that, Doyle. I swear it'll never happen again."

"Dan." Sam set her hand on the armrest. "I appreciate you wanting to try, but we don't have to pretend, either. So long as we can all just get along, there's no need to act like we're family."

Dan's eyes were red as he looked at her, and he nodded. "I'm sorry. I really am. But I was thinking about it"—he scratched his shaven jawline—"and you're just as much my sister as Jen is. I've been a horrible brother to you. Fact is, I haven't been one at all. But I want to be better. To get to know you. Even though you don't trust me right now."

Sam exchanged a look with Garrett. That Dan Klein could be so conciliatory and open was . . . shocking.

She wanted to say no if she was being honest.

But in the woods, she'd said, ". . . *it's only going to keep hurting us both if we don't fix it.*"

Squaring her shoulders, she met his gaze. "All right, Dan."

A smile curved at the corners of Dan's mouth. "Thank you. And thank you for saving Colby. I'll never be able to repay you." He patted the side of the truck and stepped back. "But actually, I had another reason for stopping you. Would you all mind following me? There's something I'd like you to see."

He walked away without waiting for a response.

Sam stared over her shoulder. "What the hell?" She shook her head with a chuckle. "Who knew Dan Klein was more than a meathead?"

"Well, that's a fine way to talk about your new brother." Garrett couldn't keep the laugh out of his voice. "He's trying. It's touching."

"Yeah, I guess so. We'll see where it goes." As Dan passed them, Garrett pulled out behind him. "The possibility exists he's leading us both somewhere that ends in a shallow grave. Should we really be following him?"

Garrett didn't answer. The only sound in the cab was the soft Christmas music playing in the background. Sam squinted. "Wait a second. Do you know where he's taking us?"

"I'm just the driver. I know nothing." Laughter twinkled in Garrett's eyes.

"Hey, you do know!" She gaped at him. "Where are you

taking me? Ah, crap, am I going to wish I had put makeup on for this?"

Garrett winked at her. "You're beautiful without it."

Where on earth were they going? She thought Dan had surprised her. That he and Garrett were in on something together floored her. She fished around for her purse—thank goodness Mom had brought it to the hospital. She had makeup in it she could use.

Flipping the visor down, she looked for the mirror, but she didn't see one. "Don't you have a mirror?"

"Now why on earth would my truck need a mirror there? You think I'm putting on makeup in my passenger seat before I hang drywall? Unless you're saying you think I would look better with makeup?"

"Oh, shut up, you." She resisted the urge to playfully swat him. "Where are we going?" Quickly, she opened her compact and started on some powder foundation.

Dan flipped his lights back on as they drew closer to Main Street. Crowds gathered on each side of the street, and Sam gave Garrett a confused look. "Is the Christmas parade today?"

Garrett turned onto Main, heading toward the town square. "Darlin', all these people . . . they're here for you." The people on the streets were cheering and waving as they passed.

Sam slunk into her seat, mortified.

For me?

No, no, no.

Dan pulled up to the town square, and Garrett pulled in beside him. Sam's heart was racing as she looked around. The town square was just as crowded as Main Street had been, though it appeared the people who had been on the sidewalk were approaching the square. The town Christmas tree was in the square and unlit.

She covered her face. "It's the tree lighting, isn't it?"

"Yup. And a welcome back party for Brandywood's favorite heroine." Garrett got out of his seat and exited before she could respond.

Outside, globe lights on the square lit the paved area while families and couples carried hot chocolate in paper cups and congregated under propane heaters. Some of them even lit sparklers, throwing starry light into the mix.

Sam didn't know whether to laugh or throw up. All of this was for her?

Garrett led her from the truck and helped her onto the sidewalk. Christmas music played from speakers, and a cheer sounded as Sam drew closer. The crowd parted, and Garrett led her up toward the bandstand, where Mom and Laura waited, along with Mark and the kids. They all wore huge smiles on their faces.

Jen and Colby stood there too.

Unexpectedly, Sam's eyes filled with tears at the sight of Colby. He smiled and came running toward her. She caught him in a hug as Jen approached. "I'm so glad you're okay, buddy," she whispered in his ear.

Releasing him, she straightened, leaning on her crutches. Jen had tears on her cheeks as she leaned forward and hugged Sam. "I owe you everything. You saved my whole life. Thank you, Sam." She sniffled and pulled back, wiping her eyes. "And if you don't mind, I would love it if Colby could call you Aunt Sam. I mean, you almost are anyway."

Sam scrunched her face, her cheeks wet with tears. None of this felt real. "Of course."

The town mayor, Bill MacKintosh, approached, and Sam stiffened. Was Katie here too?

Somehow, she doubted that Katie would come for this. Especially something that was celebrating Sam. The memory of the rage that had been in Katie's eyes threatened to steal the joy in her heart.

Mayor MacKintosh shook her hand. His smile was genuine and warm. "Don't worry, Sammy. She's not here. I can't say I'm proud of how she acted toward you, but I think there's room in Brandywood for us all, isn't there? Shall we go light the tree?"

It wasn't an apology, but then, *he* didn't owe her one. And she doubted Katie would ever give one.

Garrett slipped his arms around her waist, holding her back as Mayor MacKintosh made his way to the platform.

"You okay?" he asked, searching her eyes.

She nodded, then smiled teary-eyed. "If you did all this to convince me to stay in Brandywood . . ."

He chuckled as he pulled her into his arms. "Hell, woman, even I couldn't pull this off. But you know what I think?"

With her arm around his neck, she rested her weight against him. "What's that?"

"Redding, I think you should stay." He kissed her deeply, eliciting whoops and hollers from the crowd. She wished they could just go home already, her body churning with desire. When Garrett pulled away, she closed her eyes, basking in his warmth and love.

"Maybe I will, Doyle." *Maybe this is my home. With you.*

CHAPTER THIRTY-TWO

One year later

THE FIRST LIGHT of dawn crept across the bedroom, and Sam peeked one eye open, then crept out of bed toward the window. Her heart fell. No snow.

After the record-snowy winter the year before, she'd gotten spoiled. But it hadn't stopped her from hoping for a white Christmas. Still, it was cold, and she bounced, ready to hop back under the covers.

She slipped back into bed and smiled at Garrett's slumbering form. Sidling up behind him, she put her cold feet on the backs of his thighs.

Garrett jolted. "Ah!" He flipped, grabbing her wrists as she laughed.

"Merry Christmas?" she offered, giving him a sneaky expression.

"Devil woman." He pinned her beneath him, then dropped

a kiss to her lips, his hands releasing hers and sliding down her T-shirt. He found the hem, then pulled the shirt over her head. Lowering his kisses to her breasts, his lips covered one nipple, then the other. "Now it's a Merry Christmas."

She pulled him back toward her and slipped her arms around his neck. "I guess what I really should say is Happy Anniversary. Of sobriety. And marriage." In some ways, she was prouder of the former. He'd been faithfully attending AA for a year while she'd gone to an Al-Anon family group with his mother, who was like a mother to her now.

He pushed his boxers from his waist. "Does this mean that I get lucky three times? On account of Christmas and all these anniversaries being combined?"

Rolling her eyes, she gasped as he found her entrance, pushing inside her. "Don't act like you're a sex-deprived bachelor," she moaned. "If that were true, I wouldn't be late."

Garrett stopped, mid-thrust. He drew back, his arms on either side of her, his gaze locking with hers. "Are you . . ."

She'd only found out the night before but had been sure of it for weeks. But holding the positive test in her hands, she hadn't known if she could wait until morning to tell him. "Congratulations. You're going to be a dad. Merry Christmas."

Garrett gathered her in his arms, pulling her off the bed. He whooped, his embrace tight, then as though unsure of how tightly to hold her, he pulled away gently and kissed her forehead. "You know you're setting impossible standards for Christmas."

A bubble of laughter erupted from her, and she slid her arms around him, straddling him. "Where were we?"

This time when they came together, their lovemaking wasn't frantic or playful. But there was something else there now that carried them through each challenge they'd faced over the past year: hope.

When they collapsed onto the bed, spent, a scratching at the door made Garrett lift his head. "Charlie!" He buried his face in the comforter. "I'll take care of him."

"We should probably get ready to go to Mo—" Nearly thirty years of calling home one thing, the change to a new name would never get easy. "Laura's." Her throat thickened a bit.

Garrett glanced at her as he pulled on a pair of sweatpants. "You okay?"

"Yeah. You know. It's Christmas. Always harder to think of celebrating these things without her." Sam brushed away a stray tear.

Her mother had lost her fight with cancer on a beautiful summer's day in late July. It had seemed so unfair that someone so bright and vivacious should die at all, let alone on a sunny day. It should have been gray and bleak, just like they'd all felt when she passed. Laura and Sam, Mark and Garrett had been gathered around her, playing her favorite songs as she took her last breath. It had been horrible, a moment she'd never forget, but Sam had been thankful that at least she'd had those seven extra months with her. She'd been grateful that her mom had seen her baby girl marry.

That time had brought Laura and Sam closer and had begun to heal a rift Sam had feared would never end. *But God, I miss Mom so much.*

"I'm not ready to have a Christmas without her, Garrett." Sam brushed away a stray tear. "And I'm hormonal."

"We can stay here. I'm sure Laura would under—"

"Laura would *not* understand." Sam gave him a doubtful expression. "But it's okay. I want to be there. I've missed enough Christmases. Plus, Rachel wants to pop in from her cabin." Rachel had been so thrilled with the experience the year before that she'd been determined to come back and do Christmas Brandywood-style again.

Rachel had taken over Sam's job in New York and seemed happier working under Maren than Sam had been. The freedom of being a contract photographer had been eye-opening, though. She'd also been able to sell more of her pictures through various art galleries on the East Coast, which was providing a nice income on its own. But Sam now shot and styled food images for major magazines all over the country . . . and half the time, she didn't even have to leave Garrett's house. *Their* house. They came to her—or sent her a recipe—and Jen was happy to cook anything Sam couldn't handle.

"Is she staying until New Year's?" Garrett headed toward the door. Charlie, a fully grown Great Dane, came bounding into the room as Garrett opened the door. His tail swatted the dresser, sending Garrett's wallet flying.

"I think Peter's Christmas special is on the twenty-eighth? So I'll have to ask. She might want to wait until traffic leaves town anyway." Peter's seasonal specials with *This Charmed Life* had become a tourist attraction at this point. He'd opened a gigantic shop on Main Street to capitalize on his claim to fame.

Not that anyone was complaining about it now. The tourists meant business for everyone, including the Redding Cabins, which the magazine had done an article highlighting.

Garrett grabbed the leash and clipped it onto Charlie's collar. A moment later, he was flying down the stairs, cursing as he tried to keep up with Charlie. Sam giggled as the front door slammed. She placed her hands on her belly and hugged it gently. "I love your daddy."

STANDING on the front porch of Laura and Mark's house, Garrett raised his hand in greeting as the car doors closed. Warren and Alice followed behind their kids, who raced into the house. Dan followed them, carrying Colby, while Jen balanced Christmas presents.

Garrett took a sip of his coffee and made a face at Sam, the bitter taste acrid. *She must have only put one tablespoon in.* "You trying to cut back on my sugar?"

Sam winked. "Maybe." She turned her attention toward the arriving guests. "Merry Christmas!" Sam called from beside Garrett.

Garrett laughed as Warren sighed. He looked exhausted.

"We've been up since five," Warren said with a shake of his head. "And they're only going to get more presents and candy from my parents' house tonight. All parents on Christmas should get an IV of coffee."

Colby escaped Dan's arms on the porch and came flying at Sam with open arms. "Merry Christmas, Aunt Sam!"

Sam and Jen exchanged a warm smile. "You were up early too?" Sam asked her.

Jen nodded. "But that's every day." She came over and held Colby's hand. "Let's go find cousin Carson!"

Dan greeted them. "I'll come out and join the non-parents club here soon. I have a feeling it's going to be loud."

As the door closed behind him, Garrett raised a brow at Sam. "Should we tell him?"

"We've come a long way with Dan but I am not telling him about the baby before we tell my sister," Sam said, laughing.

"Speaking of family . . ." Garrett slipped his hand into hers, setting the coffee on the rail. "Can we take a walk? I have something for you."

She gave him a curious look. "What is it?"

"You'll see." He tugged at her hand and led her off the front porch. Charlie noticed them leaving and barked from the window. They'd brought him to the celebration because everyone seemed to love him—especially the kids who seemed to think he was a small horse. Garrett waved at the dog and kept walking.

When they stopped at last, in front of a cabin, Sam's brows came together. "Cabin twelve?"

He shrugged. "I rented it for the night. I know it's silly, but I figured it's where it all started."

"That's really sweet, Garrett." She kissed his cheek and let him lead her inside. "Is this your way of trying to have sex again?"

"We can play strip poker later tonight." He grinned, then squeezed her hand, a nervous feeling in his chest. "There's something else. I thought it might be better to give it to you when we were alone." He pulled an envelope out from the inside pocket of his jacket. "I know you said you wanted me to give this to you, and I didn't know if today would be good or not, so I can hold on to it until you're ready."

Sam stared at the envelope, her smile fading. Her mother had written on it, *"For when you find out you're having a baby."*

Out of all the envelopes, it was the only one Sam had told him she dreaded opening. The thought of her mom not being here to meet her grandchild made her cry, and Garrett worried that Sam was right about how the content might affect her.

Sam's shoulders lowered as she exhaled. "Open it, I think I'm ready. But can you read it to me?"

"Of course." Garrett tore open the seal with his thumb. Mrs. Redding's neat handwriting filled one side of the cream-colored stationery.

Garrett cleared his throat.

"*Dear Sam,*

I noticed the other day that you still wear that snowdrop ring

I bought you when you were a teenager, so I thought this would be a good time to tell you about it.

I bought it for you because you're my snowdrop.

When I brought you home from the hospital that March day, snowdrops were blooming in the yard. It made my heart happy. Because there were always flowers blooming in Venezuela—no matter what time of year it was—and here it was, the middle of winter. Flowers blooming. Just like you. My winter flower . . .'"

Sam brushed a tear from her cheek with her knuckle and sniffled.

Garrett lifted his head from the paper, closing it. "You doing okay?"

"Yeah, I just . . . that's really beautiful. Keep going."

"'The metaphor goes deeper, Samantha. Snowdrops are the most resilient of flowers. Deep freezes and snow don't bother them. Things that would kill other flowers, and there they are blossoming. You're not a daisy. Not a rose. You're a snowdrop. You can survive things that others can't.*

Motherhood isn't easy. But it is wonderful. The part of my life and myself that I am the proudest of. Because I'm proud of you and know you will be a wonderful mother. Congratulations, my love.

Love,

Mom.'"

Garrett closed the letter and handed it to Sam. She opened it, stared at the words, then smiled tearfully. "This is the best one yet." She laughed, the sound magical to his ears, thawing the knot of tension wound around his heart.

He pulled her into his arms. "Your mom had a way with words."

"I know." She pressed her cheek into his chest. "Garrett?"

He rested his chin on the top of her head. "Yeah, Snowdrop?"

She laughed again, then snuggled closer.

"I'm so glad I came home."

THANKS SO MUCH FOR READING! If you enjoyed this book, please consider leaving a rating or review. I'd really appreciate it so much and ratings help me to continue bringing you new books. To keep up with all my current releases and grab bonus material (bonus scenes for all series are coming soon) sign up for my newsletter!

And don't miss the next book in the *Brandywood Small Town Romance Series*, I'll Carry You, available now!

NEWSLETTER AND NEXT BOOK

Want to keep up with me and hear what's going on in Annabelle's Fun World of Writing? Join my newsletter on my website! I have freebies and giveaways, exclusive content and, of course, you get to hear all about upcoming book news, my life, and my love of pizza.

I hope you enjoyed Sam and Garrett's love story. Thank you so much for reading; my readers really are what make this possible and I am so grateful for you! If you enjoyed this book, I'd love it if you took the time to leave a rating or review at your favorite book retailer. It truly goes a long way.

And if you'd like to stick around and see more of the world of Brandywood, you can! Jen's story continues in I'll Carry You!

ACKNOWLEDGMENTS

I'm going to start differently and say thank you to the *Creative Penn* podcast and Joanna Penn—when I was stuck in writer's block with another book, one of your episodes helped get my butt in gear and work on something else! And not only did that lead to this book being completed, but the creation of this whole series (plus me resolving the block and finishing the other book).

...the point is, things have a butterfly effect. When I opened up that podcast while folding laundry that day last December, I didn't have another series on my radar. But I did something useful to me creatively anyway (listened to a podcast) and that really ended up having a big impact.

Now for the INCREDIBLE team that got me here:

Marion Archer, my absolutely fabulous editor who not only said yes to my semi-stalkerish email but also found room for me in her packed schedule. You are amazing and brought this book to an absolute shine. I promise to work on those em dashes, haha!

Julie Simms, Amanda Coleman, and Julie Deaton, for fantastic copy-editing and proofreading that was outstandingly professional and thorough. You're wonderful!!

Susanne Lakin, who always knows how to bring about the best in my writing and has been the most wonderful mentor, too. Thanks for always fitting me into your schedule.

The Red Pen Crew (Jaclyn, Anne, Matt) thanks for always

being my first-string readers who not only encourage but give me great direction. And thanks for keeping up with me when I was flinging new books at you every five minutes.

Lisa Boyle, you have been such a great source of support, cheerleading, venting, amazing beta reader, and writer bestie. Thank you, thank you.

To my beta readers, who helped me figure out what direction to take this in at the earliest of stages. I'm so grateful!

To my cheerleaders at home: Cora, Andrew, Evie, Victoria, and Graham, the older four who came peering over my shoulder about three thousand times to find out if I'd finished and sold enough copies to take them to Disney World yet. Soon, kiddos. I promise. (And thanks, Cora, for helping me pick the blue for this cover!)

And once again, last on this list but always first in my heart and really deserving of all the credit, my investor and sounding board—Patrick. Thanks for bankrolling me, babe, and for not getting too frustrated with me when I stare blankly at you from behind a computer screen. Love you!

ALSO BY ANNABELLE MCCORMACK

The Windswept WWI Saga:

A Zephyr Rising: A Windswept Prequel Novella

Windswept: The Windswept Saga Book 1

Sands of Sirocco: The Windswept Saga Book 2

Whisper in the Tempest: The Windswept Saga Book 3

The Brandywood Small Town Romance Series:

All This Time

I'll Carry You

Once We Met

Until Forever Ends

Ever With Me

Winnick Contemporary Romances

See You Next Fall

He Loves Me Knot

Don't Forget to Write (Coming Soon)

To find out the latest about my new releases, please sign up for my newsletter or Facebook Reader's group! I love hearing from readers and have some great offers lined up for my subscribers.

ABOUT THE AUTHOR

Annabelle McCormack spins you tales of epic historical adventure, heartfelt romance, and complex family dynamics with strong female protagonists to make things interesting. She is a graduate of the Johns Hopkins University's M.A. in Writing Program. She lives in Maryland with her "very punctual" husband, where she serves as a hot mess mom for her (mismatched-socks-wearing and late-to-everything) five children.

Visit her at www.annabellemccormack.com or http://instagram.com/annabellemccormack to follow her daily adventures.

9 798986 529400